Gael Harrison was born in Malaysia
She qualified as a primary school t
living on the west coast of Scotlanc
Ukraine and Qatar, and has recently
married with three grown up children and now ....

Other books by Gael Harrison:
The Moon in the Banyan Tree (available from amazon.co.uk)

The Highland Games

GAEL HARRISON

SilverWood

Published by SilverWood Books 2012
www.silverwoodbooks.co.uk

Copyright © Gael Harrison 2012

The right of Gael Harrison to be identified as the author of this work
has been asserted by her in accordance with
the Copyright, Designs and Patents Act 1988.

All rights reserved. No part of this publication may be reproduced,
stored in a retrieval system, or transmitted in any form or by any means,
electronic, mechanical, photocopying, recording or otherwise,
without prior permission of the copyright holder.

This is a work of fiction. Names, characters, places and incidents either are
products of the author's imagination or are used fictitiously. Any resemblance
to actual events or locales or persons, living or dead, is entirely coincidental.

ISBN 978-1-78132-047-1

British Library Cataloguing in Publication Data
A CIP catalogue record for this book is available from the British Library

Set in Sabon by SilverWood Books
Printed on responsibly sourced paper

*For Mary and Catriona, whose friendship I treasure,
and for John, for just everything*

It is only contact with people and places, with situations and conversations, that fertilizes the germ of any idea sufficiently to sprout the seed that finally grows into a book

Robert Ruark

CHAPTER 1

James MacTavish was looking for a wife. He was in the habit of setting out each morning, dressed to kill as some might say, in his Highland tweeds and sporty deerstalker hat. His step was full of purpose, his blue eyes were sharp and bright, and his nose jutted out with the look of the hound dog. For his entire life he had lived in the small Highland village of Drum Mhor, and knew each and every one of the population. He had courted many local girls over the years, but sadly now they were of an age when they prattled about grandchildren and marrying off their own sons and daughters. James MacTavish was a proud man and at fifty-two he hadn't given up on the idea that some day his perfect woman would appear. Each June and July the tourists would flock to the long beach in front of his house and he would reach for his binoculars to spy on the potential wife material. Later in the village pub he would lean casually on the bar, raising his glass and nodding sagely at lady walkers up from the cities showing off their developed calf muscles and sturdy boots. James MacTavish appreciated a well-turned calf.

'Do you see that branch that hangs over the church, just there by the corner?' he would say. 'You can't miss it... well, it was on that branch that they hung old Charlie McLean during the clearances. On a windy night, when the moon comes out from behind a cloud, you can sometimes see him still dangling there. I swear it's not good to walk alone round by the church corner after dark. Aye...' He would tip back his whisky glass and turn to Donnie. 'I'll have another if you don't mind, and maybe these young girls would care to have one with me?'

Donnie the barman would chuckle as he listened to the well-developed and familiar chat up lines that the ageing Casanova would spin to his wide eyed audiences. Donnie, at thirty, was a strapping lad who had come up to the Highlands at eighteen and had stayed on to manage the Pipers Inn for his parents, who preferred the city lights to this quiet, lost glen beside the sea. Donnie could never understand how the sweet young things would dally with the old roué in preference to himself. It was a constant source of irritation that when James MacTavish was in the room they hardly gave Donnie a glance.

He would fill the glasses, knowing fine well that in a minute the trio would move over to a table by the fire and James MacTavish would start spinning his yarns and old legends of the glen. It was a very rare summer season that MacTavish did not end up promising all sorts of a rosy future to his chosen sweetheart, usually involving sitting on fish boxes and living a life by the kerosene lamp. The romantic ideal appealed to them while the sun warmed the stones and the bees buzzed in the heather but a return visit in the autumn, when the equinox turned the tides and the raw winds flattened the rowans, saw the Highland man and his small stone house lose their idealistic glow, relegated to a memory. In years to come these city girls would smile fondly as they thought of that enchanting walking holiday and the equally enchanting Mr MacTavish.

James MacTavish was not a tall man; indeed many would say he was of a stocky build, the kind of gentleman that wore a kilt or the tweeds well. His green check jacket and matching knee length breeches showed off his broad shoulders, and he was known to boast about his strong, shapely legs. He prided himself on his highly polished brogues; a reflection of a man's character, his mother had been fond of saying. James had inherited her pale blue eyes and sandy hair, which was parted severely to the side; a throwback to when he had been marched to school, his hair wet from his mother's ministrations. Now it was tinged with the inevitable strands of white that marked the passing of the years. He kept his deerstalker down over his smooth, unwrinkled brow, and his apple-red cheeks were ruddy from half a century of exposure to the sea winds and rain of the Scottish West Highlands. He had an honest face, with a *couthieness* about him that could persuade the birds to come down from the trees, or so said many in the village. That, and the twinkle of mischief that lit up his eyes, made a cunning combination to woo and charm the unsuspecting. The summers passed and James MacTavish was still a bachelor with indefatigable good cheer, the reason being that he was a bachelor with a mission.

As James prepared to go out on this gusty August morning, he gave a cursory glance at the form that he had filled in at the suggestion of Morag at the surgery. She had made a great fuss of drawing his attention to a page in one of her women's magazines. To his surprise he saw that it was dating form. She had told him that nowadays there were plenty of ways to get a wife or a husband. You could advertise in the *Exchange and Mart*, a very reliable method, where you could probably get some hens and some fencing at the same time, or, as she'd heard from Mrs McAlister, the more modern way was to use the internet. James shied away from that invention but he was intrigued by the idea, nevertheless. Morag believed he could order an exotic lady from Thailand or Belarus or some such place, just by ticking the appropriate box. 'Fancy that,' she had exclaimed, 'I wouldn't mind a trade-in for my Archie!' James was still in a state of agitation about the whole subject. He had bought a copy of the magazine and pulled out the relevant page and ticked the boxes, just as Morag had said. He had even addressed the envelope and put a second class stamp on it. He eyed it now, sitting there on the shelf, held down by a tin of treacle. I might post it later on, or maybe tomorrow, he assured himself.

'Well, Mother, it could be today, for I'm away to wear out some more shoe leather in pursuit of a wife.' James always addressed the severe portrait of Nell hanging above the old organ in the hall. Her Bible lay open at the Book of Kings. It had been her habit to randomly open the book in the morning and read the verses that appeared, as though they were messages sent directly from God Himself to help guide her through the day. James shuddered, re-reading the verses that told the story of Jezebel, a right madam by the sound of things, not only turning her poor man, King Ahab, from God, but making him worship a pagan. Aye well, he thought, pulling his hat down firmly over his brow, she got what she deserved, that hussy.

James closed the door behind him and set off along the track down to the beach. Even from a distance he could make out the shape of unknown female figures, and seeing one now, he rushed back to the house for his leather-encased telescope. Gasping to catch his breath, he squinted through the eyeglass. Sure enough, there in the distance he could see a woman, staring out at the horizon as though she was communing with a sea captain. Not a man to waste a God-given opportunity, James scurried over the rocks, slippery with bladderwort and a motley collection of shiny mussels, and made a beeline towards the statuesque young woman. He took in her fashionably styled coat, in a rather loud shade of turquoise, and admired her profile and her long twisting ropes of hair, the colour of cream pouring from a jug on to his porridge. Her skin was white as porphyry, and her features just as sharp, as though carved from the stone itself.

'Well, hello there!' he shouted across the wind. 'Are you seeing anything interesting? Perhaps you would like the benefit of my spy glass here?'

The girl turned to him and James stepped back from the fierce stare.

Never one to be daunted for long, he persevered. 'Sometimes there are otters near the shore and we've had a basking shark marooned with the tide. All sorts of catastrophes happen here if you only know where to look. Now, I live up there, in that wee house. I have a grand view of the beach from there.' He turned and pointed to the small stone cottage nestled into the hillside by the side of a dense pine forest. 'I have lived there all my life, and do you know something? I know every single body that lives in this little village. I even know their cousins in Glasgow and their aunties in America, as well as whose dog is pregnant with pups, but there is something I don't know, and do you know what that is?'

She shook her head, and seemed mesmerised by the lilt of his gentle singsong Gaelic accent.

He smiled and looked into her cornflower blue eyes. 'I don't know you, lass! Are you here on holiday, or are you just stopping off on your journey? Did you just take a notion to come and smell the sea?' James inhaled deeply. 'It's grand, is it not? And look over there! Did you see that fish jump? Now, I have a boat and a net and if I knew you better I would ask you for some assistance. We could row out and circle the salmon, for that is what they are out there… they make a run for it up the river to spawn.' He saw her eyes light up, as he knew they would. The novelty of rowing out and setting nets and hauling them in with a good catch of the silvery fish was a novelty to city girls, and he chuckled to himself when the girl grinned broadly and nodded eagerly.

'Can I really help? I would love to do that. I'm staying up there at Iona MacPherson's croft just along from you.' Gone was her initial coldness; now her body jumped about with enthusiasm, and he was pleased to see that she had a good set of teeth.

'Are all your teeth your own?' he asked, a look of concern causing his brows to gather under the rim of his hat.

'What? My teeth? Of course they are my own,' she answered indignantly, looking at him sideways.

'That's a good thing. A man judges a horse and a woman by their teeth; you should know that, especially in a country community like we have here. And by the way, I hope you don't mind me asking, but are you spoken for?' He continued to stare at her expectantly.

She turned on him. 'What is this? I am not a piece of livestock, you know! I only came down here to look at the sea, not to be looked over as though I was at a cattle show!'

James raised his eyebrows in mock astonishment. 'Now, don't get me wrong, lass…' but his words were interrupted by the sound of the scrunching of loose shale. The two realised they were no longer alone, for a small dark figure had insinuated itself between them. An old shepherd, well past his three-score-years-and-ten, clad in a ragged herringbone overcoat and dark plum trousers tied at the ankles with frayed bits of twine, stood staring at James and the young woman expectantly. His face was as russet as a shiny Cox's Pippin, and his black eyes squinted out from deep-creased recesses. Straggly strands of iron-grey hair escaped from a bright red pancake-shaped woman's bonnet.

'Aye, James, I was just hearing what you were saying, and you're right to ask. A man must never be too careful. Women are cunning creatures, aye, they are that.' The old man gave a hacking cough and wiped his mouth on his sleeve.

The young woman grimaced, and automatically held the back of her hand across her nose and mouth to shield herself from any stray spittle.

Unconcerned with any social niceties, the old man sucked through his teeth and gave her a derisive look. 'Aye, they will befuddle a fellow with their lipstick and rouge and swanky bits of finery that they like to doll themselves up in. But as sure as death, when the clogs are beneath the bed, then the truth is found out and usually by then it's too late.' Looking out at the far horizon, his crinkled eyes seemed to have conjured up his own private image. He sighed and went on, 'By then the poor man has signed up for life with a woman who leaves her teeth in a tumbler and has her belly held in by a great swathe of elastic corsetry.' He nodded his head bitterly and the red bonnet threatened to blow off in the next gust. He looked around and snarled at his collie dog that had appeared proudly dragging the corpse of a crow. 'Put it down, Charlie, for God's sake, do I not feed you enough?' He turned back to the young woman and squinted into the light, looking at her appraisingly. 'No,' he continued, 'I always like to be upfront myself, I like to put my cards on the table, as you would say, and I expect the same from the fairer sex. Talking of which, if you were interested in marrying me one of these days, for I have been widowed these past twenty years you know, then I can assure you I would not be disappointing you. Although I hate to blow my own trumpet, I can guarantee that my manhood is big enough for three seagulls to perch upon.' He grinned lasciviously at the young woman, revealing his incomplete set of brown-stained teeth. He shook his head sadly and added, 'But the last one might have to stand on one leg...'

'Oh!' The girl gasped; visibly shocked by the way the conversation had turned. She swivelled on her heel and ran back to her car, slipping and sliding across the stones in her haste to get away.

James MacTavish called out to her, 'Come back, lass, come back! Don't pay any heed to this dirty old man.' But it was to no avail; she kept running until she was out of sight.

'Och, well,' James sighed heavily, 'it was nice to meet you anyway and I'm sure we'll be running into each other again shortly.' James turned to look at the old boy disparagingly.

'What kind of courting ritual was that, Hector Ogilvie? Is that how you used to woo the lassies in your day?'

'Aye and it never used to fail. Mind you I usually liked to have a wee dram first, before I went out. Do you not think my charms worked very well with that hoity-toity one?'

'What do you think, you daft old gowk?' James growled.

Hector coughed and spat again. 'Och well, I'll away and see to the ewes, then I have to give Jimmy Macdonald's cows a look, and seeing this weather promises to be fair, I'll cut some of the rushes up by the croft. Be seeing you, James.' The old fellow turned to look for his dog, now rolling around on the corpse of the crow. 'Come here, Charlie, you smelly devil. For God's sake, will you stop shaming me, just when I was winning with the lassie too?'

James watched the duo make their way along the beach.

He remembered a time when old Hector's wife was still alive. The pair had looked like two peas in a pod, living in their ramshackle house up by the woods. Old Kate was touched with fairy magic, some people said, and some swore by the cures she concocted, brewing up the old highland herbs and potions to treat sick animals. His own mother used to visit Old Kate to get remedies for himself, he remembered. Ah well, thought James, they're all gone, and Hector has made a life of sorts for himself and his dog.

James MacTavish slowly turned back to his own house and walked up the path to the door. He decided that he would give the fishing a try, seeing as how they were jumping. He unlaced his smart brogues and padded into the living room and through to his bedroom. All was Spartan and clean, just as he liked it; the big oak bed, made up and covered with a heavy white eiderdown, the tallboy full of neatly pressed shirts and the wardrobe, large and imposing, dominating the wall opposite the window. He pulled back the light curtain and could see the girl fussing with her car, still puffing and blowing with indignation, but he knew that he would be seeing her again. He unbuttoned his breeches, put on his wet weather gear and then padded out to the porch and pulled on the rubber boots that he kept for the boat. He reached for the hook by the door and took down 'the killer', a handy length of driftwood he kept for stunning the fish; then he made his way outside again.

'Sown a few seeds, Mother! Maybe this one is wife material; we shall just have to wait and see. I am off now to catch a fish or two for her tea!'

The portrait glowered back at him as he slammed the door.

James strode down to the beach and over to his wooden boat that he had roped to a huge rock down by the water's edge. Pushing it over the shingle of the low tide, he ran round to the front and heaved to free it from the sucking sand. When at last it floated free he clambered into the rocking craft and sat himself down on the wooden seat at the centre. He grasped the oars and started to pull strongly against the wind, soon finding his rhythm between the surging waves. Only when he was a fair distance from the shore did he start trailing the long net overboard to let it fall down to the seabed. James had the optimism and good nature of a schoolboy, along with an almost angelic smile, so he waited calmly, bobbing like a cork on the choppy water, fantasising about the girl he had met so briefly and knew so little about. I shall have to go slowly with that one, he pondered to himself. No doubt she will be asking about me, and that Donnie will not have a good word to say.

Then he was suddenly alert as he saw the arched body of a salmon leap clean out of the water. Immediately he started to row, turning the boat back towards the shore. He felt his muscles pull and strain as he turned the boat in a half circle against the tide in order to trap the fish in his net. When he got the boat back into the shore, he rammed it on to the beach and leapt into the shallows to retrieve the end of the rope that he had left tied to the rock. Hand over hand, he hauled on the ropes to pull in the net, feeling the tension and adrenalin flowing through him at the sight of the frothing tails and silver snatches of the slippery bodies desperately trying to escape. As soon as the net was beached, he grasped his 'killer' and whacked each fish hard on the back of the head before lining them up for inspection. Five big ten-pounders! A good day's work, he complimented himself. Three would go to the estate where he worked as a gamekeeper and stalker and one would go to his brother Iain, who lived up the glen with Jenny his black eyed wife and their three black eyed children. The last, of course, would go straight into his own freezer, nicely chopped into steaks, ready to serve up with some good wine. His future wife, as he had taken to calling her in his head, would never be able to resist a good plate of salmon and the vintage stories and fables he would spin around her as effectively as any cunning spider. All he had to do was wait.

Suzannah Richardson was a study of indignation. Her mouth was pursed tight and her eyes flashed under scowling brows. She revved up her engine and took off with alarming speed, sending a spray of gravel and sand up in her wake. Her only audience for such a tantrum had been some placid sheep peacefully cropping the windblown grasses growing close to the shingle. The slamming car door and erratic speed of her departure made the woolly group disperse in all directions. Suzannah drove furiously along the single-track road to the newly built croft house that sat amidst a long strip of land that rolled down to the sea. She parked next to a red tractor and let herself into the garden, remembering to latch the gate behind her. She knew she would suffer the wrath of her landlady if any sheep got in amongst the precious flowers, tenderly nurtured against incredible odds, for the fierce west winds blew directly in from the sea.

Suzannah stormed into the kitchen. 'I have never been so insulted in my whole life. I can't believe anyone would say such vile things. How dare he presume that I would listen to such talk?'

'Hush, lass, just calm down; you've blown in here like a stormy black cloud. What am I supposed to think? With all that noise you're making, I would have thought you'd been at the point of a knife or something. Dearie me, you had better tell me all about it.' Iona MacPherson cleared a bag of knitting off the chair by the Rayburn stove and ushered her lodger into it. She took Suzannah's smart city coat and hung it out in the cloakroom where it lit up the other drab outdoor clothing and dull tweeds like a bright blue beacon. 'Now, I shall make us a good strong cup of coffee and you can tell me who has been ruffling your feathers. Was it those forestry lads that sit around in their van at the first signal of a rain cloud? I know they can be full of cheek when they like.' Iona filled the kettle and arranged the mugs on a tray. She had a wry smile on her face because she knew her new tenant was already the subject of much speculation in the village.

'No, it was not the forestry lads; it was much worse. I was just talking to an older man. He lives down by the beach, well over there,' she indicated, 'under that hill. He offered to take me fishing then suddenly we were interrupted by the most horrible, dirty old man. He started telling me how long his you-know-what was. It was disgusting; he must be over seventy.'

'Oh, now I understand!' Iona exclaimed, 'You've met the village Romeo, James MacTavish, and the old boy would be Hector Ogilvie, the shepherd who lives up by the woods. No doubt you would have had the seagull story. He must have been quite taken with you. He's quite direct, I'll give you that, probably because he's such a loner. He's forgotten all the social norms. But a kinder man with animals you have yet to find. It's always to him that I run if I have difficulty in lambing time; he's like a local vet in his own way, full of the old magic and he seems to have such a healing in his hands. Poor Hector, don't be too hard on him, lass. I wish you could have met his wife; we used to run to her when we were little, with all our aches and pains. "Make it better, Granny Kate," we'd cry!' Iona busied herself with the tray and grinned out to sea where she could see the distant figure of James patiently sitting in his boat. She continued, 'As for that James MacTavish, believe it or not, that man manages to hook the girls as easily as he manages to pull in the mackerel.' Iona chuckled as she spooned three teaspoons of sugar into her cup. 'Though I think he just enjoys the chase, has done for the last thirty years. Never married; some say he can never find a woman that could replace his mother. What a harridan she was... kept poor James tied tight to her apron strings. If the truth be told, I think no woman would have cared to take on James, knowing that the old *cailleach* would be in the marriage as well. Anyway she's dead now, so I think James is renewing his pursuit of a wife. It galls him that his brother Iain has settled so well and has fathered three fine-looking bairns. You'll find that James is very old-fashioned, and quite a gentleman. Maybe when you meet him again he'll show you his other side.'

Suzannah looked at Iona and nearly choked on her coffee. 'There's not a chance I'll be talking to him again; you can bet on that. I am not up here for some wife market where strangers ask me about my teeth. Oh, I'm so embarrassed that I got enthusiastic about going in his stupid boat. This is not how I had planned spending these months up here. I have to study, and prepare myself. I also have to get ready for school; the term starts next week.'

'Och, lass, relax, you're not in the city now, and these months before you go away are a gift. Let the glen take you in and let your hair down a wee bit. We'll both go to the Pipers tonight for a drink, and I hear there's a dance on at the weekend. The summer dances are always good fun, and you will meet more of the locals there. Once they do meet you they will stop gossiping about you. It's always worse being the subject of the gossip. Just think, in a couple of months you will be at it yourself!'

'Well, I hope I never have to look that old man in the face again,' Suzannah pouted, striding off down the hallway to her room.

Oh dear, she's got a lot to learn, coming up here with her high fallutin' ways, thought Iona. I wonder what else MacTavish said to her; maybe I'll have a word with him in a wee while. She took the binoculars from the window ledge and focused on the figure sitting out in the bay waiting for the fish to rise. Yes, she decided, I might even go down after he's brought in the net; might persuade him to part with a wee fish. After rinsing the cups, Iona pulled on her green Barbour jacket and her wellingtons. She filled a bucket with pellets and stepped outside to feed her pet lambs that were frolicking in the field by the kitchen window. 'Come on girls, come and get your tea!' The four little orphans raced to where Iona was banging the pail and soon were butting each other on the head, trying to get the cobs. 'Poor wee things, with no mammy to feed you. Well, you'll soon be big enough to join the rest of the flock and then maybe I can get some peace.' Iona straightened up, waved at a car that drove past her field and went back into her kitchen. All was quiet, so she planned on having an hour to herself, knitting the jumper that was destined for Murdo, her husband, who was away for a few days on a fencing job on the Black Isle. Iona was a striking woman in her fifties. Her salt-and-pepper-coloured hair was permed tight and her body was still as lean and fit as a girl's.

Her ivory-coloured skin was soft from the rain and moisture that had nourished it over the years and her eyes were as violet as the delphiniums that grew by her front door. Her earnest expression beguiled all who met her to part with their secrets; a necessary talent to assuage her perpetual curiosity for all that was going on around her. Picking up her needles she glanced, as she so often did, at the framed photographs of her daughter occupying pride of place on the mantelpiece.

Suzannah lay back on her bed and surveyed the room that she had rented from Iona MacPherson for the next six months. A very individual style, she thought wryly as she gazed about her. Mauve and pink sweet peas wove themselves around the walls and bright yellow curtains framed the wide window. In the distance, her view took in the giant rocks and boulders that lay like a barricade against the ocean. The walls were adorned with pictures depicting Persian cats and Skye terriers and the carpet was a riot of green ferns. Iona had brought in a gate-leg table and a chair for her to work and keep her books and papers on and already, with her make-up on the dressing table and her clothes hanging in the pine wardrobe, she felt she had settled in. Oh Lord, she wondered, what have I done? I seem to have set myself adrift on a course that I would never have predicted. How on earth did I end up here? And this is just the start of the adventure, she reminded herself, for what on earth will be waiting for me in March? Suzannah wriggled to the side of her bed and pulled a photograph frame from the drawer in the bedside table. The image was that of a serious-looking man who, although not yet forty, had a head of iron-grey hair. Roderick Carruthers' cold grey eyes stared passively back at her. She spoke aloud to her one-time betrothed. 'You would love to see me fail, I know you would, and you would be laughing at my hysterics this morning. I can't even handle the amorous overtures of a Highland shepherd. How on earth will I cope in a country where I don't even speak the language?'

CHAPTER 2

Later that evening, after the dogs and hens and sheep had all been fed, Iona and Suzannah sat down to a good meal of herring and bread and butter, followed by homemade gooseberry fool.

'That was delicious, Iona; was that local fish?'

'Oh no, lass, that comes with the fish van from over Aberdeen way! All the fish and prawns that are caught up here are shipped off to Spain or somewhere. Unless of course you befriend the local gamekeeper! Failing that, you could try your luck in the river. Anyway, now that we have cleared up here, we should go and put on our glad rags and see who is down in the pub. Are you still keen to see your new local? I'll be able to tell you who's who, so you will be prepared for the weekend when we put on our dancing shoes!'

Suzannah went back to her room and slipped into a long, patterned gypsy skirt and a black V neck sweater. She brushed her hair down over her shoulders and it gleamed like platinum laced with golden threads. Iona was smart in tight blue jeans and a navy Guernsey jumper. She had put large silver hoops in her ears and painted her long nails scarlet.

Suzannah was fascinated with the older woman's manicure. 'How on earth do you keep your nails so long, working on the croft and weeding your garden? Look at mine; they're as brittle as sea shells. There is no justice.'

Together they sat at the bar and ordered glasses of red wine. Guitar music was being played by two lads in the corner; one of them was Chinese and sang and spoke in a broad Dundee accent. The barman brought the wine and smiled knowingly at Iona.

'So, are we to be introduced to your friend, Mrs MacPherson?' he asked, grinning broadly at Suzannah. He reckoned that, like himself, she might be around thirty and already he had noted her gleaming hair and the nervous flick of her head. 'Pleased to meet you; I'm Donnie MacKinnon. How are you enjoying the west coast rain?'

Suzannah laughed in spite of herself. 'I am, thank you, and for once it was dry today so I got out for a walk this morning. It is very busy in here; are they all tourists?'

'Aye,' he replied, 'a lot of them are but they'll be off soon, in about another fortnight I imagine, and the glen will be as quiet as quiet. I hear you are staying over the winter. Iona was saying you are a teacher; you'll be covering Mary Beth's maternity?'

'Yes, that's right. I shall be here working with Mrs Munro, and then I have another job lined up for March.'

'She's off to Russia, Donnie, so you had better get in her good books or she'll be sending these mafia types after you!' Iona chuckled knowingly.

'Russia! Well, what are you going to be doing there?' Donnie forgot that he was supposed to be serving, and a stout man with a bushy beard coughed discreetly at the bar.

'Are you telling everyone?' Suzannah turned crossly to Iona. 'Why don't we just tell the local barman to stand up on one of these stools and announce to everyone all my business? Do I not have any right to privacy?'

'Och, away with you, lass, keep your wig on. It's Wednesday night and we're out on the town, and you're here to enjoy yourself. I'm going over there to see Maureen, she who drives the old folks' bus. She was going to be getting me more wool at the shop in the town. You'll be fine here for a minute or two.'

Suzannah scowled into her wine, wishing she wasn't so sensitive. She became aware of a strangely familiar voice breaking into her thoughts.

'Well, who's been throwing her toys out of the pram, then?'

Suzannah nearly dropped her glass when she realized it was her tormentor from the morning. 'Not you again! I don't want to hear any more from you.' And she spun round on the stool and glared fixedly at the rows of malt whiskies that lined the shelves behind the bar.

'Och, come away, lass, I live here too, you know. We can't be enemies, and I'm sorry if I said anything to offend you this morning. You missed a grand catch, by the way. I brought in five bonny salmon and I kept one aside, thinking maybe I could make amends with you. We have a long winter ahead and I do sincerely want us to be friends. I am sure we could find a whole lot of things we could talk about? What do you say?'

James MacTavish's eyes twinkled, his smile was sweet and Suzannah could not believe that she was finding herself relenting.

'Now let me assist you and top up your glass. That Donnie is a very neglectful barman. Look at him there, fussing over crisps and shandies when the most beautiful woman in the room is sitting nursing an empty glass.' He pulled up a stool, sat down beside her and whispered conspiratorially, 'Now tell me, what is your name?'

'Suzannah.' She pursed her lips, and trying to be flippant, tossed stray strands of hair over her shoulder.

James smiled and studied the lines on the palm of his hand. 'And how are things with Iona MacPherson? She'll have you eating her pet hens next. Every time I see her she bends my ear about her lambs or ducks and chicks. When my mother was alive, she would get eggs from Iona, and was treated to great long stories of how Lucy was laying, or how Bella was losing her feathers, and then the next thing Lucy and Bella were on a plate complete with a bit of broccoli and peas. Aye, she's a hard woman, and knows everything that's going on hereabouts. When I see her coming down the field with a jar of jam or something that she's been making, I know that the jungle drums are about to beat. But you'd have to look hard in this world to find a kinder soul.' James drank back his whisky and put down his glass and shouted over to Donnie, 'Another whisky, lad, and the lady here would like another glass of wine. What do you say we move over to the table by the fire, Suzannah? Beautiful name, I remember singing about a Suzannah when I was at school. Now, how did it go?' He made a play of lifting his eyebrows and running his hand through his hair, then sang softly, 'Oh Suzannah, oh won't you marry me!'

Suzannah laughed at the brazenness of the man. His sheer effrontery was like a warm balm after the years of engagement to her aloof, reserved banker. Perhaps she should come down from her high horse and relax and enjoy the ambiance of this friendly village pub. Taking a sip from her second glass of wine, she felt the warmth ooze through her body and she let herself be led down from the stool and over to a chair by the fire. Across the room, Iona and Maureen winked at James, and from behind the bar, Donnie wiped a glass dejectedly.

'How does that old rogue do it?' he muttered.

CHAPTER 3

The next few days saw Suzannah sitting hunched over her desk, preparing books and papers for the new school term. At regular intervals, Iona brought in tea and scones, her eyes sweeping the room for any further clues about her lodger.

'Did you have a good job in Edinburgh?' Iona asked casually as she made a great show of shooing a wasp out of the window. Never actually looking at Suzannah or giving her eye contact, she appeared not to be interested in her reply, thus luring her into a false sense of security.

'I did, yes; I worked with immigrant children who are learning English. So many come into the schools and need extra support. I just helped them get started and cope with the British curriculum.'

'Oh, fancy, I never thought of that, though we hear plenty about the country being over run with people coming from the European Union. I suppose you got tired of all that though, did you, although it does sound very interesting?'

Suzannah sighed and closed her book, unwilling to be drawn further into the conversation. Instead she asked whether Murdo would be home for the weekend and if he would he be going to the dance on Friday night. 'Why is it on Friday, and not Saturday? In Edinburgh the main night for going out is always Saturday.'

'Well, it's because of the Sabbath. Here on the west coast the Church is still strong, and the Free Church of Scotland especially is very strict about what goes on on Sunday. Just ten years ago, I would never have dared to hang out my washing on a Sunday, and many would not have lifted a finger all day. Everything would have been prepared on Saturday night. I have seen men nearly weep, watching the sun shine on a field that has been rained on all week, totally forbidden to take a scythe to cut the hay on the Sunday, but things are changing and slowly the Sabbath is losing its power. Anyway,' she went on, 'Murdo will be home on Saturday, so he will miss the dance, but that won't stop me from going out to enjoy myself. We'll have a lovely time, you'll see.'

On Friday evening Suzannah dressed for the dance in a long green skirt and red polka dot T shirt. She tied her hair back in a half pony tail, and added green eye shadow and scarlet lipstick to match her clothes. Ready and waiting, she thought, but for what? Ever since she was little she had loved the anticipation of dressing up for a party, and smiled to herself at the fleeting memory of stiff net petticoats scratching her legs under soft pastel shades of cotton. White socks and black patent leather shoes would have completed the ensemble. As her thoughts drifted, she gazed out at the dark, looming shapes of the giant boulders down by the water's edge. The sun had set and the sky became a picture of purple and blue swirls, darkening as the shades of evening gave way to the deeper tones of night.

Five hours away, down in Edinburgh, her one-time partner would also be going out. She imagined him in his smart jacket and crisply pressed trousers. She recalled his caustic wit and his beautiful manners. He was so in control of his feelings that he had stifled her, and it was after a reckless argument that she had pursued the idea of leaving her job and taking up a position overseas. She knew she needed to get away from the cosy familiarity of Edinburgh's streets and Roderick's confines, and the day her application had been accepted she had danced wildly round the bedroom. Ukraine? Where on earth was Ukraine? And Kyiv? She knew it only as a recipe involving chicken. Immediately she had signed up for Russian evening classes and had started learning to read and write the Cyrillic script. Gallina, her Russian teacher, had been strict and severe and her teaching style was one that discouraged time-wasters. Suzannah found that she lived for her Tuesday class, and drank in all that Gallina could tell her about Kyiv. She listened to language tapes from the library and fantasized as the deeply masculine foreign voice took her through the unfamiliar vowels. She read books about the Tatars, revolutions and Stalin, and was inspired by the more recent Orange Revolution, born of the ordinary people's demands for change.

Suzannah felt a fleeting ache of regret when she remembered Roderick's face, and the pain that she had inflicted the night she told him that she had been offered the job overseas.

'I don't believe it! I'll wait and see if you resign from your school here first,' he had sneered over the restaurant table. 'You couldn't survive in Ukraine. My goodness, you can't even cross London by yourself!'

She remembered the fury she had felt at his response and the sense of triumph when she had resigned, to be followed by feelings of frustration when she had heard that the school in Kyiv would not actually need her until March the following year. That meant that she was virtually unemployed, and needed to find something to keep her independent for the intervening months. She wanted a clean break from Roderick. She shuddered, recalling his haughty expression when he had said bitterly, 'Well, I suppose I'm entitled to a final fond farewell beneath the sheets before you take off?'

It was, therefore, with some feeling of victory that she had found the job in Drum Mhor, and subsequently the miles between herself and her former fiancé had become an unbridgeable chasm.

I wish I had done something like this years ago; for the first time in my life I feel alive! She hugged herself, and feeling the chill of the bedroom, grabbed her elegant black pashmina and made her way down the hall to the kitchen. The future was full of excitement and even this funny little village was testing her in ways that she could never have imagined. Picking up her bag, she stepped out into the porch to wait for Iona, who was outside stepping gingerly through the hen run.

'Bloody chicken shit all over my shoes. Oh for God's sake! I have a good mind to wring your throats right now.'

Nothing could have prepared Suzannah for her first Highland dance. Iona drove them to the village hall, only to find it half empty. There were a few ladies buttering rolls and heating up soup. The accordion and fiddles were playing a dirge, and two elderly couples were waltzing sedately round the floor.

'We'll go and get a dram first; the dance won't start properly until the Pipers closes, so we'll just park here and walk. No point risking driving with all the special constables in a state of high alert!'

So the two women fought their way into the heaving pub. People were squashed against the bar, desperate to fill and refill their glasses. Donnie was rushed off his feet and the local girl assisting him was equally busy filling all the carry-out orders. Young boys stood swaying, their eyes already glazed with alcohol, clutching their brown paper bags full of tins of lager. In their back pockets it was easy to make out the shapes of their half bottles of whisky.

Suzannah smiled and nodded to a few familiar faces, friends that had come in to see Iona. Pushed and squeezed amongst the throngs of people, she waited apprehensively for Iona to get them drinks, willing her to come quickly.

'I got you a triple gin. I thought it would help to put some fire in your step! Now come over here and meet Wee Eck and Paula. She's not long arrived in the glen, and she's a good laugh. Oh look! Eck's having a right to-do with that Scandinavian tourist lady. He's taken a right shine to her apparently, him that's only about five feet high and her that's close to being a six-footer. He's sitting on that bar stool beside the snooker table.'

Suzannah looked over and saw a broad-shouldered young chap in a plaid quilted shirt and blue jeans. A row of broken, uneven teeth flashed beneath his lecherous grin. His glazed blue eyes, just a little too close together, stared fixedly from above his swollen nose, broken last week during a shinty tackle when the team were up against Kingussie. The Scandinavian woman was intent on proving to Wee Eck that she was the stronger of the two. They were now arm wrestling, their hands locked together and their elbows fused to the green baize cloth of the table as they strained mightily, each attempting to flatten the other. The crowd around them had formed a gallery and were cheering them on in a drunken fashion. With one last breath, the Viking woman pushed hard and Wee Eck's arm went over. As a consequence she raised her arms in victory and chanted, 'I am the winner! I am the winner!'

Not to be outdone, Wee Eck picked himself up to sit on his bar stool. Putting his feet on to the cross rail, he shot up fast, imitating a rocket on its way to the moon. Just for a moment he had raised himself taller that his opponent, but the speed of his lift-off brought his head sharply into contact with the wooden beam of the ceiling. Suzannah groaned when she heard the sickening crunch of the impact and watched him fall like a corpse.

Iona, who had been watching all this action, rushed forward shouting, 'Oh my God! Is he dead?'

The Viking took a swig of her black rum and announced to the audience, 'If he's dead it was suicide, not murder. You saw it. It was self-inflicted and the motive was… was utter madness!'

'Oh, Eck! Oh, Eck! Are you OK?' Iona continued to pat the lad's unconscious face.

Suzannah found herself beside Paula, and both young women started to giggle at the strange sight in front of them.

Paula grinned and cried, 'Imagine making love to him and gasping: "Oh, Eck! Oh, Eck!" '

At that, Wee Eck opened one eye, and looking up lasciviously into Paula's tawny brown eyes, he gave his crooked grin and winked. 'I imagine it fine!' Then he passed out cold.

At closing time, Suzannah and Iona went with the throng back through the streets of the village to the hall. The musicians had picked up and people were forming into sets up and down the room. Soon a *Strip the Willow* was in full swing. Suzannah found herself partnered with the owner of the village shop, Doris's lanky husband Derek, and she could feel his muscular arms beneath the tweed of his jacket as he whirled her around. She knew a fleeting moment of fear when he released her to literally fly on to the arm of the next man. Gasping for breath, she left the dance and staggered over to her friend, who passed her a bottle of orange squash. She took a mouthful, only to taste the strong flavour of gin. The sedate and careful steps of the Highland dancing that she had experienced in the Assembly Rooms of Edinburgh seemed a long way from this frenzy of drunken activity.

Over by the door, the youths stood swaying in their leather jackets. They leered at the young girls, they tipped back their lager, they laughed, and eventually they were sick without ever venturing into the lit-up hall.

Suzannah danced all night till she was giddy from gin and exuberance. She stood arm-in-arm in camaraderie with her new friend Paula, with whom she had bonded during the fracas with Wee Eck and who now was happily sharing her paper cup of wine. They stood by the rows of chairs that held the more senior members of the community, and exchanged deep personal confidences. She found herself telling Paula about her broken romance, and then giggling uncontrollably about the story of the Highland chat-up line: 'Three seagulls, but the last one had one leg up!'

'Three!' shrieked Paula, 'it was only two when he tried it on with me!'

The two young women were in hysterics and it was not until they heard Iona's outraged shriek that they realised another drama was unfolding.

'Oh, for God's sake, Donald John, you spun me so fast my false tooth flew right out of my mouth. It's gone skittering off under those chairs, and blooming Maggie from the Women's Guild is sitting right over them. What if it's broken? What am I going to tell my Murdo when he gets home tomorrow? It'll cost a bloody fortune!'

Meanwhile, in his small stone cottage up by the woods, Hector Ogilvie was writing his diary for the day. It was a ritual he had performed for the last fifty years, and as regular as the setting sun, he jotted down the main events of the day:

Beauty of a day. Shifted cattle over to the nursery. Young Macleod's funeral in Broadford. Football final in Portree. Sprayed the hall sheep. Dance in the village.

He put his little green diary back into the dresser drawer and slowly made his way through to his bedroom. There he undressed down to his combinations. The once-white body suit adhered to his flesh for weeks on end, morning and night, and it was only after much consideration that he would occasionally decide to give the lot a wash in his new twin-tub machine. It had been a gift from Kathleen at the Tea Room, after she had treated herself to a new deluxe model that apparently did everything, or so she was known to crow.

CHAPTER 4

James MacTavish was a clean and tidy man. He liked order in his house and he was noted in the community for always showing meticulous adherence to detail. Iona MacPherson often laughed at him from her kitchen window, her vantage point so to speak, from where she would watch him through her binoculars. Well, I see the grass is being cut within an inch of its life, she thought. No doubt the tape measure will be out when he comes to trim the bushes. God forbid if a stray branch dares to grow out of the symmetry! She noted that today he was weeding his vegetable plot. It was an overcast morning in September, and a greenfinch sat eying him from its perch on the fence. James counted the onions growing in straight lines; he had thirty-three exactly; round and fat and just ready to be harvested. He was afraid the frosts would come and ruin his crop and he knew he needed to get them up before the rain came. Looking up at the stormy clouds brewing in the west, he decided to lift them and dry them in the shed. Already he had his carrots stored in a box of sand. He would then be able to dig over the plot and leave it dark and ready for its winter hibernation. At the weekend he would gather seaweed from the beach and use that to protect his roses from the cold winter months to come. He frowned when he looked at his Brussels sprouts and broccoli and winter cabbages. Bloody sheep had got in and had a right feast and left him with only half his crop. The rest were being eaten to death by some pest or other. 'I'll have to get into the race myself and have them for my dinner as soon as I can,' he muttered to himself.

Later, leaning on his spade, with a box of smooth brown onions at his feet, he looked at his watch. Twelve o'clock already, he noted; they'll be here any minute now. Stepping into the shed, he laid his onions carefully on to the work bench to let them dry off. He then walked round to the front of the house where he sat down on the old pew he used as a garden bench. Across the fields he could see the figures of his brother's wife and her youngest child making their way towards him. Standing up to greet them, he called out and waved, 'Hello there!'

'Uncle James, I've brought my pens and I'm going to work with you!'

'Good afternoon, Rosie, did you have a good morning in your nursery school? I think I can see some bonny blue paint on your collar and your knee... Was there any left for your picture, I'm wondering?'

'Of course, silly! My painting was so good that Fiona hung it up on the wall, or I would have brought it for you to see. She said she just couldn't help herself. She just wanted to look at it for days or maybe even for years.'

'My word! It must have been a masterpiece. What was it of? Was it the blue sea or maybe a blue house?'

'No, Uncle James, it was a baboon. Did you like it, Mum?'

Jenny smiled down at her daughter. 'I did, lass, it was the best baboon in the nursery. Now you be a good girl for your Uncle James and I'll be back to pick you and your brother up at six o'clock. Here, James, here's Billy's clothes for him to change into when he gets back from the school. Cheerio, then!'

James and Rosie waved goodbye as Jenny headed back towards the village. She was a care assistant in the old people's home and, although usually she worked only in the mornings, they sometimes gave her an afternoon shift as well. James was happy to help out with the children, for his brother Iain was away driving his bus, criss-crossing the Scottish Highlands, and often he was not home till six or seven at night. Their older son Jonathan was away at school in Inverness, and didn't get home until the weekend.

His own job on the estate had flexible hours due to the very nature of the seasonal work involved. Despite the hectic time of the deer stalking, he had a week's reprieve before the next party arrived to go out on the hill. He looked down at his little niece. She was a picture in her bright yellow raincoat and red welly boots. Her short-cropped hair was almost as black as a raven's wing and her eyes were big, dark brown pools of sombre contemplation.

'Come on Rosie, my wee darling; let's see what we can have for our lunch. I suppose you'll be wanting your favourite, spaghetti snakes on toast?'

'Yes please, Uncle James, can I draw with my pens while you make it?'

'Not a chance, young lady, for I have a special job for you. You have an appointment in the bathroom with a big bar of soap. I want you to get those hands nice and bubbly and I shall smell them to make sure you didn't miss any little places when you come back. We want no grubby nursery germs to contaminate our fancy lunch now, do we?'

While they ate, the sky grew dark and the rain started to lash down on the windows.

'Well,' said James, 'that means we won't be going for a walk after all. I was going to show you where the otters come up to play, over by the rocks, and where I found a sandpiper's nest in the shale on the beach. It will have to wait now till the weekend.'

'We can draw then, instead?' Rosie was not at all put out by the change of plans. She adored sitting in the dark and cosy wood-panelled sitting room, on a fish box with her knees tucked under a small wooden table that her uncle had constructed from bits of driftwood from the beach. It was the perfect size for her four year-old form, and she liked to sit beside him, mimicking his actions at his polished oak desk.

James MacTavish had a passion for lighthouses. Books lined the shelves by the fireplace; specialist books with architectural drawings of the lighthouses around the British Isles. Ever since he was a boy of Rosie's age, James had felt himself mesmerised by the twinkling lights that dotted the coastline of his own Highland home. Long ago his father had rowed him out to the lighthouse nearest Drum Mhor and had held him as he grappled with the iron steps that led up the sheer cylindrical wall. Up and up they climbed, high above the jagged rocks that were as sharp as teeth below him. He remembered looking down at the dark water breaking over them. When they had climbed inside, his father had patiently led him up the spiral staircase to the watchtower, a dome of glass which housed the great light that must never be allowed to go out. James had looked out at the gulls wheeling in the wind. Around him he took in the panorama of water and sky and he marvelled at the men who lived in these structures and protected all the ships that sailed by the rocks that were just waiting to smash them to smithereens. Later he had been given a cup of cocoa by the then-resident keeper. He was everything that James could have imagined. He had a white beard, a sailor's cap, a ribbed jumper and yellow boots. The day had imprinted itself on the boy's memory, until now, nearly half a century later, he still collected books and writings and drawings of the structures. The wonder had never left him, so as he had grown up, he had made a point of visiting as many lighthouses as he could around the Scottish coast. Things had changed of course. No longer were the wick and candles of the last century used, for electric generators now provided the electricity to light these beacons. In recent years, James had seen even that age pass, and now there were few manned lighthouses left. Instead the automated lighthouses were run by computers.

Today he was sketching a photograph that he had taken of the Eilean Mor lighthouse in the Flannan Isles. Beside him, Rosie sat copying a print of the Bass Rock lighthouse near Edinburgh. She was very intent on her work and her small face was a study in concentration. He noted that she showed a good eye for detail. After completing her drawing, she proceeded to colour it in, purple of course, with a bright orange window at the top. The sun dominated the top half of the page and she had even thought to give it sunglasses and a smiley mouth with teeth.

'What a beautiful picture, Rosie! But what about a boat? Maybe you could put a boat or a fish in the water?'

The clock on the sideboard ticked away the afternoon. James noticed that the rain had stopped, and went into the kitchen to make a cup of tea. He took down a bowl and gave Rosie a packet of chocolate powder to empty into it. He then poured in some milk.

'Now you just whip that up, young lady, and we'll have a nice pudding for our dinner.'

When the bowl full of creamy chocolate whip had been placed into the refrigerator to set, he stepped out to the garden to cut a few bits of broccoli for the evening meal. The grass was soaking and he made a detour to check on his shed, for he had noticed there was a leak there during the last downpour. He reassured himself that the few drips would keep for another day, and finally went to cut the broccoli heads. When he came back into the kitchen, he spotted his small charge standing by the fridge, her face covered in chocolate mousse. James pretended ignorance and walked past her, heading straight for the sink where he started to wash the broccoli.

'It's as well I came back in,' he said, keeping his eyes averted. 'I was out there in the garden, just down by the wall, and there were a whole lot of mushrooms and toadstools that I had never seen before. Big fancy poisonous ones, you know the kind? The red and white spotty ones that the fairies live under?'

Rosie's brown eyes were growing to the size of saucers.

'Well, dearie me, if I didn't see one! All tiny and dressed up with wings and what not. She shouted to tell me to hurry back into the house because there was someone stealing from my fridge! Imagine! Well who could that be? Do you think someone has been at the chocolate pudding?'

Rosie's eyes darted to the window. Her small mouth pursed in a look of grim determination. Eyebrows drawn down, she marched straight for the back door and pulled on her red welly boots.

'Where are you off to in such a hurry? Are you not going to help me find out who it could be?'

In silence Rosie opened the door and stormed out to the garden. James chuckled gleefully to himself while he scraped potatoes and put the vegetables into the pots. It wasn't long before Rosie returned. She sidled into the kitchen and pulled off her grass-smeared boots, trying to appear nonchalant.

'What have you been up to, young Rosie MacTavish?' he asked her sternly.

She looked away, wiping her chocolate-smeared mouth with the back of her hand. 'I just stamped on those fairies,' she muttered grimly, almost to herself.

James averted his face to suppress a chuckle, and busied himself at the sink.

Just after four o'clock, the peace was shattered when Billy came clattering back from school. At eight years old, he was full of energy and his cheeks were red from running.

'Hello, Uncle James, I'm starving, have you any biscuits or has Rosie eaten everything?'

'Come in, boy; my goodness me, I've seen better manners from a wolf.'

The dynamics changed as the lad ran through to James's bedroom to change into his blue jumper and jeans. He seemed to bring the wind and wetness in with him, as well as all the noise from the playground.

'Well, I can see you've had a good day, and you are obviously all set to keep going. Now come here and have some milk and some of Iona MacPherson's gingerbread. After that, why don't we go down to the river's edge? With the water so high after all that rain, we might be lucky to get a wee brown trout. What do you say?'

'Fantastic, Uncle James, but Rosie has to get the worms. She's the best at that.'

Once more dressed for the weather, the little group spent a few minutes raking through James's tidy compost heap of old grass cuttings, and soon found a good selection of juicy worms. Rosie kept all of hers in a pail, since she wanted to keep them as pets.

She carried the landing net, for the trio were very optimistic that their fishing would bring in a huge salmon as well as a shoal of trout. Billy was adept at fixing the worm on to his hook and cast out expertly into a dark pool overgrown with alder and hazel trees. Drips from the afternoon's rain soaked his back as he bent down under the hawthorn bushes that lined the river bank.

'Now you stay here away from the edge, pet, and play with your worms. I don't want you falling in and getting an early bath. Your mother would give me an awful earful if I gave you back all soaking wet.'

'Not only that, her face and big feet would just scare off all the fish, wouldn't they, Uncle James?' Guilelessly, the boy continued to stare into the ever-increasing circles that rippled around his lure.

James liked to fish with Billy. The boy had the patience for the sport; ever since he was a little lad he had accompanied his uncle either with the rod or the darrow, or even helping to pull up the salmon nets. He showed no sentiment when it came to killing or gutting, and the long companionable silences were therapeutic to both man and boy.

'School OK?' James asked him now, as he cast expertly beside him.

'Yes, though I wish I had the new teacher, Miss Richardson. I have Mrs Munro this year; Miss Richardson has all the little ones. She's nice. She doesn't make them do any work. They just paint and get to dress up and only have to do easy stuff. Not like us, we have to work all the time and we never get to play with the blocks or anything. I think there should be a law against it, don't you?'

'Oh, I am sure she makes them work sometimes, but what do you like best at school, Billy? Are you doing the chanter this year?'

'Definitely, I am going to be a great piper, and I am going to the wars as part of the Royal Scots Regiment and I shall play the pipes. Grand job that would be. Susan Mackay's big brother is doing that now. All you have to do is wear a kilt and march about playing. Maybe on the odd day you might have to do some shooting, but that will be OK. I don't think I'd like to do it every day. We get to play shinty this year as well.' He went on. 'Mrs Munro is so funny when she runs around showing us how to tackle. She has a big woman's skirt on and she looks a right sight swinging her stick in the air! I think we should have a man teaching us.'

Behind them, they could hear the murmur of voices. They suddenly realised that Rosie was not talking to her worms as they imagined, but to someone else.

'No, they don't have names; they are just worms, don't you know that?'

'Well, when I was a little girl I used to name all my pets; I had frogs and butterflies and I called them Bob and Betty, and Oh! I can't remember all of them. I just thought you might have names for your worms. Willie might be good for one of them?'

'No,' said Rosie, decisively. My brother will just stick them on his hook in a minute and then I'll be sad. I would be even sadder if I thought of a fish eating Elizabeth or something.'

Billy hissed at his uncle, 'It's the teacher!'

'Hello, Billy,' Suzannah smiled. 'Are you having any luck?'

'No, Miss Richardson, still trying; we've only just got here. The fish will have had a fright with us crashing through the bushes and so on.'

'I didn't know you were allowed to fish in this river; I thought it was private.'

'Good afternoon, ma'am.' James emerged from the hawthorn. 'You are right about the river, but it is permitted for folk to fish this part of the river where it's tidal. It's further up that the regulations come in, and you have to pay a tidy sum for the privilege.'

'Hello, James, I didn't notice you there. I see you have your brother's children with you today. I'm sure they must keep you busy. Well, I must get on. I needed some fresh air, and it's nice to get out after being cooped up all day. You see, Billy, even teachers need to get out sometimes too.'

'Why don't you pop down some evening? Perhaps I could

interest you in a wee drop of home-made elderberry wine? Maybe later this evening, when these skallywags have gone home?'

Suzannah was on the point of refusing, then seeing the look of expectation in both Rosie's and Billy's face, she relented.

'Why not? I haven't had home-made elderberry wine for years.'

'You are going where?' Iona asked, her eyes opened wide in disbelief.

'Well, I met him with the children; they were fishing, and somehow it seemed quite a natural thing to do. What is he going to do? Eat me? I think he is really quite a nice man. Every time I see him I learn something else about him, and he is not as crass as I once imagined.'

'Och, you were a bit hasty that first time, but I must say you are mellowing, lass, not as snooty as you once were.'

'I was not snooty,' Suzannah snapped back indignantly. 'You know you told me that Eric the plumber was fishing that river, and you said he was poaching? Well, James told me just now that it's fine to fish down there near the sea. What did you mean?'

Iona smiled as she recollected the story that had passed around the glen last season. Eric had not been fishing down near the sea. In fact he had been fishing up past the big pool on the other side of the bridge, which was definitely not tidal. A permit was required to fish in that part of the river. Further along the bank Eric glimpsed a grand toff, up from England, dressed to the nines with all his fancy gear on. When he saw Eric, looking like a right ruffian in his old jacket and wellington boots, he shouted over, 'Do you know that I paid £400 to fish in this river, my good chap? Have you paid the same?' Eric had taken great pleasure in answering, 'Well now, who's a bloody fool then, eh?' Iona laughed as she recounted the story that no doubt would go down in village legends. 'Anyway,' she continued, 'you'd better not tell that to James MacTavish. He is the gamekeeper after all, and he would report anyone, local or not, for poaching on his precious river.'

'I won't say a word. See you later, Iona!' Suzannah pulled on her waterproof and her new wellington boots and trudged through the long grass down towards the sea, where the little house sat in the lee of the hill, surrounded by its fence and neatly partitioned garden.

'Come in, lassie, come in.' James had banked up his fire and tidied the house after his day of child minding. Rosie's picture of the lighthouse was pinned on the wall by the Rayburn in the kitchen. Suzannah took off her coat and hung it on the hook by the door in the hall, where she glanced at the dark-hued portrait of a woman of a bygone age.

'That is my mother, a modern day saint, sadly passed on just two years ago,' James explained as he ushered her into the warmth of the house. 'She made all her own jams and pickles and what not. Raised six boys and buried three. I miss her yet.'

Suzannah looked around the kitchen and took in the stark white walls, the black-and-white chequered linoleum. Open plan shelving held James's provisions as neatly as though they were in a shop. Pots and pans were all on display, scrubbed and polished.

A white stone sink stood in the corner, above which a window looked out over the back garden. Suzannah peered out at the vegetable plot, all neatly dug over. James passed her two glasses to carry into the sitting room while he himself brought in a bottle of rich red wine, and a plate of crackers and slices of cheddar.

'I thought perhaps that I should have the cheese stuck on dainty sticks with cubes of pineapple. Is that not how you city folks entertain?'

Suzannah smiled, momentarily remembering her evenings with Roderick Carruthers. He used to produce plates of brie and stilton, fat olives and exotic pâtés that came from Edinburgh's finest delicatessens. She sat down in a deep leather armchair by the fireside. Across from her, James settled himself into a matching chair and arranged their refreshments on a fish box that had been covered with a plum-red velour cloth. Suzannah gazed in wonder around her; the book shelves, the range of titles, the large desk, the soft glow of the table lamps and the warmth that came from the hot, burning peat on the open fire.

'Oh, how lovely it is in here. And lighthouses! Do I see books and books about lighthouses?'

'I've always had a notion for them, ever since I was a wee lad and my father took me to visit one. I remember it fine, climbing up the iron rungs on the ladder and seeing the sea so far below me. I have been collecting information about them for years, and have compiled enough to write my own book.'

'You're writing a book?' Suzannah arched her eyebrows in surprise.

'Aye, I am that. There's a lot of interesting stories that go along with the facts, you know. A bit like life, wouldn't you say?' His blue eyes followed her as she gazed around at his books and pictures. She was a striking girl, he thought, and he liked the way she curled her legs under her as she sat. Obviously feels at home here, which is a good sign, he decided.

'Now do you see this lighthouse here?' he gestured to the lighthouse that he had been working on during afternoon.

'Looks very wild and windy,' Suzannah commented, viewing the rocks and waves around the slim structure.

'Well, this lighthouse holds a mystery, even spookier than the story of the Marie Celeste. Do you want to hear about it?'

Suzanne nodded, intrigued at such an unlikely subject for an evening's conversation.

'Well,' began James, with relish, 'the lighthouse at the Flannan Isles is away on the west coast of Lewis in the Outer Hebrides. Its local name is Eilean Mor, and it's on the largest of a group of small uninhabited islands in the Atlantic, about twenty-two miles west of the mainland. You can only get to it by boat; can you see it here on my map?'

Suzannah picked out the lighthouse's position on the exposed coastline and nodded.

James studied the picture he had in his hand. 'It's a mystery, lass, that's what it is. No one knows for sure what happened, and many have their theories and their ideas, but still no one can say. It was on the fifteenth of December 1900 when the steamer Archtor, on its way from America to the port of Leith, passed the islands in wild weather, and the captain observed that no light was visible. He reported it, but owing to terrible winter storms, it wasn't until Boxing Day that the relief vessel could get to the island. The lighthouse was always manned by a three-man team, with a rotating fourth man spending time on shore. Well, when the relief boat eventually arrived, they not only found the flagstaff bare of its flag, but what's more there was no sign of the lighthouse crew.'

'My goodness! What happened?' exclaimed Suzannah.

'God only knows,' declared James. 'A boat was launched, and Joseph Moore, he was the assistant keeper, was put ashore alone. He found the outer door to the lighthouse locked, but he had a set of keys and when he entered he found the place deserted, the beds empty, the clock stopped, the fire out, and food left on the table. There was even a set of oilskins, suggesting that one of the keepers had left the lighthouse without them, which was really strange considering the severity of the weather. There was plenty of evidence of a storm hitting the island, but of the keepers themselves, there was no trace, neither inside the lighthouse nor anywhere on the island.'

'Do you think they might have been blown off the cliffs and drowned?' asked Suzannah, her eyes opened wide with interest.

'I doubt we'll ever know now,' replied James seriously, 'there was that much speculation about what might have happened, but it's generally accepted that somehow the sea claimed them.'

'Were no bodies found anywhere?' Suzannah asked, thinking they might have been washed away during the storm.

'No.' James shook his head, and making a steeple with his fingers, he reiterated what the press had reported. 'No bodies were ever found. I suppose the loneliness of those rocky isles might have lent itself to some feverish imaginings. There was even a ballad written about it. Now wait and see if I can find it for you.' He got up and went to his desk, rifling through his papers, until he found a book about the islands. 'Here it is, you might like this, it was written in 1912 by Wilfrid Wilson Gibson, and it's called simply *Flannan Isle*. He refers to a half-eaten meal on the table, indicating that the keepers had been suddenly disturbed:

> *Yet, as we crowded through the door,*
> *We only saw a table spread*
> *For dinner, meat, and cheese and bread;*
> *But, all untouched; and no-one there,*
> *As though, when they sat down to eat,*
> *Ere they could even taste,*
> *Alarm had come, and they in haste*
> *Had risen and left the bread and meat,*
> *For at the table head a chair*
> *Lay tumbled on the floor.*

James sighed and closed the book and put it down by his chair. He reached for his glass and took a sip of his wine. Both remained silent. Finally, breaking the mood, the fire crackled and a log rolled on to the hearth. Quick as a flash, James knelt down and with the tongs, retrieved the glowing ember. Suzannah caught sight of a stereo player on a shelf by James's desk. Above it was a row of neatly arranged tapes and CDs. No doubt, Suzannah thought, they will all be in alphabetical order. She remembered that Iona had said how pernickety he was.

'What music do you like?' she asked brightly.

'Well my favourite is pipe tunes,' James announced unexpectedly. My uncle was a great piper and was asked to play for royalty once when the Britannia sailed past here one summer.'

'Pipe tunes!' Suzannah grinned. 'Do you not find them a bit noisy for the house?'

'Oh no, not at all,' exclaimed James. 'I like to have a good medley going, loud as I like, especially when I'm in the bath. They're inspiring as well when I'm out in the garden seeing to the cabbages!'

Suzannah frowned as she studied James's face in the firelight. His twinkling eyes were bright, his mobile features constantly changing expression. One minute he was looking soulful and concerned, the next as though he was on the verge of a fit of laughter.

He took another sip of wine, considering for a minute, before he went on, 'I do like that fellow Leonard Cohen. Grand soulful stuff, that!'

Suzannah laughed. 'I haven't listened to him since I was at university! I think he appeals to the angst we all feel, and the songs are all so sad. Do you want to play some now?'

James got up and went over to his collection of music. 'I have some good Country and Western too; maybe you'd like to hear some Patsy Kline?'

'No, put on some Leonard Cohen, that might be nice.'

James inserted the CD and fiddled with the controls. He came back and sat down, waiting for the song to play. The quiet room was suddenly flooded by the lugubrious tones of the singer as he intimately caressed them with his probing words. James had selected *I'm your Man*, and sat back with half-closed eyes, imagining that it was himself singing the words, full of innuendo of course, to his lovely visitor.

Suzannah smiled over at the old charmer. 'Next you will be playing the song about taking Suzanne down to the river!'

'Aye, well, you did say you wanted to hear him,' James reminded her. 'A man must act on the hints he receives!'

Shaking her head, Suzannah got up and looked through the music selection herself. 'Let's have something less melancholy,' she suggested, tipping her head a little to read the titles on the spines. She finally selected Dvořák's 'New World' Symphony.

James took a poker to the fire and mused with satisfaction at how easily she was making herself at home. The music swelled around them, soothing and harmonious, filling the room with the cadences and ripples and haunting melodies. The two sat quietly, relaxed and content. Slowly they exchanged confidences, tentatively probing and questioning each other about their lives and their interests. Their eyes were warm, their faces flushed from the wine and the flames of the fire.

Suzannah told James the sorry tale of her broken engagement to Roderick Carruthers, and how she needed to get away to start a new life.

James told Suzannah that Nell MacTavish had brought six sons into the world. Two had died in infancy; another had drowned while fishing off Aberdeen. Lewis had immigrated to New Zealand, leaving only James and his brother Iain to live with their widowed mother in the old house. Then Iain had got married and James had continued living with his mother until the day they carried her in a pine box to the windswept cemetery on a hill overlooking the troubled sea. There she was interred with her wedded husband, long since dead. He had left her widowed on a summer's night over forty years ago. Drunk from a night of communal ribaldry after a day's sheep clipping, he had been gored on the horn of a neighbour's cow.

Later, after Suzannah had closed the door behind her and stepped out into the dark night, James went back to the stereo player and replayed his recording of Leonard Cohen. While clearing away the plates and rinsing the glasses he hummed along to the words of *I'm your Man*. He smiled contentedly. The day had gone very well. Maybe, just maybe, he might throw away that form he had tucked away on the shelf, beneath the tin of treacle.

CHAPTER 5

October came in blustery and wild. Gales blew the leaves clean off the trees and made a hearty attempt at lifting the roof right off James's house. Billy and Rosie were full of the madness that wind seems to inject into children, especially on Saturday mornings when there was no school. They rushed about making their plans for the day. Since there had been a break in the squalls of rain that lashed against the gable end of his house, James had decided to spend the time securing the tin roof on his shed. Jenny had called down earlier to drop the children off, for she had to go to Inverness with her older son, Jonathan.

'You're full of glee today, aren't you? What has your mother been feeding you? I think you must be on a diet of those jumping beans, by the look of you. At this rate you are going to be wearing out all my grass with your running back and forth like that.'

Rosie shrieked excitedly, 'We're going to dig a pit to trap… '

'To trap a mammoth,' cut in Billy. 'I know all about mammoths and sabre-toothed tigers. Can I borrow your spade, Uncle James? I think we'll dig up the field just a wee bit, so that we can camouflage it properly.'

Unthinkingly James let them have what they wanted and went back to his job of fixing the roof. When he was happy with his repairs, he walked down the path to see where the children were. He grinned to himself while surveying a pile of earth growing like a giant molehill amongst the grass. Billy was making good progress and had dug to a depth of about a foot. I have my doubts he'll be entertaining any elephants in that great hole, James thought. He'll be lucky if he catches a mouse or a vole. If I'd asked him to turn the earth in my vegetable patch there would have been great huffing and puffing and sulking, but to dig to catch a mammoth, extinct for a few million years, well he seems to have the energy of five men!

'You'd better be careful, Billy-boy,' James called out to his nephew, 'at the rate you are digging I'm afraid you might be getting close to Australia!'

'Don't be silly, Uncle James. I have to get to the centre of the earth first and that's filled with fire.'

'But it's OK, Billy,' nodded Rosie, her eyes big as saucers, 'we have lots of sea nearby so we won't burn, nor will the mammoth when it falls in, will it?'

'Right, well you two just carry on, I have things to do.' James went back inside and filled the kettle. He was expecting company later in the afternoon. Suzannah, Paula and Iona were coming round, as well as Donnie from the bar. Paula had decided to stay on in Drum Mhor, and had taken a lease for a cottage that was adjacent to the row of whitewashed houses in the village. She was a right bright spark, full of the notions of putting on a drama in the hall. Many muttered behind their curtains that the hall saw enough drama as it was, without anyone planning more shenanigans. James had allowed himself to be talked into being a founder member of the group and soon he surprised himself by looking forward to the rehearsals and planning meetings that led to closer proximity to the ladies.

It was an unexpected pleasure that filled up the back end of the year. Usually by October, when the nights drew in, the folk from the village retired behind their front doors and huddled by their firesides. This year James had done little work on his lighthouses; he had been far too busy learning his lines. The group were putting on a play about a Middle Eastern sultan. The star of the show was going to be none other than the Reverend Jeremy Wilson. Paula had coerced him into it one Sunday morning after a rousing service, and the man was more than happy to be persuaded. The minister brought with him his grand, deep voice and his flair for the dramatic, and had singlehandedly transformed the play. James was relieved, because previously that part had been pencilled in for himself. He had since been relegated to the role of eunuch, which he was not too happy about, but had decided that he would have himself described in the programme as the 'keeper and protector of the sultan's harem'. He felt it gave him a little more dignity, though goodness knows what Paula would have him dressed up in. He just hoped that he could have a nice long robe to hide behind. James was not the sort of man who liked to show off his naked torso, especially in front of the village in winter time. Suzannah had rounded up several budding actresses, mostly young mothers, who were all set for the belly-dancing classes that Paula was going to teach, and so the harem was now cast. Donnie was to be a wicked king who had designs on one of the ladies of the court.

Today though, the group were coming round to discuss the scenery. Iona's Murdo had some grand big sheets of polystyrene they thought they could use. Suzannah said that it was very 'arty' to just have black and white scenery; then the costumes would look very bright and fetching in front. It would be a good contrast; she'd seen something like it during the Edinburgh Festival. James was delegated as the painter, seeing as he was good at lighthouses. He didn't quite see the connection himself. That bossy Paula had sent away for a posh box of theatrical face paint and some costumes that you could hire from a fancy dress shop down there in England. Even wee Rosie was to have a part. She was to walk on to the stage carrying a cushion.

James had quite forgotten about the children, he was so taken up with his reverie, so it was not until they burst in, their faces red and windblown and eyes full of excitement, that he remembered the trap that was going to catch a mammoth. 'Come here, you rascals, go and wash your hands and then you can eat this good bowl of Scotch broth. After that I want you to go and fetch me a bucket of mussels from the beach. I am having the drama group visiting this afternoon.'

The children were happy to comply and after eating their soup and two scones dripping with syrup, they flew out of the door and down to the beach, where they chased the seagulls along the line of the shore.

'Quick, Rosie, get as many as you can. We have to go back and keep watch!' Billy was in a fever of excitement. He had it all planned, for it was not a woolly mammoth that he hoped to catch, but Iona MacPherson. They had dug the hole on the path that led down from her house. Making their way back up to their uncle's cottage, they skirted their way around the rocks and hid their buckets, half-full of the shellfish, by a rock pool. Then, scrambling over the stones, they wriggled like Indian redskins along the grass until they came to the carefully placed, upturned drinking trough used by the sheep in the summer.

'Get under, Rosie, pull in your leg. Now me, move over. I'll put this wee log here to keep it open. We need oxygen to breathe, you know, and then we can see when she falls into the trap!'

The children did not have long to wait, for soon the members of the newly formed Drum Mhor Drama Club strolled down through the field to James MacTavish's stone cottage. They had all met at Iona's, so now they came down as a group, and it was with alarm that the boy hunter spied them from his post beneath the water trough.

'Oh, no! I thought it would be just Iona, I don't want to capture that Donnie from the bar; he'll skin me alive if he finds out it was me.'

Billy need not have worried for, as luck would have it, they all stepped around the carefully disguised mantrap, the pile of freshly dug earth being a dead giveaway of recent excavations. The children were so proud of the camouflage. Billy had made a lattice of branches and sticks and then covered them with some pages from *The Press and Journal*. On to that he had gently sprinkled some sand and then finally he had replaced the turf back on top. But it had all been to no avail. The adults disappeared safely into the house and he was left feeling forlorn. There was nothing else to do now except continue picking the mussels from the rocks down on the windswept shore.

'Look, Rosie! Look, there's old Hector! What's he looking at?' The children dropped their buckets and ran up to the old shepherd.

'Hello there, young Rosie, and what are you and your brother up to today?' Hector asked kindly.

'Nothing any more, we just tried to make a trap to catch Iona, but she walked around it. It's not fair.'

'A trap? Well, I've made a few of those in my time. It's just all trials and tribulations. But look up there, Billy-boy, do you see that?'

Billy squinted into the darkening sky, and only noted the dark clouds ballooning and mushrooming with the gusting wind.

'See what?' he asked, scanning the hills and open sea.

'I see, look!' shrieked Rosie. 'Over there!'

Across the swirls of yellow-gold they could make out the magical forms of the geese, flying away in their characteristic vee.

'The first of the season,' Hector told them. Later he would record it in his diary.

The drama meeting and rehearsal went well. The group, duly fortified with birch-sap wine, ran through their lines with growing confidence.

'I think this play will be fantastic!' James enthused. 'It's great that the minister is taking part. Imagine the Reverend with all those skimpily-clad lassies! How are the belly-dancing classes going, Paula?'

'I have ten girls in the harem, including Iona and Suzannah here, and they are coming on a treat! I only went once to a class myself so I don't have much of a clue, but so long as they do a bit of shimmying and wiggle their hips about it will be a lively enough spectacle!'

'I have the black gloss paint, and I've drawn out four scenes that will provide the backdrop, so if you all give them your approval then I'll get on and paint them this week.' James took down the sketches and everyone was impressed with the patterns and filigree tracings that he had used to give an impression of a sultan's palace. He had managed to give the illusion of steps with urns and pots of ferns and trailing plants. He had drawn archways with patterned motifs running alongside stone imagery that could have come from the Middle East.

'That is brilliant, James, and as Suzannah said, with the colourful costumes and the scatter cushions and the grand red Persian rug that we're borrowing from the doctor, everyone will think they are in Arabia!'

'Well, I hope my veil is pretty thick. Can I not get a black burka and sit at the side like a granny or something?' Iona lamented. 'What if my false tooth falls out again during the bit when we all have to dance around? I'll just have to keep my veil up over my face.'

'You are doing very well, Iona,' soothed Paula, 'you have natural rhythm, but if you're worried, I'm sure you can buy some special cement to glue it in.' Paula handed out the rehearsal schedules for the week. 'I will be seeing Reverend Wilson at church on Sunday, so I'll remind him that he has a rehearsal with the belly-dancers. I'll have to keep my voice down, though – imagine if anyone heard me making such a racy assignation!' She mimicked herself. ' "Lovely service, Reverend, are you free Tuesday night to work with your ladies of the harem!" '

They all laughed and James filled the glasses and passed around oatcakes spread with Crowdie cheese. The afternoon wore on and eventually it was time to bring the meeting to a close. The dark was settling over the glen when the visitors took their leave. Billy and Rosie had sneaked in earlier and were warm and snug in James's sitting room. Suddenly a blood-curdling scream broke the peace. Iona had fallen into the children's trap. Fortunately for her, the pit was only as deep as her knee and Donnie and Suzannah were able to lift her out. Luckily for Billy, no major damage had occurred.

'Oh my goodness!' exclaimed James, 'I think that was meant to catch a mammoth!'

'Bloody kids!' she roared. 'They should be put in a cage, so they should.'

CHAPTER 6

Three weeks later Suzannah swiped the top off her boiled egg and watched her landlady limp around the kitchen. She was still making heavy weather of her wrenched knee.

'Are you seeing Paula after school today? Could you tell her I should be all right for rehearsals next week? I think I need to put my leg up again for a day or two.'

Suzannah nodded and bit into her toast. She knew that with this stormy weather, the pull of the fireside and the heavy wool on the knitting needles was the real reason that Iona was shirking the humiliating gyrations of the belly-dancing class.

'Och, lass, there's nothing to it; I can do it myself in front of the bathroom mirror. Just tell Paula I shall be as right as rain next week… maybe.'

Suzannah looked forward to her afternoons with Paula. The two young women had become firm friends over the last few months. They enjoyed meeting in Kathleen's Tea Room in the centre of the village. Being situated right next to the village shop, it was very convenient for people to buy their groceries and then drop in next door for a tea or coffee and a pancake behind the lace curtains.

Kathleen, a comfortably proportioned spinster in her mid-fifties, was the exuberant proprietor of the cosy establishment. She skilfully manoeuvred her ample girth between the closely spaced tables, her laden tray held high above her customers' heads. She showed a preference for loud, flowery overalls, and her helmet of white hair seemed at odds with her girlish fringe. Pink powdered cheeks and bright cerise lipstick just added a further dash of colour even on a mid-November day such as this. Kathleen had her own ideas of how a tea room should be set up. She was not a woman who favoured tea bags, and only stored a small collection of fruit varieties which she kept out of sight beneath the counter. She only produced these under pressure and even then with a certain amount of tutting or perhaps an audible sigh should a tourist request them during the summer season. Instead, on the wall behind the counter, she had six shelves on which she proudly kept a collection of forty-two tea pots in all colours and varieties, shapes and sizes. She encouraged people to sit and strain their tea, and eat her home baking and stay as long as they liked. The room was cosy, and her six tables were covered with creamy crochet cloths. Naturally, the tea sets were of old-fashioned china decorated in old-fashioned roses. The ambience was gentle and belied the often vicious gossip that was whispered back and forth between the nodding heads of the village matrons.

'I don't know who that Paula thinks she is, coming up here and turning everyone's head with all this drama nonsense,' Dolly MacBride leant over her plate and hissed, 'and if she thinks that I am letting my man go to watch a load of lassies showing off their navels, she's sadly mistaken!' Dolly puffed herself up, her substantial bosom threatening to burst the buttons on her military-styled gabardine coat. She ran one of the very successful bed and breakfast businesses in Drum Mhor during the summer and was a walking advertisement for her own good, plain cooking. At home, her somewhat diminutive husband and sons lived in fear of the phrase that she had been bandying around for the past ten years, 'It's my time of life.' Her docile husband, Ronnie, seemed to be shrinking while his wife burgeoned, and he was once heard to mutter under the bonnet of his car, 'Hormones, hormones, they've ruled my life for the past thirty years; now they've up and gone and my life's worse than ever!'

Dolly's friend Lottie MacDonald, a shrivelled widow of sixty, wore iron-grey hair, pinned to the side with a Kirby grip, which framed a face soured by a life of disappointment. She glared across the sugar bowl, her eyes like small black marbles flashing in a network of pleated lines. She pursed her lips and hissed, 'I can't believe that a man like James MacTavish would have allowed himself to be talked into such folly, and even worse, the minister!'

'Honestly, Lottie,' exhaled Dolly piously, her eyes rolling around in their sockets, 'I had just got over the shock of hearing about Joan Maclauchlin's lassie being in the family way, now this!'

The two women clucked and whispered, their heads bobbing like conspiratorial pigeons, at the same time trying to outdo each other with snippets of news currently on the grapevine.

Suzannah entered the Tea Room, a tinkle of the bell announcing her arrival. She nodded politely at the two ladies before taking a seat at a corner table. She looked at her watch and wondered where Paula could have got to. She was glad that Paula had decided to make the move north; their two paths might never have crossed otherwise.

Paula was from London where, she insisted, she had merely 'existed' for the last five years. Initially she had just wanted a holiday, well away from the pressures of her highly paid job in a photographic model agency. She had certainly not meant to stay on in Scotland, but the beauty of the beaches and the slow pace of life were working like a balm on her fraught nerves and she realised that there was really little reason to go back. She had saved enough money to maintain a modest way of life, and before leaving London a friend had suggested she get a job which made better use of her English language degree. She had recommended Paula to a colleague who hired professional freelance readers for a well-known publishing house. In her small cottage, piled up on a table by the fire, were three manuscripts that required her attention. Now every evening she would look at them, then at her watch, then instead of sitting warm by the fire with a large brandy, ploughing through the prose, she would run out into the rain or sleet to the cold village hall to harangue the intrepid cast to move upstage or down, enter or exit, or shimmy and gyrate. The show was in just four weeks and everyone was starting to panic.

The shop bell tinkled again and Paula herself burst in, her face bright and her cheeks red from the wind. 'Oh, it's so cold; did you see the snow on the mountain tops? And there is a bad forecast for the weekend.' Shivering, she removed her coat and hung it over the back of her chair. 'I think we should bring extra heaters to the hall for our rehearsal. Last night there was ice on the inside of the glass!' Hardly taking a breath, she looked around and smiled broadly at Lottie MacDonald and Dolly, before joining her friend. 'Have you ordered yet?' she asked.

'Not yet,' smiled Suzannah, 'but I'm gasping for some tea. I am just so glad to sit down. Those children have me on the go all day, and Meg Munro has persuaded me to put on a Christmas performance with them, so that's more drama! I shall be glad when it's all over.'

Kathleen brought over a tray with a bright yellow tea pot and a plate of freshly made pancakes with dishes of butter and raspberry jam. 'I have a lovely apple pie, just out of the oven. Maybe you would like a slice after you've had a pancake or two? You drama folk can afford all the extra calories, since you will be doing your belly-dancing again, no doubt! Is it not too cold in that hall? Now me, I don't like to leave my fireside all winter long!'

Paula chatted easily with the older lady, then winked discreetly at Suzannah when Kathleen bustled off towards the two gossips and leant down close while she made a play of lifting their side plates. 'More belly-dancing!' they heard her whisper and they smiled at each other as they listened to the three 'tutting' quietly, their lips pursed tightly in disapproval.

'I do love it here, with all these funny folk, don't you?' continued Paula. 'It takes me about two hours to make the tiniest journey; I continually meet people who want to tell me about the weather, or ask me if I am fine. I also think I have a fan in Wee Eck. Do you remember the night he hit the rafters and we all thought he was dead?'

Suzannah grimaced, 'Yes, I almost felt it, the poor man.'

'So you remember I said how funny it would be to make love to him and call out: "Oh, Eck! Oh, Eck!" and then he woke up to see my face over his! Bless him! Well, now he's always at me to honour my promise!'

Suzannah looked over at her very tall, stunningly beautiful friend. Her toffee coloured hair, once cut so elegantly in London, had outgrown the once geometric shape. Now, soft wisps curled around her ears, falling softly onto her jacket collar. Her eyes were yellow and tawny as a lioness's, and Suzannah was filled with envy at her friend's strong bone structure and perfect aquiline nose. When Paula's wide smile totally lit up her face, she was a very difficult person to say no to, as most of the village community could testify.

'Do you realise we are halfway through November? There is only one more month before you leave for Kyiv. Why Kyiv? Can't you change your mind?' Paula beseeched as she demolished her third pancake and jam. 'Everyone is going to miss you here: the school, the children, Iona and of course Donnie, who can't keep his eyes off you. And what about me?' She waved the tea cup at her, 'What am I going to do without you?'

'I know,' agreed Suzannah, 'I never expected to feel like this about Drum Mhor either. I only came here to get away from Roderick. It was only meant to be a stop gap, and anyway my contract with the school is only temporary; the permanent teacher will be back soon. She's had her baby and is due back in action in January.'

'James will be devastated. I think he imagines that you will marry him!'

'Oh, Paula, you are outrageous. James MacTavish may be looking for a wife but he is over twenty years older than me. To be truthful, I must admit I am fond of him. We have become good friends. Maybe when I leave, he may decide to make you his wife!'

'No, he won't be looking my way. I won't be sending out any "available" signals. For, you see, I have already found the perfect man,' Paula looked over at her friend impishly, 'though he doesn't know it yet! I shall just have to go very slowly, as they say!'

'Who? I can't imagine who you have seen. Not the fish man, the one who comes round in his van?'

'I'll only tell you if you promise not to tell a soul, especially Iona MacPherson.'

'I promise. Now, who is it?' Suzannah was almost squealing in anticipation.

'It's Rob from over the hill. He has a house down by the water, beside the avenue of giant sycamore and lime trees. He invited me in one day when I was out walking. He saw that I was soaked and he let me dry off and sit by his fire. He makes fiddles and composes music as a hobby, and during the day he runs his croft. He has sheep and a few cows, as well as a boat that he takes out in the summer for loch cruises. Suzannah, you should see him. He is so tall, and all brown and craggy and as gorgeous as a bear. His eyes and hair are jet black, and he has the most beautiful eyelashes. I think I fell madly in love that afternoon. Is that possible?'

'Oh, Paula, I am so jealous. He sounds wonderful, and you have all the time in the world to get to know him. Promise you will write to me with all the news of the village and your love life and just everything.'

'I will, though I do wish you weren't going. I think you should stay and marry James MacTavish, and we can be neighbours and put on drama productions every year from now on!'

'I told you, he's too old for me. I want to feel like you do when you talk about your black-eyed Robert. I want to feel dizzy with love. I haven't felt a spark with anyone here; perhaps my Mr Right is waiting for me in Ukraine. I shall go to Kyiv and see what the future brings. Who knows? I might meet a handsome Cossack and learn to bake bread and watch him dance. We may go for holidays to the Crimea, and I will dip my toes into the Black Sea.' She paused lost in thought, and then she came back to the present. 'About James… I hope I can stay friends with him. He is so funny, and sensitive. But do you know? Although he professes to want a wife, I think in fact that a woman living with him full-time would drive him crazy! He is so domesticated and set in his ways.'

Paula smiled. 'I have a feeling you're right. He certainly seems to enjoy the chase though, doesn't he?'

CHAPTER 7

December came at last, and with it blew the winds of winter. Snow flurries whirled around the window panes, making the inside of the houses seem the most perfect place to stay. The drama group was the exception. Each night the individuals taking part in the show stepped outside and, bent into the wind like arctic explorers, they made their way through the village to the hall. Rehearsals had stepped up a pace now that the production date was drawing near. The single Calor Gas heater generated a pitiful amount of warmth, but excitement and nervous energy kept the group warm and vibrant with adrenalin.

Paula rang James MacTavish one Thursday morning. 'Has the paint dried yet, James? I know you said you were using black gloss to paint the scenery. How does it look?'

'Oh, fine and arty, don't you worry. I even have the plants and steps all painted on. It looks quite the thing you know, these great sheets of polystyrene all through my cottage. I'll be glad to get them out, I can tell you. Fair gives me a fright when I come in for my cup of cocoa at night.'

'Well, that was what I was wondering. Could you bring them over to the hall today, do you think, and then we can get them fitted up? We need to have a proper dress rehearsal with scenery and costumes. Can I leave you to organise that, James?'

'Oh, it's no bother to me! I'll have them over there in a jiffy!' James decided to give his neighbour a shout. He could see him out there in the field. Maybe he could spare an hour to give some assistance.

*

'Oh for God's sake, James!' Murdo MacPherson was getting a little edgy as he teetered against the wind, carrying the first large sheet of polystyrene from the cottage out to the waiting transit van. The wind threatened to snap the picture in half but the two men persevered and carefully manoeuvred the unwieldy object safely into the van and arranged the blanket to protect it. Back to the house they went to get the second sheet.

'Och, I think we'll have a wee dram before we tackle the next one, Murdo, what do you think? The wind might ease up a bit, you just never know.'

'You know me, James, not one to say no to a good drop of Talisker.' The two men sat down at the kitchen table and companionably sipped the neat whisky, sighing contentedly.

'Just the job, Murdo, though I think I might just take the bottle with me tonight. A wee dram might help with the Dutch courage. I don't know how these daft women managed to persuade me to get all involved with their nonsense. Now what do you say, shall we try the second sheet now?'

Fortified against the wind and weather, they managed to get the second and third sheets safely into the back of the van without incident. Quite brazen with confidence, they stepped out of the house with the fourth, but just as they turned to get the huge sheet at an angle, a sudden squall of rain and wind snatched the sheet from their hands and it shot straight up to the sky like a giant kite. James watched his masterpiece of Persian artwork rise high and aim straight for the clouds. With awe he turned to Murdo, his eyes wide with shock, and both men uttered simultaneously, 'Well! In the name of the wee man! What are we going to do now?'

'What goes up, must come down,' said Murdo helpfully, eyeing the sky as carefully as he did when searching for eagles over the high peaks.

'It's away to sea,' said James, full of dejection. 'Look at that, speeding along like Concorde itself.'

Sure enough the piece of scenery was making off towards the white horses of the stormy sea, the wind keeping up its force and driving the white sheet like a sail. They watched it fly up over the neighbouring field, up high as the clouds. But then, just as suddenly as it flew up, it suddenly flew down again, before snagging itself on the barbed wire fence at the edge of the beach just inches from the wash of the vicious waves.

'Were you praying, man? For if you were, James MacTavish, you've certainly had an answer. I've never known a man with such a jammy streak of luck that just seems to run right through you!'

'Och, away with you. Come on man, run, we'd better get it off the fence before the wind decides to snap it in two… that would be a real calamity.'

The two men dashed over the field to the fragile polystyrene, hanging precariously on the sharp wire barbs. Gently easing it off the fence, they held the sheet with the narrow edge facing into the wind and walked back towards the van. All seemed well but tragedy struck once again. The moment they manoeuvred the sheet into the van, there was a mighty crack and the picture snapped with a sickening sound, right through the middle.

'No, James, I take it back, you are not in the Almighty's good books at all. So now what do we do? Do you think a tube of Superglue will do the trick? And do you think the lassies will notice? It's a nice clean break after all; maybe we should have another wee dram just to discuss the next move, what do you think?'

The big opening night arrived and the village was in a state of jittery excitement. Soft flurries of snow were falling on Wee Eck as he marched towards the hall. Through the lit-up windows of the houses along the main street, he could see the local inhabitants bedecking themselves in their finery for a grand night out. Paula had given him the job of stage manager, so it was with a certain responsibility that he strutted along with his chest stuck out and his shoulders back. He had heard there had been a bit of disaster with one of the scenery flats, but hopefully it had all been resolved by now. He opened the side door of the hall and walked up on to the stage. Paula was there, scowling at the semi-circle of polystyrene sheets that had been clamped together with braces and brackets. The intrepid producer was weak with nerves, but her adrenalin had her fired up and she was all set for a night of resounding success.

'So you're here at last, Eck. I thought you were coming to help me get the props on the stage and to test the curtain?'

'Och, I had things to do. I had to take a bath and put on my Sunday suit for the occasion. You can just relax, I'm here now.'

'For goodness' sake, Eck, you are behind the scenes; nobody is going to see you. Now go and sort out the rest of the props and help anyone that needs it. I have to see to the actors. I just hope that James MacTavish sobers up before he goes on stage.'

The small room at the side of the hall was bustling with action. The doctor had lent them his two examining screens to give privacy to the actors and actresses while they changed into their costumes. Paula immediately started bustling around with her box of special tubes of makeup, telling everyone to apply a good coat of number six. She then added blobs of red and smidgeons of white to their faces in readiness for their stage debuts.

'I've come a long way from the photographic models!' she laughed while painting black lines around the minister's eyes, turning him from a rosy cheeked Scot to a swarthy Rudolf Valentino. 'Now you look quite the sultry womaniser!'

Meanwhile on stage, Marie Wilson, the minister's wife, was setting the cushions and pot plants tastefully around the chaise longue that had been lent by an elderly lady in the parish. Eck stood by importantly, somehow out of place in his dark suit, last aired at Jo Patterson's funeral and now smelling sharply of moth balls. There was an almost hysterical buzz in the air. Monika, the props lady and official prompt, was testing the curtains. They had not been used for years, and it was an effort to pull them, but with a mighty tug she managed to close them only to reveal considerable damage by moths and silverfish. We'll just not keep them closed too long, she thought optimistically; we don't want people gawping at the curtains all night. Now, I shall just put a nice bunch of chrysanthemums here on the brass table by the chaise longue; I'm sure Paula will appreciate a nice woman's touch around the sultan's palace.

Paula looked over the stage and was quite pleased with the overall effect. James's four sheets of black and white depictions of a sultan's palace stood stark and proud and very 'arty', just as Suzannah had predicted.

At a quarter to eight, the audience started to arrive, shaking the snow off their coats and stamping their boots at the door. Grace from the Post Office was in charge of the cash box at the door. With an air of importance she issued the tickets and handed out the brave attempt at a programme that Suzannah had printed on the school copier. Soon the seats filled up and there was a hum of expectant murmurings as folk looked about and called over to friends and neighbours. Peeping through the moth-eaten curtains, the cast shrieked at each other, 'There's your mum, Caroline! And look, there's Mrs Munro sitting beside the doctor.'

Paula felt sick. Nerves and tension were engulfing her. She couldn't remember ever feeling so fraught or as vulnerable in London as she did now. Suzannah, standing beside her, dressed in lilac gauze with satin harem pants, also reflected on the turn her life had taken. What would the wonderful Roderick Carruthers say if he could see her now? James was as calm as any eunuch could be. He had downed three double whiskies and stood swaying gently.

'How are you, James? Is the scenery going to hold?' It was Murdo, his partner in the crime of the afternoon, peeping in from the side door.

'Och, I'm as happy as a bumblebee in a pot of honey! Look around you, man! Girls dressed in all the colours of the rainbow, naked arms and bellies in the middle of December, and my grand scenery taped and glued and standing as proud as any standing stone in the glen. You are looking at a happy man, Murdo MacPherson! I shall say my few lines and just enjoy myself and gaze at my future wife.'

'Oh, and which one have you got your eye on tonight, you daft old Romeo?' cut in Donnie, walking past carrying his turban.

'You will just have to wait and find out, you young pup you, now on you go and finish putting on your make-up.'

Wee Eck strode out from behind the curtain and made his way up through the audience. He could see that there was a bit of a commotion going on at the front door of the hall, and as stage manager he was the man to deal with any situation. 'How's it going, Grace? Is there a problem here?' he asked imperiously.

'Well, yes,' she hissed at him, her eyes darting about like a light on a pinball machine. 'You'll never guess, but two big tour buses have turned up out of the blue! The folk are from Northern Ireland and are here on holiday, some Christmas and New Year deal in the Highlands. They heard that there was to be "live theatre" being put on here in Drum Mhor so they've travelled fifty miles to come and see it. Murdo-John and Allie Shaw are getting some more chairs; that's another ninety folk for goodness' sake! Oh, what am I going to do about programmes? Can you not go and ask Meg Munro if we can't get into the school and do some more?'

'Leave it to me, Grace lass, I am the stage manager, and I shall see to the programmes.' Off he marched straight back to Paula for a consultation.

'Ninety people!' Paula laughed, 'are you having a joke with me, Eck Morrison?'

'What ninety people?' Caroline, one of the young-mum belly-dancers, shrieked.

All the girls turned, eyes wide, fear suddenly gripping the young amateurs. They calculated the numbers and estimated an audience of over 180 folk, and most of them strangers. They had not expected that when they signed up in the autumn.

'Calm down, everyone,' Paula called from the top step leading to the stage. 'We have done well and the rehearsals have been great. Just remember that we are all in it together and everyone knows what to do. And you remember what to do with your cushion, don't you, Rosie?'

The little girl, completely transformed into an eastern princess, nodded seriously and stood close to Suzannah. Her uncle was fumbling in his holdall. No doubt he would be having another sip of his Dutch courage, as he liked to call it. Through the curtain they could hear the rising hum of people talking, the volume swelling along with the audience. Eventually Wee Eck reappeared, flushed from running backwards and forwards and over to the school for more programmes.

'Five minutes, everyone, and then it's curtain up!'

'Right, into your places,' hissed Paula, 'and Monika, I shall say a few words then you and Eck will open the curtains. Break a leg everyone!'

Rosie looked up at her uncle. 'That's not a very nice thing to say, is it, Uncle James?'

The hall was dark. Paula stepped out into the spotlight in front of the moth-eaten curtains. She gulped at the sight of the room completely packed with bright expectant faces. Taking a deep breath, she smiled radiantly. 'Good evening, everyone, we are delighted to welcome you out on this cold, snowy evening to Drum Mhor's very first drama performance. We hope to transport you to the land of the exotic, where you will be in the company of a sultan from Arabia and enjoy the intrigues that go on in his harem. Afterwards we invite you for a cup of tea, provided of course by the ladies of the SWRI. Half the proceeds from tonight's show will go towards future performances of the drama group and half will go towards the Village Hall Fund. So please, sit back and enjoy the show!'

There was a ripple of applause, but as she stepped back behind the curtain Paula thought she heard a snigger from the front row. She could not be sure, but she thought she heard one of the forestry lads say, 'That's if we don't ask for a refund!'

The curtains opened, rather jerkily at first, until Wee Eck gave a mighty heave and they shot back in a cloud of dust. Without further ado, Paula pressed 'play' on the music system and the amplifiers took up the sound. Murdo, who knew something about electrics and was in charge of the lighting, now switched on the footlights and immediately the stage was suffused in a rosy glow, transformed into a scene from 'Scheherazade.' Egyptian wailing music emanated from the wings and suddenly Iona MacPherson, clad in a long red satin caftan, came snaking in, arms weaving about above her head, her nervousness robbing her face of expression. Following her danced the sinewy half-naked bodies of the young women of Drum Mhor, arms rising and falling as though their elbows and wrists were made of bendy gel. The music changed pace into a fast, frantic caterwauling with a persistent drum beat. Keeping time, the girls shimmied up to the front of the stage and threw their silky scarves out to the side, then spun like dervishes, creating a blur of colour before striking a languid pose on either side of the chaise longue.

'Very dramatic, I must say,' whispered Kathleen from the Tea Room, her mouth pursed in disapproval.

'Very!' agreed her friend Dolly, ensconced beside Lottie Macdonald, who was eyeing up the naked midriffs and who, unusually for her, had nothing further to add. In spite of the stern critics in the third row, everything was going very well until Iona, with a triumphant wave of her scarlet streaming scarf, collided with the unfortunate piece of scenery that was precariously held together on the back with a criss-cross application of brown parcel tape, courtesy of Grace from the Post Office. Wee Eck, eagle-eyed and alert, saw the polystyrene teeter and heard the crackle of the tape pulling apart. Like a stunted gazelle, he leapt behind the large sheet of scenery. The audience caught only a fleeting glimpse of the funeral-suited stage manager diving into position. For the remaining one-and-a-half hours of the performance only the four fingers of each of his hands were visible while he physically held the show together.

'I see they found a use for that wee nyaff after all,' murmured Lottie MacDonald, 'but I think he could try and stand still. That big bit of white sheeting looks as though it's doing a dance all on its own!'

The audience watched with growing amusement as another drama seemed to be unfolding, one which they could only assume was quite unrehearsed. James MacTavish, the guardian eunuch of the sultan's harem, caught his large scarab ring in the gauze of Suzannah's headdress.

'Oh for God's sake, lassie, will you hold still until I can get it out!'

The forestry lads in the front row let out a great guffaw and chortled to each other in their predictably lewd manner. There was nothing else for it but for James to kneel down beside the girls and deliver his lines while trying to free himself from the offending veil.

The coach party started to laugh quietly when they heard the disembodied voice of the stage manager come from behind the scenery.

'Get yourselves over here when no one's looking, I'll have you free in no time.'

His good intentions were unceremoniously interrupted with frantic '*shhhh!*' sounds coming from behind the curtain. The play moved on without further distraction until the final denouement. It was only a small hitch that occurred during the well-rehearsed scenes involving the carpet. The set was a rare visual delight but unfortunately, due to his exuberance, Donnie the wicked king miscalculated when he rolled up Suzannah. Instead of leaving her head free so that she could shout and be heard, he rolled her up tight, leaving only her long silky blonde hair in view. Her protestations and carefully learned lines were lost in a muffled hum of protest.

'Quite a mighty physique, that young lad has!' commented Dolly to Kathleen.

'Aye, he does, and I wouldn't mind being rolled up in a carpet with him.' Kathleen started to giggle quietly, her plump shoulders and silver hair bobbing. The three women had mellowed during the course of the light-hearted entertainment. Just for a few minutes the brittle barbs from their tongues had relaxed and at last they were enjoying the show.

Behind the white sheet of polystyrene, Wee Eck's bladder was strained to bursting and his poor fingers had turned as white as sun-bleached bones. He was more than relieved to hear the play come to the finale, a love scene to be acted out on the chaise longue. The cushion was carried in by the little princess, and the sultan started to declare his love and devotion. Suzannah, her face close to the minister (himself a picture of stoic subservience), tried hard not to flinch under the onslaught of his toxic halitosis. The audience, now openly laughing, were treated to yet another delightful piece of bad stage management. Monika's efforts at creating a warm, homely atmosphere with her large vase of chrysanthemums succeeded in totally eclipsing the tender love scene. The wonderful declarations were uttered behind the golden blooms, and the actors were completely obliterated from the near-hysterical audience.

'What a wonderful evening,' one man was heard to say to his wife, 'the best play I've seen in years. I don't remember when I laughed so much, and I don't think it was meant to be a comedy!'

The clapping went on for several minutes, and the forestry lads at the front were the loudest in the hall, shouting out their appreciation for the local girls. 'Grand job, Caroline, any chance of a private viewing!'

Eventually the tea urns were brought out and sandwiches were served. Lottie MacDonald bustled around the table, encouraging everyone to have a little refreshment. 'So you've come all the way from Belfast? Well, fancy that, did you hear that, Dolly? They've come from Belfast. And how are you enjoying our snow here? I think we'll have a bonny Christmas right enough. Now just enjoy your sandwich and your tea, there's no need to rush away. What's that you're saying? You think I should have been one of the dancing girls! Ha ha ha… If I knew you a little better I would give you a wee look at my varicose veins, but you can be sure, I've seen the day when I could have danced until the dawn, but now I think I'll leave all that nonsense to the young ones.'

'You! A dancing girl?' exclaimed Kathleen.

'Well if Iona MacPherson can do it, I don't know why we couldn't have been asked.'

Kathleen smoothed her white bobbed hair. 'I might like to have a go in the next drama; what do you think? I have to say, they looked as though they were having great fun up there on the stage.' She caught sight of Hector Ogilvie who was sitting alone at the end of the back row. He must have slipped in after the play had started. Kathleen poured a mug of tea and put an egg sandwich on a plate and took it over to the old man. 'Well, Hector, did you enjoy the drama?' She handed him the plate and mug.

'That's very kind of you, Kathleen, how much do I owe you?'

'Oh, be quiet. You just enjoy it. Will you be all right walking up that road in the dark? Maybe one of the forestry lads could give you a lift up in their van?'

'No, no, I'll be fine; I have my stick and I'll just take it easy. I think I need a bit of time to cool off anyway. My heart has had a bit of a rattle tonight with all these naked girls up there on the stage. I could just manage a couple of them on my knees right now. Maybe one of them would like to come and tuck me in.' He sucked on his tea noisily, and then let out a loud laugh, spluttering with the thought.

'Come on, you dirty old man, you just get home to your bed and start counting sheep. I'll see if young Iain will give you a run to your house. I see you haven't been giving the twin tub a go recently,' Kathleen commented, rubbing her nose as she made her way through the crowd of people to find the lads.

Outside the snow was thick, yet the visiting coach parties were reluctant to leave. The bus drivers were impatient to be gone because the night was late and they had a precarious journey to complete, with single track roads, and little hope that the snow plough had been out in the intervening hours. Eventually the hall was cleared and all the people including the locals had gone, full of goodwill and enthralled by the exotic music and the dancing girls shimmying and entrancing with their blackened eyes and gauzy veils. Backstage, make-up was removed and costumes packed away. The group donned their boots and scarves and headed out into the snow and made their way to Paula's house. The party afterwards went on into the small hours, with everyone chipping in with their own versions of the night.

'A few glitches, right enough,' acknowledged Wee Eck, 'but the best show ever seen in these parts, and I want to say it's all thanks to Paula. As the stage manager, I want to drink a large glass of Black Navy rum to her, and as the stage manager I definitely deserve a kiss.' He lurched over and stretched up as she leant down and unsteadily they clutched on to each other, until she started to laugh.

'Oh Eck! Oh Eck!' and everyone laughed with them.

Not to be outdone, James MacTavish announced, 'I want to prove tonight girls that I am not the eunuch that I have led you to believe that I am. Now, just take your time,' he went on, 'one at a time, mind, don't rush at me, but who will be coming to kiss me goodnight, then?' He stood swaying gently, his angelic smile belying the lascivious look in his eyes.

'Oh, all right then,' said Caroline, 'don't want the old goat to feel he's lost it!'

'Come on then, you randy old thing,' and Monika lined up too.

Donnie hit his head in exasperation. 'Why? How? He can barely stand up and they're still all over him.'

All the girls were treated to a kiss and a very close embrace with the village's most reluctant bachelor. They all giggled as they took up their seats around the room.

Suzannah winked at Paula, and made her way over to James.

She did not speak, instead she smiled and closed her eyes and pursed her lips. He looked at her, flushed and sweet, her mouth wide, her nose small and straight, the long line of her neck creamy and disappearing into the shadow of her blouse. Slowly he encircled her in his arms and lowered his head to hers. Softly he touched her lips with his own, soft like a bird's wing. She did not pull back, and gently he nibbled her lips and opened them and pulled her to him. Heat suffused her, the earth started to move and she felt herself falling and falling into a wild black kaleidoscope. The evening had disappeared, the drama was forgotten.

'Come on, Suzannah, come and join the party; Murdo-John is going to sing.' Iona yanked her away. 'Have you got a drink, lass? Give her a vodka, Murdo. She likes triples usually!'

Suzannah listened to Murdo-John singing about Loch Awe and Ben Cruachan, and she herself hummed along, but she was aware of the blue eyes behind her. The electricity was jumping between them like live wires, and until now she had no concept of what astral planing was all about. Now it was as though a part of herself had left her body and she imagined the two souls melting together somewhere on the ceiling.

'Give us a song then, James MacTavish.' Murdo leant over and filled his friend's glass.

'We've a lot to celebrate today, what with flying scenery and a great Hollywood production...'

'Aye, held together by yours truly, don't forget that!'

'Oh, Eck,' giggled Paula, 'come here and sit on my knee, we can do a good ventriloquist act next.'

James went over to the mantelpiece. He took a sip from his glass and cleared his throat.

'I shall sing my favourite song from our great national poet, Robert Burns: "Ae fond kiss, and then we sever... " ' He looked around the room and gazed fondly at the girls as he sang. He avoided Suzannah's eyes and she felt hurt and confused. Only a moment ago she had been laughing and immune to such teenage feelings of angst. Now, just after a kiss, her world had turned on its head. She felt betrayed and angry. Were the feelings that she had experienced not mutual? James acknowledged the applause and sat down again at the window. Monika sang a rousing song from the islands, and then Grace from the Post Office sang a sad, quavering ballad in a high, thin soprano, all about leaving Scotland during the Highland Clearances.

'Oh my goodness, we shall all to be going home crying at this rate; what about a song to cheer us all up? Suzannah, what did you learn down there in the nation's capital? They must have taught you a tune or two?'

Suzannah suddenly remembered a song called *Dainty Davie* that she had learnt in Edinburgh. It was also Burns, but not a song for the parlour. Her friend Irene used to sing it, full of wicked innuendo and flirtation. Tonight Suzannah was in just such a mood and the blood in her veins seemed to be flowing with fire. She walked to the front of the room to begin her rendition:

It was in and through the window broads
And a' the tirlie wirlies o't
The sweetest kiss that e'er I got
Was from my Dainty Davie.

Oh, leeze me on your curly pow
Dainty Davie, Dainty Davie
Leeze me on your curly pow
My ain dear Dainty Davie.'

Suzannah mimicked the antics of her friend as she had sung the song, late one night in a pub in Edinburgh, and just as Irene had flirted with an unsuspecting gentleman, Suzannah made her way over to James and sat on his knee and hugged him tight around the neck. Huge applause broke out, to which Suzannah arose and made an exaggerated curtsey.

Iona, still laughing, also got up and said, 'Come along, Murdo, my own dear Davie, take me, take me, before I'm sick!' She lurched out, then remembered, 'What about you, lass, are you coming?' She held out her arm to Suzannah.

Suzannah looked over at Paula for guidance, but her friend still seemed to be occupied with Wee Eck, so she turned and looked at James. He just looked back at her, his eyes hooded, giving no indication of how he felt. With a heavy heart she mumbled, 'Yes, I'll just get my coat.'

When it was all over, Paula stayed in a cloud of exuberance. She could hardly sleep for excitement. All the weeks of rehearsals and preparations had been worth it. When eventually she did get to her own bed, her mind continued to race and sleep eluded her. She had seen Robert, the black-eyed giant from across the hill. He had been sitting close to the back of the hall and by his side was a woman. Not a good omen, she thought, but not worth getting upset about, not now anyway. Just before sleep did overtake her, she laughed into her pillow remembering the silly double act that she and Wee Eck had performed.

As the snow fell and the clock struck three in the morning, Iona smiled wickedly at her husband of thirty years, and with her eyes still black from the kohl and her head still spinning from too much champagne, she danced enticingly across the kitchen floor, and took Murdo's hand and gave him a knowing wink.

'There's still life in the old bird yet!'

'Aye, *cailleach*, I can see that, and so could the entire village. They'll be saying I'm a lucky man having the best of the sultan's harem to bed whenever I like!'

Together they made their way just a trifle unsteadily up the stairs, and tiptoed past Suzannah's bedroom. Suzannah had fallen asleep in a glory of unsated lust and confusion. Worn out by the excitement of it all, she had fallen asleep as quickly and easily as a child.

CHAPTER 8

Christmas day dawned wet and grey. A squall was roaring up the sound and Suzannah woke to the noise of her landlady shouting at her sheep to come for their breakfast. She stretched lazily and let the lashing of the rain and the baaing of the sheep convince her that she could lie in bed for a little longer. Just as she was drifting off again to the drumbeat of the rain, her door was opened unceremoniously and Iona burst in wet and dripping from her outside chores.

'Come away, lass, I need you to do something with this goose. Murdo shot it this morning and you can see what these fancy recipe writers advise us to do with it.'

'Oh no, Iona, I don't know how to roast a goose. I just buy them ready-to-go under cling film from the supermarket. Ring up Margaret, she'll know. She knows everything.'

'Come on, no lying about now, I need a hand and we can do it together.'

Wearily Suzannah felt for her slippers and her dressing gown, shivering as she made her way to the bathroom. This was not what she had in mind for Christmas Day. Paula was invited to join them this afternoon for the meal and Suzannah was glad that they would be together for Christmas. When eventually she appeared in the kitchen she found herself facing three workmen in overalls, all sitting with a dram of whisky with Murdo.

'Happy Christmas!' they all chorused. 'Grand day, if you don't have to go out!'

'Happy Christmas to you too, I shall just have a coffee before I start the goose. Does it need stuffing or what?'

'Stuffing?' said Murdo, 'Good God, lass, it will need plucking first!' and they all laughed at the expression on her face.

'Just give it a good soaking in boiling water and then the feathers will come out no bother at all. You'll be pleased to see that I've already gutted the bird, so you don't have to get squeamish about that.'

'Well, lads,' said Murdo, 'we'd better get going or Mrs Cormack will be fretting all day about her chimney. I'll be back by four for dinner, see you then.'

Suzannah looked at the bird, and then by habit she picked up the binoculars on the window sill and peered through the lenses down the field. She saw smoke curl from the cottage under the rock, but no other sign of life.

'What are you peering at?' Iona asked briskly. 'Any boats out there today?'

'No, I thought I saw some curlews over there at the bottom of the field. Take a look, what do you think?'

Handing the glasses over, Suzannah pressed her cold hands against the hot flush of her cheeks. James would be spending Christmas with his brother and family. She hadn't seen him since the drama evening, except through the lenses of the binoculars. Instead of walking on the beach in front of his house, as she had been in the habit of doing, she had taken to going up the river and skirting around the big bend and up over the hills. From the high viewpoint she could see down over the bay and stare out to sea. She was free to be alone with her thoughts.

'Oh, Iona, I don't know how to do this.' She stared at the dead carcass of the beautiful grey goose, its neck long and ropey, the beady eyes opaque and black. 'It's going to take me till the New Year to get it ready, and I don't think I'll be able to eat it after all this.'

'Don't be such a softie, just fill the basin with boiling water, just as Murdo said. Now, dunk it in and leave it for a bit and we'll have a cup of coffee and then we'll plan the stuffing. It'll be the best

Christmas dinner you ever tasted. You just wait and see!'

Suzannah gingerly lifted the body, surprised by its weight, and lowered it into the scalding water. Bubbles arose, and with a wooden spoon she pushed the body down.

'Now just put this jar of beetroot on the top to keep it under and we can have a wee *strupach*!' She took a sip of her scalding coffee and passed the milk over to Suzannah.

'There's a mighty storm brewing I think; I might put my wee lambies into the shed. They're so tame they just come when I call them now. Do you know how my father used to call his sheep in the winter time?'

Suzannah shook her head, knowing that she was about to be told.

'Well, he would get his bagpipes, and head to the hill and stand at the bottom and march up and down playing every Highland tune that he could think of. The skirl of the music would catch in the gales and sure enough the sheep would come down, baaing and crying, and then follow him over to the feeding troughs, just like that story of the Pied Piper. It was a grand sight seeing my old father doing that, right up till he was in his eighties.'

Suzannah got up and returned to her task at the sink. Rolling up her sleeves she tentatively dipped her hand into the water and felt the soft feathers. She took a hold of one between her thumb and forefinger and gave it a sharp tug and sure enough it came away. A bit like plucking her eyebrows, she thought. Iona left her to it, and came back about half an hour later only to find about twenty carefully arranged feathers on the draining board.

'Oh for goodness sake, what am I going to do with you? At this rate it will be fish fingers and chips for our tea. Come here and I'll show you.' Iona's strong hands went to work and before long, great fists full of feathers joined the few singly placed trophies. 'Now, we have to wash it out and stuff it and get it ready. Let's get the vegetables prepared, maybe you can do that? Will you run out into the garden and get me some Brussels sprouts?'

'It's pouring; can't we just have frozen peas?'

Suzannah took one look at Iona's face and made for the door, muttering about the madness of living in such an antiquated place where there didn't seem to be any modern conveniences. The village shop was closed for four days. Wistfully she remembered her life in Edinburgh, where the local Pakistani shop stayed open for almost twenty-four hours. The wind whisked her hair as she padded round to the back of the house and a cloud of rain released its contents directly over her head.

'Happy Christmas, Suzannah! I can see you are having a good day so far!' James MacTavish veered over to the garden fence from the middle of the road where he had been walking. 'I was just out to get some air before going up the glen to see if Santa has been good to Rosie and Billie. No doubt they will all be up to high doh by now. Oh my goodness, what weather! Come over to the garage, you will be drowned out here.'

Suzannah obediently turned back and went towards James. Before she could protest, he caught her by the shoulders and lifted her wet face and kissed her softly on the lips. Rain lashed against them, and again he sought her lips and pulled her to him. Breathlessly she stood in his embrace, lost in time. Was this what it meant when you were swept off your feet? He could have lifted her now and ravished her on top of the sodden vegetable patch, for all she wanted was his mouth and hands on her. Again he lowered his head and again she felt herself falling down into the black swirling abyss where nothing else existed.

'I had to be sure,' he said at last. 'I thought you had bewitched me, but no, I think this is it. This is what we both want.'

'I want you,' she said. Her eyes looked at him, bright as jewels, and warm as a blue sea reflecting a summer sky.

'I want you too. But go now. I'll be seeing you soon.' And he leant over and kissed her softly, so softly on her open lips. Remembering just in time to get the Brussels sprouts, Suzannah ran back into the house and found the goose all ready for the oven. Iona was busy with the potatoes and Suzannah threw down her contribution and went straight over to the mirror. Her eyes were sparkly, her face pink from the onslaught of icy rain, and her hair, tangled like rats' tails, dripped on her red and black striped jumper.

'Well, you are a picture!' exclaimed Paula, bursting in and bringing in more rain. She whisked off her heavy Barbour jacket. 'What are you so happy about?'

'I just ran into James MacTavish out there; he just wished me a Merry Christmas.'

'What!' Iona's head nearly swizzled off her shoulders as she turned to look at her lodger. 'You only went out for a few minutes, what did I miss?'

Suzannah sighed. 'It's the first time since the drama party. I haven't stopped thinking about him since, but I was afraid. I thought, maybe it was just all on my side, but no, he seems to like me too.'

'Well, good for you, lass, but don't get your hopes up, he's a right Romeo and a confirmed bachelor.'

'I know all that,' said Suzannah, running a brush through her hair. 'All I am saying is... it feels right.'

'This is all very sudden.' Paula looked serious. 'You know of his reputation. He's renowned for his holiday romances with sweet young things up from the cities. They say he always has great plans to marry them but somehow manages to wriggle his way out. And what about you and your new job? What about going to Kyiv and your adventure there?'

'Oh whatever,' laughed Suzannah. 'If it's a romance, well, I just want to enjoy it. I certainly haven't felt so full of lust for a long time!'

'It's the chase, that's all. You find him attractive now because you think he might be a challenge. I know exactly how you feel,' smiled Paula. 'There's a certain man that intrigues me as well.'

'Well I'm just glad that I'm a happily married woman,' cut in

Iona. 'Now, it's Christmas Day and we have everything prepared so let's just sit down and relax for a wee while.'

The three friends sat around the Rayburn stove and drank sherry while the afternoon ticked by and the smell of roasting goose filled up the kitchen. Outside the wind and rain continued to roar and the fields turned into soggy waterlogged lakes.

Suzannah could not remember feeling this happy since she was a child. And like a child, she experienced again the joy of sitting around a Christmas table with the moist slices of goose piled on to their plates. On their side plates they put the small pieces of lead shot fired from Murdo's shotgun into the unfortunate bird.

'You lassies take care that you don't lose your fillings on these hard slugs. Damn nuisance!' Iona cautioned, discreetly spitting another pellet into her hand.

Silently Suzannah prayed that these precious moments could be preserved forever. 'I don't want to go away, I want to stay here.'

Murdo raised his glass of sparkling white wine. 'I have only made about fourteen toasts so far, so another won't hurt, but I want to propose a toast to you, lassie. Go away and stay away for a year or so and then come back to us if you are sure. Like many before you, you are in love with the Highlands and the novelty of it all, but it's a hard place to live and you owe it to yourself to know that you are ready to settle here. I daresay James MacTavish may be the man for you, you just never know, but he's been waiting a good many years for his perfect wife; I am sure he'll wait another one.'

'I'll drink to that,' agreed Iona, her eyes already a little unfocused.

Paula nodded in agreement and smiled at her friend. 'I'll keep an eye on him while you're gone!'

Suzannah smiled fondly at her friends and knew that they were right. She also knew that she would count the minutes until she would see him again, and lifting her hand she gently ran her fingers over her lips.

*

That night as folk gathered round firesides and curtains were drawn to shut out the cold night, Hector Ogilvie sat alone by his fire, listening to his clock and watching his dog lie sleeping at his feet. His watery eyes were misty from the extra glass of whisky that he had treated himself to earlier. Pictures of other Christmases danced in the firelight, of Kate and their two fishermen sons, all now resting in the graveyard. His entry to his diary read:

Mild, odd shower. In church in the afternoon.

CHAPTER 9

The New Year blew in on a strong, cold north-easterly wind, and continued to blow through January. Snow showers were frequent, but they didn't lie. Instead the mountains and hills glistened with a festive frosting. The mornings saw a harsh frost, and the temperatures plummeted during February. James MacTavish sat as usual in his wood-lined study. The fire was red and crackling. He had found an old fish box on the beach and some driftwood that he had dried and now the sharp acrid smell of wood was blowing back down the chimney in gusts from the stormy gale outside. He was busy making a drawing of the Ardnamurchan lighthouse, Great Britain's most westerly point. He had been recently challenged that it was in fact somewhere in Cornwall, but he had been quick to point out that the man had been seriously off the mark. He found the page in the book describing where the lighthouse stood on the rocky outcrop called Corrachadh Mor, just over half a mile south of Ardnamurchan Point. He squinted and looked at the photograph. The tip of the peninsula extended out like an accusing finger between the islands of Mull to its south, and Eigg, Rum and more distant Skye to its north. James idly followed the route that would lead to such a lonely outpost. He imagined that it must feel like coming to the end of the world, for he'd heard that Ardnamurchan was a wild, lonely and stunningly beautiful place. That is, he thought, if you like wild, rock strewn and bumpy landscapes.

Just then, he heard the door open and her now familiar voice call out, 'James! It's me, can I come in?' She found him warm and studious, bent over his papers and books. 'What are you doing, then? Oh that is so beautiful, and what a place. Tell me about it.' She dropped a kiss on to his forehead, and he pulled her on to his knee.

'You are looking a picture of loveliness today. How was the school? Have you taught them all their lessons and sorted out that young scallywag who put the magnet on to the computer?'

'Yes, everything is fine. The screen eventually returned to normal and so we are all off the hook, thank goodness. Now tell me about this lighthouse.'

'Well, as far as I can make out, it was built in 1849 with stone from the island of Mull, one of fourteen constructed in Scotland by the Stevenson family. Its particular claim to fame is that it is the only lighthouse in the world built in an Egyptian style.'

'Fancy that!' Suzannah looked more closely, and saw that there were also photos depicting the keeper's living area in the 1940s. There was the uniform hanging on the back of the door and even buttered toast on the table.

'There are no keepers now, though?' she asked him.

'The boring answer to that, my dear, is no. The Ardnamurchan Lighthouse was automated some years ago. I was thinking maybe we could go for a trip to visit it some day. Would you like that?

'Nobody has ever invited me to visit a lighthouse before. I can't wait!'

As had become the habit, James had made dinner for them both. They ate the simple meal around the kitchen table, then went through to his study and sat for a while in front of the fire.

Suzannah fidgeted. There was only a week left before she had to leave. 'I don't want to go.'

'Then don't.'

'I want you.'

'So come here,' and his eyes crinkled. He reached for her hand, pulling her down between his outstretched knees, holding her close to him. In the heat from the fire, he traced the outline of her neck and lifted the soft shiny wisps of hair away from her face. She willed him to beg her not to go, but to stay with him. Instead he pulled her to him and their mouths met, and she felt herself falling and falling, deeper and deeper into the now familiar swirling blackness of passion.

CHAPTER 10

There was a queue in the post office and Paula found herself standing behind Dolly and Lottie Macdonald.

'Oh you just go ahead, dear, we're in no hurry. We have to get our pension then we'll go and have a pot of tea at Kathleen's Tea Room. How are you keeping? Did I not see you coming out of the doctor's surgery yesterday morning? I hope it's nothing serious?'

'That's very kind of you; if you don't mind, I do want to get these parcels off. No, nothing serious, just a spring cold.'

'Oh, I see you are sending things to Suzannah,' the postmistress commented. 'How is she getting on out there in Russia, or is it Ukraine? Not the Soviet Union anymore is it? Is she liking it?'

'Yes, Grace, she seems to be enjoying herself,' smiled Paula, wondering how they always managed to find out everything without actually coming out and asking.

'Lovely girl she was, and such a good teacher. And will she be staying long out there in Kyiv?' Grace asked, pulling out the appropriate sheet of stamps from the leather-bound folder.

'About two years, though I don't know if she'll stay that long. She wrote that the weather at the end of February when she arrived was bitterly cold. Minus thirty she said, and everyone all dressed up in furs.'

'Fancy that!' sighed Dolly. 'It's hard to imagine. I don't think I could be doing with such a cold climate. It's bad enough here. Look at it now, May already and this is the first dry day we've had. I'm so tired of all this rain.

'Right, Paula, that's everything done, why don't you come

round tomorrow night for some supper, if you're free?'

'Thank you, Grace, I would like that. See you then.' Paula waved goodbye to the remainder of the people in the queue and let herself out of the shop. Standing out on the street, she saw that a new advertisement had been stuck in the window.

WANTED
Part time labourer for a month
Telephone 482400 – Robert Ross

Paula smiled ruefully and made her way back to her house. Spring, as Dolly had said, had arrived at last. Tentative shoots were trying again to brave the winds and rain. Buds hung heavy on the dripping branches of the rose bushes, and primroses dotted the sides of the roads like small heralds of the sunshine that was filtering through the clouds. Paula took note of the clumps of nettles growing rampantly outside her front door. Not very welcoming, she thought; perhaps now was the time to try out a recipe for nettle soup. Surprisingly she had heard it was very tasty. Inside newspapers lay on the floor, manuscripts were spread across the sofa, the fire had not been cleaned out and ash and cinders were piled up. Where the sun burst through her window, she could see the heavy coating of dust that had accumulated over all her furniture. Unmoved by the detritus around her, she picked up the telephone. 'Hello? Is that Robert? It's Paula here. I saw your advert in the post office window and wondered if I could be of any help.'

'Er, um, hello, Paula. Er, so you're interested in doing some labouring, is that what you're saying?'

'Yes!'

'Mm… It will be quite hard work, you know…'

'Yes, I can do hard work!'

Paula found herself grinning as he told her to report for duty that very afternoon. 'Oh God, I just hope he doesn't expect me to shovel manure or anything like that,' she muttered, tugging a brush through her hair and pulling the straggling locks into a pony tail. Gone completely were her smart London coiffure and any remnant of the tailored clothes that had once been such a priority. Nowadays she padded around in thick socks under her jeans and wore a selection of bright woollen jumpers that were for sale in the post office, knitted by old Jenny who lived in a tiny house not far up the road from James MacTavish.

At two o'clock Paula drove over the hill and along the avenue of beech, lime and sycamore trees until she came to the stone house that sat at the road-end of the croft that ran up to the foot of the mountain. The loch lapped gently on the other side of the road, and she gazed about at the beauty of the scene in front of her.

'So you are here for the labouring job are you?' Robert came out to meet her with two border collies barking at his heels. 'Sit down, Roy! Come here, Ben!'

Paula looked at the trio and nodded enthusiastically at her new boss. Robert was indeed a tall man, well over six feet, strong and strapping as they would describe him in the village. His dark hair was curly with just a few streaks of white and he had let it grow long on to his collar. His eyes were as black as pieces of onyx, fringed with lashes that gave his face a striking, foreign appearance. She guessed that he was a couple of years older than herself, probably around forty or forty-four, it was hard to tell.

'I have two jobs for now. Can you come into the kitchen and feed my twin orphan lambs? Then I need you to go around the field and pick up all the scraps of wool that the sheep have shed. I just put the flock out to the hill last week, and I need the field cleared so that the hay can grow. I don't want wool catching on my blades when I come to cut it in July or August. Can you manage that? I imagine you'll get a couple of bags, and there's plenty stuck to the fence as well.'

Paula took the bottle of milk that Robert handed her, and copying him she approached the hungry lambs. She took hold of the other twin and felt the sharp tug at the teat and laughed as the lamb drank and sucked as though it was the last meal on earth. 'Good grief!' she laughed, 'what a hungry creature! Do you have names for them?'

'Aye, that one you have is Dot, for obvious reasons. Do you see that black spot on its head? And this one is Holly. I don't know why, it seemed like a good idea at the time!'

After the feeding, Paula was then dispatched to the field where she spent the afternoon bending over the grass, picking up the long swathes of wool that had caught around the fence posts and rocks. The day grew warm and the sun burnt her forehead and forearms. Occasionally she stretched and smelt the salt wind from the sea loch, and stared up to the pinnacles of the mountain. Buzzards soared high on the thermals and crows eyed her fiercely from the branches of the surrounding sycamore trees. She felt glad to be alive.

Meanwhile Robert climbed up on to his tractor and whistled for his dogs and chugged off down the avenue towards his boat shed. With the tourist season beginning, he decided to pull his boat out and see what needed to be done to get her ready for her trips on the loch. He ran his hand through his thick hair and surveyed the wooden hull. A good paint job would be necessary, he thought, just to liven her up. She was still up on her trailer where he had left her in the autumn, so he decided he would take her out in the sun and give her a closer inspection. He pulled on the trailer but was met by strong resistance.

'Ach, bloody tyre is as flat as a cowpat,' he informed his dogs.

For the next hour he struggled with the tyre and then hosed down the boat, thick with cobwebs. When he returned to his croft he espied his labourer sitting by the stone dyke gazing up at the hills. The sun was hot and he noticed that the field was still dotted white with sheep's wool. Robert whistled jauntily while he boiled the kettle and made two mugs of tea. He frowned, wondering if she took milk, and considered taking a tray with the sugar and some biscuits as well when suddenly his dilemma was resolved.

'I take it black with sugar, sometimes with a slice of lemon, that is if I am not being too presumptuous imagining the tea might be for me?' Paula stood framed in the door of the kitchen.

'I thought you might be glad of a break from sitting in the sun! It's grand and warm out there. Come, we'll sit out by the fence and then I will have to leave you. I have to go to the town and get some paint and some varnish. My boat is in a sorry state and needs a lick of paint. I might as well take advantage of this dry spell.'

'Oh right! I'm sorry but I'm afraid I didn't get much done, I just couldn't stop staring up at the mountain tops. I'm sure I saw a golden eagle.'

Robert smiled to himself and quietly gave thanks that he hadn't agreed to pay her by the hour. 'So you will be back tomorrow? When you finish the field and of course the fence as well, I have a few more jobs for you, that is, if you are willing?'

'I would love to help, though in case you haven't noticed I haven't done any outdoor work before. I seem to get a bit distracted; there are so many things to look at.'

'What did you do in London?' Robert asked her, studying her smooth, beautiful hands.

Paula grinned as she read his mind and stretched out her long slim fingers into a star. 'Actually I worked in a model agency. I recruited photographic models and organized their schedules and marketed them for agencies. It was all very fast and cut-throat and I'm afraid I lost sight of the small things. I found I was in the office in front of a computer for most of my working day. I forgot to take the time to smell the roses, as they say.'

Paula took a sip of her tea and studied the man in front of her. She took in the hypnotic black eyes, and the brow etched with three deep lines. It was a face that had weathered the years, and she imagined him staring out at the horizon, eyes screwed up against the sharp light reflected on the sparkling lilt of the waves. Looking at him now, stretched out on the step of the back door and listening to her talk of London, she saw that his expression was full of interest and compassion. Idly she glanced at his hands, large as she expected, masculine and rough. Not for the first time did she feel the unmistakable stirrings of attraction in the pit of her stomach. She remembered the similar rush of feelings when he had taken her in and dried her off during the rainstorm back in the autumn.

She took a deep breath and continued, 'I also got involved with a man who swore love and devotion.'

'Ah! I thought there might be a man involved.'

Paula smiled. 'I met him in London. He was from Cyprus and was doing his medical internship. We were together for over six years, and I honestly thought we would get married eventually. Just last year he dropped the bombshell on me. He admitted that he had been promised to some sweet young thing back home in Limassol. The parents had arranged the match when they were children apparently. I was left looking like a right fool. I had to get away, so I decided to take a break and got six months' leave. I saw the holiday cottage here for rent in a magazine, and decided to take it.'

'And now?' enquired Robert. 'I believe it's more than six months, and you are still here. What are your plans now? I'm afraid I can't pay you the same as those bigwigs in London town.' He smiled at the thought of the meagre wages she had agreed to accept for her hard work labouring in the fields.

'No, don't worry, I am doing some freelance reading for a publishing house, and I still have income from my flat in London. It's rented out so I shan't starve. In the meantime I would be happy to help you with your chores, that is, if you still want me?'

Robert reflected that he could have finished the field in a couple of hours, and predicted that with Paula doing it, he would be lucky if it was ever finished. Looking at her now, he admired her soft toffee-coloured hair falling in wisps around her forehead, her face fresh and covered by a light smattering of freckles across her nose. He liked the criss-cross of lines around her eyes and the sharp crease around her mouth that he imagined was the result of her happy disposition. He found he liked the idea of her proximity and decided that she might in time be quite an asset to the croft.

'Aye, you'll do, but I expect you to finish that field by the end of the week and then you can give me a hand with painting the boat. Now I must be on my way but I'll see you tomorrow.'

CHAPTER 11

The next evening Paula soaked in her bath, tired and sunburnt from her day spent toiling on the croft, as she saw it. In truth it had been another day gazing around at the birds and bending over trying to identify wild flowers and grasses. By lunchtime she had felt overcome with the need to lie down under the lime trees to listen to the buzzing of a swarm of bees. Robert had found her there. He had crossly exclaimed that time was money and what on earth was she doing? He had been quite indignant at her explanation, but she had calmly extolled the pleasures of stopping and listening and taking just a few minutes out of each day. She had told him that it stopped stress from taking its toll. Hitting his head with his hand, he had admitted defeat and eventually sat down beside her. Together they had listened to the splashing of the waves against the rounded boulders and the lazy drone of the bees high up in the tree canopy.

Paula smiled to herself as she remembered the peaceful interlude during the afternoon. Now, luxuriating in the steam and inhaling the sweet fragrance of the bath salts, she closed her eyes and let her mind drift over the contours of Robert's neck and the outline of his strong back. Only when the water began to cool did she become aware of the passing of time. Shaking herself mentally to return to the present, she rose from the bath in a great tidal rush, splashing the floor as she stretched for her towel. It was time to motivate herself and get ready for dinner with Grace. Dressed in a long skirt, a colourful gypsy stole wrapped around her shoulders, Paula walked briskly up the street to where Grace lived in her little house behind the post office. From an earthenware casserole dish she was served a portion of venison with mashed potatoes, carrots and peas. The smells wafted up from the table and Paula declared that she was ravenous after her day spent outdoors.

'Fancy you working for Robert Ross,' commented Grace dryly, fingering the white crochet collar that she had made last winter after being inspired by a lecture at the SWRI. 'Did he ask you himself?'

'Oh no,' Paula replied, 'I saw an advert at your post office so I kindly offered my services. I only have to gather the wool and do a bit of painting, nothing too arduous. Why?'

'Well, dear, I was just wondering how Margaret will be feeling, knowing that you are spending so much time with her intended. They've been an item for quite a few years, you know.'

'Margaret?' Paula asked sharply. 'Robert hasn't even mentioned her. I didn't know he was involved or was serious about anyone.' She took a sip of the red wine that Grace had been pleased to bring out of the cupboard and pour. 'I don't think I'm a threat to anyone, working in the field in my old clothes. If they've been sweethearts for so long, why have they never got married?'

'Och, there's always been something.' Grace screwed up her face, as though in disapproval. 'For one thing, Margaret was away at the college in Glasgow, and then she had a job in Stirling, only coming back to the glen every now and then. She seemed to expect Robert to be chasing after her the whole time. Now she's at home living with her elderly parents, and she's quite the little madam, full of her fancy ways, thinking she's one of the gentry, if you ask me. But I'll tell you, she's got quite a way to go to be a lady, that one.' Grace leant over her plate and almost whispered at her guest. 'Did I tell you about Anne-Marie and Angus's wedding last year, just before you arrived? No? Well!' and she sat back and wiped her lips with her red and pink seersucker napkin. 'Margaret told us all one night at the bar that she intended to get Robert to pop the question, so she made a plan. She told us she was going to Inverness with the notion of buying something that might seduce him. She thought maybe some posh lingerie would do the trick. I'm sure you will know what I mean, being from London and all that.' Grace took a forkful of venison and chewed it vigorously.

Paula mimicked Grace's prim expression and suggested, 'Fancy knickers and peek-a-boo bras?'

Her hostess just rolled her eyes, looking faintly disapproving at the thought of such sorcery. 'Well I was married once myself, my dear, and I can tell you I didn't need all that nonsense to persuade my Andrew to keep me warm on a winter's eve, quite the opposite actually, but I won't go into that now. Don't want to speak ill of the dead.'

Paula's eyes widened at the unlikely thought of Grace the Jezebel. She thought she might delve deeper into the postmistress's past another time. In the meantime she persuaded her to go on with her story.

Grace leant over and continued, 'Now Margaret is small, and I have to say quite tubby, with thighs that look all the better for being hidden away, if you know what I mean?' The older woman's eyes were bright and her lips took on a pursed look of prudishness.

'So what did she buy?'

'Well, I'll tell you! Suspenders! A white suspender belt with white stockings! Oh my dear, she had plans, I can tell you that, and not only suspenders did she buy, but she rang up the pharmacy in Inverness and asked for an order of two gross of condoms… two gross! Imagine!'

Paula nearly choked at the thought of Grace discussing condoms. While she herself wasn't quite sure what a gross was, it sounded a lot. 'Why so many, I wonder?'

'Stupid girl thought a gross was twelve. For all her fancy schooling and her la-di-da ways, you would think someone would have taught her how to count!'

They both drank the wine and Grace filled up the glasses, her eyes bright and gleeful as she recalled the rest of her story.

'Well, the wedding reception was going great guns, and everyone was in the hall dancing and having a grand old time. I was sitting by the side with Dolly and Kathleen from the Tea Room, and Margaret came whirling round, half flying she was on Robert Ross's arm. Her pink dress just flew up, and we were treated to a rare sight! Big white knickers that went all the way up to her waist, and then there were the suspenders, pulled to breaking point, for the stockings had slipped down to the tops of her knees, and all that white fat flesh just about bulged over the top! What a sight it was!'

Paula laughed and for a moment she felt a passing flicker of sympathy for the poor girl. She could just imagine the spectacle she must have made of herself in front of the village worthies.

'Well that was last year,' Paula reminded Grace, 'and they still haven't married. Maybe the seduction with all those condoms was just too much of a challenge. Robert seems happy to me just being single.'

Walking home later that evening Paula reflected on the gossip she had heard. She just wanted her life to carry on without any domestic dramas. She enjoyed living in the village and being part of the community. Most especially she had come to love the mountains and the sea, and the wildness and freedom of the birds and animals that she had encountered. She did not want to be the cause of some poor girl's unhappiness. That was not something she relished, but she did feel a strong attraction to the man. She had felt it from the very first time he had taken pity on her and rescued her from the rain. Actually I think he finds me very useful, she thought optimistically while turning the key in her front door. Oh God, I must do something about these nettles.

CHAPTER 12

The wet days of spring led into the most glorious months of summer. Days seemed never-ending; the nights descended only in streaks of deep indigo. The quiet lasted for only a few short hours before the yellow dawn returned. Children were soon released from the strictures of the schoolroom and hay grew long in the crofts around the village. Old folk sat out on benches and greeted one another as they made their way from the shop to the post office to the doctor's surgery. Tourists and visitors came and went, exchanging news from towns and cities for the more pressing gossip that was enacted within the village. Who had died? Who was to be married? It was a constant source of entertainment with everyone feeling their own sense of importance, each being a key player in the ever-evolving drama.

Hector Ogilvie liked to cycle down to the post office to collect his pension. From there he made straight for the Pipers Inn where he ordered a pint of Guinness. As the thick, dark liquid slipped down, Hector smacked his lips and wiped the creamy froth from his unshaven bristles. Spying the tourists eating chicken-in-a-basket and scampi and chips, he scoured the room with a speculative gaze. He'd had a good morning, and although it had been wet with heavy showers at times, he'd admired the fields and sea in the distance and thought they were beautiful even. Two loads of silage had been delivered and he'd made a good effort at raking and shovelling the stuff into the barn. After his two pints of Guinness he returned to his bicycle, unclipped his collie dog and began his journey back to his croft house.

'Hello there, Hector.' He heard the booming voice of his friend

Johnny Macdonald. 'Here's a wee something for helping out with that cow last week,' and he handed over a brown paper bag containing a half-bottle of whisky. 'Now make sure you drink it all at once!'

'Aye well,' smiled Hector, 'it looks as though I shall just have a wee rest now, and I know just the place. Up by the caravan site, where all the tourist lassies like to parade about.' Smiling lecherously and eyes darting around, he weaved his way along the avenue on his rickety old bike, followed by the faithful Charlie.

Robert continued to find jobs for Paula to do, knowing that she was hopeless at just about everything she undertook. As the summer progressed, Margaret took to driving over to see him and she made a great performance of fussing in the kitchen whenever she came.

'Robert loves it when I am here. He knows I make such good cakes and he likes his tea here at the table. Will you be working here for much longer, Paula? I expect you will be missing all the bright lights of London?' Without giving Paula a chance to reply she ran on in her continuous monologue. 'Robert was so unhappy when I was working in Stirling. He couldn't stand being cooped up in the city. He would stay a night and then be pestering for me to go home with him. So here I am, looking after my old mam, but I can see Robert is happier having me in close proximity. Of course he would never insist that I do any of these nasty jobs he sets you.'

Paula smiled at that, for recently she had been busy creosoting the fence posts. Wee Eck too had taken to dropping by. He, by contrast, was a welcome diversion for he brought the latest village gossip to the small croft by the loch side.

'Have you heard the news?' he announced one morning when Paula and Robert were preparing the boat for the day's sailing trip. 'The minister is so fired up after the winter drama production when you made him a star of sorts that he's wanting to put on his own drama!'

'No! I haven't heard that. What is he planning to do?' Paula stopped loading the life jackets into the boat and looked with interest at her former stage manager.

'He is going to involve all the school children and the Sunday School, and he's going to put on a pageant about Bonny Prince Charlie. He was telling Grace in the post office, and he's put up a notice inviting anyone interested to go for a meeting in the hall tonight. He's just full of excitement about it all. Maybe we should go and see if he wants our assistance?' Wee Eck looked at Paula questioningly, with a certain amount of puppy-dog adoration in his gaze.

'Yes, of course, I would love to get involved. I wonder if he has a script.' Paula looked at Robert. 'What about you? Will you go?'

'Not me, that's not my sort of thing. You can tell me all about it tomorrow, or will you be wanting time off for rehearsals, do you think?'

Paula and Wee Eck arrived at the hall that evening in good time for the meeting. The Reverend Wilson and his wife Marie were already sitting together around the long table. Meg Munro and James MacTavish were there too. Paula greeted them all with enthusiasm, noting that James coloured slightly when he saw her. She knew that he always associated her with Suzannah, and she felt vaguely uncomfortable at what her friend had written in her last letter to her.

I just love him, Paula. I never dreamt that I could walk on air and yet still feel my feet on the pavement. I don't know whether to laugh or cry. Is it the city, the river or all the wonderful things that I am seeing and doing? I just know that I have never felt so completely and utterly in love. His name is Sergei...

Poor James, she thought.

The minister cleared his throat and started his welcome speech. 'Thank you for attending, everyone, and giving your time. I have been very busy putting together a drama for the children, and would appreciate it if you could all assist me. Now I will give you my vision if you like. I see the play being a simple re-enactment of the return of the Prince to the Highlands, his arrival at Glen Finnan and the gathering of the clans. I can see a few village scenes with women spinning and grilling fish, and men tending the cattle, then there will be the call to arms.'

'Will adults be involved in the scenes?' Paula enquired.

'Yes, they will be allotted a group of children and will be dressed up. I thought you and some of the village women could drape yourselves in tartan travelling rugs or something.'

'I could be a woman who runs around with the clans,' volunteered Marie helpfully.

Paula's eyes met James's as they both pictured the large frame of the minister's wife running anywhere. A muscle clenched in James's jaw and he suppressed a chuckle.

The minister nodded importantly. 'Yes, dear, of course, and don't forget we need the Red Coats. I see them marching about and then of course there will be the big charge at the end, with the Highlanders all falling dead in the field of Culloden with their targes and claymores at their side.'

Iona broke in then, having just arrived in the hall to hear the last words. 'Perhaps we could have a piper play a lament?'

'Yes, very good, Iona, and what about a few songs as we go along?'

Meg Munro offered to teach the children at school some appropriate Gaelic songs for the village scenes, for spinning and fishing.

'It sounds wonderful, Reverend,' said Paula enthusiastically. 'I would love to be involved with any art work. What about a castle for the Red Coats and I know James would be willing to help with any shields or targes?'

'Aye, I would that,' agreed James. 'I have a few books in the house that would help me design them.'

'What about costumes?' asked Paula, ever-practical.

'That one is easy. I have bags of jumble in the church hall, and have access to every home in the glen. I am sure I can get folk to part with a tartan shawl or a bit of plaid,' Marie replied. She turned to her husband and continued, 'So when shall we hold this pageant of yours, Jeremy?'

The minister nodded and spread out a calendar on the table. 'Let us say in two weeks. That will be enough time to get the children rehearsed and we can have working days over in the field by the sea. Perhaps Murdo and Wee Eck could erect the tent that we use for the Highland Games? We could set up somewhere to paint a bit of scenery and weapons and such like. Now Iona, do you think you could have a word with Murdo about arranging the gala tent to be erected in the corner of the field? We could use that as our base?' He then went on waving his finger up and down as though he was lecturing in his Sunday morning sermon. 'There are plenty of talented children and they can help with the painting and so on. I thought of young Harry MacDonald for Prince Charlie and Rory Campbell as his assistant. I shall have to get the rest of them together to divide them into Highlanders or Red Coats.'

Robert saw little of Paula over the next few days. She was breathless on the phone when she telephoned her excuses for her absence. 'I know I have to finish creosoting. Don't you think I know that? My hands look as though I have some horrible disease and there is still a stink that comes off them. You are lucky to have such a devoted labourer that doesn't mind ruining her hands for the sake of a few stupid fence posts.'

Robert coughed at his end of the phone. 'Those stupid fence posts, as you insist on calling them, are vital for keeping the sheep and lambs safe during the spring, in case you had forgotten. But you just carry on traipsing around a field dressed up like some mad Highland woman and I shall just have to find time to paint them at eight o'clock at night when I'm finished with the tourists.'

Muttering to herself, Paula ran out of the house and down the street. She had agreed to meet James and start painting the castle and supervise the making of the targes.

'Hello! At last you've shown up. Billy here is desperate to get painting and Rosie has been cutting out hundreds of circles from my silver baking foil. She's doing a grand job, are you not, pet?'

'Yes, I am. Sally at the shop gave us lots of old bits of cardboard and some boxes. We are going to make shields, once Mr Wilson comes. Those are really called targes; did you know that, Paula?'

'Yes, Rosie, I'm learning lots of things. What about the claymores? Ah here he comes, the Reverend himself.'

'Good morning, everyone, well we can all get started as we have a lot to do. Unfortunately I have a burial this afternoon. One of our very senior citizens sadly passed away and the funeral is today, so you will have to do without me for a few hours.'

'Did you bring the paint, Mr Wilson?' Billy asked expectantly.

'Yes, and it's gloss, so you will have to be very careful you don't spill any on your clothes.'

'I'm a good painter too, aren't I, Uncle James?' Rosie looked up beseechingly.

'You are, Rosie my wee darling, but I think you will be better off helping Paula paint the big castle nice and grey. They are using water paint for that, so you and the soap can arrange to meet in the bath afterwards. What do you say?'

Rosie looked crestfallen for only a second, for she saw Paula lift some large sheets of cardboard cut to the shape of crenulations along the top. Immediately the small girl ran over to where she was allowed to paint with abandon for the rest of the morning.

'What about swords and claymores?' asked Iona, who was cutting out the circles for the targes. Cardboard won't be any good. Far too floppy I would have thought. And we'll need some rifles for the English Red Coats.'

'Och, just leave it to me. I have a plan for that,' said the minister, 'but first I have to see the rest of the group who are making the village scenes, and check a few things with my wife, then I had better be going. I'll see you all later on.'

The church emptied slowly to the sonorous sounds of the organ. The small number of relatives and friends gathered together outside before making the traditional procession to the graveyard. The coffin was placed in the hearse and Hamish, the joiner and undertaker from the next village, sat stiffly beside the driver. The mourners, led by the minister, walked sedately behind the funeral car until they reached the cemetery gates. Hamish organised the pall bearers to carry the coffin and set it down on to the green felt beside the open grave, then he went back and walked beside the Reverend Wilson. Together they walked towards the final part of the ceremony.

Holding his Bible to his chest, the minister, without once breaking his step, turned to the undertaker and with his face straight and serious asked, 'Can you make me twenty two wooden claymores and twenty two rifles by Thursday?'

    Hamish blinked, but kept his eyes to the fore. 'Aye, and what size would you be needing?'

    'Just for the children, you know, for the pageant?'

    'Oh, right you are then, not a bother at all,' agreed Hamish, his face impassive.

    'Dearly beloved, we are gathered now ready to lay our poor sister to rest...'

The day of the pageant dawned cloudy and grey and a wild wind threatened to blow the fine castle straight out to sea. The crowds that had gathered to see this re-enactment of one of Scotland's most famous stories seemed envious of the young actors cosily wrapped up in their warm tartan shawls. Marie Wilson and her twenty or so Highlanders took up their posts, creating scenes of rural country living. The Red Coats, including Rosie and Billie, were dressed fine with tall hats and wooden cut-out guns. Their welly boots were all in marching order, waiting for the signal from their commander-in-chief, the very Reverend Wilson. Prince Charlie and his aide arrived, by sea of course, in Robert Ross's boat. Paula stood proudly watching as Robert gently helped the young prince ashore. Wee Eck and Paula were dressed in the tartan, as were Iona and James. Their job was to blend themselves into the tableau and guide the youngsters throughout the pageant. Margaret and Dolly watched Grace and Marie Wilson grilling fish on a disposable barbecue.

'Hope they get it done before the daft Englishmen make their charge. At this rate with all this wind, I wouldn't be surprised if that barbecue didn't blow over and set the whole place on fire. I'm sure the fire engines would be quite bemused being called out to a great fire in the glen. That would put the wind up the minister's kilt, would it not?'

'Aye, and isn't it just typical of Grace to have marinated the mackerel first; she is such a show off with her cooking. For goodness' sake, is that not soy sauce that I'm smelling? She would have been better off serving coffee to all these tourists who've come to watch. They look frozen stiff.'

Meanwhile Bonny Prince Charlie marched diagonally across the field, stopping to talk to the clans people, trying to persuade them to come and form an army. The children in their bits of ragged clothes met at the far end of the field for the tragic end of the story.

Finally the signal was given and Robert Ross, from his stance behind the cut-out cardboard statue of the Prince at Glenfinnan, got a fine view of the skirmish and tragedy that would be forever associated with Culloden Moor and the dissipation of the Highland clans. He saw claymores being raised and colours of cloth weave in and out as the children ran head-on for each other. Leather look-alike targes with their shiny metal studs glinted in the bursts of intermittent sunshine and blue Glengarry bonnets united against the cruel formations of the King of England's Red Coats. Robert watched the Highlanders, who were outnumbered, untrained and ill equipped, fall and die. Soon the field was littered with the bodies of the village children, huddled and separate, falling where they had been shot. He saw his grown-up friends too fall amidst the carnage and soon there was stillness. The English troops fell into formation and marched away. From the side of the field the kilted Donnie came out with his bagpipes, playing a lament that would have broken anyone's heart. When he ceased, there was only the splash of the waves, and the scream of the gulls. The silence persisted, and still no one stirred. People were so moved that they forgot to applaud.

CHAPTER 13

Rosie MacTavish was enjoying the halcyon days of summer. Her home was a confusion of teenagers and noise and doors being slammed as her brothers came and went with their entourage of friends. Nobody was interested in her. Not even Billy. Her mother always seemed to be at the end of her tether and if she wasn't working her shifts at the nursing home she was dragging Rosie off to the shop where they had to collect loaves by the dozen to feed so many extra mouths.

'Can I go and see Uncle James please?'

'Aye, if he'll have you, I know he's not working today. Be a good girl, and on Saturday we'll go to Inverness on Daddy's bus and buy your new things for starting school. Would you like that?'

'Yes, but please please could I have that special pencil case that has the sliding cover? I don't want Billy's old one.'

'Away and play; I'll take you over to Uncle James when I've hung out this washing.'

Rosie decided to spy on her two brothers. Jonathan, or 'Joker' as they called him, was now fifteen and as tall as a lamp post. He was sitting out in the barn with an empty plastic lemonade bottle. Billy was kneeling beside him holding a bottle of vinegar. Rosie crept up behind them but she could not see what they were doing; the two black heads were too close together.

'How much do we need?' she heard Billy ask.

'Just a wee bit, I think, till it fizzes. Right, I'll put in the vinegar, and then we have to put in the stuff we got from the chemist.'

'Will we put it in now, or later?' Billy asked.

'Later. We'll take our bikes and some matches down to the river, and we'll do it there,' explained Joker. 'We'll make a fire and have a feast afterwards.'

'Can I come, can I be the cook?' Rosie blurted out.

'No you can't, go away! You're too small,' Joker said unkindly. 'Come on Billy, let's get our bikes.'

'I'll tell! I'll tell Mum you took her cooking stuff.'

'You'd better not, or I'll put rose hips down your back and then I'll put real spiders in your socks and they'll bite you.'

'You're a mean bully, Joker MacTavish.'

James MacTavish was sitting on his pew when Rosie arrived. She was breathless from running down the path, and he admired her sun-browned face and wild black hair. He noticed that it was growing longer and she had a real air of the urchin or gypsy about her.

'Well my little darling, how are you today? Are you counting the days until you go to school?'

'Not really, Uncle James, Billy said I won't get to paint and he said the other minister makes us pray all Thursday morning. I like the Reverend Wilson; he really likes painting and things.'

'Aye, but school is famous for something else, lass, and do you know what it is?'

Rosie turned her dark eyes up to him, wide and questioning.

'Custard!'

'Custard?' repeated Rosie, disappointed.

'Aye, lassie, school custard is the best in the world. And you get it all over syrup sponge and roly poly pudding and apple crumble. Oh my goodness, it's making my mouth water just to think about it. Your Granny, her that used to live with me here, was the school cook for as long as I can remember, and I never had a day without a good lashing of her custard.'

'But she's dead,' pointed out Rosie, in her matter of fact voice.

'Aye, she's passed on, right enough, but before she retired, she whispered her secret recipe to Phyllis who cooks at the school now.

So it's like a magic potion passed on from generation to generation of school cooks!'

'Is that true?' asked Rosie, doubtfully.

'It's as true as true,' confirmed her uncle.

Rosie sat quietly on the pew beside him. She played with her fingers, twisting them and lacing them, obviously weighing up some deep thoughts. Eventually she came out with what was bothering her. 'Uncle James, if you put vinegar and soda and something from the chemist in a bottle what will happen?'

'It will blow up; now why would you be mentioning this? Did you see something, or just hear something?'

'Nothing,' she replied.

'Rosie?'

'Well, it was Joker and Billy. They went off on their bikes and they said they were going to make a fire and cook things.'

'Come along, my little Sherlock, you did well. I think you and I should go for a nice walk.'

James knew every bend and pool of the Glen Mhor river. Silently he led the way, climbing over the fence that separated him from his neighbour's croft. Rosie lagged behind him, suddenly afraid of what her brothers might say when they saw her with Uncle James.

'Uncle James, please don't say I told you, or they'll put spiders in my socks.'

'If it was the last century they would be sent to Australia for poaching, and my goodness they have big spiders over there. Don't you worry, lass.'

Soon they came to the bend in the river. The bushes were thick, heavy with foliage, and it was hard to make out the two bikes leaning against two trees, camouflaged by the thick branches.

'Sssssh, quietly now, I think I see them.' James could hear the voices of his two nephews. They had discarded caution to the wind; the excitement of what they were doing had them dancing about on the sandy embankment.

'Right!' shouted Joker. 'Here we go.' He added the solution and shook the bottle and put the cap on it. Just as he was about to lob the bottle, he heard the loud voice of his uncle.

'What do you think you are doing, Jonathan MacTavish?'

'Bloody hell!' the boy froze in fear. Realising that it was his uncle, and what the consequences might be, he panicked and shouted, 'Run, Billy!'

'Stay where you are, both of you!' thundered James.

At that moment, a muffled bang came from the river. The bottle had sunk beneath the calm brown surface only to explode violently. Floating to the top, along with the ragged remains of the plastic bottle, came four large trout and two tiny minnows.

'Get the net, Billy, and pull them in,' instructed his uncle.

'I'll be taking those, Joker my lad, and I'll be giving them to your mother to present at the old people's home. It's a shame to waste good trout, but if you ever do that again, the police will be involved. You are damaging the river's environment, and displaying a lack of sportsmanship. Poaching is illegal, and I am disappointed in both of you. You have always been keen fishermen, displaying patience and skill. I cannot believe you would have the nerve to blow up my river. As the river's legal guardian I have always turned a blind eye to some of the activities that go on here, but explosions are not in keeping with our village traditions.'

'Did Rosie tell?' asked Billy in a small voice, a sinister look finding its way to his wee sister.

'No, Billy, as you know she often comes walking with me. Did you know that poachers used to be transported in ships to Australia? You should be grateful those times have gone. I don't know how you would have got on out there, either of you.'

'Incy Wincy Spider,' sang Rosie, gleefully. 'Can we go now, Uncle James?'

James called in to see Murdo and Iona later that evening and recounted his story of the two boys caught red-handed with their home-made explosives.

'Clever, eh?' Iona exclaimed. 'Why didn't I ever think of it? Might have saved me a few midgie bites over the years. How many hours do you think we've stood there and waited and waited for a bite, when all we had to do was toss in a stick of dynamite!'

'Aye, well I gave them a good thundering. I just hope they don't retaliate and get little Rosie.'

'She'll be so excited, that one. She's starting school soon, isn't she?'

'Aye, she is that. I'll miss her in the afternoons. She was telling me that she would be helping you on your stall in this year's Highland Games? She says it's a big secret.'

'It is, and I won't be telling you either. What are you doing this year?'

'Well, surprise surprise! I shall be on the gardening stall. Maybe for once we might get a good lot of produce to sell. These last few years have just been a wash-out with all the rain. I hear the big heavies from Inverness and Tain are coming over for the hammer and caber events. Did you hear that, Murdo?'

'I did, James, but I think I'll be helping judge the beauty contest myself.'

'Oh will you, indeed? Does that mean I'll be winning?' Iona smiled saucily at her husband. 'I'd better make sure you have an early night!'

'What about another wee dram, James?' Murdo leant over to take his friend's glass.

'Well, you know me, I won't say no!'

'Another year gone by, James, and you're still single. How has the talent been this year? No walkers or bird watchers to your fancy?'

'Aye, one or two,' James ruminated, 'but you know? I think I'm getting fussy in my old age. Now thank you to you good folk, but I might just wander off down through the fields; it's grand, walking and smelling the hay on a warm summer evening.'

'Well, don't take your time or the midgies and clegs will eat you alive! Some of them are as big as helicopters!' Iona waved to her neighbour as he let himself out of the gate.

James opened the door of his house. He stopped in the hall and glanced at the portrait of his mother above the organ. He randomly flicked through the pages of the open Bible, and found himself looking at the Book of Proverbs. He scanned the words telling him that the fear of the Lord is the beginning of knowledge, and only fools despise wisdom and instruction. That's about it, he thought, we just have to keep learning from our mistakes.

Sighing deeply, James walked through to the kitchen and poured one more glass of whisky. A night cap, that's what I need, he decided. Wandering over to his desk, he looked out of the small window that faced out to sea. In the distance he could make out the flickering lighthouse. The water was calm as shimmering silk and in the foreground his garden was neat and orderly. A hedgehog snuffled its way across the cut lawn and disappeared beneath the heavy foliage of a peony rose. Oh, Suzannah, he sighed, where are you? Why did I let you go? He remembered the day she left. He could still see her eyes, so blue and filled with tears.

'Why, James?' she had said, over and over again.

'I'm too old for you, lass, you need a younger man. I'm not the marrying kind.'

'Well, just you remember, James MacTavish, that it was you that said that, not me. I have never mentioned age or marriage, but it must be very important to you. For goodness' sake, you even have an application up there on your shelf for finding a bride. If I remember correctly, I seem to have satisfied many of your requirements. I even have my own teeth.' She had smiled and for a minute they both remembered the morning of their first meeting. 'All I wanted was for us to be together.'

'No, Suzannah, I won't spoil your life. Go to your new job, learn about the Russians, meet new people and fall in love with someone your own age.'

Suitcase by her feet, her forlorn figure, wearing the same bright blue coat in which he had first seen her, had watched him walk away from her without once looking back.

James gave himself a shake and picked up a card that had arrived that morning, and which he had been reading when Rosie had come by.

James, my dear James,
His name is Sergei. He is young and works in the military hospital. He is a heart specialist and he trained in New York.
I am happy, I love it here and my job is full of challenges but I miss Glen Mhor and I think of last winter with such joy.
Warm thoughts from your Suzannah

James MacTavish went to bed. He lay on the white sheets and heard the crying of the gulls and the bleating of the sheep. Your Suzannah. For a long time he could not sleep.

CHAPTER 14

The last Saturday in August dawned fair. The night had seen a persistent rain but a good fresh gust from the east had scattered the clouds and so the morning heralded a brisk breeze and smatterings of sunshine.

'You can't wish for anything better than that,' remarked James to Donnie, who was opening the wide wooden gate that led into the field where the gala was to be held. He remembered the days gone by when Glen Mhor had hosted real Highland Games in which all the big heavyweights came to compete. Nowadays only big centres like Drumnadrochit and Braemar and the like were deemed worthy of such goliaths. Still he was content that the village committee had somehow organised themselves and the gala this year would be a good crowd magnet for visitors and locals alike.

'Aye James, I have the clipboard here. I see you have stall number twenty-one for your garden produce.'

'Very good, Donnie, I'll away and set up now. I see the field is a wee bit damp yet, so I hope the races can go ahead. I hear those big lads from Tain have seen fit to honour us with their presence.'

'I saw that too, and a couple from Muir of Ord and Dingwall. I just hope nobody expects us to compete against them.'

'Well, I've seen the day, Donnie my lad, but I doubt I could even hold a big tree up, let alone heave it up in my arms and hurl it across the field!'

'I'm going to preserve my strength for the *Strip the Willow* later on at the dance tonight. I've got my eye on a lass from Skye, and that's all I'm telling you, James MacTavish.'

'Don't you worry about me, I'm keeping a very low profile. There's a lady here who has got the scent of me, and I shall be dodging her all day, I think. It's a hard life being pursued, but now I must away and set up my stall. Maybe I could interest you in some curly kale?'

Donnie smiled as he watched his old rival making his way slowly across the muddy field, then turned back to his task of allocating the stalls to the various participants.

Kathleen at the Tea Room was in a frenzy of activity. She had been up since five, baking and packing up her pies and cakes and pastries. Some she had arranged to sell in the Tea Room, for she suspected there would be a lot of casual visitors in the village. She did not want to have to resort to Mr Kipling or his other cake cronies. 'I'm not one that likes to serve manufactured cakes,' she was often heard announcing to her customers in her lofty fashion. Today, however, she had taken the precaution of having a few coffee and walnut slices under the counter – 'Just in case, you understand'.

'Will you be all right, Lizzie, just for a couple of hours?'

'Of course, Kathleen, I know what to do. You go and set up your stall and have a wee look about. I can take care of the Tea Room while you're gone, then I can go to the gala in the afternoon. I like it better then anyway.'

Lizzie flicked her wavy brown hair back from her face and pulled on the sugary pink overall that Kathleen handed to her. At twenty, returning to her home village to work in the Tea Room had not been her number one plan, but she found the will to leave grew less pressing as the months drifted by and she became absorbed in the weave of daily dramas that made up the village tapestry. Her mother and grandmother were pleased to have her home, so the three generations of the McEwan family lived together in a small cottage off the main road. Sadly there was no man of the house. Her father had taken off with a hill walker about ten years ago and had never been seen since. From her stance at the door, with the bells tinkling, Kathleen frowned at her assistant momentarily then proceeded to carry out the cardboard box full of her baking and strapped it on to the back of her motorcycle. Today she was a vision in mauve. She had even clipped on her matching ear rings. They looked like shiny sweets and gave her face a fresh pastel look, coordinating well with her cerise lips and pink powdered cheeks. The elegance of her newly blow-dried white hair was sacrificed to the practicalities of her silver crash helmet.

Lizzie immediately brought out the array of flavoured teas and tuned the radio to a music channel while she waited for the kettle to boil. She quite relished a slice of one of those nice cakes under the counter, perhaps with a 'frowned upon' strawberry and mango tea bag. Tonight she was determined to get her hooks into Donnie. She knew he was keen on the vet's assistant from Skye, but she didn't think it would pose too much of a problem for she had a quiet confidence in her own powers of persuasion.

Meanwhile Paula looked out of the gala tent at the events that were occurring in the field. She observed the comings and goings of the visitors who had descended upon Drum Mhor for the events. Was it really only a year since she had left London to come up here? So much had happened while she had weathered the cycle of the seasons. She had made friends, had become involved, and no longer could she imagine a life lived behind an anonymous front door in an impersonal city.

Gazing about her, she saw family groups clustered around the raised platform where the Highland dancing competition was underway. Girls as slim as pencils with hair scraped back into ballerina buns were dancing and kicking and flicking their arms, their fingers frozen in a thumb and middle finger clench. Kilts swirled and tilted as the dancers leapt about, heeling and toeing to the skirl of the bagpipe beat. The usual crowds gathered to watch the big strong men throwing hammers and lifting telephone posts and tossing them into the air as though they were toothpicks.

She could see the girls and boys running races around the track. Over on the far side of the field, Paula could make out the pens containing the livestock. She knew Robert would be there. The plan was that a few crofters were going to display their expertise at some sheep dog trials with six sheep. The said sheep looked very incongruous. Newly clipped, they appeared slim and athletic with muscular bodies and sporting long spindly legs. They did not contribute to the familiar picture of a woolly flock at all.

Suddenly she saw Margaret, dumpily marching over to the enclosure and leaning over the fence. She was obviously saying something to Robert. Paula grimaced, and wondered if Robert was completely blind. Could he not see that the woman was just trying to beguile him with her more than adequate cleavage and her Wonderbra? Paula pulled down her own sweater over her thin, boyish frame and turned back to the tent in disgust.

Hector stood at the sheep fank, studying the ewes that he had clipped and dipped the previous week. He enjoyed being amongst the other crofters, standing about waiting for the event to start. It was a good time to exchange snippets of news. Hector was a fount of knowledge about hay and silage deliveries. His red bonnet was in place and he held his head down, staring at the ground or tilted slightly to the side so as not to have to look anybody directly in the eye. He noted the drizzle in the morning and felt that a north wind might pick up later in the afternoon.

'Are you competing today, Hector?' Robert shouted over from the other side of the fencing.

'Aye, well, I put my name down and I think I will.'

'Oh well, I doubt if any of us will stand a chance then,' laughed Robert good naturedly.

The old fellow hardly needed a dog, for his grunts and whistles seemed to communicate to his sheep and they would do his bidding like old friends.

'Come away now, Charlie, just get yourself over there, now… good dog. Now sit, for God's sake will you sit for once and do what

I tell you. Now come on, girls, over to the fence, there you are. Now, move yourself, Charlie, just do as I say… get over there and give them a wee nudge.'

Robert knew if old Hector was in for the event, everyone would come over just to enjoy his repartee with his dog and the sheep.

Back in the tent, Paula and Wee Eck had set out a nature discovery corner for budding young scientists. A long table was set up with saucers containing spoor from different wild creatures. At the end of the table were photographs of birds and animals labelled A, B, C and so on, and the participants had to match the animal with its correct droppings. Wee Eck had been in his element devising this activity and had cajoled the Forestry Commission to donate many of the offerings. For the last hour he had been supervising his table, explaining to grannies and postal workers and information technologists as well as a multitude of children just what an eagle's droppings might contain, compared to those of an owl or a puffin or even a mammoth, in answer to a question from Billy!

Paula felt like a witch sitting by a large black cauldron perched on a portable gas ring. Beside it she had science beakers and next to them an array of different plants and berries. Participants were invited to find out about natural dyes, and were given squares of cotton or hanks of sheep wool to dunk into their chosen liquids. She smiled at the children's faces gazing in wonder at the colour of onion skins, lichens and the crottal that grew on the rocks down by the beach. When they had passed through the tent earlier, Dolly and Mrs MacDonald had been full of their local knowledge, telling Paula that it was crottal that mothers and wives dyed their men folks' jumpers in if they were going to sea. While Paula was busy assisting a small boy from Glasgow to dip his white cotton square into a beaker of beetroot juice, James MacTavish appeared by her side.

'I'm looking for Rosie and Iona MacPherson. Haven't seen them yet, have you?'

Paula started to laugh.

'What is it?' asked James. 'I saw Billy and for once he's fine and behaving and that Joker hasn't been far away from the venison burger stall, but where's Rosie?'

'Hang on a minute,' urged Paula, 'till Little Lord Fauntleroy here has hung up his square to dry and I'll show you where they are. Eck, will you keep an eye on this cauldron? I won't be long.'

Together they made their way over towards the beer tent. James frowned at the direction they were taking, but instead of venturing into the dark and fetid interior, they veered down the side where there was a big sign, painted in red paint, garish and blood-like:

PREDICT WHERE THE CHICKEN WILL SHIT
50p A GO

An old table had been covered in a red cloth, and on it a large board was painted to represent a checker board. Numbers in blue were painted on the squares.

'Rosie! What are you doing?' exclaimed her uncle.

'Hi, Uncle James! This is the best game in the world; do you want to try, and you, Paula? It's only fifty pence and if you win you get a prize. And guess what the prize is?'

'Don't tell me, it's not an egg, is it?' asked Paula laughing.

No, silly, it's a goldfish! Look! We have lots of them and little bags.'

'We haven't been giving a lot of fish away, so far,' grinned Iona. 'Our little red hen is a very contrary chook.'

'Do you want to have a go, Uncle James?'

'Very well, here we are; daylight robbery I think.'

Iona leant down and lifted the cover off the box at her feet. She lifted Miss Peggety out and put her on to the board. She then covered her with a perforated plastic laundry basket.

'Place your bet please, sir!' Rosie ordered in the manner of a seasoned croupier.

'It will have to be legs eleven.'

'Wait,' said Paula, caught up in this new game, 'here's fifty pence and I'll bet forty-two.'

Four pairs of eyes watched the chicken stalking around the board. Its beady eyes stared back at them, and its neck twisted about trying to see through the limited viewing holes.

'Maybe she doesn't need,' lamented Rosie, 'she's already been quite a few times.'

'No no, just be patient, we've been giving her lots of snacks.' Iona grinned encouragingly at her prize earner. Suddenly the chicken clucked and ducked her head and flapped her wings and there was a splat. Everyone craned over the laundry basket to look.

'Forty-three! Oh bad luck! Do you want to try again in a minute after she has recovered?'

'No, no, but I think you may have to buy an aquarium with all your winnings to take care of the fish you can't get rid of!'

'Och away with you, James MacTavish, the day has only started. Our Miss Peggety and her friend Goldie will just keep hitting those numbers and we'll have a gold mine!'

'What's this then, do I hear the sound of gambling in the vicinity of the beer tent?' It was the minister.

'Good morning, sir, and how are you today?' Iona smiled sweetly. 'Just thought I would get this pest of a chicken to earn her keep. She spends her life making a mess all over my flower beds, so I brought her here to entertain the crowds. Would you care to have a go?'

Reverend Wilson smiled indulgently, and looking over his shoulder to check there was no one else about, he nodded. 'Why not, just a little flutter, as it were!'

'What number do you want?' whispered Rosie, busily washing the board clean, ready for the new contestant.

'I'll take number three for the Trinity, if I may.'

Rosie took the money whilst Iona set the other chicken up for action.

Goldie strutted about, and being more of a show girl than her feathered friend, she splayed her wings and ran for the sides before settling down to a more sedate stroll around the arena. Craning her head forward she scratched the chequered surface and let a watery deposit fall on the already stained board.

'Number three! Well done, Reverend, you have the luck of the Almighty!'

Everyone shook hands, quite overcome with excitement, forgetting for a minute that they were congratulating the minister for winning the chicken shit competition. He departed quite exhilarated with his little goldfish, but wondered how he would explain the new member of the family to his wife.

CHAPTER 15

Wee Eck sat on a barrel in the beer tent. He had already had a skin full of lager and was now swaying gently to a tune that only he could hear.

'Look at him,' Murdo MacPherson nudged James MacTavish. 'I doubt he'll make it to the dance tonight. What about yourself, are we going to see you lead off a *Strip the Willow?*'

'I thought I just might have a wee gander and see what's doing. I see Jenny got back from her shift at the old folks' home and hauled her kids off home. That Joker is just running rings around her; I think she's counting the minutes till he leaves home!'

'Good-looking boy, that one. What age is he now?' enquired Murdo, tipping his glass and draining the last few drops of beer.

'He's sixteen. Says he's going to finish the school in Inverness at the end of the year. He wants to do a joinery apprenticeship apparently. I think that would suit him; he always was good with his hands. Somehow I thought he might have got a job at the fish farm. Young Billy will miss him of course, but maybe he'll buckle down now. Rosie had a good day today with Iona. They only had three goldfish left, and guess who has ended up with them?'

'Aye, I thought you might! She couldn't really keep them herself with all those cats they have running about at your brother's place. Now I had better be on my way and get some dinner before the dance tonight. Why don't you join us, James? I think Iona is making a roast so there will be plenty.'

'That sounds grand, Murdo, I'll take you up on that. Are you all right, Eck, do you need a lift home or are you staying here for the night?'

'I've got to go home. I need a bath. I promised I would see Paula there, but maybe I'm needing a wee bit of courage first. I'll just have one more dram before I go.' His head flopped forward and he appeared to have fallen into a snooze.

The two older men left him, shaking their heads. They passed Dolly, Kathleen and Mrs MacDonald who were waiting outside the wooden gate.

'Grand gala, ladies,' commented James. 'I must congratulate you on your cakes as always, Kathleen. Food fit for monarchs. Now if you have any crumbs to spare, you know where you can bring them. Any time now, don't be shy!'

Kathleen coloured slightly at the attention, and then noticed her friend Dolly's pursed lips.

'I see the minister was gambling behind the beer tent with your wife, Murdo MacPherson, and with your young niece, James MacTavish. Brazenly walking about he was with that goldfish, just as though he had come back from Monte Carlo. I have a good mind to send him a reminder of how Jesus swept the sinners away from the temple.'

'Oh come now, Dolly,' cajoled James, lowering the pitch of his voice. 'It's the gala and it was all innocent fun. Maybe you could save me a dance later on. We were always good at the St Bernard's Waltz, do you not remember?' and he winked at her, smiling into her eyes.

Paula came running up to them, her face flushed. 'Do you know where Eck is? He's supposed to help me load up all the stuff into the Forestry Commission's truck, and then I promised Robert that I would help him get his sheep back in the trailer. Oh this is not fair, where is he?'

'Don't worry, lass, I think he said he was going to get a little refreshment. You run along now, and I'll see that he gets home.'

'Yes,' agreed Kathleen sweetly. 'I'm sure Robert will be needing you. Did I not see Margaret leave about an hour ago? She was talking about getting all that muck off her feet and beautifying herself. She wanted to smell nice for Rob at the dance tonight. Cheerio then, see you all later!'

Robert chugged through the village on his tractor, pulling the trailer with his six sheep behind him. Paula trudged behind with Robert's dogs, tired and mud splattered after her efforts to get the boisterous creatures up into the box.

When they eventually reached her house, she waved at his departing figure and wearily let herself in to the comparative calm of her living room. 'I am mad,' she muttered, turning on the taps of the bath and then squeezing a glob of bath essence into the steaming water. She took a sip from the tumbler of Lucozade that she had poured herself, hoping for a jolt of energy. She screwed up her nose as it made contact with the fizz, and padded back to the kitchen where she topped up the drink with a good two inches of gin. When Paula eventually emerged from the bathroom, she felt woozy and sleepy, and decided to fry herself an egg which she ate on a piece of bread covered in tomato sauce. She stood at the kitchen worktop while she munched through her meal, leaning over to avoid the dripping yolk. Feeling a little revived, she dressed in a clean pair of jeans and a long-sleeved cheesecloth shirt that she tied at the front, leaving her midriff bare. She fluffed up her hair which had grown long and curled softly on to her shoulders, then peered into the mirror above the fireplace and dabbed on some eye shadow and mascara. Her lips looked pale in her suntanned face so she applied a thick coat of Rising Dragon Red on to her wide mouth. The effect was startling. She looked stunning. 'Now, a splash of Issey Miyake, another quick gin, and I'm off,' she declared to her reflection.

She stepped out on to the street and looked across the rippling surface of the sea. Although it was nine o'clock already, it was still light. She knew that soon the autumn leaves and mists that herald the long winter would swirl and surround them but for now it was as though the summer was reluctant to leave. Paula entered the village hall, her eyes searching for just one face.

'Paula,' Iona cried, 'at last you've arrived! We were going to send a search party out for you. Look at you! What is it? You look different somehow. Oh, you smell divine, and I love that blouse. I had one just like it that I wore and wore until the cotton was as fine as a spider's web. Then one night it ripped right down the back, but lucky for me I was wearing my green velvet waistcoat. Well if that bitch Dolly didn't say to everyone in her big loud voice: "Oh, Iona, what a beautiful blouse, take that green thing off so that we can all admire it!" I tell you now, I just fixed her with a stare that would have turned your milk to curds. I could have taken her outside and flattened her. Well, talk of the devil, here she comes now.'

Paula and Iona turned and smiled sweetly at Dolly as she approached with Kathleen, followed closely by Lottie MacDonald.

'Great turn-out, Iona, isn't there?' Dolly said. ' I think we've made a real killing today with all the sales and entrance fees, and what with your illicit gambling as well. You look very nice tonight, Paula. Is that make-up you're wearing? Is it from your drama production?'

Iona dug her nails into Paula's shoulder and both women continued to smile broadly at their adversary.

Dolly continued, 'I see Rob is here with Margaret. Lovely dress she's wearing. So feminine, don't you think, Kathleen?'

'When is the dancing going to start?' Paula asked Iona when the three had moved away. If I don't do something physical I think I might have to flatten someone too.'

For the next three hours the music filled the air and the dancing took on a life of its own. Paula whirled with the postman, the shopkeeper, the doctor, several tourists, and even with Iona after sharing another slug of gin that she had spirited away in her handbag. The two friends waltzed around the floor together.

'This is the best dance ever,' cried Iona. 'The gala dances are always the best, but this one is the best yet! Oh I wish Suzannah could be here now. Have you heard from her this week?'

Paula nodded and laughingly quoted, 'Sergei Sergei Sergei! Can't get any sense out of her at all. Oh, I think there's a baby on the way, but keep that to yourself!'

'That's fantastic!' shouted Iona, pulling her friend off the floor.

'Look!' she shouted. The young rock band musicians from the island of Eigg were taking their places on the stage. 'Now we're in for some wild sounds. Might need my ear plugs for this lot.'

'No, you look!' Paula was gesticulating wildly, her eyes riveted to the stage.

Wee Eck had possession of the microphone and was making a real mess of untangling the cable linking it to the amplifiers.

'What is he doing up there?' hissed Paula.

The screeching of the microphone filled the air, and behind him the band was making perfunctory sounds with their guitars while they waited for what should have been their introduction.

'Ladies and gennelmen, great to see you.' Eck flashed his row of serrated front teeth and grinned into the whirling disco lights. He seemed to have forgotten what he had to say, and his eyes appeared glazed as he tried to focus. 'I want to sing a wee tune. Come on, guys, help me with the back-up. Come over here, Roddy, and I'll whistle it to you. Right, here we go. Are you ready, lads? I'll count you in, one and two and three… Tell Paula I love her! Oh yes I do…' He swayed then turned to check on the band, obviously forgetting the rest of the words. 'Tell Paula I love her!' he repeated, turning back towards the hall. His feet seemed heavy and he looked down, confused why this should be so, and as he did so, the cable which had looped itself several times around his ankles strained and Eck fell from the stage, much as if he was bungee jumping. Amidst the confusion that followed, the band leapt off the stage to rescue the amplifiers, while Paula and Iona rushed to rescue poor Eck, now comatose and forgotten after his brave attempt at romantic chivalry.

'Come on, we'll haul him up on to the chairs,' ordered Paula in a no-nonsense voice. 'You take his feet and I'll take his shoulders.'

Together they managed to stretch him out across three chairs and Paula knelt beside him trying to sooth his brow with her tissue wet from the tap. She looked up and saw Margaret sail past in Robert's arms, a triumphant smile on her face.

'Oh well,' thought Paula, 'I should never have allowed myself to hope.'

Lizzie, who worked at the Tea Room, came over and sat with Paula and Iona. 'Hi,' she said, 'have you seen Donnie at all?'

'Aye, I did,' replied Iona indifferently, 'he was behind that bale of hay in the beer tent with the vet's assistant.'

'Oh,' Lizzie looked crestfallen. 'Did they come to the dance together, do you know?'

'We haven't seen him all night, but then that's what happens at the gala. People meet up and get into that beer tent and when they come out, it's as though they've left their brains behind.'

'Oh, yes, I see what you mean. I saw Wee Eck fall down. Is he all right now?'

'Oh, he'll have a sore head tomorrow, that's for sure. Hopefully he won't remember any of it, but no doubt someone will remind him,' said Paula ruefully. She felt a kinship with the girl, and a strong feeling of sympathy.

'Do you want some gin? I'm in mourning too, I suppose.'

It was not until the silvery streaks of the dawn broke over the hills around the village that the residents of Drum Mhor slowly made their way back to their houses, closing their curtains against the rising sun and pulling their duvets over their heads. For most it had been a good gala, for some it had been very good, and for some it had been heartbreaking.

Hector Ogilvie blearily recorded the day in his green diary:

Got half a bottle for winning the sheep trials. Wet in the morning, heavy showers at times. Better and drier for the gala. A topper of an evening.

CHAPTER 16

For the next few weeks of September Iona was in heaven. She had heard so much gossip and rumour at the dance, and all of it required further analysis and discussion with her contacts. Murdo shook his head each time he passed through the kitchen, for his wife had become a permanent fixture by the kitchen sink, the telephone pressed against her ear and her eyes scanning the road for passing vehicles. 'Is that right? Well, did you ever? No?' Her voice kept up a constant litany while her ears absorbed the latest snippets of news from the wagging tongues at the other end of the line.

Still shaking his head, Murdo made his way to the bottom of the field where he was repairing the fences that bordered the seashore. He knew that Iona would be down shortly with his afternoon mug of tea, and would share her news of the village with him then. He pretended not to be interested, but he waited to hear the latest scandal eagerly. It was while he was gathering his tools together that he glimpsed a female figure surreptitiously making her way towards his neighbour James's house. Aye aye, he mused, what have I been missing? I didn't know that young James has taken to entertaining Grace from the Post Office, although I did think they were a bit friendly at the badminton and he was quite the gent seeing that she got home all right, but this is definitely new. Hmmm... And he knelt down to hammer in the brackets that would hold the wire.

Soon Iona came trudging down towards him. She was a sight in her waterproofs and boots, a headscarf holding her new perm in place. 'Did you see what I saw?' she called out as soon as she came within shouting range.

Murdo waited till she settled herself down beside him, 'Now Iona, you be quiet about this. Grace may have a very good reason to visit with our neighbour and I don't want any half-baked stories to go around about our friend.'

'Aye aye, just you hold on a minute Mr High Ground Person and wait till you hear what I have to say.'

The two sat leaning against the strainer post, holding their mugs of tea in their hands. They squinted out at the same view they had enjoyed for the past thirty years together. Each day it changed with the mood and the swell of the sea and the colours of the mountains and flirtations of the seasons. Only the peeping of the curlews on the brow of the hill disturbed the rush and scrape of the tide pushing the beach stones further down into the sea.

'Well, what is it that couldn't wait till I got back up to the house?' Murdo asked.

'God, it's cold in this wind.' Iona fumbled in her jacket pocket and pulled out a chocolate biscuit. 'There you go now, that should give you a wee boost till dinner time.'

'You're not a bad wife when you try. So what new scandals have you to tell me? I can see your eyes are lit up like a merry-go-round.'

Iona made a clicking noise with her tongue, dismissing her husband's insinuation but so overcome with the latest episode from the village gossip merchants she couldn't hold back for any longer. 'You know Phyllis the school cook's son, Ross?'

'Yes, of course. He's got a job in the forestry. What of it?'

'Well, he came home last night all agog.' Iona nodded her head, her eyes wide with insinuation.

'Agog, was he? And why was that, *cailleach*? Did he have to do some work?' Murdo chuckled into his mug.

'No, you daft so and so, he saw a ghost, they all did.'

'Oh, this is rich,' guffawed Murdo delightedly, 'and it's not even Halloween. Was he listening to James MacTavish by any chance? You know how he likes to spin his tales to the ladies in the pub?'

'Just listen, will you?' Iona commanded indignantly, the tight curl on her forehead threatening to unravel. 'It was a car, a ghost car, honest to God. Phyllis said the boy was as white as a sheet when he got in. He said they had been driving up over the hill when they saw a grey sedan coming down towards them, you know, on that stretch where it's single track? Nothing unusual about that, so they pulled into a passing place as you do, and waited for it to come down. Well, they waited and waited, but just before it reached them, the car they were watching completely disappeared. It was like a David Copperfield magic trick.'

'Oh, get away with you woman, you've been watching that old *Brigadoon* film on the telly again, all that romantic nonsense with folk disappearing into the mist. Whatever next? I think those forestry lads might have been having a wee tipple seeing it's near the weekend.'

'Well, just be as cynical as you like, you old gowk, but they all saw it. Johnny Campbell who was driving thought at first he was hallucinating, but all six of them told the same story. They can't all be seeing things, can they?'

'I'll tell you what I think, I think it's time you made my dinner. We've the hogs to feed, and mind you bring in the hens and make sure they are all secure for the night. Don't want that pine marten getting in and having a feast.'

Iona picked up the flask and mugs and muttering under her breath, marched back up to the house. She would ring Ellen in the village and see if there had been any other sightings.

October came in with a howling gale. Paula sat at Robert's kitchen table drinking a mug of milky coffee. Robert sat opposite her, munching a digestive biscuit with a slice of cheddar cheese on top. Outside the clouds were banked up in an angry black barrage and the rain lashed horizontally against the window panes. Lightning streaked through the trees, accompanied by thunder violent enough to make the house shudder. Paula had discarded her wet boots in the porch, and the pervasive smell of Eau de Cologne mint emanated into the warm kitchen. In her rush to get out of the rain she had run across the overgrown path by the normally placid stream that separated Robert's garden from his field. During the summer Paula had planted the mint amongst the grasses by the stone dyke which bordered the stream. She remembered telling him how wonderfully pungent the smell would be when people crushed the mint as they crossed unsuspectingly from one area to the other. Now as they sniffed the sharp aroma, they smiled at the memory of that summer morning.

'Where's Margaret today?' Paula asked judiciously, trying to pick up the telltale sounds of another presence in the house.

'I asked her not to come today, though I doubt she would have anyway. The rain and the ghost car are enough to put her off.'

'Oh,' breathed Paula, silently giving thanks that she would be spared the irritating presence of the would-be lady of the house.

'What do you think of the ghost car story, Robert? Do you believe it? Have you ever seen it?' She tilted her head to one side, wondering if he too would be as cynical as Murdo MacPherson.

Robert helped himself to another biscuit from the packet on the table. 'I do believe it, for you see, it has happened before. It was quite a few years ago now, but I remember my granny saying at the time that it was a sign, a premonition. A car was seen by all sorts of people, always disappearing as it got closer, and it was thought to herald a terrible accident.'

Paula's eyes grew large. Unconsciously she shivered. 'And was there an accident?'

'Yes, there was. Not long after a local man went over the edge while driving home. He was driving a grey car, just the double of what people had been seeing. It was such a tragedy.'

They both sat in silence, each thinking their own thoughts while the sweet aroma of the mint wafted around the small room.

'And what of walking ghosts?' asked Paula at last. 'Are they also a warning, do you think? Isn't there supposed to be a grey lady that walks in a hotel on the way to Inverness? I've heard that she frightens the staff half to death. Mind you it may be a coincidence that she's only ever seen when they sneak in at dawn and are probably full of booze.'

'Well, booze does heighten our awareness of the senses. Look how Wee Eck seems to show all his feelings towards you when under the influence yet can barely look you in the eye when he's sober!' Robert laughed at the expression on Paula's face; pursing her lips in disapproval she gave a good imitation of Dolly.

'I don't want to talk about Eck any more. Go on with what you were saying.'

'Very well, but it was quite a spectacle and took a lot of bravery on his part. Anyway, about grey ladies. I do know the one you're talking about. They say she walks the flagstones by the back door of the hotel. Apparently she was one of the gentry up on a shooting party. Her husband was accidentally shot on the hill and they say she is still waiting for him to return. When she heard he'd been killed she took an overdose. She's still waiting, poor thing.'

Again the two sat quietly lost in their own thoughts. Finally Robert stood up and walked through to his sitting room. He lit the table lamps and opened the iron door of the wood burning stove, raking the smouldering ashes, causing a gush of woody smoke into the room. He opened the lid on top and dropped in some more logs, then sat down on one of the wooden chairs beside the fire. Paula stood framed in the doorway. She watched him adjust his long legs and stretch behind his chair for his guitar. She took in the cosy room and listened to the rain beating on the small square window. There was a piano against the wall with a large bookcase shoved in beside it. She walked over to the window and sat behind the table that held his books and music scores. The two dogs had been left out by the Rayburn in the kitchen. She wondered if he remembered that other rainy afternoon twelve months ago, when they had first met and enacted this very same tableau.

Robert strummed a chord, then he expertly plucked the strings and Paula drifted with the melody that magically filled the room. It was the theme from the film, *Braveheart*. She had been to see it in London. She listened. He was good, very good. She looked out at the dark shapes of the mountain and listened to the angry wash of the tide and constant splattering of rain on the glass. She turned round and saw Robert in profile, his dark head, and the curve of his nose and the olive tones of his cheek. His hands were large and his fingers long and bony. She shivered.

Suddenly the music stopped and he turned to her. 'Come here. Sit here where I can see you.'

Paula knelt down in front of him, unaware of her lioness-like beauty. Robert's eyes caressed her face, fresh and flushed from the heat of the fire. He wanted to touch the amber gloss of her hair. Instead he smiled into the warmth and trust of her topaz coloured eyes. He turned his attention back to his guitar and experimentally strummed the instrument. Soon she recognised the notes that were coming through, and then he started to hum softly. It was the song everyone sang drunkenly at dances and in the bar. Paula knew it well. She felt a lump in her throat, for never had she heard it sound like this. Robert joined the melody with the words and sang softly: 'Will you go, lassie, go?'

She smiled and whispered, 'Sing it all, please.'

He continued strumming as softly as before, then sang the folk song to her, his voice full of meaning, striking chords in the depth of her heart. When he had finished he put down his guitar and leant over and cupped her face in his hands. 'Well, Paula, will you? The summer's gone, and the autumn too. Will you go?'

Inexplicably her eyes filled with tears. 'No,' she breathed as his lips found hers.

'Never?' he whispered into her hair.

'What are you asking?' She kissed the warm skin of his neck, feeling the heat of him beneath his collar.

'Stay with me.' Words got lost as his arms tightened and she found herself lying back on the red rug, pinned down by his strong body. 'Hush,' he whispered urgently, 'no questions, no answers.'

'Yes,' she panted, 'no questions, no answers.'

CHAPTER 17

James MacTavish was feeling his age. He tried to ignore the ache in his joints each night when he returned from climbing the hills on the estate. Nothing that a wee drop of whisky won't put right, he told himself. He topped up his glass for the third time. Nearly November already! This blustery weather was designed for keeping folk indoors and not for chasing up the mountains to cull old stags. He surveyed his kitchen and the empty saucepan of pea soup that was soaking in the sink. 'Och, I'll get to that tomorrow,' he muttered. He lifted the large orange pumpkin and placed it on the table ready to be carved in preparation for the Halloween visitors he was expecting. Just as he was settling down by his fireside, he heard a chapping at his door. He knew it couldn't be Iona or Murdo because they never knocked; they just called out and let themselves straight in. He hauled himself out of his chair and stood up, his face screwed up in pain from his aching back.

'I'm coming; I'm coming, just wait a wee minute, whoever you are.' James walked out to the hallway and opened the door. He stared out expectantly and then grunted, for framed in the darkness was Grace from the Post Office. 'Well, come in Grace, come in, and what can I do for you this evening? Did you leave something when you were here last?'

James turned awkwardly towards the shelves in the hall, his beady eyes searching for some book or leaflet that might have been misplaced or forgotten from a previous visit.

'No, I didn't leave anything, James, apart from those magazines I gave you, but I don't want them back. I actually brought over another article that I had in the house. It's about the Bell Lighthouse; I thought you might find it illuminating… '

Grace chortled at her own joke and James momentarily forgot his stiff joints.

'Very kind of you, Grace, I must say. Well, come in, come in. I was just having a wee dram; perhaps I can offer you something. There are my home made vintages or I have sherry?'

'A sherry would be nice,' Grace replied, her lips curling tensely.

'Very good, very good, well I shall have another wee one myself to keep you company. Now come through to the warm and tell me about your day. I was just enjoying the fire. Why don't you sit over there and get warm? It's such a wild night out there; I'm hoping the wind dies down for tomorrow night.' Smiling at her over his glass he went on in his friendly fashion. 'The kids had a grand time at the Halloween party. Rosie was so proud to have won the best costume; she was a great wee witch.'

'Yes,' replied Grace, 'and Billie was good as a mummy from the crypt. First time I've seen him stay so quiet or still for so long. Mrs Munro from the school said it's a pity he couldn't wear the costume to school.'

'Jenny had the right idea with those bandages; she only left holes for his eyes when she was wrapping him up. Pity she couldn't do the same for Joker!'

Grace looked around the wood-panelled room and the desk piled high with papers. She took in the shelves of books and then her eyes were drawn back to the hypnotic flickering of the flames. James felt the warmth of the whisky slowly make its way down to his fingers and on to anaesthetise his limbs. An angelic smile lit up his cherubic face while trying to focus his gaze a little hazily on his guest. He observed her good red cardigan with the bright gold buttons and her brown, scratchy tweed skirt. His eyes travelled down to the heavy orthopaedic-style shoes and the sheer stockings in a shade too pale for a winter's night. It must be cold for a woman in this weather, he thought charitably, but then he noticed the black hairs that had matted in the lea of the shin bone. He screwed his eyes up tight, before downing the last drop that remained in his glass.

'Another wee dram, Grace?'

Wordlessly she nodded, licking her lips and dabbing the corner of her mouth with a tissue retrieved from the bulging sleeve of her cardigan. Obviously she has the contents of the whole box stuffed up her arms, James thought as he lurched unsteadily towards the kitchen to fetch the bottles. Grace shifted shyly on the sofa. She had been aware of James's eyes roving over her body. It had been a long time since her husband Andrew had gone to meet his maker and she had forgotten how intimate it was to sit in such close proximity to a man that made her heart flutter whenever he came near her. She had all but swooned when he partnered her at the badminton tournament. Since then she had replayed word for word all the idle conversation that had passed between them. She had heard for years that he was looking for a wife, but it seemed he could never settle on one. She knew that if he just gave her the chance she could show him what a real woman was made of. When he returned from the kitchen she coyly tilted her head to one side, in the way she had seen the late Princess Diana do. She looked towards him through the lenses of her tortoiseshell-framed spectacles and smiled with the new-found courage that a glass of sherry always gave her.

'I'm so glad we have found so much in common, James. All these years we have lived as neighbours and I never knew you had such passion… ' she broke off and tittered into her glass, '… for lighthouses.'

James regarded her with an emotion that was close to fear. Was this woman seriously offering herself as a sacrificial lamb to his lust? She was part of the very weave of the community; he had known her since she had arrived from Inverness as a bride and later stood by her as she buried poor Andrew. James knew he had to sober up as quickly as he could and appease her feelings so that she would not feel rejected.

'Now, Grace, I have a problem here with my pumpkin. I have drunk so much of this delightful libation I don't think I could possibly wield my carving knife. Would you mind very much if you could cut me some eyes and a big jaggy mouth into it, so that I can put the lantern in the window for tomorrow night?'

Beguiling as ever, James cajoled his visitor through to the kitchen and set her to work. He switched on his stereo player and put on a CD of Kenneth Mackellar singing some heartfelt ballads, and then when he saw she was absorbed with gouging out the eyes into sharp diamond shapes, he gently told her that he was in love with someone else.

'The heart is a funny thing, Grace. You think you have control over your emotions for years and then something happens and another person enters your life and the chemistry changes and you don't know anything. I never believed all those folk who told me that. I just thought I was destined to be the old Romeo, whom everyone laughed at. But then suddenly it happened to me, but I found out too late. I thought I would forget her, but I can't.' He broke off, and picked up a piece of the pumpkin and bounced it on the palm of his hand.

'Suzannah?' Grace asked tentatively.

'Aye, Grace, I lost my heart to Suzannah but I let her go. She's away with that Cossack or whatever he is and Paula was telling me that she's expecting a baby in the New Year.'

'Oh, James, I'm so sorry, I didn't realise. I mean I knew you two were close, but well,' she laughed shrilly to hide her embarrassment, 'you do have a reputation.'

'I know, but I don't want you to feel sorry for me, Grace. So if you have finished gouging out my eyes, I shall do the rest tomorrow. It's late now and you should be on your way home. Will you be all right walking up the path? Have you got a torch?'

Grace smiled back at him. 'I do, and thank you, James,'

'What for?' He looked at her, his eyebrows raised artlessly.

'For being so honest.'

Grace put on her coat and striped bobble hat and pulled on her matching mittens. Switching on her torch she turned back and smiled at James, silhouetted in the doorway, his mother's picture framed on the wall behind him.

'Goodnight, James, I hope you have a happy Halloween.'

It was not until two Sundays later that he could sit down peacefully at his desk and take out the writing paper he kept in his top drawer. Taking his Parker fountain pen he started to write:

Drum Mhor, the second Sunday in November
My dear Suzannah,
I sit here and look out of the window and can still see your face staring out to sea. Do you remember that day when I met you on the beach, just down from my house? The image is clearer than any photograph that I have of you.

You write about your life with Sergei, and your school and the children you are involved with. Your letters are full of your adventures and I want you to know I love hearing about the parks and the chestnut trees and churches and iconic paintings.

And now you are to have a baby. Oh, Suzannah, I wish you so much happiness. Take care of yourself my dearest girl. Will you come back and visit us do you think?

Life here has been colourful. I had a houseful of young guisers at Halloween. They came all dressed as goblins and witches for the most part, demanding sweets by the lorry load. That funny child Lucy who lives up the glen came all dressed up as a pink fairy. When she took off her duffle coat I couldn't believe my eyes. The rest of the children looked a right ragged bunch in comparison. You will remember Clara Johnson? She arrived as a green faced witch, and she had a tame barn owl on her shoulder. It wouldn't leave her, and even tiptoed down her back when she was on her knees at the zinc bath, ducking for apples. I thought I had seen everything but obviously not so.

Rosie and Billie went off with my 'Jack o' Lantern' when they left and Jenny made some grand soup for me, so I feel as though I had a good start to November.

The annual bonfire went off well with the usual display of fireworks, and a grand Guy Fawkes on top. We all had a good trawl along the beach beforehand, looking for firewood and collecting all the rubbish washed up by the tide, adding it to the old broken boats and junk that was collected over the year. I'm surprised you didn't see the flames from Ukraine.

We all miss you, my dear, but we wish you happiness. Before I sign off I shall look out of my window again at the sea. As I write I notice the waves are angry, frothing white spume into the air. There is a cruel wind blowing, and just smatterings of snowflakes have started to fall.

Goodbye for now, my dearest,
James

CHAPTER 18

Shovkovichna, Kyiv. December
Dear Iona,
It is so cold here now, but inside the apartment it's boiling. The heating pipes snake from one block to another all around the city, all heated from a central plant, and it is the same with the hot water supply. Outside it is about minus thirty degrees and now I realise why people invest in furs to keep them warm.

We have been talking a lot about the birth, and we have finally and maybe belatedly decided to have the birth in Scotland. I cannot bear the thought of climbing these stairs to our fourth floor apartment after the baby is born, with pushchair and all the shopping.

I was wondering if we could come and stay with you for a short time until we find a house to rent. Of course then we will have to return to Kyiv as Sergei will have to resume his work here at the hospital. He has been given a visa in order for him to attend a medical conference in London at the beginning of January. It would work out perfectly so that he will be there for the birth.

I would so love for us all to have Christmas together but please let me know if this is too much of an imposition on you.

Write as soon as you can. With lots of love to you and Murdo,
Suzannah

Iona re-read the letter then folded it and replaced it into the envelope. She stacked it on top of the pile that she had tied up with a tartan ribbon. Looking at her watch she decided she did have time for a cup of coffee and a few minutes to herself before going over to the shop to get something for dinner. She carried her coffee through to the dining room and pulled the end of the ribbon and looked again at the envelopes. Suzannah's curling script, in various coloured inks, spilled around her. Iona picked one from the beginning of the pile and relived with her friend her impressions of her new country.

February, Kyiv

My dear Iona,
I have just eaten something with about a million calories, a delicious burnt almond thing, and I am writing this in a café in Independence Square on the main Kreschatyk Boulevard. The square is dominated by a fantastic flying angel statue marking independence. There are so many fabulous sights everywhere I look, old women selling flowers, gorgeous girls in bright, eye-catching coats, marchers looking as though they have stepped out of a scene from Dr Zhivago, and severe militia wearing lovely furry hats.

I came here with very little knowledge, or expectations, which I think is good, so I will not be disappointed if the experience doesn't live up to anything that I had expected.

The city of Kyiv is thriving and quite grandiose. It has been burnt and bombed and destroyed and rebuilt so many times, I will take weeks just figuring it all out. Some of the new buildings are fantastic, imposing, classical and colourful. Most of the buildings away from the centre are less colourful and at this time of the year everything is brown, grey or black and dreary. People at school have told me that the snow has just melted, and where it was once all white and sparkling, now there are just piles of vile filthy slush. In time spring will bring forth the blossom and grass I hope!

I love the words for the months of the year: March is 'Berezen' and means birch forests begin to bud, May is 'Traven' which means grass begins to grow, and June is 'Cherven' which means worms crawl from the earth!

Iona sighed as she replaced the letters and stacked them neatly. Only one did she leave out in order to read again. It was a letter Suzannah had written very early during her stay in Kyiv.

March, Kyiv

My dear Iona and Paula,
Forgive me writing this to you both on the computer at work, but I have to share this with you. As you know I write my newsy letters full of my impressions of the opera and the city and people I see in my day-to-day life, but I didn't ever write and tell you how lonely I was, or how much I missed the village and your friendship. I know it's natural to miss friends when you go to a new country, and you cling to the familiar while you adjust to the unfamiliar. My heart was sore leaving James, and everything I saw or experienced I wished he could have been by my side. I know he is fond of me, but it would seem not fond enough, for he let me go. Perhaps I was just another holiday romance for him.

I went out with some Swedish and American girls from school not long after I arrived. We had shashlik (a mutton kebab) and vodka and then drifted to a bar that was deep in a basement. Beer flowed like water, and in a recess at the back was a band of Ukrainian singers. They had the usual guitars and drums, but there was a double bass and saxophone as well. The music just took over everything;

it was as though the walls were throbbing and our heads and ears became part of the rhythm. I remember dancing with a tall Ukrainian guy, he was lovely, skinny and dark. I didn't even know his name all night, but I kissed him and we seemed to become part of the music and the room and the city and the country. I do know him now. His name is Sergei. He is a doctor and I am having his baby.

Iona went back to the kitchen and rinsed her mug. She gazed out at the frozen field in front of her, seeing without seeing the black branches with their skeletal witches' fingers etched against the bleak grey morning sky. Her thoughts were with her friend and today's letter announcing her plans for giving birth in Scotland. Iona was thrilled at the prospect, and checking her calendar, she calculated how long it was before the young couple's imminent arrival. She must write to Suzannah today. In the meantime however, she reached for the telephone. While she dialled, she leant over the sink to see whose car it was that was passing her gate: 'Paula? How are you today? Are you doing anything just now? No? Good, then get the kettle on, lassie, I'm coming over!'

CHAPTER 19

Sergei hummed to himself in the kitchen of the Kyiv flat, relieved that it was Saturday. This weekend he was not on duty in the hospital. He peeled a long strip of speckled skin from an apple then sliced the damp sphere into sections and tossed them into a bowl that already contained segments of orange and pungent cubes of sweet yellow melon. In a tea cup he was soaking some thick-skinned purple grapes which he now delicately dried on a piece of kitchen towel. '*Harasho,*' he complimented himself, and picking up the bowl and two forks he strode through to the bedroom. Suzannah was propped up against the pillows, a novel in one hand and her book of Russian verbs in another.

'*Dobroye utro,* my beautiful lady, I have prepared a plate of sunshine for you.' He kissed her on the forehead and sat on the edge of the bed.

'*Spasiba,* thank you, my very good doctor; it is so nice when you get a day off. I hope you don't do this to all your patients?'

'What? This?' And he burrowed under the covers and started kissing the soft flesh of her inner thigh. Suzannah squealed, and wriggled away.

'Stop it, Sergei, not now, I can't hold this bowl and have you down there. Anyway aren't you put off by my big tummy?'

'What big tummy? You look like a normal *babushka* to me; I love big women.'

'I'm not big, stop it; stop your teasing and come and eat some of this melon; it always gives me indigestion. What are we going to do today? Has it snowed any more during the night?'

'Yes, and still it snows, but the sun is shining. Look! So fantastic. All white like a dream place. I am going swimming this morning. Do you want to come?'

Suzannah blinked. 'Where? At your gym? I thought you were going to spend the day with me?' She looked crestfallen for, although she had protested at his erotic idea of a morning kiss, she still hungered for his body even though she was seven months pregnant.

'No, it is a big surprise. I will not tell you, but we must get going soon. Come, eat up and then dress very warm and we shall go out.'

Suzannah glanced at the suitcases open around the room. Already she had started packing for the pending trip back to Scotland and she could not wait to have her baby and introduce Sergei to all her friends in Drum Mhor. Just for a second she thought of James, but quickly dismissed him from her thoughts. I shall think about that when I get there; anyway James is a gentleman and everything will go well, I'm sure of it, she convinced herself.

She gave herself a shake and padded through to the bathroom where, holding her protruding belly, she threw one leg over the bath and heaved herself upright and turned on the shower. As the hot water belted down on her shoulders she felt the baby turn a somersault and she ran her hand over the rippling skin of her stomach.

Where on earth was Sergei going to take her to today? Each outing was like a magical mystery tour. With his guidance she had eaten Georgian food, seen the inside of seldom-seen churches, had signs translated for her that made her laugh out loud. She remembered seeing a holy well in the courtyard of a monastery where pilgrims from all over Ukraine and Russia came to pay homage. They touched their faces with the holy water, and prayed as they crossed themselves. Sergei broke the spell for her when he read the Cyrillic script beside it: PLEASE DO NOT DO LAUNDRY OR WASH FEET IN THIS WELL.

She soaped her arms, and thought of how he had opened up the city for her and taken her away from the tourist bars and cafés. She loved the out-of-the-way galleries in Podil where artists voiced their concerns for their freedom and political voice in lurid images of nudity, vibrantly painted in sulphuric yellow and nauseous shades of green. She was lucky. Sighing over the magical few months she had spent in Kyiv with her eccentric young surgeon, she towelled herself dry and walked naked back to the bedroom.

She dressed in a pair of pink and white padded ski trousers and a flannelette shirt that belonged to Sergei, then pulled on her jacket and tugged at the straining zipper. Laughingly she looked down at her boots.

'I can't reach below the bump.'

'You would make a terrible peasant; how do you think those women manage when they are pregnant?' Sergei cast his eyes to the ceiling in mock exasperation. 'You just want to live like a rich capitalist princess and what about me? Am I just your slave?'

Suzannah laughed, looking down at his brown curls while he knelt in front of her to lace her sturdy boots.

'Stop complaining. It's your fault I'm in this predicament.'

'Oh is it now, my wild girl? Did you not seduce me with beer and wild music? My mama warned me about Scottish girls. Take care, my little Sergei, she told me when I went to New York, don't be tempted by foreign girls, and I was not. I had to come back to Kyiv and meet a girl from Scotland. My poor mama. She forgot to warn me about the dangers of living in our own city.'

'Are you sorry?' said Suzannah, her blue eyes full of mischief.

'What do you think, my beautiful Suzannah? You are my destiny, my life, and I love you.'

He got up from his knees and kissed her and together they swayed in the dark hallway by the door.

'Now, enough of this,' Sergei kissed her again lightly on the nose. 'I think you are ready. Now we must get to the Metro and cross the Dnipro and then I am going to show you how real Ukrainians keep strong and healthy. Hold on to me and mind you don't slip. We shall be all right once we get down under the ground.'

On the escalators at the Arsenala metro station, descending deep into the earth, they listened to the rousing patriotic music flooding from the speakers and watched the streams of sullen-faced people arising from the depths. Sergei stood on the step in front of her, and with little inhibition reached for her and kissed her deeply whenever the mood took him. After one such embrace Suzannah smiled fondly at the back of his head. She liked his ways, his warmth and his open, boyish love for her, and the excitement of her new life in general. He was so very different from Roderick, her one-time fiancé in Edinburgh, she thought wryly. There were never any stiff, awkward moments with Sergei; in fact she often felt herself restraining him as nothing was too much of a novelty or adventure.

Today she followed him out of the exit of the metro station to the Hydro Park. It was a fun venue built on an elongated island that nestled between the two forks of the river. In summer it served as a Riviera playground with white sandy beaches, kiosks and cafés that sold beer and shashlik. There was even an open-air dance floor. Suzannah remembered their previous visit one summer evening. They had watched elderly couples dressed in elegant evening wear dance the old ballroom favourites to an accordion played by a dapper middle-aged man. These matrons were presumably looking for love and friendship and on a summer evening Suzannah liked to watch them pair and regroup around the open air dance floor. It made her feel good to see people of all ages take the time and trouble to dress up so elegantly for each other and enjoy a few hours of companionship.

Now it was winter, the accordion player was gone, and the dance area was an arena of white snow. Suzannah looked around, her eyes sparkling. Today the Hydro Park was wonderful, everywhere frozen and beautiful. The sky was sapphire blue and the temperature maybe twenty below zero but, she thought, with such a crisp day Sergei was right; there was no way they could have stayed indoors. Trudging through the pine forests they felt enshrouded in silence except for the swishing sound of a cross-country skier traversing the snowbound paths.

Sergei wrapped his arms around her. 'We can pretend we are in the middle of Ukraine. Far away from cities and towns, where it is like this everywhere you look, just trees and snow and great plains of flat land that goes on and on. One day I shall show it to you.'

Fortified after a cup of hot green tea they continued across the island where they found scenes reminiscent of a Holbein painting. The river was partially frozen. Suzannah wanted to follow a group of men, armed with metal hooks and fishing gear, to see where they intended to break the ice and start fishing. However Sergei turned her away from the main path to a different section of the river. Suzannah stopped in her tracks and gasped at the scene before her: over twenty nudists were dipping in and out of the freezing water.

'Oh my God!' she exclaimed. 'The temperature must be at least minus twenty, and Lord knows what the wind chill factor is. I'm freezing, and look at me, wrapped up in layers and layers of clothing and leather boots. But look at these crazy people stripping off! Why don't their hearts just stop with the shock?'

Suzannah watched appalled as trousers, jumpers, socks, shoes and finally bras and underpants were removed and then left in a sorry heap on the snow. Men and women walked boldly into the ice, pushing great slabs of ice out of their way, before submerging and jumping up and down like arctic sea lions. While she stood watching, she was totally entranced by the incredible scene as boobs and bums and wilted willies emerged from the freezing water. She laughed delightedly to share the moment with her lover when it suddenly dawned on her that she was standing alone.

'Sergei? Sergei, where are you?'

It was then that she focused on a body that had become very familiar over these last few months. She stared at the muscular back, the tight buttocks and the strong, sinewy legs. Her handsome, respectable and buck-naked cardiologist was beginning the slow and sedate walk across the snow without even a wince. Suzannah gasped in surprise at the sight of him edging his way in up to his chest. He smacked the ice around him and tossed the sheets to the side, and then he started to jump rhythmically before he disappeared under the surface.

'Oh my God, Sergei, where are you?' Suzannah called out, feeling momentarily anxious, then laughing with him as he reappeared between the chunks of ice and his torso rose in a spray of cascading bubbles.

'Well done! Well done!' she cried, running over to the water's edge, and pulling out the towel from his backpack.

Sergei rubbed his skin till it glowed red with the friction. His eyes were shining and he was full of exhilaration. 'That was fantastic, I feel fantastic. It keeps you young. I am going to live forever!'

Muttering about mad rituals, Suzannah led the way back into the woods, trudging through the glistening layers of new snow. More feathery flakes fell on their faces, and laughingly they opened their mouths like children, savouring the metallic tang of the frozen droplets. They cut across to the shore on the other side of the island and found the strangest set of fishermen dotted about on the frozen ice, sitting on boxes with pick axes and fishing poles and staring down into the black water below. Suzannah reflected that she could have been looking at a painting, for the image seemed to freeze time and the present became one with the past.

The snow continued to fall throughout the day and on into the night. Suzannah lay, wide-eyed, looking out at the soft flurries twisting and dancing in the streetlights. She felt the baby move and a small foot jab out at her waist. Beside her, Sergei's breathing turned into gentle snores. His hand still held hers, just as it had done when he drifted off to sleep.

They had made all their plans and would be flying to Edinburgh in two weeks' time. There they would spend a few days with her father in the city before hiring a car and driving north to Drum Mhor. She felt a prickle of excitement at the thought of seeing Paula and Iona and all the people that she had befriended last winter. She tried to envisage her Ukrainian man in the bar or at a local dance, and wondered if he would do that Cossack dancing. She had better get a recording of the music just in case. Content and happy, she gazed sleepily at the mesmerising snowflakes, yawned deeply and finally closed her eyes.

CHAPTER 20

Drum Mhor was crackling with the news of Suzannah's return.

'I don't know why we bother having a daily newspaper,' muttered James MacTavish crossly, filling his basket with tins of beans and tomato soup. 'The grapevine seems more supercharged than any telegraph pole I have ever encountered.'

'Och away with you, it's great having our own spy in the village, a real Russian spy.' Wee Eck's eyes were alight with excitement. He was a fan of all the James Bond films, and he relished the idea of the Cold War being reignited in his own Highland glen.

'A spy!' laughed Kathleen who was waiting her turn in the queue for Doris to ring up her basket of provisions. 'There are no spies nowadays; I've heard there's no need for 007 or The Man from Uncle any more.'

'Oh, Kathleen, now you're showing your age.' James chuckled.

'I do know this,' she went on, 'there are great big telescopes in outer space and they have everyone in their sights, even you, Wee Eck, though no doubt whoever has the job of watching you must find it hard to keep their eyes open.' The older woman shuffled forward and watched her jars of crystallized ginger and maraschino cherries being rung up on the till.

Wee Eck stared at her, his head twitching with indignation. 'I'll have you know, Kathleen, there is a lot that goes on in this village that would keep those fellows out there in America or Russia busy for weeks.'

*

When Suzannah finally arrived she looked radiant and seemed oblivious to the fact that she was the main source of local tittle-tattle. James had taken an immediate liking to Sergei when he and Murdo had initiated him into the Pipers Inn during his first weekend in the village. Sergei's immense tolerance to large quantities of vodka immediately won him enormous respect with the forestry workers and even more so with the fish farm workers. Donnie watched with awe from behind the bar as the respectable doctor from Kyiv downed glasses of vodka at alarming speed and still stayed upright. His Scottish co-drinkers soon showed the telltale signs of a good night out, their brain cells dying before each other's eyes. They wove between the toilets and the bar and eventually out through the door where they hoped to make it home without falling down and possibly freezing to death. Sergei laughed heartily on the walk back across the fields, with James and Murdo singing noisily behind him.

Sergei was a lover of Robert Burns; he knew all his poems and songs. He told his new friends that St Petersburg, where he grew up, and Moscow were some of the first places ever to honour the socialist Scottish poet. The then Soviet Union had enforced the learning of Burns's songs in the schools, hence the ease with which Sergei had been able to recite and sing throughout the evening.

Suzannah was delighted that her exotic Sergei had been so well accepted by her closest friends. Iona was quite mesmerised by his accent and enjoyed taking him out and showing him the towns and villages neighbouring Drum Mhor.

'You must come to Kyiv, Iona. Don't you think so, Suzannah?' Sergei smiled down at his landlady affectionately after they had returned from a visit to the butcher's shop in the town.

'Oh, I don't think so, thank you anyway,' demurred Iona, looking warily at them both. 'I'm not one for the city life; I just can't sleep with all that noise you get in the morning, what with the milk floats and so on.'

'What?' laughed Suzannah, turning to Paula who was flicking

through a glossy magazine on the sofa, 'Milk floats?'

'You don't get milk floats any more Iona.' Looking up, Paula added, 'Milk comes from the corner shop or the supermarket as far as I'm concerned, so that is one less worry for you when you go off on your holidays to eastern Europe.'

Sergei leant over and kissed Suzannah, '*Do svidaniya*, I am going out now, I want to take some photographs before it gets too dark.'

After he had gone, the three friends settled themselves around the fire, and sat for a while in companionable silence.

'Listen,' began Paula, 'I heard the ladies gossiping in Kathleen's yesterday. They've started a knitting club in Dolly's house, up the glen. Do you think they would let us join in?'

'Maybe, though it would depend on how many wanted to go. Her sitting room is quite small. It would be better if we could do it in the school or maybe even in the dining room off the pub. We could ask Donnie. I didn't know you were a knitter, Paula?'

'I'm not, but it can't be that hard, and you're an expert; you can teach me.'

'What about you, Suzannah?' Iona looked over at Suzannah who was looking very ethereal by the light of the fire, her soft blonde hair tumbling over her shoulders.

'I made a jumper at school and the odd scarf, but maybe I should try and make a little hat for the baby.'

'Right, that's settled then; if we can't join the witches up the glen we'll start our own little knitting coven here. We can get a bottle of wine in and all the men are banned, how's that?'

'Excellent,' laughed Paula. 'I wonder if Margaret will be joining in. No doubt she'll knit some fantastic Shetland masterpiece for Robert, and I'll only manage a blanket to line his dog kennel.'

'How are things there?' asked Suzannah gently. 'I thought you and Robert were a couple. I mean you did say that things were wonderful.'

'They are,' agreed Paula, 'but Margaret continues to assume

that she is the one that Robert really wants, and that his feelings for me are just a passing phase.'

Iona shook her head, twisting her mouth into a derisive line. 'She's in denial, that one. Everyone can see that the pair of you are madly in love, even poor Eck, bless him, but Margaret has a stubborn streak, just like her father, and she will cling on like a limpet. I heard she tried to spy on you and Robert; is that right?'

Paula started to giggle, and turned to share the story with Suzannah. 'She did; talk about your Sergei being thought a spy. Margaret is much more clandestine than any character in a Stieg Larsson novel.' Paula leant forward to stoke the fire then slid off the sofa to sit on the footstool at Suzannah's feet. She could see that her very pregnant friend was uncomfortable trying to twist her body in order to face her. 'Well,' she began, 'you know that Jenny, James's sister-in-law, works in the old folks' home. It seems that Margaret borrowed a hearing aid from the home – you know that when you put it on, you are supposed to be able to hear voices from quite far across a room. Apparently, according to Eck, she brought this gadget to Robert's house when she knew I was there. She is so eaten up with jealousy, I think she wanted proof that we were lovers and then she could have a big scene and recriminations and so on. Well, Robert and I were completely unaware of what was going on outside; we were upstairs in bed. Then we heard a loud squealing noise, followed by a cracking noise and a dull thud. Robert got up to the window, but it was five in the afternoon and dark already, so he thought it was just a cat leaping about. It wasn't until later on that Eck told us what had happened.' Paula smiled ruefully at the recollection. She went on, 'Margaret had managed to get herself up on to a branch of the sycamore tree that grows just outside the house. She had used an old table used for the sheep clipping – it usually sits out by the barn – to hoist herself up there. She then turned her listening device as high as it would go, causing the screeching noise that we heard. It was while she was edging along the smaller branch near the bedroom window that the bough snapped and down fell poor Margaret, hearing aid and all!'

'Oh no! Poor girl! She must have been mortified,' Suzannah exclaimed. 'Was she hurt?'

'Yes, but nothing major. I think she wrenched her ankle and cut her knee. It was lucky that Eck was passing in his jeep. He saw her limping up the road and gave her a lift to the doctor's and he patched her up.'

'And do you think that has put an end to her grand passion?' asked Suzannah, her eyes wide with sympathy.

'No way,' cut in Iona, 'she will be after him and plotting with Dolly and Kathleen how to get him back.'

'I'm glad Wee Eck has taken it so well,' commented Suzannah. 'He did hold quite a candle for you, Paula, right from the start.'

'Yes, I feel a bit bad about that. He's a real friend, that one. I hope he finds the love of his life one of these days.'

'What is that?' asked Suzannah, her voice soft in the darkening room, only the flickering fire causing shadows to play on the faces of the three women sitting around its warmth.

'What is what?' asked Iona, ' "The love of your life?" '

'Yes, I mean, can we love in different ways? We all have so many facets to our personalities, and we know how different we become when we interact with different people. Does the love for one person mean you have to stop loving another?'

Paula considered before answering. 'I think it's a conscious choice that we have to make. The person that is right for you in Cairo when you are backpacking at the age of twenty might not be right for you when you are a high school principal at thirty five. People bring out different traits in you. Some will make you feel musical, some you will want to laugh with all day long, some you will just want to study the fine lines that are etched around their eyes. It's all love, in its own way. Past loves seem to disappear as time passes. I think they have to go in order to reassure the love of the present.' She stared for a minute into the fire before continuing, her voice soft. 'It's like the colours gradually fading from an old photograph. Feelings that were once so strong, that you thought would endure forever, become just a strand of memory. It's sad, but inevitable.'

Iona gently put her hand out to Suzannah. 'Sergei is perfect for you, lass. He is bright and optimistic. You made a good choice. Don't you have any regrets, now!'

'I know, I don't, but just sometimes I wonder how it might have been with James.'

Iona sighed deeply and got up to switch on the table light. Immediately the room was suffused in a warm, pink glow. 'I don't know about you girls, but I think I'll put on the kettle. We have to plan our knitting club. I'll have to go to Inverness and get some wool for baby clothes. That wee one in there will need a brand new wardrobe.'

Suzannah ran her hand over her bump and spoke to her unborn child. 'Poor thing, having to wear your mother's first-ever attempt at a knitted tea cosy, and your Aunty Paula's excuse for a scarf. Oh dear, oh dear.'

CHAPTER 21

The following Thursday night at eight o'clock, Wee Eck and Robert were drinking beer, embroiled in a conversation about spies and satellites and the possibility of Sergei having a hidden identity. Eck craved a drama and if there was nothing happening in the village to keep the cogs of his brain whirling on high alert then he was forced to use his imagination. This evening the two men sat facing each other across Robert's kitchen table. The kitchen smelt of fried food and peat smoke. The remains of a sausage lay congealing in a mess of tomato sauce and Eck pushed the plate further away from him. It did not occur to him to clear the plates into the sink. Where he lived, with his ageing mother, he still enjoyed the status of being head of the household, and was thus spared any domestic duties. In return he kept the outside immaculate and his skills as a handyman and gardener extended beyond his own house. His advertisements in the local papers, and his flyers at the chemist in the town, ensured that he was well-known in the district.

Robert sat with one of his dogs between his knees, patting the soft, glossy coat. He was laughing softly at Eck's flights of fantasy. 'For goodness sake, Eck, the man's a doctor. He drinks vodka and can sing and recite Burns better than you or I can. I don't think he has anybody to spy on up here.'

'Maybe,' agreed Eck, 'but how do you know he's not here to learn the lie of the land. I know spies need to find out about coastal regions and where they can land their submarines and so on. Maybe the Burns thing is just a cover.' He decided to change tack by introducing a new theory. 'Maybe he's on the run? Or maybe he needs to make contact with his base. I've heard that there's a Russian Mafia; you never know, they might be after him. You and I, Rob, we should start patrolling the village. We'll need to keep our eyes and ears open for any strangers in black leather jackets and with foreign accents lurking about. It should be easy this time of year, since all the tourists are long gone.'

'Here, have another beer.' Rob reached over for Eck's glass and turned to fill it from the black plastic keg he kept on the table beside the cooker. 'Get that down you and stop all this nonsense. It's just all in your imagination.'

Eck swallowed loudly and then wiped his sleeve across his mouth. 'I'll have you know that I saw him walking about with his camera down on the beach next to James MacTavish's house. I thought maybe he was going to organize a getaway or maybe a rendezvous.' Eck's eyes were alive with excitement as he trawled through his memory for spy themes in the comics that he had read in school.

'For goodness' sake, Eck, get a hold of yourself; the man's a tourist – he's never been to Scotland before. What's wrong with taking a few photographs? I don't want to hear any more of this. I know Paula and Suzannah would just skin you alive if they knew what stories you were coming away with.'

Eck grunted. He acknowledged his setback with the statuesque Paula. It was obvious, even to him, that she and Robert were well on their way to marital bliss. He had taken the blow of her rejection with his indefatigable good nature and consoled himself that the right woman for him was just there to be found, and he was going to enjoy the search. He knew that Margaret was not as forgiving, and had aligned herself with Dolly's knitting group up the glen.

Robert and Eck sat quietly, letting their thoughts drift from cameras and spies to the women in their lives.

Robert broke the silence. 'I hear the knitting sessions are going on tonight. Two groups I believe, one up at Dolly's and one at Iona MacPherson's. I would like to be a fly on those walls,' and he smiled, then his brow creased. 'Well, maybe I wouldn't.' He stood up, and made towards the door. 'Come on now, Eck, you get off home. Drive carefully for there's a frost and the moon is full... and you've had three beers. Take it easy on those bends now and I'll see you tomorrow.'

While Robert and Eck were enjoying the quiet camaraderie by the fire, Dolly's gathering was in full swing. The pins moved like pistons as wool travelled from one needle to the next, the fragments of knitting growing in a complexity of patterns, woven in hues of glorious colour. Beside each woman a glossy pattern lay open illustrating the finished article, the black instructions jumbled across the page like some ancient Sanskrit.

'You're making a grand job of that jumper, Margaret. Would that be for Robert's Christmas present?' Kathleen asked solicitously.

'Yes, he used to love it when I made him jumpers,' she sniffed as she knitted her tight little stitches, an urgent tension emitting from her small plump body and her mouth pulled as tight as the wool. She lifted the heavy sleeve hanging from her needle to the other side.

'Well, at the rate you're going, lassie, you'll have it finished by Saturday. You'll have to make a pair of socks to go with it if you want to stay in the knitting club,' laughed Dolly.

'Aye, it's a wonder you're not getting sparks off those needles, at the rate you're going,' observed Lottie MacDonald.

'I hear they've started knitting down at Iona MacPherson's as well,' added Doris knowledgeably. Her status of working in the shop often gave her snippets of news that the ladies in the Tea Room missed out on.

'Well, Iona is a good knitter. I expect she'll be busy making a layette for the new baby, but I can't imagine the other two knowing which end of a needle is which.'

They all laughed cosily, picturing the two city girls trying to emulate the skills displayed in Dolly's warm and stuffy room.

'You won't have to worry about competing with Paula's knitting, Margaret, but I think maybe you should sit back for a while. Your ankle is still strapped up and we don't want to see you overdoing it, lass.'

'Aye, talk about getting hurt, I think that Suzannah is just asking for trouble, flaunting her condition the way she is. And not even a squeak of her getting married. It's her that's hesitating, they say, for you know what he did in the pub last week?'

'No, tell us; what did he do?' asked Doris, peeved that she had not been invited to join them for a drink last weekend.

'Well, he stood up, so handsome and foreign, quite made me swoon just watching him… ' announced Kathleen smugly while touching her silver coiffure delicately, 'and he turned to Suzannah and sang all of *My Love is Like a Red Red Rose,* in perfect English mind you! It was beautiful and she just sat there and smiled, like a pregnant Madonna. I hear from Iona that she won't marry him. I can tell you, if I was thirty years younger I wouldn't have to be asked twice.'

'It's the fashionable thing these days, though. Morals are gone and just debauchery everywhere you look. All these young girls having their wicked way and the poor young men just don't know what they're supposed to do. Not like in our day.' Lottie MacDonald pursed her lips in a disapproving line, a pronounced furrow ploughing its way between her heavy black brows. 'That James MacTavish is not setting a good example to the young generation either,' she added. 'It's about time he settled down instead of trying to bed every young woman that comes into the glen, and all in the pretence that he is looking for a wife.' She tut tutted noisily over her knitting. 'Him and that Suzannah are a right pair.'

'I think it's time we had a cup of tea,' interrupted Dolly. 'Come and help me, Margaret, and give those fingers a rest.'

Dolly and Margaret retreated to the kitchen to boil the kettle and collect the sumptuous spread that Dolly had prepared earlier. There was lemon curd cake, coconut macaroons and snickerdoodle biscuits. Of all the women present, Dolly felt closest to Margaret and felt a genuine sympathy for the younger woman's predicament. Dolly had been slighted years ago by a dashing English gentleman who had wooed her during the autumn months of stalking, and whispered love poems into her ash blonde hair and kissed her fresh pink lips. It was only after he left that she found out about his fiancée in London. Further tears had gathered on her pillow when she discovered that he had left her with more than a memory. She had had to make a soul-searching decision, but one that she had never regretted.

Ruefully, Dolly looked over at Margaret. 'Maybe if you look about, lass, you will find the right man for you. Robert was never right or the pair of you would have married years ago. Look at me and Ronnie, married all this time and yet for a while before I was so blinded by someone else I nearly didn't see him. You might be the same, and already know your man and yet not realise he's for you, just like I did.'

'You're right. I appreciate it that you understand. It's just hard to let go, and I hate the thought of him being with "her". It's just so hard.' Margaret sniffed into one of Dolly's tartan paper serviettes.

'I know, lass, but look at me and Ronnie. Haven't we been blessed with our two sons, Michael and Ruaridh? Life is all about decisions. Let him go, lass. Now wipe away your tears and we'll have a nice cup of tea, and you can tell me how you like my cake; I might even give you the recipe.'

Further down the glen and along the road to the shore, Iona's knitting circle was made up of less professional knitters. Paula struggled with a red scarf, dropping more stitches than actually knitting them. Suzannah giggled at her friend's attempts and patiently tried to help her get the knack of crossing the wool and slipping it off the needle. By contrast Iona knitted like lightning, hardly giving the work in her hand a look as she chattered and laughed and passed around the bottle of white wine. The small jacket that she was knitting grew like magic in her hands. Grace from the Post Office was delighted to have been invited. She was one who knitted quietly and efficiently. She had begun a masterpiece, a shawl for the baby in the softest creamy-white. The texture was fine and lacy, as delicate as a spider's web.

'My mother told me that a shawl should be so soft and light that it can slip through a band of a wedding ring.' Grace looked over at Iona. 'Did you not hear that too?'

'Aye, I did, Grace, but look at these two lassies, not a wedding ring between them. I think it will have to be up to you and me to see if it will go through! Now come on and have another wee drop of this wine before the men come back from the pub. No doubt they will be demanding sandwiches and tea when they get here.'

Donnie stood behind the bar polishing the glasses and whiling away the quiet hours of the evening with various men who were exiled from their homes and firesides. Games of pool and darts were taking place and a couple of forestry lads sat companionably passing the time with him. There was a feeling of calm, quiet contentment. Old Hector sat quietly by the fireside, his dog Charlie by his feet. He seemed lost in his own reveries as he watched the logs spit and burn.

Sergei had been en route to the Pipers Inn, but changed his mind and decided to visit James MacTavish instead. He enjoyed the company of the older man and found his house a haven after all the comings and goings at Iona and Murdo's home. Chickens, cats, dogs and sheep seemed to be demanding constant attention. People called in at all hours to visit Suzannah and the phone was constantly ringing. James greeted his visitor cheerfully and ushered him through to his sitting room. Sergei stretched out his long limbs in front of the fire and felt the heat of the peat burn into his legs. Lazily he surveyed the panelled room and tilted his head to read the titles of the books and magazines that were piled on James's desk. He breathed in the fumes of his double malt whisky, savouring the peace of a masculine den.

'You must be used to bad weather where you come from?' James asked, after loading another peat block into the flames.

'Yes, but in the city it is not too bad; we have machines to clear the snow and the houses are warm and we have lots of hot water. In the country it is bad, people there are so poor. Not enough to eat, few of them have cars, it is a difficult life. Many old people die of the cold. The temperatures drop to minus thirty and the snow stays for a long time. Even in the city the homeless die like little sparrow birds in the snows.'

'Yes,' said James, 'I read about that, and of course I have learnt quite a lot about your history, especially since Suzannah went there. Your people have suffered so much; so many invasions, then Stalin, and then the bad years following. And now, after your Orange Revolution, do you feel there is more hope for the future?'

'We hope, of course, but still we have the great divide. Since Perestroika the rich are getting richer and the poor are still suffering, just as they have all through history. Look at me, a cardiac surgeon, and I earn less than Suzannah was earning at her language school. Yet when you look around you, everyone has mobile phones, people can afford to go skiing and have holidays. Perhaps this new government will find the best solution. We can only live in hope.'

James sighed deeply, letting the words sink in, and a silence fell over the room. Only the gentle whistling from the fire disturbed the quiet.

'You seem to love lighthouses,' said Sergei, looking at the framed pictures on the wall. 'I remember Suzannah telling me but now I see you have so many books about this subject.' He gestured towards the bookcase.

'I do, always have done; probably comes from living so close to the sea. To me, there seems something heroic in those little structures jutting out above the rocks.' He sipped from his glass, enjoying the picture that he was conjuring. 'Aye, only a glimmering light in a great expanse of ocean. Just a wee light to warn sailors of dangers lurking like sharks' teeth beneath the surface of the water.'

Sergei looked a little bemused, missing some of the imagery in the translation in his head. Nevertheless, he could understand why someone could become passionate about such structures.

At ten o'clock that same evening, as James and Sergei mused over the trials of sailors at sea, Wee Eck drove home along the dark roads leading away from Robert's croft. He reflected that there was more traffic than usual on the road, but deduced it was probably due to the two new knitting clubs that had started up. He waved jauntily at Paula who was walking home along the deserted village street towards her little house. She was all bundled up in a ski jacket and woolly hat and scarf. He smiled at her retreating figure in the side mirrors; he couldn't imagine her as a knitter at all. Passing the village hall, the road led him out of the built-up area and on to the bridge crossing over the river. All he could see were pin-pricks of light coming from crofts scattered across the land and up the hill. Eck drove on round the deep bends that led to the fork in the road, marked by a chestnut tree. He changed down a gear and hummed tunelessly as he drove up the single track road that circled the glen. Here there was no light, only the luminous glimmer from the full moon. Eck was conscious of being alone and his eyes shifted to his rear view mirror but there were no other lights to be seen. Grasses were encased in frosted coats of icy armour and reeds rose in sharp formation, appearing to form a black battalion standing at attention by the side of the road. Suddenly ahead he saw a car approaching with its headlights on full beam.

'Bloody moron, can you not dip your lights? How can I see with all that dazzle in my eyes?' he muttered, changing down again to pull into the lay-by to allow the oncoming car some space in which to pass.

The car approached steadily, still showing no indication of dipping its lights. Eck shouted futilely at the vehicle, 'For God's sake, you're blinding me!'

Then as he looked, his eyes still squinting into the glare, the car completely vanished. Eck blinked, and blinked again. There was nothing on the road, just empty space. He looked to see if there was a turn-off, but he knew there was not. There was no place for the car to have gone. Hairs rose like prickly splinters all over his body; he felt fear invade his car like a cold, damp cloud. Soon, he would describe the experience in the comfort of the warm pub, where Donnie would pour him a restorative whisky and he would find some bravado in the telling. But for the moment, when he realised he had confronted the ghost car, he felt only fear and the need to reverse and get back to a place where there were folk he knew. He did not want to be alone; he was scared to death.

A few minutes later, leaning on the bar, Donnie sympathised with him. 'Aye, it sounds like the ghost car, and we know now it means a premonition, but you are the only one that's seen it at night. You just drink that dram down and I'll give you a run over to Robert's. I'm sure he'll give you a bed for the night. I don't suppose you fancy driving over that hill again after all that drama.'

'Drama,' said Eck, 'I was just talking about drama tonight, didn't imagine I would feature in one quite so soon.'

Hector, his eyes bright as two black coals, nodded sagely and spat into the fire.

As the night settled over Drum Mhor, Suzannah cuddled closer to Sergei. His hand softly caressed the bump that lay between them. She smiled sleepily and said, 'Paula was telling us that Eck is convinced you are a spy.'

Sergei chuckled. 'Spies, lighthouses, ghost cars. I hate to think of how the KGB would interpret my letters and the phone calls that I make to my mother. She always warned me about foreign girls, and now here I am dwelling with one. Kiss me, my Mata Hari, but don't bother trying to seduce me tonight; James has drugged me with his powerful Scottish whisky.'

'It's supposed to make you frisky,' Suzannah giggled, kissing his shoulder. Receiving no response she smiled affectionately and softly smoothed the hair from his forehead. Moonlight filtered through the thin curtains into the room. Suzannah studied her lover's face, the long lashes, and the full lips pouting in sleep. She caressed him with her eyes and snuggled into his warmth. Slowly she felt herself drifting into the black corridor of sleep, only the inevitable rumble of his soft snores marking the end of another day.

CHAPTER 22

There were only two weeks left before school broke up for the Christmas holidays. Rosie's head was full of the forthcoming celebrations. She spent the evenings at the kitchen table instructing her mother on how to make snowmen and Christmas tree decorations, just like the ones she was busy with at school. Jenny patiently helped her fold the paper while her youngest child chattered about all her activities.

'So you are learning symmetry now, are you? My goodness, soon you'll be doing Joker's homework. He'll be glad of your help, I'm sure.'

'By the time she could help me, I'll have finished with both my school and my apprenticeship. I'll be a fully served joiner by then; I start my apprenticeship next year, don't forget.' Joker sat at the other end of the table, engrossed with Billie in another of their secret and no doubt mischievous science projects. Jenny was happy to see her children content to sit away from the television for once.

'What are you boys making anyway? There seems to be a lot of whispering going on.' She looked up between cutting coloured strips of paper for candles.

'We're just making electrical circuits using a battery. Look at this, Mum, you wire it all over the board like a spaghetti junction but when you hit this peg, which is really the switch, the light comes on. We're going to need more wire though. Can we borrow some of Dad's?' Billie looked up at her wide eyed with enthusiasm.

Jenny nodded. 'I suppose so, but don't forget to tell him; he'll be mad if he goes looking for it and it's disappeared.' She turned again to Rosie and said, 'And what else do you do at school, apart from symmetry and making decorations?'

'Nothing,' muttered the small girl, 'it's just God, God and more God.'

'What does that mean?' Her mother looked at her sharply, her brows raised in surprise. 'Do you mean the Christmas story and Bethlehem and things like that?'

'No,' Rosie scowled, 'I like that bit, it's the other minister that makes us pray for hours and hours and we only get to sing Psalm 100.' She began to sing in a dirge-like voice, 'All people that on earth do dwell... '

The boys laughed and Billy sighed dramatically, 'It's true, Mum, that's all we get from the Free Church minister. My neck gets sore from praying so long.'

'Oh well,' said his mother, 'maybe it will do you some good and keep you out of trouble. I'm looking forward to the ceilidh that you're putting on for the old folks. I'll be able to enjoy it for once. I'm not working that night, so I'll be able to sit and watch you. Have you been practising?'

Rosie immediately lit up and started chattering about the coming performance. 'The big ones are doing war songs that the old people know, like *Tipperary* and *Pack up Your Troubles in an Old Kit Bag* and other ones.' She added lamely, 'Billie is in that, and he's doing a poem with his class, and I'm dancing with Morag and Kirsty. The wee ones are singing some Scottish songs like *Ally Bally, Ally Bally Bee* and *Maire's Wedding*.'

Billie cut in, 'Mrs Munroe is going to be dressed in a tartan dress with a long wifey scarf thing on her head. She is going to sit on the stage like an old granny and tell the audience what's coming next. The doctor said she could borrow his rocking chair specially.'

Jenny laughed at the idea and asked Billie what poem he was learning with his class.

'It's *Lord Ullin's Daughter*. I know it already. It's all about a ferry and a girl getting drowned.'

'Yes, I know that one,' said Jenny. 'Not really what I would expect for a Christmas show though. Do you not have any Christmas things in it?'

'Yes,' said Rosie with a hint of exasperation, 'we have made up a song about the twelve days of Christmas and made paintings to go with it. Shall I sing you some of it, Mum?'

Her mother nodded, and Rosie began:

On the first day of Christmas, my true love sent to me,
A tree from the Forestry-ee,
On the second day of Christmas, my true love sent to me,
Two silver salmon and a tree from the Forestry-ee.
On the third day of Christmas, my true love sent to me,
Three steaks of venison, two silver salmon and a tree
from the Forestry-ee.

She continued to sing, not noticing that her two brothers had packed up their things and had tiptoed out of the room. The Rayburn cast out a warm glow in the homely kitchen. Only the sound of the soup simmering on the stove interrupted Rosie's tuneful carol. Jenny wished her husband Iain was home to hear this rendition, but glancing at the clock she knew it would be another half-an-hour before she would hear his bus approach.

Upstairs the boys were plotting their latest cunning plan. When Joker had arrived home for the weekend earlier that evening from his high school in Inverness, he had been excited on hearing from Billie the gossip that was circulating the village. His eyes had lit up when he heard how Suzannah had returned to Drum Mhor with a Russian spy. Immediately both boys were on high alert and wondering how they could intercept any messages that might be sent.

'We can get a listening machine when we go over to the old folks' home. Remember I told you how that crazy woman Margaret fell out of a tree trying to spy on Robert Ross?'

Joker laughed at Billie's account of poor Margaret's shame.

The younger lad continued, full of importance, 'Eck was saying to Uncle James that he was sure Sergei was here on undercover business, so all we have to do is track his every move and take notes. We can listen to any secret phone calls he makes and then we can catch him red-handed.'

Joker listened attentively while he unwound the wire that he had liberated from his father's workshop in the garage. 'Aye but we'll have to keep very quiet about this, and you'll have to keep me fully informed during the week. Let's get on with making this now. We have to make a signal so that if anyone comes close to us when we are spying, they will step on the wires here and then the bulb will light up. No one will suspect that we are really counteragents because we can just say we are practising our science homework.'

Both boys were bent over the wires and bulbs, so intent with their plotting that they didn't hear their little sister enter the room. She listened to their plan to lay the wires under the door of the cupboard next to the bedroom that Sergei and Suzannah shared in Iona's house. She just knew that they were up to no good. Quietly she retreated and pulled the door closed again. She decided to keep a watch on Billie and follow him wherever he went. If they could spy on a spy, then so could she.

The following Friday, Mrs Munroe and Mary Beth were enjoying a cup of coffee in the school staff room. They could see from the window the comings and goings of the various groups that made use of the village hall during the day. The badminton ladies were just leaving, looking hot and flustered, with breath coming out of their mouths like old puffer steam trains.

'They'll be off now to the Tea Room for some of Kathleen's chocolate cake,' sighed Mary Beth, nibbling her Rich Tea biscuit delicately, with more than a sense of superiority. 'I can just taste it, all moist and dripping with chocolate icing.' She sighed again, and looked down at her solid figure that had shown no sign of reducing since the birth of her baby a year ago. The yoga classes on Saturday mornings were not working at all.

Mrs Munroe eyed her colleague over her gold rimmed glasses, her fiery red hair like a forest blaze above her thyme-green suit. 'We have the ceilidh tonight at the old folk's home, so we should meet here and walk over decorously together as a school. I don't want all the children arriving like a rabble and giving the old folk unnecessary excitement. I just hope for everyone's sake that they don't fall asleep in the middle of it. You know what they're like when we visit on Tuesday afternoons.'

Mary Beth smiled at the image of the old lady with one leg who had the habit of smiling sweetly at the children, saying a few words then lurching over to the side of her chair and falling asleep. The first time she did it, everyone thought she had passed on. It had been very disconcerting and quite upsetting.

'Yes, I agree, and I'm looking forward to it this year. It's good that so many people have bought tickets and can come and support the children. I hear Suzannah will be there as well with her new man.'

'Yes, quite a novelty,' concurred Mrs Munro, her lips tightening.

'And we'll have the pipers as well.' Mary Beth smiled cheerfully.

'Oh don't remind me! Six of them, so I'm told. I just hope they have learnt how to keep in time this year.'

'And in tune!' laughed Mary Beth.

The two teachers responded to the sound of the bell clanging out into the icy playground. The children ran to the doors and lined up, their faces red from running, their eyes as bright as colourful marbles.

'Come along, my little Rudolfs, you can come in first today. Do you want to lead the way, Rosie?' Mary Beth ushered her infant class into the warmth of the passage where they hung up their jackets and stacked their boots under the bench. There was an air of excitement in the school. Christmas was coming, decorations were hanging from the ceilings and the walls, but more importantly, school books remained closed in readiness for the final rehearsal that was scheduled for tonight's ceilidh performance.

Sergei was bemused by the ceilidh. Since his arrival in Scotland he had taken to carrying around a small red notebook that he kept in the breast pocket of his jacket. In this he noted new English words or expressions that he did not previously understand. By taking notes he could remember to look them up later in his dictionary. Sometimes he drew pictures of things he saw or of things that interested him. He had built up quite an eclectic collection. He had copied diagrams of some of James's lighthouses, each one annotated with their pertinent details. He had recorded the number of fighter jets that flew over the sea to Skye. And he had drawn a very good likeness of a deep-sea prawn-fishing boat.

Tonight he sat beside Suzannah in the overheated community room of the old people's home. The dining room that was connected to this room by sliding doors gave a perfect stage area for the children to perform. The audience from the village sat in rows around the twenty-four orthopaedic chairs that the residents sat in. Billy and Rosie were part of the performing group, but Joker was free to sit where he wanted. He placed himself next to his Uncle James who was sitting beside Sergei. Thus it was with a certain amount of excitement that he saw Sergei reach into his jacket and retrieve a red notebook. Joker caught sight of diagrams of a fishing boat, a Tornado fighter jet and a lighthouse. His eyes were riveted to the book. He saw Sergei reach into his pocket for a pen. With eyes that were straining in their sockets to see to his left while still facing towards the show, he read the word *kay lee*. He watched mesmerised as Sergei proceeded to write a lot of strange unfamiliar letters that Joker knew to be Russian. Joker felt sick with excitement.

Meanwhile Mrs Munroe took her place in the rocking chair. She was dressed in a long brown dress and had draped a tartan shawl around her head.

Jenny smiled and noted that Billie's information of how his

teacher was to be dressed was totally wrong as usual.

'Look at her,' sniped Dolly facetiously, 'no doubt she'll be wanting to be in the Drama next.'

'If you ask me,' countered Lottie MacDonald, 'she looks ready to be a resident in here.'

The row of the village matrons snickered companionably, enjoying the show even before it had begun.

Paula, sitting beside Robert, turned to the back row in order to wink at Suzannah. Both young women grinned at each other as yet another village entertainment started to unfold.

Nobody noticed the small dark figure of Hector Ogilvie sitting quietly by himself at the back of the room. His rheumy eyes stared as though into the distance, and he gave no indication that he recognised anybody in the gathering. His hands, stained brown from dirt and weather, were clasped on his knees. Dolly had remarked as she had come in that it was a fine night, to which he had replied, 'Aye, but I see there are wintry showers on the top.'

Rosie's class came on first, holding their paintings in their hands, and waited for Mary Beth on the piano to strike up the chords of the *Twelve Days of Christmas*. James MacTavish clapped the loudest when the carol was complete and Rosie was gratified that he had seen and admired her beautiful painting of the Christmas tree. He looked along the row at Jenny and his brother Iain and nodded at them. It was good they were both able to attend.

James nudged Joker beside him. 'Keep your eyes ahead, lad, what are you trying to do, see sideways?'

Sergei, while clapping loudly to welcome the young pipers taking to the stage, had inadvertently dropped his notebook from his lap. Only one pair of eyes had witnessed this fact. Joker MacTavish watched and waited, frozen with anticipation, for his moment to retrieve it unseen.

The ceilidh proceeded with the rehearsed dancing and singing and poetry reciting. After the children had completed their programme there was much cheering and clapping and the adults seemed unwilling to leave. Finally Mrs Munro stood up and in true Highland tradition she requested that someone from the assembled community should perform for them.

'Oh, well! What about you, Suzannah?' laughed James. 'You are a good singer as we have already found out.'

'Not me, I don't think I want to be made any more conspicuous than I am already.'

They turned back to the stage. One of the forestry lads was making his way up to the front, ready to perform. Clearing his throat, the lad began to sing an Irish ballad, *The Fields of Achinry*.

'Look at the old folk!' whispered Jenny. 'They are all swaying in time, and even old Hilda is singing along. Normally she's fast asleep by now.'

Sergei was mesmerised by the singing and camaraderie within the packed room. He held Suzannah's hand and whispered, 'I wish I could show my mother how it is here. She would love to see Drum Mhor.'

Suddenly they heard the forestry lads call out to him, 'Sergei, Sergei, Sergei!'

'What? You want me to do something? But I cannot sing.'

'You could dance,' Suzannah smiled mischievously, taking the CD from her handbag. She had brought the Cossack music, just in case he was ever asked to perform. Sergei stood up, laughing good naturedly, his tall frame dominating the room.

'All right, I will dance. After I dance, I will challenge all of you to dance with me.' He pointed to the six tough young forestry men sitting together by the side of the room. Turning to the old people in their semicircle of chairs, he stood tall and straight and bowed deeply. 'I pay you much respect, and now I will dance for you.'

Mary Beth placed the CD into her stereo and turned the music up. The pulsing rhythm filled the room. The Ukrainian man slapped his thigh and kicked a heel up and slapped it with his other hand. He then stepped lightly to the right, then left, then turned and jumped high, then he dropped down on to his haunches. Never breaking from the rhythm, his legs jutted out alternately; crunching his thigh muscles and bouncing low on the floor. As the music whirled faster, Sergei rose and danced wildly, picking up the tempo until his body and feet were a blur. The audience clapped with him and for a few moments the spirit of the Steppe and the Urals and the wide plains of southern Ukraine filled the small Highland room and transfixed the audience. Suzannah put her hand on her belly and felt the restless kicking of her dancing child, as though impatient to be released and join in the festivities.

Beside her, Joker transferred the red book from his back pocket and hid it inside his jacket.

CHAPTER 23

James MacTavish stood gazing thoughtfully at the portrait of his mother. He looked down at the Bible, which as usual lay open on the organ beneath her picture, and flicked the book shut before letting it fall randomly open again. He scanned the verses that revealed themselves before him, looking for a sign that might give his day direction, and then smiled wryly as he selected the story of Bathsheba and David to read. He looked up at the portrait again and couldn't resist speaking to the old matriarch: 'Well, Mother, you don't miss a trick, do you? You're thinking that I want rid of that Ukrainian usurper, aren't you? Yes, I remember that Bible story of David tricking Bathsheba's husband, and sending him away to war so that he could steal his wife. Are you sending me messages, you canny *cailleach*?'

He took a step back and looked into the hooded eyes that stared back impassively, half expecting an answer or a knowing wink. Clicking his tongue, he put on his tweed jacket and deerstalker hat, and went back into the kitchen to collect his bottle of Famous Grouse whisky that he had set on the table. Today was the first of January and he had the serious business of First Footing to attend to. He stepped out to the porch and opened the outer door. He inhaled deeply, breathing in the fresh winds that came whistling in from the sea, smelling the sharp tang of the seaweed and tasting the salt in the spray. A new year; I wonder, what will it bring, James thought. Will the winds blow a wife into Drum Mhor for me? I have a feeling in my bones that this will be the year that one of those lassies I take to my bed in the summer months just might stay the course. I will make it my New Year's Resolution. Before this New Year becomes an old year, I will have found myself a wife.

So it was with renewed vigour that James stepped out and headed up to his nearest neighbour. He noticed the smoke coming from the chimney and he could make out the shape of Murdo on the croft carrying a bag of pellets, about to feed his sheep. The two men shook hands again, though it had only been a few hours since they had parted at the village hall.

'How's the head, James?' Murdo asked him solicitously.

'Been better, but just had a grand breakfast of fried black pudding and eggs and sausages all washed down with two Ibuprofen. I'm all set now for bringing in the New Year with yourself and your good lady.'

'Just you go on in, James; I'll finish here and I won't be long. The house is full already: Jenny and Iain are down with their kids, and Sergei and Suzannah are just back from a walk on the beach.'

James strode over to the house and knocked at the kitchen door. 'Hello, is there anybody in?' he shouted.

Iona threw herself into his arms and gave him a big squeeze that nearly dislodged his bottle. 'Hello Romeo, do I not get a better kiss than that?' And she proceeded to glue herself to his mouth.

'For God's sake, woman, behave yourself. Do you want to put me all wrong? Your husband will have the shotgun out in a minute. Here, come here, and I'll give you a wee cuddle in the shed out of sight, how would that do?' and he gave her a knowing leer.

'Come in you daft old gowk, and you can try and behave in a gentlemanly fashion, like your younger brother sitting through there in the sitting room.'

James found himself pouring whisky and toasting the New Year to all in the house. He kissed Suzannah chastely on the cheek and smiled down at her ballooning belly. 'Someone is going to have a memorable year, that's for certain,' he laughed, then turned and shook hands with the tall figure of Sergei. When at last he settled down on a chair facing out to sea, he became aware that young Billy was missing from the company. 'Where's Billy?' he asked Joker, who was swaying precariously near the fireplace in the sitting room.

'Iona said he could go upstairs and play with his batteries and bulbs. He's been up there a while now.'

'You look a touch green, boy, what were you drinking last night?' James studied Joker's face, and noticed the eyes that were bloodshot and out of focus.

'Och, just had a can or two with my mates up the glen.'

'Aye, a can or twenty-two,' quipped his mother crossly. 'He was sick all over the back step. It's a wonder he can even stand today.'

The door bell rang again, and Grace from the Post Office arrived, her face fresh and ruddy from the brisk walk in the biting wind. More greetings were exchanged, and her heart did a little flip as James pressed her hard against his chest. Over Grace's shoulder, James watched Suzannah get up from the hard chair on which she had been perched, and signal to Sergei. She was flushed, and James thought she had never looked so beautiful. She was dressed in a royal blue corduroy maternity smock, with a lighter shade of blue polo neck beneath. She had pale matching tights and brown leather clogs. Her long pale hair was loose and her cheeks were flushed pink. Forgetting that he was still holding the palpitating Grace to his breast, he watched Sergei follow Suzannah out of the room. Joker, from his place by the fireside, also noted the exit of the young couple and heard them climbing the stairs. Subconsciously he felt the outline of the red book in the back pocket of his jeans.

Billy heard the footsteps on the landing and saw the couple's bedroom door close behind them. As quick as a flash he let himself into the airing cupboard, positioned his listening device wire and plugged in the ear pieces.

'What do you want me to do, Suzannah? Shall I get Iona?'

'No, not yet, but I think it's time. We will have to tell them soon.'

'All right, but I must send a message to Kyiv. You rest here for one minute and I will go outside and see if I can get a signal.'

'Don't be long, please.'

Billy's eyes were like saucers. When their bedroom door opened the light flashed on his warning pad, but he stayed as motionless as the lizard he had watched on a boulder by the river last summer. When he heard the retreating steps of Sergei disappearing out of the front door, Billy let himself out of the cupboard and ran down the stairs two at a time. He opened the sitting room door, his eyes spinning with excitement, and indicated to his brother to come out to the hall.

'He's going to signal!'

'What?'

'I heard him, he's going to signal Kyiv. He's gone outside.'

The two boys ran out of the back door and crept to the front of the house, searching for a sight of the black leather jacket that Sergei always wore. They ran up the road, then down by the field, but he was nowhere to be seen.

'He's obviously gone somewhere secret. Spies do that.'

'What spies are you talking about?' The deep foreign accent broke into their exchange.

'Oh, hello there. We were just out for some fresh air,' stuttered Joker.

'Looking for spies? Tell me, what do they look like?'

'They look suspicious. They usually make signals and they contact jets and boats and things,' Billy volunteered.

'I see, and do they write things down?' Sergei asked menacingly.

'Usually in code,' Billy went on.

'I see, and would the code book be red?'

Joker blushed scarlet. 'I'm sorry, I found your book. I just thought you might be here spying on fishing boats and things.'

'Not a problem; I am just sorry I am so ordinary. There is nothing very special about me. I am a doctor and my girlfriend is about to give birth. I wanted to tell my mother, and to inform the hospital where I work that I will be back in about three weeks.'

'Oh.' Billy looked crestfallen, and Joker looked mortified.

'Maybe your father could help me get Suzannah to hospital. I think we still have enough time.'

'Sure, I'll go and get him.' Joker ran back into the house.

'Are there no spies in your country, then?' asked Billy, mightily disappointed.

'Of course, and in yours too, but a good spy is never found out; even the people in their own families never know who they are working for.' He winked and looked at the boy menacingly. 'So you see, Billy, a spy could be anyone you know, anyone at all; you just have to stay alert.' Sergei nodded conspiratorially at the small boy and, whistling into the cold wind, went back into the house.

Suzannah gave birth to a boy in Raigmore hospital in Inverness at four minutes to eight that evening. As she held her newborn son and watched his fierce little gums search for her nipple she felt overwhelmed with love and wonder. She stared up at Sergei standing beside her and beamed at him, sharing the inimitable moment. The horrific journey in the back seat of Iain's car, clutching Sergei's hand each time the pains wracked her body, was over. The memory of the labour was wiped clean. Miraculously, instead of the pain, she now gloried in the unique joy that was hers. She was a mother.

'What shall we call him?' she smiled up at Sergei.

'I would like to call him Anton Yaroslav.'

'Yes, I like that. We are not married, so he will have my last name, Anton Yaroslav Richardson. Is that all right?'

'It is perfect. We will marry in the summer, in Kyiv. Yes?'

'Yes, when the chestnut trees are out and the parks are so beautiful. Sergei, I am so tired. I need to sleep, I am so sorry.'

'Sleep, my Suzannah, Anton is already asleep. *Ya tebya lyublyu, ti takaya krasivaya.*'

Sergei stepped out of the room and found Paula, Robert, Eck, Iona and Iain waiting for news.

'It is a boy and he is magnificent. His name is Anton Yaroslav. Suzannah is well but has fallen asleep. I don't think she will sleep for long, so you will be able to see her soon.'

'Congratulations!' Paula hugged him tight, and the men shook his hands. Sergei was so overcome with the novelty of becoming a father that he broke down. Tears ran down his face, and he sat with his head in his hands.

'Are you all right? Is the baby all right?' Paula asked him, her face full of concern.

'I am a happy man, that is all.' Sergei blew his nose loudly, regaining his self-control. 'I am a very happy man.'

Paula slipped into Suzannah's room. She crept silently towards the bed and gazed down at the sleeping forms of the mother and child. Her friend was flushed and her hair was damp. She looked exhausted. Nestled in her arms, Paula could make out the pink round face of the newly born baby; his head snuggled beside the exposed nipple. His tiny puckered mouth was still open from when he had let go, when sleep had claimed him.

'Hello,' smiled Suzannah, groggily, catching sight of her friend. 'Aren't I clever? I can't believe he's here, and he's perfect. Sergei is so happy.'

'Yes,' agreed Paula. 'He's the most beautiful baby, and look at that blond hair!'

Just for a minute Paula gazed at the peaceful scene before a nurse marched through the door, disturbing the serenity.

'Hello, dear.' The nurse leant over and gently stroked the cheek of the small, swaddled bundle. 'He's a bonny bairn, that's for sure, but he needs to be bathed and dressed and so do you. We have to make you all fresh for your visitors. Don't you worry; I'll help you with the baby and Nurse Dora will see to you. I see you've brought everything in your case.' She bustled about. 'I'll just go and get everything ready.' She marched out of the room in a swish of starched uniform, her crêpe-soled shoes barely making a sound.

'How long do you have to stay in hospital?' enquired Paula, looking around the room with distaste.

'Only a day or so, then I can get back to Drum Mhor. Sergei is going to stay in a guesthouse in town. That way he can visit me and be here to take me home. He was supposed to go to London tomorrow for a meeting with some other European heart specialists, but he cancelled because the baby came early. It is a little worrying as that was the official reason he was granted a visa to come here, to attend the conference. He will have to phone the Ministry of Health in Kyiv and see if he can meet up with one of the delegates.'

'But there's no need, Suzannah. Robert and I, or Iona can take you home. Really, let him go. My goodness, we are all here for you, surely you know that?'

'I do, and thank you. It is very important to him, I know.' Suzannah smiled up at her friend.

Just then they were interrupted by another nurse breezing into the room. 'Hello dear, I'm Nurse Dora; I am just going to help you have a wash and get into your own nightdress. Is this your case here? Right, I'll fill the basin and put these screens round you.' She turned to Paula as she crisscrossed the room, collecting all the items she needed for Suzannah's bed bath. 'Perhaps you could come back in just a few minutes?'

'See you soon,' Paula winked as she let herself out of the room, 'and don't worry, I'll have a word with Sergei.'

The following morning Sergei arrived at the hospital with Robert. Instead of staying in the guesthouse as he had planned, Sergei had gone back, at Paula's insistence, to Iona and Murdo's house to collect his suit and papers that he required for the conference. Robert then drove him back to Inverness where both men made their way to the Maternity Unit at Raigmore Hospital. Snow was falling like clouds of soft feathers outside and the roads were treacherous. Robert helped himself to a paper cup of black coffee in the waiting room outside, giving the young couple some moments of privacy before he drove Sergei to the airport.

'How are you today, and my son?' Sergei beamed down at the excited face propped up on the pillows. Suzannah was dressed in a dark pink nightdress; her long silvery hair was brushed and shone like silk. Her blue eyes were as bright as a china doll's.

'Just look at him, Sergei! He cried to be fed at five then fell fast asleep, and now it's nine. Shall we wake him so you can hold him? The nurse is going to show me how to bathe him later and then I'll be ready to take him home.'

'Yes, I want to hold him; I will be very careful.' Gently he eased his large hands under the sleeping form of his son, and keeping the fleecy blanket around him, he carried him to the bed where he studied the small flushed face. 'He will have a British passport; he will be free to go where he wants. Anton Yaroslav.'

The baby opened his eyes and stared up at Sergei with a funny, quizzical expression.

'What dark blue eyes you have, my boy. But I must go now, my darling Suzannah. I don't want to leave you, but perhaps it is better that I attend. We don't want to cause any trouble with the Immigration Department, do we?'

Suzannah smelt the cold air on his hair and face as he kissed her goodbye. He paused at the doorway and looked back at the bed. Suzannah had opened her nightdress and was offering Anton her engorged breast. The nipple was hard and the tiny mouth searched blindly before clutching like a vice with his strong gums. Sergei closed the door and made his way to the waiting room where he met up with Robert.

'They are well, and they will go home tomorrow. I cannot thank you enough, Rob, for helping me and Suzannah at this time.'

'Think nothing of it,' laughed Robert. 'Let's get you to the airport. I just hope this weather doesn't hinder you on your journey.'

Robert dropped Sergei off at the airport and drove back into Inverness. The snow was still coming down, and he had his doubts about the roads being clear enough to transport Suzannah back to Drum Mhor tomorrow. He stocked up on supplies for his croft at the North Eastern Farmers Store on the outskirts of Inverness. Just as he was about to go to the check-out, he noticed a wire basket containing a selection of thick Icelandic socks. He decided to buy a pair each for Suzannah and Paula. He selected a pink pair and a green pair and took them over to the counter. It's important to have warm feet, he thought. He chuckled to himself as he remembered how cold Paula's were when she snuggled close to him in the middle of the night.

CHAPTER 24

Sergei walked to the check-in counter and showed his ticket and passport to the middle-aged airline representative.

'Good morning, sir. The flight is delayed by half an hour, but the weather in London is good. There should be no problem once you are on your way.' She checked his passport and smiled at him. 'From Ukraine? This weather will be no surprise to you, sir.'

Sergei nodded. 'Snow can always be disruptive, but we are perhaps a little more used to it in my country. Unfortunately it stays with us for much longer.'

Checking his boarding pass, he picked up his bag and made his way through security and found an area of the lounge where he could be alone. He took out his mobile and turned his back on the room. '*Da, da, da. Harasho, do svidaniya.*' He snapped his phone shut and slipped it back into his pocket. He checked the time on his watch and strolled over to the window where he could see the snow-covered runway. His face remained impassive as various passengers complained volubly at the delay, but after an hour or so, the announcement came that the snow had abated sufficiently for the runway to be cleared. With his shoulders squared, he listened to the loudspeaker announce that the flight to London was ready for boarding. With a fixed gaze he proceeded towards the waiting plane and was finally seated into a window seat.

The journey was uneventful. Sergei used the time to carefully read through the papers that he had taken out of his briefcase. They were unintelligible to anyone who could not decipher the Cyrillic script.

Arriving in London, he immediately took a cab to Earl's Court.

Again he reached for his phone and hit his last number redial. He alighted outside the Exhibition Centre and waited for his contact, his steely blue eyes scanning the faces of passersby. He turned on hearing an appreciative wolf whistle coming from across the street. A woman was approaching. He watched her strut towards him, the high heeled boots making a sharp tapping sound as she walked. Her long blonde hair was plaited down her back and her cheek bones were high and Slavic. Around her swirled a long black woollen cape that fell dramatically to her ankles. She tossed her head, aware that he was watching her. Without breaking her step, she flicked one side of her cape open, revealing a cream tight-fitting suede leather jacket and matching miniskirt. Sergei sauntered towards her. Their eyes flickered over each other, but both feigned a cold indifference. Without a word, she turned and he followed her back the way she'd come from, past a school, then over the road, before walking down a wide residential street. Finally she stopped beside some wrought iron railings and spun round to face him.

'Is Vladimir here?' Sergei asked.

'Of course,' she replied abruptly. 'He is working just now, so we can be alone.'

The woman led the way down to the basement flat and groped in her purse for a Yale key. She let herself into the flat and turned on the lights. The hallway led into an open plan lounge and kitchen, from which two bedrooms led off. The apartment was warm and comfortably furnished. Artificial sunflowers beamed brightly in a vase on a card table that had been covered by a Provençal cloth decorated with olives. Pots, pans and groceries were scattered on the kitchen worktops. Sergei glanced around at the blue carpet and mauve and pink scatter cushions, the silky hangings and bejewelled table lamps. There were two opulent blue sofas placed at right angles to each other.

'Who lives here?' he asked.

'I do. I rented it from a woman who is working in Kenya. It is secure. It has been checked out.'

Sergei walked around the room. He pulled a curtain across a glass door that presumably led out to a back garden. He walked into the bathroom, tiled in turquoise mosaic. His eyes took in the female clutter of shampoos, moisturizers and tanning creams. He took the opportunity to relieve himself, then rinsed his hands and looked in the cabinet above the sink. There were two packets of contraceptives. How convenient, he thought. He took one packet and tucked it into his trouser pocket before walking back into the lounge.

'Come here,' he commanded.

The woman walked towards him, her face impassive. Her ice-blue eyes were cold and unblinking, and her head was tilted in a challenging pose. 'Business first,' she said.

'What's the matter, Tatyana? It's not like you to want to wait.'

'It's been four months, Sergei. I have been undercover here for four months, waiting, waiting. Now you have your child and your perfect alibi. That was clever of you to impregnate that girl. Now you can marry her and your child will be British and you will be the perfect agent. I have access to all the contacts you will need for our research, and each man's secret scientific investigations. The conference you will attend tomorrow will be full of representatives from Switzerland, the United States and Germany, as well as from London and Paris. It is imperative you make contact with the agent I have just visited in Switzerland. He is based in Basel, and has the vital drug that we need. It is essential you meet with him tonight.'

Sergei nodded, familiar with what she was saying, but displeased with the information that he would have to go out. 'I need to meet him tonight?' he grumbled.

'Of course, it must be tonight.'

'Why so soon,' he growled, I thought I would be with you tonight?' Sergei smoothed a lock of hair from her forehead.

Tatyana brushed his hand away. 'It is crucial that you perform your part of the contract tonight.

'I understand.'

'Now then, do you remember Mikhail Isakov?'

'Of course,' Sergei sighed deeply. 'What about him?'

'He is coming here for the conference and we suspect that he will cause a lot of trouble unless he is stopped. He intends to give interviews with the press about how some of the scientists are engaged in espionage and corruption. Is he not a colleague of yours?'

Sergei nodded. 'Of course, he is a fool. He thinks that by talking up all his big shot ideas he will change everything. Someone should make him shut up.'

Tatyana looked at him from half-closed eyes. 'Tonight the agent from Basel will give you tablets that are so strong they will cause death within minutes. The symptoms will be of a classic cardiac arrest. Perhaps Mr Isakov might benefit from a small cocktail?' she suggested, her cold eyes glinting up at him.

Sergei lifted one of her long slim fingers and kissed the perfect rose-painted nail. He said nothing.

Tatyana continued, 'You will meet with the agent tonight. I have the details of the bank account that he can access for his payment, after the transfer of the drug and its formula of course. Tell him to memorise the reference number. Make sure you leave nothing on him that could lead to his association with us. This drug will be invaluable for elimination of our enemies. No longer will we look foolish in the eyes of the world with our crude methods of assassination.'

'And Vladimir?' Sergei asked.

'He has been working undercover as a chauffeur at the Embassy here in London. He and I have formed good links for you scientists to perfect your work. The snow and your new baby will have distracted anyone that suspected you might have another agenda.'

In spite of himself, Sergei smiled. He remembered the innocent speculations in the village of Drum Mhor, and the excitement on the face of that young lad Joker when he thought he had cornered a spy. Bringing himself back to the present, his eyes smouldered as he focused on the woman in front of him.

Tatyana removed her cloak and went to hang it over the back of a chair. She retrieved a paper from the inside of her bra. 'Here is the number of the Swiss contact. You will meet him tonight in a bistro near Pimlico. It is essential that you are not followed, so Vladimir will take you on the tube. Have you brought jeans and casual wear with you?'

Sergei nodded.

'Good,' nodded Tatyana, 'I think that is the business concluded for the moment.' A tentative smile slowly threatened to unfreeze her perfect red mouth. As Sergei watched her, he could see the warmth travel up to her arctic eyes. 'Some vodka?' She smiled knowingly. 'And I have some caviar; perhaps you need reminding of the flavours of your own country? But I am forgetting, for should we not have some champagne? You have to celebrate the birth of your child, do you not?'

His eyes hooded as though hypnotised, Sergei watched her walk over to the refrigerator and take out a bottle of Dom Pérignon from which she expertly eased out the cork. He watched the spume of silver bubbles cascade into the chilled glasses and felt the familiar arousal stirring in his loins. Before she could turn round, he moved up behind her and undid the tight plait, allowing the pale hair to fall down over her shoulders in a stream of liquid satin. Gently he ran his hands down her body, firmly smoothing the perfect line of her hips. Her short skirt rode up with the friction of his body and Sergei's breathing quickened. Turning her around in order to kiss her, he was ready for a smooth capitulation. Instead Tatyana stepped back, out of his arms, and handed him his drink. They clinked glasses and savoured the champagne, gazing into each other's eyes as they drank.

'Do you love her?'

Sergei noted the pained expression on her face and shook his head. 'No, it's just a job, my darling. We are committed to what we do. We have been since we were students. Now this is the real test and we must keep strong. I like her. She reminds me of you; that is why I chose her, but she is nothing like you. No fire, no ice, no passion. I love only you, my beautiful Tatyana. You are my life, my soul. I need only you.'

'And your son? What about him?'

'He is my passport, my darling. That is all. Suzannah gives me credibility. Without her I would not be allowed to travel so easily. What about you? Do you think I don't ache with fear and jealousy at the thought of you living here with Vladimir?' He narrowed his eyes, looking at her over the rim of his glass. 'Do you think I don't wonder what you do in the nights?'

'Very well,' she nodded, 'let us just enjoy now. No more accusations, all right? We must keep faith in each other.' She raised her glass. 'To us!' She smiled flirtatiously, 'And to you, Sergei, my dearest love.'

Sergei groaned as her hands pulled his face down to hers and he tasted the wet mouth, sweet from the wine. 'My darling, I can't wait any longer.'

Tatyana took the glasses and indicated to Sergei to bring the bottle. 'We have all afternoon and I have to show you many many times just how much I have missed you.'

Sergei took the glasses from her and set them on the table. He dropped to his knees and held her slim hips and warm belly to his face, burying his face into her softness before pulling her down on to the carpet. Facing each other on their knees, he drew her towards him, kissing her hard, and then bending her back, he manoeuvred her long legs up over his shoulders. Tatyana lay beneath him, her long, silky hair spread out over the carpet, her eyes partially closed in anticipation, listening to the sounds of him unfastening his belt. Her body strained up towards him and she moaned, 'Now, I am yours, now…'

CHAPTER 25

Showers of windswept sleet continued to fall upon London. In spite of the weather the medical conference was a resounding success. On the second day Sergei's research paper on the cardiac effect and treatment of poisoning was well received. Muted applause and polite questions followed his report. Isakov approached him and insisted they sit together at lunch. Sergei kept his head averted during the soup course, preferring to talk to the French delegate about her work. She was due to speak later in the afternoon.

Surreptitiously he glanced to his left, where Isakov was relishing a portion of steak pie. Seeing that he had Sergei's attention at last, Isakov said, 'You did a good job on that research, my friend. I know you are one of the most honourable men in our profession, but I have my suspicions that some are not as scrupulous as you. This evening I am going to see a journalist I met last night and I am going to share with him some of the problems we have in our work.' His voice lowered to a whisper and he glanced over his shoulder. 'You know what I am talking about.'

'Yes, perhaps I do.' Sergei wiped his mouth with a linen napkin. He went on, his mouth still hidden behind the white cloth, 'But do you think that is wise? Do you not think people at home might be displeased?'

'There are many who are watching the progress of our country and they are alert to some of the more underhand tactics that are involved. I don't think anyone would dare to harm me, especially after such a high profile event such as this. I was interviewed at the airport when I arrived,' he preened, and added, 'and my face was on CNN last night.'

Nervously the scientist glanced about him and unseen, Sergei dropped the prepared tablet given to him by agent into Isakov's wine then promptly filled up the half-drained glass. He motioned for the other man to drink a toast with him, and together they clinked the crystal tumblers.

'To our country,' Sergei smiled over the rim.

'Yes, I will drink to that, my friend. Good paper, Sergei. Excellent.' Within seconds he shook his head and blinked rapidly, the effect of the drug making him woozy. I am sorry,' Isakov mumbled, almost inaudibly. I am suddenly not feeling so well. Please, if you will excuse me, I really feel terrible.'

'Shall I help you get a cab back to your hotel? I plan to leave shortly myself. I have to get back up to Inverness. My girlfriend has just had our baby. Do you remember my Scottish girlfriend Suzannah?'

'Yes, of course. I thought she reminded me of your ex-girlfriend, Tatyana. What happened to her?'

'God knows,' replied Sergei, looking away quickly.

'I feel very dizzy; perhaps the pre-luncheon champagne was stronger than I thought.' Isakov's eyes glazed over and his speech slurred. 'I must lie down.'

'Of course, let me help you. Take my arm,' said Sergei solicitously.

Sergei walked with the sick man out of the room, supporting his drooping body with his arm, but out by the lift, Isakov fell backwards, crashing on to the marble floor. Immediately Sergei knelt down and felt the pulse in his neck. He made to resuscitate the man and performed the necessary actions in front of the waiters who had gathered.

'Help him!' the French delegate shouted. 'Someone, please call an ambulance!' She had followed the two men from the table and was worried by the sudden deterioration in the Ukrainian scientist's condition.

'It is too late, I'm afraid. It seems that the man has had a massive heart attack.' Sergei stood up, shaking his head, his face a mask of concern.

After the removal of Isakov's body, the afternoon session of the conference was cancelled. Carrying his overnight case, Sergei made a silent exit from the building and took a taxi to the airport; just one more anonymous, impersonal businessman. No words were exchanged with the doorman or the driver. He sat back in the seat, lost in his own thoughts as the London sights passed his unseeing eyes. He felt a moment of passing regret that he would not have the opportunity to listen to the Frenchwoman's paper. He shrugged and closed his mind to the taunting thought of the long black-silk-clad legs that had pressed against his own beneath the table as they had played with their food. At the airport Sergei made his way over to check in for his flight to Inverness. The runways were covered by a dusting of snow but there were no major delays. He picked up his overnight holdall and slipped his boarding pass and ticket into the top pocket of his suit jacket. Seeing that he had plenty of time, he decided to unwind with a drink before proceeding to Departures. He strolled over to a café counter and ordered a coffee.

'Make that two,' a familiar voice added.

Sergei spun round and stared into a pair of Gucci sunglasses.

'I had to see you before you left, just one more time.'

'Two coffees, both black.' Sergei ordered the Polish waitress.

Tatyana carried the tray over to a table and pulled two chairs close together. 'We have an hour, my darling; you know I couldn't let you go without seeing you. Don't give Suzannah any reason to doubt your identity. It is imperative that you maintain your cover.'

Sergei nodded, stretched over to take her hand and lifted it to his lips. Looking into her eyes he saw the cold crushed-ice quality that she reserved for their professional business dealings.

'I will get in touch with you by the usual means when we need to use you again.'

'And if I need to use you again?' he added, a mischievous glint in his eye. He took her hand and kissed her rose petal nails.

Tatyana's face softened and she stroked his hand and stared into his eyes. Her own blue eyes glittered. 'It is imperative that we remain apart for some time, you know that?'

'Perhaps,' Sergei agreed, 'but it is so hard, for you are my love, Tatyana, you are my destiny.'

'I know, my darling, I know, but I worry now that you have a child. You may be tempted to leave our organization.'

'I have just killed a man on your orders. I am leaving you only because you have ordered me to and I have no idea when I will see you again. It is I, Tatyana, who should be worried. Do you know what it is like living with a woman that I don't love, and never knowing when I will see you again? I will tell you. It is hell. You are sending me to hell.'

Tatyana looked at him dispassionately, at his tall figure, his strong, beautiful face, his immaculate charcoal suit. She studied him, imprinting him on her mind. 'Kiss me, Sergei; *ya budu vsegda lyubit tebya.*'

When Sergei landed in Inverness the daylight was gone. He picked up an evening paper on his way to hire a car, and frowned at the stark headlines:

UKRAINIAN SCIENTIST DIES OF HEART ATTACK AT LONDON CONFERENCE

Forcing himself to compartmentalise his thoughts, he tried to concentrate on the road west and the community that awaited him. Leaving the lights of the town behind, Sergei followed the snow banked shores of Loch Ness, the placid water of the loch the colour of ink and no doubt, he thought, hiding its own dark secrets. The road was dwarfed by forests of tall pine, and above him half a moon gleamed through a troubled sky. Sergei felt a sudden overwhelming longing to return to the small Highland glen and to the simplicity that was Suzannah and his new son. He reflected on the juxtaposition of his character, which altered like a Machiavellian prince from one persona to another. As he drove, the weather worsened. It was hard to focus through the myriad of snowflakes dancing in the headlights. The road snaked round sharp bends and through dark forests of conifers. Snow lay heaped on the branches, turning the scene into a magical fairyland.

Sergei struggled as sleep weighed heavily on his eyelids. Opening a window he let the freezing cold permeate the car and he started to sing loudly a song from his school days. An hour passed, and still he remained hunched over the wheel, squinting out into the white flurries. His shoulders ached and he felt mesmerised by the falling snow. Tension, that's what it is, I am too tense, he told himself. Once he got out and jumped up and down by the roadside to revive himself. Another hour passed and still he met no traffic on the lonely stretch of road.

It was with relief and impatience to be back in the Highland glen that he finally turned off the main road and headed over the hill and down the long single track towards Drum Mhor. Sergei's eyes strained as he peered out into the night, desperately trying to avoid skidding on the lethal surface. He continued leaning forwards trying to see out of the windscreen, heavy with falling flakes, the wipers hypnotic in their metronomic rhythm. He imagined he saw the face of Tatyana in front of him. He could hear her voice and images of her legs, her breasts, her beautiful mouth and long silken hair flashed before him. Sergei's eyes were drooping, exhausted from two nights of fiery passion.

Forcing himself back to the present, he put the car's headlights on full beam to take advantage of a lull in the snowstorm. Just as he took one hand off the steering wheel to open the window again, he felt the car swerve furiously towards the verge. Panic immediately sent the adrenalin rushing through his veins and he frantically pulled at the wheel which was already rigid in a tight lock. It was too late. The car hurtled down the embankment, rolling over and over before settling with a sickening thud on its roof. The night continued black and silent and the snow continued to fall. No one else drove over the hill that night and the temperature plummeted. Soon the telltale signs of the car's fatal tracks were obliterated.

It was only when dawn approached and the snow plough scraped its way past the scene of the accident that a shout from the raised cab broke the silence on the hill.

'Look at that, Murdo, is that not a car over there, down there on the left? Stop! There's been an accident. Yes, I can see it now, there's a grey car upside down, over there, half buried in that drift; the headlights are still on. Oh my God, it's the ghost car.'

CHAPTER 26

The snow lay muffled in white drifts. Curtains twitched at windows and faces tilted towards the swish of any unfamiliar car gliding past. Eyes were bright with excitement and curiosity. Voices were hushed and lips pulled into concerned lines of sympathy.

'Oh the poor thing, did you hear what's happened now?'

'The police have taken the body, of course, but I hear there's to be… questions!'

Kathleen's Tea Room buzzed with the soft hum of a telegraph pole. The clang of the shop's bell was greeted with all eyes turned at a possible new source of information. Doris was quite the queen, ruling over the villagers' need for sustenance throughout this tragedy.

'I hear there will be no funeral here. He'll be sent back to his own folk for that. What a fine young man he was, and what a shame. It could have happened to anyone on a night like that. They say the hill was like one of those bobsled courses.'

'Aye, but there was a warning, a premonition,' someone else chipped in. 'Remember the night Wee Eck saw the ghost car? Oh, it just makes shivers run up and down my scalp and go scooting down my back.'

'I hear she's gone already. Some fancy lawyer from Edinburgh drove up and helped her with "the enquiries". Hmmmm, makes you wonder what was going on. Maybe there was some truth that Sergei was a spy.'

'Aye, I heard that, right enough. Joker was telling his father that he found a red book, full of little notes it was, about submarines and things. There were codes and everything...'

The gossip continued and only James, Iona, Murdo, Paula and Robert kept their own counsel. They knew that the men who came and searched Iona's house and the bedroom shared by the young couple were a different kind of police than those they were used to. The officers from Inverness advised Suzannah to take her young son and stay with her father for a while until the interest had died down.

As January drifted into February and warmed slightly into March, so memories of the spy drama faded and the glen returned to normal. One bright spring morning James MacTavish hurried over his breakfast, blowing over his porridge, impatient to be out of his house. When at last he shut the door behind him, he sniffed exultantly at the tangy sea breeze. Breathing deeply he scanned the horizon for porpoises or killer whales frolicking in the bay. He saw the haze of white snowdrops and autumn crocuses that had bravely ventured out from under the old gorse, itself already showing signs of life. He could hear the flap of Iona's sheets which threatened to blow right off the washing line.

Today was the day that he was going to send off for a wife. The old letter of application had long since been binned, James having felt that the round mark of the treacle tin did not lend itself to a good character representation. The previous week he had bought another magazine while on a shopping trip to Inverness, and had driven home in quite a state of anticipation. He had settled himself down at his kitchen table with a cup of tea and studied his options, before duly circling the appropriate boxes with his requirements. Veering well away from the exotic options of the Philippines and Thailand, he had requested a lady from the south. He stated that an artistic type might be to his liking. He had a fancy for a woman who might spin her own wool, perhaps. He wrote at the bottom of the application that a woman with strong legs would be an asset, seeing as he lived in quite a hilly part of the world and was fond of walking himself.

Now James took his letter and like a man with a mission, he marched over to the post office where he demanded a book of first class stamps. Not allowing himself to be distracted by the presence of Hector Ogilvie, who was in the process of collecting his pension, James affixed the small square in place and surreptitiously left the intimacy of the small room before finally dropping the envelope like a red-hot coal into the post box. Relieved of that duty, James MacTavish jauntily walked the length of the village and detoured down to the Pipers Inn where he asked Donnie to pour him a pint of Guinness.

'Grand day, James,' Donnie greeted him. 'What are you up to today?'

'Just taking the air, laddie, and then I have to get up to the estate. A whole supply of fence posts is to be delivered. That'll be keeping me busy for a few weeks. What about yourself, are you busy, or is it too early yet for the tourists?'

'They're coming in twos and threes, not exactly droves. It's mostly just the locals keeping me going, now that all the fuss seems to have died down. Have you heard any news from Suzannah, James?'

'No, not a word. She's had a bit of a shock, but I suppose it's better for her down there in Edinburgh.'

'Aye, I heard that her ex-fiancé came up for her, and took her off. What do you make of Sergei then, do you think he was a spy, or had anything to do with that murder at his conference down there in London?'

Before James had a chance to answer, Hector burst into the bar with a look of bright expectancy on his face. His weathered skin had a glow like a russet apple that had been given a lick. 'Give me a Guinness, lad, for it's payday for me. I've got a delivery of herring from old Murchison and I need the strength to get home and salt it.'

James and the old man chinked glasses and they both took a satisfying swallow of the bitter brew, savouring the burnt flavour.

'Aaaah,' Hector sighed blissfully. Inelegantly he wiped his

mouth with the back of a grimy hand and looked in his sideways fashion at the two men. 'Are you still convinced that foreign lad was a spy?'

'No, Hector, we are not; we only know what others are saying and they don't know any more than we do!' Donnie grinned as he polished glasses and stacked them in gleaming rows on the shelf behind him.

'Well,' wheezed the old man, 'I should mind your tongue, for the place is moving with folk that I don't know. Strangers with shifty eyes.'

Just then a man who had been sitting at a table nursing a half-pint of lager approached the trio at the bar. 'Grand day, can I buy you a drink?'

Hector winked at James and nodded. 'Aye, you can. What brings you to Glen Mhor, then?'

The stranger tapped his Ordnance Survey map and smiled, 'Walking. I have come up to enjoy the scenery. I seem to be lucky with this lovely spring weather and was hoping to do a bit of a hike this afternoon.'

James tipped back his drink and nodded. 'Aye, it's a grand day for a walk. Have you come far?'

'I'm from London, actually.'

'Good God, is that the time?' Hector nudged James. 'Get that down you, James, and give me a hand to get the fish home and you just never know, I might give you a couple later on when they're done.'

The visitor watched their exit, and with a bemused look on his face, he turned back to Donnie. 'Was it something I said?'

'Well, yes, and no.' replied the barman amiably. 'You see, we've had a lot of interest in the place since a man was killed on an icy stretch of road back in January.'

'Is it so unusual to have road accidents in winter on roads such as these?' asked the stranger.

'No, but when the man is a scientist from Ukraine, and a

Ukrainian scientist has just been killed in London, and he was coming back to his girlfriend here, then yes, we have been inundated with people and police and newspapers and what not.'

'Was there a connection between the two men?' persisted the visitor.

'They say so.' Donnie lifted the flap in the bar and proceeded to collect the empty glasses from the tables.

That night Hector sat wearily by his Rayburn stove in his small kitchen. Around him were the herrings with their heads cut off, already soaked in water and now lying on their backs covered in a blanket of coarse salt.

His winter long johns and vests had been washed and duly dried in the fresh wind blowing from the southwest. Now they lay folded on a clothes horse by the side of the open fire. Tonight he was going to have a bath. The first since the autumn.

He took down his green diary and wrote:

Dry and windy. Saw the first swallows. Did a wash. Had a drink in the bar. There was a plain clothes policeman there. Salted the herring.

CHAPTER 27

That year in Drum Mhor, April began with a showery blast of cold wind blowing in from the northwest. Hector recorded that it had been blustery with fresh snow lying down low on the mountains. He was spending his days gathering the ewes down from the hills for dipping before the lambing season started.

Over the hill, on the croft that nestled by the loch, Paula sat on the stone dyke surveying the jostling sheep that she and Robert had gathered that morning. The baaing and crying and endless butting and shoving was beginning to drive her mad, and she retreated to the wall to save her toes from getting crushed by the sharp hooves.

'When is Eck coming to help you?' she shouted over the raucous chorus of agitated animals.

'Any minute. He said he'd be here at the back of ten, no doubt planning a cup of tea before we start. Are you not staying, then?' Robert looked up from the trough where he was preparing the toxic wash for his sheep.

'Well I will, if you need me, but I said I'd meet some of the women over at the Tea Room at eleven. We're planning to start a new session of Keep Fit in the hall, and we were going to have a coffee before we started.'

Robert averted his face to hide the smile. His eyes crinkled and he muttered almost to himself, 'I suppose you'll be having a scone as well?'

'Don't you start your insinuations, Robert Ross; it's very important that I support the community. All the girls that were in the belly-dancing in the play just loved the sessions and we thought it would be good to keep fit now that spring is in the air.'

'Aye well, but I hope I get some of your time as well. If you work as you promised for me, I can assure you that I will keep the fat off your bones.'

'It isn't really for me, but I'm happy to lead them in some aerobics. I did a bit in London, so I think I can work out some moves for the more athletic ones.'

Paula jumped off the wall and blew Rob a kiss. She had seen Wee Eck's jeep turn into the driveway and ran off to make a flask of tea for the two men. She then packed a small holdall with her green leotard and purple leggings and pulled on her Barbour jacket. She climbed into her small Fiat, and drove off with a shout to the men at the sheep fank. Rob and Eck both raised their eyes as though to heaven.

The jangle of bells heralded her arrival into the Tea Room and looking round she saw that two tables were already full with her potential new students for the Keep Fit and Aerobic Class. With dismay her eyes settled on Margaret, ensconced between Lottie and Dolly. Oh Lord, thought Paula, it looks like I have three sumo wrestlers on my hands. I doubt they will even manage the shoulder lifts or the head rolls, never mind the 'boxercise moves'. Keeping her reservations private, Paula cheerily called out a general greeting and went to sit beside Iona who was chastely drinking a large mug of milky coffee, complete with three spoonfuls of sugar.

'What a day! I thought the wind might just blow me up to the tree tops. I can tell you, Murdo's face was a study of scowls when I took off, leaving him with a load of sheep to dip. I called over to Hector and the old boy was glad to come and give a hand. He'll get a half-bottle of whisky for his trouble and he'll stay for his tea. Now, have you brought the music and everything?'

Paula nodded and smiled up at Lizzie behind the till. She ordered a cup of weak tea, and emphasised loudly that she did not want any home baking with it.

Kathleen growled under her breath and leant over to hiss into Lottie's ear, 'Has she never heard that bodies need fuel before exercise? I don't doubt the ambulance will be called out if folk have to jiggle about without a wee scone to keep them going. We'll all be fading away, make no mistake.' She squeezed her substantial thighs between the chairs, wheezing as she replaced the laden tray down on to the counter. 'Now, Lizzie, remember, no awful screeching music while I'm gone, and offer the newly baked Madeleine cakes if any tourists stop by. We'll be about an hour, well that's if we make it. I'm sure I'll come back just as a mere sylph, due to starvation if nothing else.'

The other ladies tittered and nodded, knotting their headscarves tighter under their chins.

The hall was cold and damp. A window had been broken by some wayward child from the play group that hired the hall on Tuesday morning. The Hall Committee had yet to make a decision about mending it. The ladies squirmed into track suit bottoms and T shirts. The wooden floor was a patchwork of brown and black stains, the legacy from generations of spilt beer, and Joanne, who had the thankless job of mopping up after the dances, had failed miserably in making the floor a place that one wanted to lie on.

Twenty-two ladies emerged from the toilets and wandered into the hall, looking around for a heater that they might press against.

Iona attempted to raise the spirits by running on the spot, and making jokes. 'When I'm finished here, my goodness there will be no stopping me, it will be on to Miss World. That Murdo MacPherson will never be able to catch up with me when he gives me the chase on a Friday night!'

The young mothers were a delight, dressed in their colourful Lycra outfits and showing off their already tight bums and thighs. Seeing the heavy set taking position at the rear of the hall, Iona waved cheerfully at Margaret who shyly fluttered a few fingers in response. Dressed in a jogging suit of baby blue, her wholesome figure was almost completely hidden and her springy brown curls were crammed fiercely into a pink satin bow. Robert is a man of extremes, Iona thought as she diverted her gaze to the lithesome figure at the front of the class. Paula wore a Green Goddess-style leotard. Her body was long and boyish and her legs were as strong and graceful as a ballerina's.

Paula called the class to order. As the music began pounding out the insistent beat from a recording of Madonna, she stretched her swan's neck to the side and arched her arms to form a graceful curve. Dolly, Lottie and Kathleen followed suit, visualizing themselves as mirroring the beautiful woman in front of them. Margaret remembered the ballet lessons of her childhood and, following Paula's lead, she stretched her back, stepped to the side, and pulled her unyielding waist over to the left and then to the right. I've seen more movement in a coffin, Kathleen thought unkindly. Not one for full-length mirrors, she imagined that her own once-pliable body had still the same allure it had when she was young.

The lesson went well, and the windows soon steamed up as the ladies of the new season's Keep Fit puffed and struggled to twist and jump and gyrate. It was during the penultimate exercise of pelvic thrusts, done en masse on towels laid on the floor, that Elvis the Post arrived with a registered package to be signed for by one of the participants. He poked his head into the hall and his eyes nearly shot out of their sockets. For the first time in his life, he saw a sea of female bodies moving in unison as they should only do in the darkest part of the night. Coughing and spluttering, and keeping his eyes from swivelling back to twenty-two thrusting pelvises, he left the precious packet from the Royal Mail, still with the unsigned receipt form attached, and fled.

When the session was over the ladies heaved out of the hall like cattle from a byre and laughed uproariously at the look on the face of the poor postman.

'He must have thought it was like a dream come true! We'll have to put a padlock on the door next time,' chortled Dolly, 'or all the men will be making excuses to come and see our gorgeous bodies. I don't mind admitting it but I think some of us have the look of a Rubens painting!'

'Aye, you're right there, Dolly,' agreed Lottie. 'Real men appreciate real women.' She sniffed knowingly at Paula's skinny back. 'I'm told that real men like a good voluptuous body, something that they can really hold on to. Look at that Titian bloke as well; he loved to paint great lumps of flesh on his angels and Madonnas. Now that is what many still call beauty. Come on, Kathleen, I think we've earned one of your scones and butter and jam.'

Paula shook her head, laughing as she wiped the sweat from the tendrils escaping her headband. 'That could only happen here,' she giggled and then saw Margaret about to leave the hall. 'Did you have fun?' she asked her former rival.

'I did actually, but I really do want to lose a few pounds. I would rather look like you than a model that Rubens might want to paint. I've been trying for years to get thin, but I just eat. Boring cottage cheese and lemon juice doesn't seem to tempt me much.'

'I could lend you this CD and you could try doing the exercises yourself during the week,' Paula offered. Then she added slyly, 'and maybe forego Kathleen's cakes for a while?'

Margaret hooted, returning to her usual confident self. 'Are you saying I should go on a diet?'

'Well, maybe I am.'

'And what would be the point? You come up here and steal my boyfriend, effectively ruin my life, and now you think you can be my personal adviser on how to catch another man. You don't half have a cheek.' She trounced around, and in her rage nearly collided with a black car with shaded windows.

'Bloody hell, see what you nearly made me do?' she yelled at Paula.

'Shut up, Margaret! Look! It's reversing back to us.'

The car came to a halt, the electric window of the passenger side hummed down and an exquisitely beautiful woman looked out. She surveyed the two hot and casually dressed women disdainfully. 'Zees ees Drum Mhor?'

Paula nodded. She took in the silver-blonde hair, falling like a silken waterfall over a black cashmere polo neck. She noted the red manicured nails and the eyes the colour of harebells in the spring.

'Are you looking for someone?' she asked politely.

'Perhaps. I look for woman named Suzannah.'

'She's gone. She left here. I'm sorry I can't help.'

'*Harasho*. I vanted to see zees place. That ees all.'

'Bye,' smiled Paula at the beautiful stranger. Together with an awestruck Margaret, she watched the black car purr towards the village.

That evening in Drum Mhor there were groans from those with stiffened limbs, unused to exercise after the long dark months of winter. Sheep huddled and bleated after the day's indignities in the dipping trough. In the warmth of the Pipers Inn, Elvis the Post shared the horrors and delights of being at the receiving end of a mass pelvic thrust. Listening avidly, Hector's eyes lit up lasciviously and he licked his lips, leaving the spittle to bubble at the corners of his mouth.

Meanwhile, by the flickering candlelight in the bedroom under the slanting roof, Paula knelt in front of Robert. The sheets were pulled back and she ran oil over his olive-skinned shoulders and down his sinewy arms. The dark eyes were in shadow; only the chiselled line of the nose and jaw could be made out. Leaning forward and straining her slim flanks she offered her breasts to his mouth. A mouth the colour of dark stained mulberries.

In a neighbouring village, on a narrow bed, Tatyana lay alone. The curtains were open and she was gazing out of the small panes of glass. It had been madness to come, madness to want to see for herself where he had died. Madness to want to see the child.

CHAPTER 28

On the twenty-eighth of April the first cuckoo was heard in Drum Mhor. The lilting call echoed throughout the glen. Crofters straightened their backs and rubbed a hand over hot brows and looked about with a sense of joy filling their hearts. Spring was here, and lambs, fluffy and full of fun, frolicked in the grass that ran down to the shore. Iona stood as still as a statue at the bottom of the field. She leant against her crook and surveyed her new livestock running races for the sheer joy of being alive. Her brow was furrowed however, for at her feet the heavy body of a ewe strained and cried as it tried to deliver an unwilling lamb. She had been watching it for the past hour, first from the kitchen window and then finally coming to have a closer look. She knew the sheep would need some assistance, and she knew she would possibly have to reach in and pull the wee thing out, but she preferred to have someone near by in case things were not as straightforward as she hoped. As luck would have it she heard the rickety sound of Hector's ramshackle bike. He was riding precariously, wobbling from side to side; Iona prayed that he had not been on the bottle. If anyone could help her, she knew he was her man.

'Hector!' she yelled as he drew near to her fence. 'Can you come and give this poor ewe a look for me?'

'Oh, well, maybe I can stop for a wee minute,' he muttered, and without further ado the old man screeched to a halt and left his bike propped up against the fence. His dog, Charlie, had been running alongside, secured tightly to a bit of string. 'Can I put him in the barn, Iona? He's that blooming helpful, I'm frightened he might grab the poor wee thing's head and yank it off.'

'Aye, Hector, you just put him in there.'

The old man walked down the field towards her and saw the afflicted sheep straining and groaning. The eyes were out of focus, dazed with pain and incomprehension. The belly was stiff and swollen and hard as a drum.

'Poor beast, I need to feel inside her, but I need to give my hands a wash, Iona lass, I'll just use your kitchen if I may.'

Before long Iona watched as the old man's hand disappeared inside the sheep. He strained, trying to keep in tune with the contractions, and then looking up at Iona's concerned face, he shook his head. 'I think it's dead, but we need to get it out. Have you any new born orphans?'

Iona nodded. 'One just; poor wee thing. I have it in the kitchen by the Rayburn. The mother died during the delivery.'

'Right, lass, go and get me a good sharp knife and bring out the wee lambie and we'll see what we can do.'

Iona dashed back to the house and soon reappeared carrying a struggling woolly bundle in the crook of one arm, and a knife and pail with the other. She carried the bleating creature down to where Hector was kneeling beside the stricken ewe. He had already heaved the stillborn lamb out of the dazed mother. Taking the knife from Iona he immediately made an incision into the back of the neck, and deftly skinned the small slippery body. Amazed at his dexterity, Iona watched him wrap the dead skin over the lively kicking orphan and gently led it over to the mother who was already struggling to get up. She sniffed and prodded her new baby with her nose. Hector leant over and pulled her teats, forcing the milk to come down. As though by magic Iona watched as the two bereaved animals were united.

'That was bloody marvellous, Hector, you certainly know a trick or two! I would have been at my wits' end, even trying to get the dead one out. Thank you for that.'

Hector just grunted and picked up the dead lamb and put it in the bucket. 'It's a grand day. A good smell in the air, and Young Polly calved over at the McKenzie place. Bonny wee thing, too. Myself and Jim have been having a few anxious moments about her. Now, where's Charlie, I must away and see to that field up by the shop. I'm supposed to be cutting the lambs up there. I'll just give my hands a wee wash if I may?'

'Right, very good.' Iona walked along beside him, trampling the patches of daisies and buttercups that were already providing a carpet for the new lambs to play on. They reached Iona's kitchen and she put the kettle on for a cup of tea.

'Many thanks again, Hector. Oh! Listen, it's the cuckoo! Does it not turn your thoughts to romance, Hector?' Iona laughed as she watched the old man lather up his arms and hands.

'Aye it does, Iona. Aye it surely does!'

While the drama of life was unfolding in the field above him, James MacTavish was treating Elvis the Post to a quick dram before he continued on his rounds.

'What a great day, James. I see you have your garden all planted and it's looking pretty good, I might add.'

Elvis got up from the garden pew and walked over to the rows of neatly planted potatoes. He bent over and read the seed packets that were stuck on a stick at the end of each drill. James smiled proudly and accepted his due praise. Elvis was the same age as himself and the two had gone through school together. By contrast though, Elvis had married young. He had been rather a dashing lad, with hair as black as the wing of a crow. He had cut quite a figure with the girls at the dances, preening in freshly ironed pink shirts and a black leather jacket that gave him illusions of being a dead ringer for Elvis Presley. He didn't last very long as a bachelor however, for Betsy Gordon had bewitched him and Elvis was now the father of six. His strong shoulders looked well in his postman's uniform and he still sported a definite swagger when he strutted from his red Land Rover to the various houses and crofts that were part of his daily round. He attached tremendous importance to his job of delivering Her Majesty's Post, together with any gossip that he gleaned from the various kitchens along the way.

His wife, Betsy, had developed into a great churchwoman, raising funds each year for the poor souls in Africa, but in the privacy of her own house, she wasn't afraid to give any of her own brood the feel of her hand across the ear. Elvis wisely kept a wide berth between them whenever he sensed that Betsy was on the warpath. So it was with a comical raising of his left eyebrow that he greeted James's news that he was expecting a lady from the south to be coming to stay for a few days.

'Well, James, don't tell me you are going to succumb at last? I've never heard of you entertaining without at least an introduction. It must be this balmy weather that has beguiled you.' Elvis laughed and drank the last of his wee dram, and handing back the empty glass, he started back to where he had parked.

'I think she'll suit me very well,' James retorted. 'You just bide your time and see. I have had a few conversations with her on the telephone and she thinks she might like living here in Drum Mhor. We'll just have to wait and see. She is arriving tomorrow afternoon so I have to go to Inverness and meet the train. She'll be staying at Meg Sullivan's guesthouse over in the village for a few days, just to see how she and I get along. I don't want us to rush things too much. Better see how we like each other face-to-face, if you know what I mean.'

Elvis threw his head back and laughed. 'You're an old rogue so you are, James MacTavish. I haven't got enough fingers or toes to count the girls you've let slip away. I don't know where you get your charm, or your luck,' he added, thinking of his own nagging wife back in his house.

Whistling and waving cheerily out of the window, Elvis drove over the bumpy driveway up to the main road. He couldn't wait to get to the next house to report the news of the imminent arrival of the latest potential wife for James MacTavish.

CHAPTER 29

Victoria Finch was bubbling with excitement. Craning her neck, she peered around the substantial bulk of her fellow Edinburgh-bound traveller in order to see the view from the window. Idly she noted the changing landscape as the express train hurtled her northwards through the English countryside. As it charged through her native Oxfordshire, she silently bade farewell to the familiar velvety patchwork of green fields. She nodded and slept for a while, her pretty head leaning comfortably on the crisp dark suit of the businessman who sat like a mannequin, politely enjoying the familiarity of the young woman's warmth against him. The jolt of the braking train woke her with a start and she noted that they had pulled into Edinburgh's Waverley Station. Victoria apologised profusely for the damp spot she had left on her gallant knight's sleeve. Politely he demurred, and retrieving his briefcase he made his way reluctantly off the train.

For the remainder of her journey to Inverness Victoria sat glued to the window seat, her face alert, absorbing all the nuances of change in the passing trees, fields and fence posts. She was mesmerised by the darkening hues of the hills that dominated the window space as the train left the fertile lowlands and climbed from Perth up through the Highlands. Her heart was hammering as she viewed for the first time a land that was stark, where snow still lay in jagged crevices on impossibly high mountains. The train thundered and weaved and crossed wide brown rivers, and whistled through stations that were gone in a wink.

Victoria was not an academic girl, having left school at sixteen to attend a home economics course in her local college, but she had read a lot of novels so she felt she knew what to expect from this adventure that she was undertaking. Ever since she had accepted James's invitation to visit she was convinced that she was doing the right thing. Her doting parents had been very supportive and as ever had been manipulated by their effervescent daughter's changeable whims. For as long as she could remember, Victoria, with her golden curls and sweet, round baby face had been the apple of her father's eye. She had grown into his delightful princess, and neither of her parents could understand why their beloved treasure had not been snapped up and married to one of the suitably rich young men in their home town. They were beginning to see that their chocolate box beauty with huge green eyes and golden ringlets lived only for herself and had no real concept of long-term commitment or fidelity. Her head swam with visions of herself as Scarlett O' Hara or Catherine Earnshaw, and she spun webs of fantasy around her rather dull life. Her parents were aware that she barely lived in the real world, thus it was that they hoped that this invitation to Scotland in order to meet a mature Highland man might be the answer and not end up as another of her many flighty adventures. They had their doubts that, at thirty-three, their darling would ever be happy with one of her suburban contemporaries.

So here she was, dressed in a girlish green and white embroidered dirndl skirt with an emerald cashmere cardigan slung over her shoulders, a picture strangely emulating a Doris Day movie of the 1950s. She had brought a black woollen poncho which was nestled beside her suitcase, ready to put on. Approaching Inverness, Victoria's eyes widened as the yellow broom beneath a raw lapis blue sky gave way to a large town that clustered along the banks of the wide, silver River Ness.

Victoria was a romantic young woman who saw her adventure rather like a scene from a film in which she was the star. When she read the profile that James had sent her, she imagined herself going to meet an older 'Young Lochinvar' and living in a rustic stone house, where she would huddle from the monsters that live in the lochs, and where she could paint, and illustrate her wildly imaginative romantic novels. She could see it all in her mind's eye. Unfortunately she had not begun to write a novel yet. She imagined it would be relatively simple once she was sitting in the cottage by the paraffin light. James had specifically asked for someone that was artistic. She took out her powder compact and delicately dabbed her upturned nose, then applied a shimmer of crushed strawberry ice lipstick to her Cupid's bow mouth.

The train finally drew into Inverness station after its long journey from the south, and passengers wearily descended on to the platform, looking for the exit, for people, or for taxis.

Victoria stepped down from the train and looked about helplessly, wondering how she was going to recognise James MacTavish and it was in this way that James, who had been standing at the barrier waiting for the London train, set eyes on his intended for the very first time. James took one look at her, and checking her image against the photograph that she had sent him, blinked at her reality. James was enchanted. Victoria scanned the faces around her and realised that a mature man of medium height had separated himself from the crowd and was advancing towards her. Dressed in tweeds, the trousers cut off just below the knees, he stood apart in the crowd. He cut quite a dash, she felt, as though he exuded confidence and self-importance. She noted that on his head was a matching deerstalker hat and in his hand he was carrying what appeared to be one of her letters and he was comparing her photograph with herself. Victoria took in his ruddy face and arched sandy eyebrows.

Taking a deep breath, she smiled at a beaming James. His angelic countenance was reminiscent of a fresco she had once seen in a church in Florence. She had laughed with her mother at the picture of a group of monks. The monk's faces had been round and good natured, with a golden fringe of hair and twinkling blue eyes. It was one of the kindest faces she had ever seen.

James stepped forward and, with a swashbuckling sweep of his arm, he took Victoria's small left hand and significantly kissed her ring finger. Looking up with mischief in his eyes, he made a show of taking off his hat then bowing in a most gentlemanly fashion.

'Welcome, my dear Victoria, to Inverness. I am very pleased to meet you and am looking forward to beginning our acquaintance.' Pausing to stare at her creamy complexion and white, even teeth, he sighed dramatically. 'My goodness, are all the girls down in the south as beautiful as you? I think I might need an armoured car to keep all the Highland men away from you, but seeing as I don't have that, I will just have to escort you back to Drum Mhor in the estate car.'

Victoria giggled at such an extravagant greeting, and simpered at the compliments. She wondered what kind of vehicle James MacTavish possessed. Perhaps it was one of those big Range Rover sorts that she had seen on TV dramas set in the Highlands of Scotland?

'Come away now, lass, first things first. We live quite a way from Inverness so I thought I would take the opportunity of doing a big shop while I'm in town. I usually like to stock up with all the necessary things, and visit Safeway and North Eastern Farmers. I hope you don't mind if we do that, then we can have a spot of high tea before we head back to Drum Mhor.'

Victoria nodded enthusiastically, imagining her new life, and wondering what he meant by The Estate. In his letter he had said that he lived in a stone cottage by the sea, but maybe in the Highlands that was a way of saying it was a small mansion. They made their way out into the May sunshine and James walked along purposefully, pushing the trolley with the bright red case and poncho and with his potential new wife following behind. She looked with some trepidation at the back of his neck, at the hair that peeped from below his hat, and at his sturdy legs. Then she saw the white pickup truck. The back was covered with a blue tarpaulin that still had a small puddle of rainwater sloshing in a corner.

'Och, I should have emptied this at home, but I was in such a hurry to get here,' James muttered, heaving her case off the trolley. 'Just you wheel this back into the station for me and we'll be off in a jiffy.'

When Victoria returned, James had already reversed out, and was sitting in the truck. Her case had been inelegantly stored in the back. She eyed the red plastic seat waiting for her, and she heaved herself up into the cab and settled down, fussing with the seat belt. Her Highland experience was already losing some of the glossy romantic notions of her daydreams.

Later, after the two had filled two supermarket trolleys full of bread and bacon and tins of meat, James politely asked Victoria what she liked to drink. 'What's your tipple then?' he said, eying the shelves and selecting three bottles of whisky for himself.

'I like white wine,' she replied, shutting her eyes at the memory of her father's well-stocked cellar.

'Very good, then I don't need to buy too much as I have demijohns full of the stuff: elderflower, primrose, rose-petal, and the best of the lot is the birch sap.'

Victoria sighed as he marched on, leaving the shelves of French, Italian and Chilean wines behind. He had selected a bottle of Blue Nun. Dinner was a treat in the cafeteria attached to the supermarket. James settled them at a bright table and recommended the macaroni cheese, peas and chips.

'Next time I promise I'll spoil you a bit better and take you to the Castle Tea Rooms, but for today I just want to get you home.' He then buttered his bread roll and set about eating with relish.

The journey over to the west was a joy. Victoria gasped as the views unfolded and lochs and castles whizzed by. James promised he would stop and let her look on another occasion. Her green eyes shone in the setting sun as she took in the mountains and glens, and James relished her small breathless pants of admiration.

'Now, here we are, home at last,' he announced as he drove down through the glen and along the road that lay parallel to the sea. 'That's my wee house there, and over there are the neighbours. No doubt the curtains will be twitching with everyone wanting to get a good look at you.'

Victoria gazed from right to left, at the empty spaces, the huge expanse of sea and the black shapes of the mountains that seemed to glower over the village.

'I asked Meg Sullivan to reserve a bed for you tonight at her bed and breakfast. Was I right to do that? I didn't want you to feel that you had to stay with me, until you felt you wanted to, if you know what I mean.'

Victoria smiled sweetly at James, and nodded shyly. 'Thank you, but I do want to get to know you. Can I not stay here with you?'

'Of course lass, I'll just give Meg a ring, and tell her that you won't be requiring her room after all. Now can you make yourself useful and bring in some of those bags. I'll get that great weight of a case in after I've finished phoning. Goodness knows what you've brought with you.'

So it was that on her first night in Drum Mhor, Victoria lay in the bed that old Nell MacTavish had occupied for over fifty years. The portrait of the old woman glowered in the hall and the Bible's pages were open at the verses telling of Joseph's interpretation of Pharaoh's dreams. With his characteristic optimism, James had dismissed the ominous messages of the days of gloom to come.

CHAPTER 30

Victoria was awakened early by the sound of a woman shouting at a dog. She lay still and registered the sounds that drifted through the open sash window. She could hear the peep and chatter of house martins in the eaves, and from fairly close the throb of a boat chugging along the bay. There was the baaing and bleating of lambs and a dog barking, and from somewhere close the sound of a kettle coming to the boil. She listened to the sound of feet approaching her door, and a gentle tap.

'Are you awake, lass? I've brought you a cup of tea.'

She smiled lazily and, shaking her head of long gold curls, she called for James to come in. 'What a beautiful day and I slept so well, it must have been the lullaby of the waves. I didn't know where I was when I woke. How are you?'

James eyed his future wife with heavy eyes. He had been awake half the night, prowling like a panther, fighting the temptation to just barge into the room and ravish her there and then. He was not a man who was accustomed to having to hold himself in check. His success with the fair sex over the years had always resulted in instant gratification. 'Oh well, you know, I'm quite weary, after the long drive and the excitement of having you here with me at long last.' He casually sat down on the edge of the bed and smelt the warmth of her body, and saw the milky whiteness of her neck and arms. I think I'll have to farm her out to Meg Sullivan after all, he thought, for if I don't, I'll be in between those sheets in a jiffy.

Victoria stretched languorously, causing her breasts to rise and taunt James further. He groaned with lust.

'Oh my goodness, it's time I was away, but I'll be back around four. You just make yourself at home and do your womanly things. No doubt Iona will be down shortly to look you over.'

'Do I not get a kiss goodbye?' Victoria looked up, her eyes closed to slits, like a cat.

God help me, thought James. Victoria closed her arms around his neck and kissed him chastely on his closed lips. The smell of her filled his head with ribbons of steam. He squeezed his eyes tight to block out the sight of her nearness, her fleshy nakedness. Never had his senses experienced such a jolt of electricity. He could not even inhale; it was as though a cloud of desire had filled his lungs and he thought he might burst. Blindly he rose from the bed and stumbled towards the door. Watching James's lumbering attempts at self-control, knowing just how he was feeling, Victoria smiled contentedly, imagining herself as a heroine on the silver screen. Later, after drinking her tea, she lay back on her pillow and closed her eyes. She let her imagination run free. With a little effort, she could almost imagine James had a look of Richard Burton, without that sultry ruggedness of course.

It was just after twelve when Iona and Paula came to inspect the 'mailbox bride' as they had taken to calling James's potential new wife. They found her rearranging his sitting room and putting new Indian-style cushions on his settee. They registered the sequins and soft silks and satins. They noted that she had added a white jute throw over the leather armchair and taken down some of his pictures of lighthouses. The room had been vacuumed within an inch of its life, the window thrown open, and all the ashes from the carpet had miraculously disappeared. There was an exotic jar full of incense sticks smoking a pungent aroma into the room.

'Hello there,' shouted Paula, competing with the loud Tchaikovsky that was filling the house.

'Hello!' shouted Victoria. 'Wait till I turn the music down; I love ballet music, it's just so romantic.'

Iona raised her eyebrows at Paula, and together they followed the apparition of Pre-Raphaelite beauty, clad in a citrus yellow caftan, out to the kitchen where she turned down the stereo. They felt quite dowdy in comparison, wearing blue jeans, T shirts and quilted body-warmer waistcoats. After the introductions they were treated to coffee which they took out to the garden. They sat together on James's pew in the sunshine. Victoria had grabbed a crocheted green shawl that she wrapped around her shoulders to shield her from the fresh wind that blew in from the sea. The visitors let her prattle about her plans for the house, and how she saw herself in the great scheme of things.

'I shall write novels, but I need to be inspired. I just want to wear my Indian clothes that I got on holiday with Mummy and Daddy last year and sit in the study and use those fish boxes covered with red cloth as my desk. It is just so perfect.'

'I think James works in there as well,' pointed out Iona. 'He's compiling a lot of research into a book on Scottish lighthouses. Perhaps you should have consulted him about the changes.'

'Excuse me, but we are to be married. I'm not sure if he told you, but James will be happy with anything I do here. I am definitely going to get rid of that dreary portrait in the hall. She puts the fear of God in me.'

'She was quite a fearsome woman when she was alive,' remembered Iona. 'I really do think you should consult with James over that; I know he was very fond of his mother.'

'Oh, it's his mother, is it?' Victoria looked surprised. 'Funny, he didn't say.'

Paula looked up as a piece of mud fell down from the eaves under the roof, catching her shoulder. 'Oh look! You have a nest of house martins. How lovely. They come back to the same place to breed every year.'

'Yes, and there's a hedgehog in the garden. James showed me that last night. He's delighted as it eats the slugs that go for his cabbages. I think I'm going to love it here.'

Iona frowned; she felt uneasy about this girl that had swept in like a fresh new broom. She heard Paula inviting her to the Keep Fit, and suggesting that they all go out for a drink together to get to know each other better. Iona looked out to sea, her face uncommitted.

'Has James had other women here, do you know?' The girl scanned both their faces, looking for clues as to why James might have advertised for a wife.

'He's very popular with the ladies,' Iona remarked, 'but he's fussy.'

'I'm quite surprised, as he's not so good looking, is he? I mean he's quite charming, and I do prefer older men, but he doesn't look like a lady's man, does he?'

'Don't judge a book by its cover,' quipped Iona. 'James has hidden depths, it would seem.'

Just then the post office Land Rover pulled up at the gate, spraying gravel as it braked sharply. Elvis jumped out, his eyes on stalks, anxious to make the acquaintance of the new young lady. He also knew that he would be reporting his findings in a lot of houses during the course of the afternoon. It was important to him that he had a good look at the new delivery.

'Grand day, Elvis,' Iona greeted the postman.

'Aye, it is that. Now I have a letter here for James, but I see he's not here.'

'I'll take that. I'm Victoria. Pleased to meet you,' said Victoria with a sense of importance. She eyed the tall black-eyed man and took in the cleft chin and chiselled features. Now that's the sort of man that really turns me on, she thought, and let her hand rest in his for a fraction too long.

After half an hour Paula and Iona took their leave, but almost before they were out of earshot, the two women burst out laughing.

'Oh my God! James has met his match. She'll eat him up and spit him out,' Paula giggled. 'Listen, Iona, do you hear the cuckoo?'

'I do. That bird has a lot to answer for; it seems to rid men's heads of any common sense they might have once possessed.' She sighed deeply, and went on, 'Poor James, I just hope he enjoys the ride before the horse bolts, for as sure as death, she'll do that.' Iona shook her head, imagining the worst.

CHAPTER 31

James MacTavish was in heaven. The sun shone brightly that summer in Drum Mhor, and the heat was so intense that big Donald Duff was convinced that he could fry an egg on his bald head, or so he kept boasting to any one that would listen.

The door of the village shop was wedged open and sometimes the odd sheep sneaked in and nosed in the basket containing out-of-date products that Doris kept surreptitiously beside the deep freeze. Some of the old age pensioners were not averse to gambling with packets of bran flakes that might be past the sell-by date.

James liked nothing better than to perambulate his new fiancée around the village. Holding a supporting arm against the small of Victoria's back he felt a certain possessive pride as they drew admiring glances and the odd wolf whistle when passing a parked forestry vehicle.

She had turned his life upside down. His house was now quite rearranged, and just last week he found the portrait of his mother leaning, face against the wall, in her old bedroom. James forgave everything, for with Victoria well and truly ensconced in his own bed his lust blinded him to all his previous reservations. Most afternoons she met him, bathed and waiting, wearing only a smile. She would lead him enticingly into the sitting room and there she would bend down and remove his boots, smiling teasingly through her feathery black lashes, waiting for the predictable rampant response to the merest suggestion of a touch to his straining lust.

The lads at work chortled as they noticed James nodding in the jeep as they drove around the estate. He had lost quite a bit of weight and his appearance was growing haggard, with his eyes lost in dark blue shadows.

'Not a bad way to go,' commented one lad, 'shagged to death by a nymphomaniac.'

'Aye, they say he got her by mail order. I think I might send away for one of those myself,' laughed his friend.

Hector, by contrast, could not look James in the eye when he was out walking with 'that woman'. He would look to the ground, pulling in Charlie the dog and nodding and muttering to himself. James was bemused by the absence of Hector's usual colourful repartee. He thought the old boy must be wildly jealous or else sickening for something.

By July the glen was simmering in the continuing heat wave. Paula was absorbed with meetings with the minister about another pageant that he had written. This year he was planning to recreate the Highland Clearances and incorporate some of the villagers as well as the children into key parts. He had hopes to stage the whole sad story on the beach, with the denouement of course being the boats arriving to take the poor evicted people away to the colonies. Paula recounted the day's events to Robert while she grilled mackerel for his dinner and poured fizzy white wine into their flute glasses.

'I told them that you would be a boatman, like you were before, in the Bonny Prince Charlie pageant. I hope you don't mind?' she smiled back at him with what she imagined was a beguiling expression. She went on, 'we should be able to get a quite a lot of support. I know Grace wants a part, and I even heard Dolly and Lottie saying they wouldn't mind being in it, seeing as they wouldn't have to remove their clothes and do any exotic dancing! Imagine that pair!'

Robert removed his shirt and threw it into the washing machine. He leant over her and kissed her neck. 'And what about the kids, what will they be doing?'

Paula wriggled out of his embrace and tossed him a loaf of

bread, laughing as she started slicing tomatoes. 'Oh the usual; they will be soldiers and Highlanders and evicting officers. The script reads well. I can just see Lottie being frogmarched off to a boat with young Billy bossing her about. He'll be in heaven!'

'And the love birds?' Robert chuckled. 'Will they be able to leave each other alone for five minutes, do you think?'

'I don't know about that,' Paula scowled. 'I doubt if James will let her out of his sight for five minutes. I'm getting sick of the way he won't take his hands off her. What's he afraid of?'

'Och, let them be. They'll come off the boil eventually. Did I hear that Eck was trying to make up to her in the pub the other night? Is that why your feathers are all ruffled? Are you a wee bit jealous that your one-time admirer has eyes for another?'

Robert laughed and poured more wine into his glass, then went out to find a clean shirt to put on. He'd heard that Margaret was making eyes at Eck, and he was hopeful that maybe she was moving on as well. Life was quite good for Robert Ross. He whistled as he clattered up the stairs, leaving Paula to stew over the way things were turning out. *Oh Suzannah, I wish you were here*, she thought for the hundredth time that day.

Rosie and Billy were full of anticipation. Their big brother Joker had offered to run them down to Uncle James and he in turn had promised to take them out fishing. It was the school holidays, and the days were long and ran into each other. The two had gorged themselves on jam sandwiches, and for the past two days had been absorbed in making a four-hole golf course on the grazing land adjacent to their house. Billy was in charge of making the greens, and Rosie spent a long time decorating the flags for the posts. Their father's unused clubs, which he had inherited sometime in the distant past, had been gathering cobwebs in the garage, so Billy had hauled them out and had practised a few swings. In truth they had more fun planning the course and digging the holes than they did playing golf.

Next week was to be the pageant and their time would be

taken up with creating another scene from Scotland's sad history. Rosie had been quite put out when she was refused a part as a soldier or an evictor. She was to be a poor child instead. She was to look ragged and barefoot and the tourists were supposed to feel sorry for her. Rosie was not looking forward to getting her feet cut on the shells and broken bits of bottle that were lying hidden in the loose shingle.

Joker eventually turned up with the truck and the children waved goodbye to their long-suffering mother who was collecting eggs from the hen house.

'Here, take these to your Uncle James,' she called. 'Tell him they're nice and fresh' and she handed Billy half a dozen.

'OK, Mum, see you later.'

The trio drove off with Joker proudly at the wheel. He had just passed his test and was chuffed that he was at last a man, having left school and about to start his apprenticeship. The tragedy at the beginning of the year had affected him more than he cared to admit. Sergei's death had been in all the papers, and the link between him and the dead scientist in London had still not been resolved. He felt just a flicker of fear when he remembered the dead man's words that morning on New Year's Day: 'You don't really know who anyone is, a spy could be anyone.'

He dropped his brother and sister at the end of the road. This was unusual for him, but he could see Victoria hanging out washing on the line and he could make out the bright skirts and gypsy shirts that she liked to wear. He saw a turquoise bra and panties that were mere strings. Joker coughed and waved, reversing the truck and making a speedy getaway. His face was suffused in a crimson glow, and suddenly he felt gauche and awkward.

Billy clattered into the kitchen. 'We're here, Uncle James, Mam sent some eggs, are you ready?'

'I'm here, boy, you don't have to bellow as though I was in Australia. I'm just getting a new darrow out of the drawer. I think the mackerel are running; the bay is full of gulls, all squawking and making a right to-do. We'd better get going if we want to get in on the action. Where's Rosie?'

They found Rosie sitting on the grass making daisy chains with Victoria. They made a pretty picture, James noted, the golden head with the tumbling curls bent close to the straight locks of blackest jet. All around the garden bumblebees crooned into the heads of deep red peony roses and snapdragons winked in clashing shades of orange, pink and lemon. A clump of ancient wallflowers rioted in deep blood colours of red and rust and somewhere in the branches of the sycamore tree an insistent chirp of a blackbird chattered to its mate.

'I want to stay with Victoria, Uncle James; I don't want to go fishing after all.' Rosie said without looking up. Instead she draped a chain of wilted daisies on to Victoria's golden curls.

'We might go and walk along the river.' Victoria smiled at him, a small knowing smile that James immediately felt his loins responding to. She went on, 'It looks dappled up there in the shade of the trees. I think I need to cool off, don't you?'

James stood still enjoying the heat of the summer day. He was spellbound at the tableau she created on the dark green grass. Her white dress, patterned by tiny posies of bluebells, was offset by the profusion of surrounding flowers and patches of clover. The rich smells of uncut hay wafted from the fields, and above them the sky was sapphire blue, broken only by the long white streaks of vapour left behind by a jet plane. James smiled into her eyes.

'Come on, Uncle James, let's go,' shouted Billy from the rocks below the house.

'Right, lad, I'm on my way.' Bending over he ruffled Rosie's hair and dropped a kiss on Victoria's smooth honey-coloured brow.

CHAPTER 32

The river bank was overgrown with bushes and grasses. Weaving in between the close-growing alder trees, taking care not to snag their clothes on the rusty barbed wire of the lichen-covered fence posts, the two girls walked in single file. They came to a bend in the river that was overhung with a dense canopy of leaves, creating a cool enclave of gloom; a blessed relief to the eyes after the bright glitter of the midday sun.

'I don't really like to fish,' said Rosie flopping down by the bank and kicking off her trainers. She immersed her feet to allow the fast flow of brown peaty water to wash over her toes.

'Me neither,' replied Victoria. She too had kicked off her sandals, and pulling up the long skirt above her knees, she dropped down beside Rosie and dangled her feet into the water. 'What bliss,' she sighed, 'this is the most perfect day.'

The two sat for a while enjoying the mesmerising sight and sound of the water.

Suddenly a dog's bark shattered the peace. A blur of black and white collie dog came hurtling from the undergrowth by the trees, its long pink tongue lolling spittle all over them in its enthusiasm to greet them.

'Oh, Charlie, get off!' shouted Rosie. 'You're going to push us in!'

'Whose dog is it?' frowned Victoria irritably, pulling herself away from the grinning fangs.

'Come here, boy, come here when I call for you.'

'Oh, it's you,' she noted ungraciously, taking in Hector's

summer attire of pale grey corduroys, tied with twine as usual at the ankles, and a Black Watch tartan flannelette shirt, done up to the throat. His red bonnet had been left behind, and his head was uncovered for once, leaving the greasy grey strands of hair exposed. Last night he had conducted a session of self-barbering with the kitchen scissors, so he felt he was respectable enough to go without the hat.

'Aye, it's me. It's a grand day. Great for you to sit about.'

'You could sit with us if you want,' invited Rosie charitably, ignoring Victoria's look of distaste.

'I've got a field of hay to cut. There's no saying how long this good spell will last and with the Sabbath tomorrow, I'd better get cracking. Maybe I could invite you to a roll in the hay, lass?' he twinkled hopefully at Victoria. 'I see that James MacTavish is safely out of the way for a few hours.'

Rosie got up and started throwing sticks for Charlie and soon wandered off out of reach.

'I hear you're a bit of hot stuff.' He looked at her sideways. 'How about a kiss for an old man?' he leered, edging towards her.

Victoria's eyes widened in horror, and she hissed, 'Go away; you shouldn't say things like that!'

'You won't be disappointed, and I see you have a grand body, proud you are of it too.'

Hector's eyes lit up at the thought that maybe he might win her over with his charm. He went on, whispering and looking about in case the magpies in the trees were listening,

'I've got a pole that reaches nearly to my knees, and by God, it's been a while since…'

He never got to finish for Victoria had already started to run, leaving her silver sandals in her haste to get away. She ran and ran, back across the field, over the stile and round by the bend in the river. She slowed down only when she reached the gravel path leading to James's house, her soft white feet protesting against the sharp stones. She ran through the house and turned on the taps of the bath. Sitting on the edge she shivered, rocking her body rhythmically, while watching the tub fill with steaming hot water.

Rosie was unaware that she was alone. She had been absorbed for a while in a game of tag with the dog until she had chanced upon a stranger to the village. Sensing that he had lost the child's interest, Charlie's ears had cocked when he heard the sharp whistle of his master. Obedient for once, he had run back through the trees to the river bank.

'Hello,' said Rosie conversationally.

'Hello yourself,' replied the man. He looked a studious sort of man, bald with intense eyes magnified by round wire spectacles that gave him a comical appearance. He seemed to be absorbed in a book. By his side a pair of binoculars lay on the grass. He too was obviously suffering from the heat, for he had discarded his chequered sports jacket and had rolled up the sleeves of his cream linen shirt.

Rosie was intrigued and immediately asked, 'What are you doing?'

'I'm a twitcher.'

'Oh,' said Rosie, sitting down beside him. 'Are you on holiday like me? What do you teach?'

'No, I'm not a teacher, I'm a bird twitcher, I like to look at birds.'

'So do I,' said six year old Rosie. 'I like drawing them too. Is this your book?'

'Yes, but don't touch.' The man pulled it out of her reach.

'Why not?' Rosie's eyes were huge, questioning. 'I just wanted to see the birds.'

Hastily removing some loose photographs and checking the pages, the stranger then handed over the book to the small girl.

'Are those pictures of your children?' Rosie persisted. She had managed to glimpse a photograph of a young girl.

'No, just friends of mine,' the man replied tersely. 'So, tell me, what kind of birds do you have around here?'

'Well we have crows and ravens and buzzards,' informed Rosie, feeling quite important. She picked up the book and started flicking through the pages, recognizing owls, sparrows and robins. 'We also have lots of oyster catchers on the beach. Have you seen them?'

The man had moved closer to her, and he looked at the pages with her. She could feel his breath on her neck; she didn't like that much so she tried to wriggle away. She didn't want to appear rude though, because he was being very kind, sharing his book with her.

She recognised lots of the birds, and was delighted to share her local knowledge of where the sandpiper laid its eggs and how she had tried to save a robin last winter when it flew into her mother's newly washed windows. The man seemed very interested, which was gratifying. Her brothers and even her father soon lost concentration when she chattered on for too long. Rosie realised that he had placed an arm around her, and was holding the book with one hand. His breath was coming in shallow gasps. She was afraid he might be having a heart attack. She knew older men suffered from those. Mrs MacDonald's husband had had one a few years ago, her mother had said.

'Are you all right?' she asked, her chocolate eyes concerned, her head tilted to the side, very like the small robin that she had rescued.

He tightened his arm around her shoulders, and she suddenly felt his hand slipping up under her skirt.

'Stop that! What are you doing?' she cried.

It was only then that she looked at what his other hand was doing. In his right fist he was holding his penis, huge, red and swollen. Rosie's mouth opened to scream, but before she could do anything, he rolled her over, muffling her mouth with his hand and jabbing her leg with the round fat end of the revolting 'thing'. Rosie closed her eyes to block out the face and struggled with all her might to get her mouth free from his hand. She froze as she felt him take her panties and rip them away from her. Rosie was more shocked at that than at anything the man had done up till then. What on earth was he planning to do? She lay still, afraid. Finally she opened her eyes and saw him above her. The big hand was still pressed against her mouth, squeezing down hard on her neck. She felt him scuffle, and put a knee between her legs, forcing them to part. As the man adjusted himself, shifting his weight, he released his hand from her mouth. Rosie screamed. She screamed and screamed. She screamed until she felt a sharp pain on the side of the head and then, for her, the sun went out.

Victoria towelled herself dry, and suddenly realised that she had forgotten Rosie. She felt a frisson of fear at what James might say if he found out that she had run away from her responsibility. Hurling clothes on to the bed, she selected a long orange Indian cotton dress that hugged her body enticingly. Before running out of the house, she had second thoughts, and remembering the lewd suggestions she had received from that dirty old man earlier, she ran back to the bedroom and pulled on a pair of jeans instead, pushing her head through the neck of a black T shirt. She slipped her feet into the canvas tennis shoes she kept at the front door, and with breasts bouncing, she jogged back to the river, hoping and praying that Rosie was still preoccupied with daisy chains. As she crossed the field, she heard the screams. They rent the air and shattered the still summer afternoon. People left what they were doing, and started to run. Iona ran down the road towards the trees by the river. On the sea, James heard the screaming and felt a fear as cold as ice manifest itself in the pit of his stomach.

'What was that, Uncle James?'

The older man locked in the oars and turned the boat towards the shore.

Victoria froze. Coming out of the woods she saw the dog. 'Oh my God, that old man has attacked the child. Someone get help, please, we must find her. He was after me, and then he must have seen Rosie. Please, oh please... Victoria started to cry and her shoulders shook with dry sobs, as she imagined the worst.

'What is it lass, what's happened?' Iona arrived, breathless from the unaccustomed sprint.

'It's Rosie, he's hurt her, I just know it.'

'Who?' Iona took her by the face and stared at her. 'Calm down, Victoria, who hurt Rosie?'

'Hector Ogilvie.'

'Hector Ogilvie? Don't be daft. He wouldn't hurt a fly.'

'He was telling me about his long pole and I ran away,' and she started to sob.

'Sit there, I'm going to find the child. Don't you move.' Iona ran through the bushes and noted the already flattened grasses where the girls had walked earlier. The dog ran with her, barking and running back towards her, trying to speed her up. 'I'm coming, Charlie, I'm doing my best for God's sake.'

Iona finally arrived at the river bank where Victoria's sandals lay abandoned. There was an eerie silence, and only the gushing river and the slanting sunlight through the leaves gave any semblance of normality. There was no other sound, not even a bird. The dog whined at her feet, confused that she had stopped. He barked at her expectantly.

'All right, Charlie, where is she?'

Wagging his tail, he trotted into the jumbled copse of alders and stopped in front of her old friend, Hector Ogilvie. Blood was on his hands, and across his knees was the inert body of the child.

Iona gasped. 'In God's name, what have you done?'

Before the old man could reply Victoria had run up, hysteria breaking out again at the grisly sight in front of her. Behind her were the village's two special constables.

'Don't say anything that might incriminate you, old man,' said Officer John when he came up to him.

'Is she alive?' the other officer queried, looking at Rosie's lifeless face.

'Aye, she's alive and unhurt, thanks to Charlie here,' the old man said quietly, but no one heard him. He looked into the distance, straining to see if the attacker was still around. 'There was a man,' he told Officer John. 'He might still be around and you might still get him. He's a wicked bastard.'

Hearing the last sentence Victoria started ranting and accusing Hector again, until Iona took charge and led her, still protesting, away from the river.

That night Jenny sat by her small daughter's bedside in the hospital in Inverness. She wept as she looked at the small skull, so fragile, swathed in a white bandage. The head wound was deep and the child was suffering mild concussion. The doctor had assured her that she had suffered no other injury, and it would seem that the rapist had been interrupted. Of course the mental scars would persist long beyond her physical recovery.

Meanwhile, in Inverness, Hector Ogilvie was in police custody, and for the first time in his life he was experiencing the loss of his freedom. He sat slumped, his head on his chest, perplexed and bewildered at the sharp turn of events.

Back in Drum Mhor, behind the curtains in the village, people whispered their opinions about Hector's obvious guilt or his tentative innocence. Officer John held his own counsel. He had known the old boy his whole life and he believed him when he had said that the rapist may not be far away. That hysterical woman that James MacTavish had brought to the village had definitely turned the public against poor Hector. Officer John did not sleep well in his bed that night.

CHAPTER 33

Rumbling black and blue clouds formed and reformed in menacing formations. Thunder roared in the sky and the sea whipped up spumes of angry white foam. The prolonged spell of heat that had hung over the glen all summer was threatening to shatter within minutes. A flash of cold wind whistled through the uncut swathes of yellow hay. People in the village were rushing about like disturbed ants, bent forward in their haste to avoid the storm.

Lottie Macdonald scurried up the path that led to the doctor's surgery. Her shoe leather was just about worn away from making this particular journey so regularly. She burst into the waiting room and announced unnecessarily to Morag, the receptionist, that she had an appointment with the doctor. Morag sighed quietly, rolling her eyes as she ticked off Lottie's name on the patient list for the morning.

Lottie Macdonald was known in the village as a professional hypochondriac. If it wasn't her lungs it was her kidneys, she thought, and if it wasn't her kidneys then maybe that twinge in her shoulder might mean there was something dark going on inside her lungs. If there was ever a woman who enjoyed ill health as much as Lottie Macdonald, then Morag had yet to meet her. Morag often wondered, maybe a touch unkindly, why the old woman never made an appointment to get a cure for the persistent ache in her jaw, caused from too much evil tongue wagging.

She peered over her glasses at Lottie, remembering how put out the older woman had been when her husband Fergus Macdonald had passed away a few years ago from a massive heart attack. The sympathy for such an untimely death was quite lost on the widow who instead seethed furiously at the poor man's passing. She had even wagged her finger at his cheesy dead face, reminding the poor man of all the years she had spent suffering from a whole assortment of diseases. Now here she was alive and having to go it alone and here he was, off to push up the daisies. There was just no justice in the world. Even now, after four years, poor Lottie still smouldered when she thought of how her husband had pipped her to the post, as it were, with no warning.

Now, her hypochondriac hobby had become her raison d'être. She took a macabre delight in all things medical, and hovered around houses that were smitten with illness. Joker likened her to a black hoodie crow, or an angel of death. Unaware of how the village as a whole viewed her, Lottie persisted with her delusions and kept thumbing through her worn-out copies of the *Readers Digest* and the dog-eared family medical reference book that she kept at hand on her bedside table. She was as knowledgeable as the doctor himself, or so she liked to inform her closest friends.

Glancing around the waiting room, Lottie nodded over to Margaret, sitting quietly by the table, browsing through an old copy of the *Woman's Own*.

'Hello there, dear,' she smiled concernedly, 'we haven't seen you for a wee while, well, not since the Keep Fit. How are you?' The older woman's eyes scanned for any vital signs that might give her a clue as to why Margaret might be seeing the doctor.

'No, I went down to Stirling. I thought I might see if I could get my old job back, now that my mother is so much better. I just got back a few days ago.'

Margaret smiled and was about to return to her magazine but Lottie was having none of that. She heaved herself up, moved over and sat down next to her.

'I suppose you've heard all the news, then?' Lottie whispered, her eyes darting over to Morag and then at the two young mothers sitting on the far wall. No doubt they're in for some contraception, she thought knowingly.

'Yes, poor Rosie. Do you know if she has come round yet? My mother said that she had been hit on the head. I can't believe that old Hector Ogilvie would interfere with a child.'

Lottie sniffed and pulled herself up, closing her eyes and turning away, her lips forming a thin line. It was clear she had no wish for the conversation to proceed further along that track. Lottie was uncomfortable discussing intimate matters that might relate to things below the waist. Margaret surreptitiously smiled and looked down at the article she was reading. Just then a huge clap of thunder nearly rocked the surgery out of its foundations, making everyone jump and one of the young women screamed.

'Oh my goodness, what a storm,' cried Margaret.

'I hate lightning!' said one of the young mums, 'and I didn't even bring an umbrella.'

'She didn't bring much of a skirt either,' observed Lottie quietly, 'and with those sling-back shoes, on a day like this, she's bound to get pneumonia.' Leaning back towards Margaret, she carried on with her whispered confidences. 'You know that Victoria, the one who's moved in and totally bewitched James MacTavish?'

Margaret nodded, taking an interest in spite of herself.

'Well,' continued Lottie, 'she said Hector propositioned her just minutes before he threw himself on Rosie. She seemed to think that if a man is in a state of arousal he'll just go for anyone. I suppose she would know. She certainly looks as though she's the type, if you know what I mean.'

Margaret coughed uncomfortably under Lottie's knowing stare, and tried to return to the problem page in the magazine. There was a letter there from a girl not unlike herself, who had lost the love of her life to another. Margaret, still unable to believe that Robert Ross was no longer hers, desperately wanted to read the reply and see if she could apply the second-hand wisdom to herself.

It was not to be, however, for Lottie resumed her fierce whispering, 'James MacTavish seems to be getting a lot of letters these days…'

Just then Morag called Margaret's name and announced that it was her turn to see the doctor, so Margaret reluctantly replaced the magazine, smiling uncertainly at Lottie. What was the old woman implying now? she wondered, as she made her way to the consulting room.

Lottie was distracted, for the storm broke in a splintering crack of light and a great wash of rain suddenly hit the windows. The deluge of water that had been brewing since dawn cascaded on the village in torrents. Preparing to sit the storm out in the waiting room, she settled herself cosily back in the chair. She picked up the magazine Margaret had discarded and started to read about the problems that had seemingly held the young woman in such thrall.

CHAPTER 34

It was the fourth day since the attack on Rosie. James had gone to work as usual, clad in his wet weather gear. He had left the house without his habitual shout of farewell. His feelings for his live-in bride-to-be had taken a somewhat negative dive. He could not shake off the memories of that afternoon when Rosie was hurt. Victoria's flagrant lack of responsibility towards Rosie was something he knew he would never be able to forgive. James also knew in his heart that Hector would never have hurt the child, and he resented the girl, who had only been in the glen five minutes, for making such a hysterical accusation against the old man. Looking out at the storm, he thought, I'll just have to weather it, there's nothing else for it. Stomping through the puddles he seethed at the thought of the attacker still being at large.

The thunderstorm raged all morning. Victoria sat curled on the settee in James's sitting room. The velour cloth covering the fish boxes sat at her feet with a pristine pad of paper waiting for her great romantic novel to materialise. Instead she was re-reading *Wuthering Heights* and her heart was beating with lust for a dark, swarthy hero to come and take her up to the hills and ravish her. By noon the sky was still dark and lightning was sending jagged flashes to illuminate the cobalt sky. She heard the rattle of the approaching vehicle reach the gate. Victoria ran to the porch and was met by a sodden Elvis the Post.

'God, what a day! I'm drenched,' he announced unnecessarily, dripping on to the stained linoleum.

Victoria opened the inner door. 'Come in,' she called sweetly, 'why don't you take off your jacket and have a cup of coffee with me? I was about to have a sandwich – you could join me?' She lifted her eyebrows and smiled invitingly. Victoria knew that the letters Elvis had been delivering with such dedication for the past week were nothing more than advertising leaflets. She suspected they were mere excuses for him to see her. She also suspected that the smouldering attraction that she had for the postman, which had begun on that very first morning when she had held his hand, was not just on her side. She looked up at him now; at his height, his broad shoulders, his thick black hair peppered with streaks of white. His craggy face was tanned and she noticed a rivulet of water running down his neck. She shivered involuntarily and swallowed, although her throat was quite dry. Her luminous green eyes caressed the contours of his strong face, running down the length of the straight nose before fixating upon his wide, grinning mouth.

Elvis smirked, knowing why her pupils were dilating and why her face was suffused in a pink flush. He let out a delighted laugh and stepped towards her. 'Come here, woman,' he said gruffly, 'I have a special delivery for you.'

With raw physical passion he ran his big hands beneath Victoria's long skirt, and lifted her up on to Nell's antique polished sideboard. The solid oak creaked while the old timbers withstood the assault of the postman as he ravished the girl who had newly taken possession of the house. His passion was hot, urgent, violent and all-consuming. Within minutes it was over. Victoria was stunned. Still sitting where he had taken her, dazed and damp from his wet shirt and hair, she watched him put himself to rights and make towards the door. 'Sorry, lass, I think that was Express Delivery!' and with a couple of strides he was gone.

Victoria paced the house in an agony of desire. To compensate for her unfulfilled lust, she filled a bucket with soapy water and scrubbed the porch floor. Next she polished the wooden furniture, rubbing till the sweat ran from her brow. Her passion still unabated, the fever hot in her veins, she cleaned every nook and cranny of the house, her body trembling, waiting for the day to pass. When James finally did arrive home, weary and soaked through, he was dragged to the bedroom with little chance to ask questions. The door was closed firmly behind them. James looked at his deerstalker that she had thrown on to the floor and momentarily thought of that woman, Lady Chatterley. He imagined he might be the lover, the gamekeeper Mellors. Poor man, thought James, I never really pitied him until now. When at last Victoria lay still, James held her close, waiting for her ragged breath to return to normal. He adjusted himself on the pillow and stared over at the steamed-up window. All I wanted, he thought ruefully, was a cup of tea and a Rich Tea biscuit. Outside, the rain beat like applause on the tin roof of the shed.

The next few days saw Victoria and Elvis embark upon a tempestuous affair. They knew that they could no longer use Meg's sideboard as their springboard to ecstasy so as soon as the weather cleared and the sun burnt up the wet puddles, they took to meeting on old forestry tracks. A lot of people noticed that Her Majesty's Post was arriving a little later every day, and uncharacteristically Elvis seemed unwilling to linger for the bit of cake or small libation that he had been accustomed to.

Victoria's eyes took on a sparkle that James had not noticed before. He was gratified that she was so enjoying life with him, and settling into the quiet life of the glen. He had been concerned that she was not making friends, and had worried that perhaps the days would seem long to her with so little to occupy her time. He appreciated her efforts at taking care of him, although he did have some reservations about the mystical theme she had introduced to his home. Occasionally he had to suppress a longing for the evenings prior to Victoria's arrival. Evenings of quiet and contemplation. Evenings spent with his books on lighthouses. Sometimes he felt the old longing for Suzannah and the familiar ache when he thought of the lovely face, white and sharply, carved like porphyry. Sighing deeply, he let the memories of her recede into the private place in his mind's eye, where they could be recalled and savoured at will. I shall just have to learn to compromise, that's all, he told himself, bringing himself back into the present tense. I'm just too stuck in my ways, that's all, and my goodness, I don't know what I am complaining about, being the envy of the village, and having a girl like Victoria who wants to hitch herself up to an old codger like myself. James smiled cheekily into the hall mirror and adjusted his deerstalker hat. He strode out of his house with a jaunty spring in his step and filled his lungs with the warm, salty air.

Meanwhile Victoria gave little thought to James. As soon as he was out of the house she commenced her rituals of self-titivation for her lover. Studying the hands on the kitchen clock, she would caress the old sideboard then pace up and down until it was time. Each day at noon, she let herself out of the back door and, careful that Iona MacPherson was not watching her through those wretched binoculars, she ran down to the beach and along the sand, shooing the oyster catchers and gulls that screamed at the intrusion. Her hair bouncing in golden ringlets down her back, she hitched up her skirt and jumped across rocks glowing pink with sea thrift. Sometimes Elvis picked her up in the van and covered her with his jacket to conceal her from prying eyes. He would then drive her up to deserted lay-bys and make short work of his passion for her.

Today however, they had arranged to meet at the deserted house that belonged to Hector Ogilvie. Just past his gate was a clearing where the track headed into a dark wood closely planted with pine. The gloom hit her as she left the heat of the sun. She laughed delightedly, for standing waiting for her, tall and rugged like Heathcliff himself, was her Royal Male. Graciously he invited her to lie down upon his uniform jacket and in the filtered sunlight she pulled off her loose gypsy dress. Underneath she was naked. For the first time his eyes ran over her perfectly beautiful body. He lay for a minute beside her, looking up at the giant trunks of the pines, soaring skyward as though to heaven itself.

'It's like being in a cathedral,' Victoria sighed.

'Well, I'd better get on my knees then,' replied the ardent postie, unbuckling his belt, 'and do a bit of worshipping!'

Since it was a week since Hector had been taken away, Murdo decided to check on the old shepherd's house. He and Iona were looking after Charlie, and he thought he would just take a wander to see that all was well and reassure himself that nobody had tried to break in, seeing as there had been such hostile feelings towards the old man. Charlie ran ahead and came straight to the postman's van, barking expectantly at the familiar vehicle. Victoria gasped as she saw the dog's beady eyes and wide grin over the shoulder of her postman and squealed for him to let her go.

'Bloody hell,' he gasped, watching her pick up her dress and run into the trees as naked as a wood nymph. Elvis struggled to pull on his trousers and hastily buttoned his shirt.

Only just in time he heard Murdo call out, 'Hello there, Elvis, are you having a wee picnic?'

'Aye, just finished. It's fine and quiet here, and dark,' Elvis replied, retrieving his jacket and making towards the Land Rover.

'You should have dropped in to see us,' Murdo persisted. 'Iona has a pot of broth bubbling away. You know you are more than welcome.'

'I know that, but I had some letters for Hector and just saw the woods and I took the notion to stop.' He ran his hand through his hair, taking the opportunity of leading the other man away from the hotspot of his passionate tryst. 'So what's the news?' he asked, lighting up a post-coital cigarette.

'Good news, actually. Very good news.' Murdo accepted a cigarette and he too lit up. They puffed for a few minutes in companionable silence.

'Well, go on then, what's the good news?' Elvis asked, blowing the smoke into a ring and trying to keep his hand from shaking.

'It's young Rosie.' Murdo looked serious. 'She finally was able to tell her mother and the police that the man who hurt her had a moustache and glasses. She said he was a bird watcher and he hit her with his binoculars. Apparently Charlie here had come barking up and disturbed him. She was even able to describe his shirt and jacket, whereas Hector was in his usual tartan shirt.

'Oh, thank God she's all right.' Elvis was suddenly aware of Victoria coming down the hill on the other side of Hector's house. Turning around so that he could see where she was going, and to prevent Murdo from spying her, he carried on talking. 'Oh, that's great news about Hector too, that means he'll be released. Poor bugger, being kept in custody like that.'

'Aye, Jenny was on the phone to Iona, and she was saying that he'll be home tonight. That's why she made the soup, and I think Kathleen at the shop is bringing over some shepherd's pie.'

'But what about the attacker? I hope to God they manage to nab him.' Elvis shook his head, imagining what he would do to him if he could get his hands on him. Although his own six children were well and truly grown, he would have killed anyone that dared to lay a finger on them. 'Paedophiles should have their balls electrocuted, and if I catch that perverted bastard that hurt young Rosie MacTavish, I would personally see to it that he was well and truly scorched.'

Murdo was nodding and puffing along with the diatribe. Elvis voiced what all the men in the village were feeling. Denied the retribution that they felt was their right, they felt frustrated at their inability to right a wrong.

'We'll just have to leave it to the police,' Murdo breathed out resignedly, 'and hope they catch him pretty damn quick.'

That night the police drove Hector Ogilvie home to his house by the edge of the woods. He thanked the officers kindly for their services and waved his hand shyly as they drove back along the road. When the motor disappeared from sight he felt the silence of the glen descend upon him. Hector sniffed the evening. He smelt the seaweed tang mixed with the innocent aroma of warm hay. Far away he heard the cry of the gulls, and the honking of the geese.

'Very good,' he said, turning to his gate. He lifted the latch and walked up his crazy-paved path to retrieve his key. He kept it in a metal buoy that hung on a big nail at the side of the house, partially covered by an overhanging profusion of white roses. He turned the key and opened his door. He missed his dog, but knowing that news of his return would already be spreading, Hector knew that Iona would be around shortly. Taking a last sniff of the evening air, and letting his eyes scan the unbroken skyline as he looked out to sea, he felt glad to be home. He stepped into the house and cast his eyes down on to the mat. 'Ah well, no letters since I've been away, I see. I'll just put on the kettle for a cup of tea.'

Later that night, sitting with his dog at his feet, Hector reached for his green diary, and made his entry for the day:

A dry and sunny day, but a cool breeze in the evening.

CHAPTER 35

The school term started with much anticipation. Mrs Munro, wearing her sage skirt and mustard twin set, stood on the step greeting her young charges as they jostled to get through the gate. Mary Beth smiled shyly behind her, holding a bunch of white daisies that young Colin Campbell had pulled up by the roots from his dad's fine herbaceous border. The two teachers were concerned that Rosie MacTavish might have some serious issues after the attempted rape during the summer holidays, but they need not have worried, for when they saw her coming into school surrounded by a posse of small girls, she appeared to be enjoying her status as a mini celebrity. All the children had been told of the incident, and renewed lessons on not talking to strangers had been reiterated throughout the glen. Rosie's head wound had healed well, and with her family's support and good humour she appeared to have made a good recovery, mentally as well as physically.

Rosie was very happy that the minister's pageant had been cancelled. The Reverend Wilson told the committee that he felt it would have been unfitting to have gone ahead with the production while Rosie was lying in a hospital bed in Inverness. She was glad because she didn't want to miss it and had been so looking forward to being in it, even though she was just supposed to be a ragged child with no shoes. Paula had told her that they would do it next year instead, when she was fighting fit. This had made her smile as she ate the raspberries that Robert brought to the hospital especially for her. She was quite excited to be back at school. Life was really looking up. Now that Joker had officially started his apprenticeship with Hamish the carpenter, he had little occasion to play with his younger brother. Thus Rosie was promoted to full membership of the spy ring and allowed to play with the special listening device that the boys had used to such good effect when tracking that wicked Sergei.

She remembered the awful morning when they heard he'd been killed in his car on the icy road; how sad everyone had been for poor Suzannah and her little baby. Then came the questions and black cars. Wee Eck had been agog when telling her dad of newspaper reports about another Ukrainian man dying in London. She had listened behind the door to her mum gossiping on the phone to her friends about what the police were up to, of how they had questioned Uncle James and the MacPhersons, and had spent hours in a room with Suzannah. They had even searched the room and fingerprinted everything. Of course, Billy and Joker were ecstatic to think that they had actually heard Sergei plotting before he had left for London. She wondered if she and Billy could try and catch that horrible twitcher that had hurt her.

Rosie felt very brave about the incident during the day time, and walking home with her friends she was quite happy to tell them little snatches of what she could remember. But at night time, when it was dark and the curtains fluttered in the breeze from the open window, Rosie would scream and imagine the face and the spectacles and the horrible thing he had touched her with. It was then that Jenny would run in and hold her, and soothe her, and lie down beside her until she slept.

CHAPTER 36

September came in with blustery squalls of horizontal rain. Showers soaked the sheep that were being readied for the sales. Crofters draped in wet weather gear battled against the wind to erect the pens ready for the sorting and then the dipping of the ewes.

Hector, Murdo and Iona were sending 141 lambs and thirty-three ewes off to the market, and together they hauled the woolly creatures through the necessary procedures before market day.

Autumn colours blazed in rare moments of sunshine, and the curling fronds of the dying bracken were soon covered by spiralling leaves, swirling in a confusion of browns and rusts and gold.

James MacTavish dressed with care. Checking the weather from the kitchen window, he noted that the clouds were scudding past at alarming speed. Perhaps we'll have a dry day after all, he mused while pouring hot water from the kettle into the mug of instant coffee. He carried it through to the bedroom where Victoria was still propped up against the pillows. Her ardour was much reduced of late, James was secretly pleased to note.

'Here you are then, my pretty girl, and what will you be doing today?' His smile was forced. 'Do you think you might try and write a few words on that paper that you have sitting through on your wee table?' he asked sweetly.

He was met by a sullen silence.

'Fine,' James nodded, seeing the black mood that seemed to have settled upon her white brow like a witch's scowl. 'I'll be late back today; Lord and Lady Walton arrived last night from the south. They will be here for a month for the stalking and the shooting season.'

'Oh, what are they like?' Victoria asked.

'Well,' James replied, rubbing his chin thoughtfully, 'I would say they both exhibit a healthy appetite for all their natural bodily needs, if you know what I mean.' He winked lewdly at Victoria, who had miraculously shed her sullen face and cheered up. 'His Lordship has a passion for the drink too. You can see it immediately in his red face and bulbous nose. Aye, he tries to cover it up, but the shaky hands and the eyes give him away every time.' James laughed, remembering many occasions spent with his employer in the past. 'He's not that fussy which bottle the liquor comes out of either, or what time of day it is; he's always happy to imbibe at any opportunity.'

'And his wife,' queried Victoria, 'what's she like? Are they old?'

James considered before replying. 'Now, let me see. They must be in their forties I would say, though maybe Dickie is fifty. Hard to put ages on them. His wife Barbara is a fine figure of a woman. She's always telling me how sporty she used to be, played some daft game called lacrosse or something like that when she was a girl, but now all she likes to talk about is her skiing and her lessons with Fritz or Splitz or some such young Adonis she gets lessons from in Switzerland. I think they both get their passions slaked on the piste,' James chortled, thinking he was quite clever to think of jokes in a foreign language.

Finally he took himself off and Victoria listened for the sound of the door closing before she leapt out bed and padded through to the bathroom. Turning on the taps, she poured some lavender essence into the gushing stream of hot water then inhaled deeply, until she was able to submerge her body beneath the fragrant froth. Savouring the steam, she shut her eyes and languorously stretched her neck. She cupped her breasts and let her hands travel down to her taut belly. Pictures of summer flickered like the sunlight through the high canopy of leaves, bringing back the hot days of wild passion. She smiled dreamily to herself. By contrast, the last few days had been difficult, for the lovers had found it impossible to meet, the weather was bad and James had stayed at home. Hence the black depression. She knew that James had seen a very different side to her nature, and not one that he relished. He likened her to a snarling, caged tigress. Today she was free, today James would be away all day, and Elvis the Post could pick her up and take her way up into the hills, along the forestry track and lay her down upon the springy heather.

While Victoria prepared for her lover, Iona phoned Paula. 'How are you today?' she asked chirpily.

'Not bad, Iona; it's always good to get a break from the sheep. Have you got yours ready for the trucks tomorrow? Robert has been out since five, so I suppose I should get a flask of tea and take it out to him at the fank. What are you up to yourself?'

Iona pulled the curtain back from her window and peered down the field to James's house. For added effect she lowered her voice. 'I saw James leave this morning, all done up like a dog's dinner in his special Walton tweeds.'

'Well, what of it? I heard the estate owners had arrived at the Lodge last night. Nothing unusual; it's that time of year, isn't it?'

'I know that,' Iona replied irritably.

'So, what are you really saying?' Paula grinned, for she knew she was in for a bit of gossip.

'It's Elvis the Post; he's been sneaking Victoria off in his Land Rover all summer.'

'No!' gasped Paula, quite shocked. She was also amazed that Iona had only just found out. She would not be pleased to know that such a dalliance had been going on under her very nose and that she of all people had been unaware.

'Yes, it's the God's honest truth. Murdo heard from the forestry lads, and he heard Hector muttering about it while we were dipping the sheep yesterday. It seems they sometimes meet up in the woods, quite close to his house.' Iona fingered her wedding ring, and still keeping her eye on the house down by the sea she added, 'Poor

James, the village Casanova, and he's the only one that doesn't know, it seems.'

'Yes, poor James,' agreed Paula. 'Should we not tell him?'

'Tell him! Are you mad? I'm more worried about that old battleaxe Elvis is married to. She might just come over and give Victoria a few blasts with the shotgun.'

'But I thought Betsy was holy?' Paula reasoned.

'Holy! Ha!' laughed Iona. 'Do you not read your Bible, girl? Where does it say that God condones adultery? She'll kick Elvis out, and then come and sort out that Jezebel down in the field there. Oh my goodness, there she goes now.' Iona's breathing came rapidly as she watched Victoria run up the track and on to the road. 'She's off on a lovers' tryst, the evil wench, you can be sure of that!'

Meanwhile at the Lodge house on Glen Gyle Estate, Lady Barbara Walton was preparing for her day. She hummed as she blow dried her blonde hair, cut severely into the contours of her neatly shaped head in an almost masculine style. Her big-boned figure dwarfed her more diminutive husband and she exuded health and a cheerful disposition. She liked nothing better than her garden and walking through the Gloucestershire countryside with her two spaniels at her heels. She was a hearty woman, favouring tweed skirts, green wellington boots and quilted body warmers, but was not averse to wearing a pair of jeans which she felt was really quite a trendy thing to do. Her two teenage daughters had made huge inroads to her wardrobe in the last few years, and had gradually weaned her away from the gaudy head squares and dirndl skirts that she had previously embarrassed them with. Lady Barbara turned on Radio Two and joyfully sang along with the mellow songs which brought back memories of her younger days. Happily she went about throwing open windows, reflecting how much she loved her time spent in the 'Bonny Land', especially during the autumn months.

*

At the same time as Victoria was surreptitiously proceeding towards her rendezvous with Elvis the Post, James MacTavish, wearing his special Walton tweeds, was escorting his Lordship over the estate. James, as his Lordship's ghillie, or special man as he might have been called in Victorian times, was an expert stalker. He demonstrated a lifetime's experience in the practice of deer stalking, and his natural instinct proved invaluable when navigating the way across peat bogs and rocky ground. Today the two tramped over the spongy mosses, dotted with tufts of fluffy bog cotton, often sending a capercaillie into flustered flight. Each year the Waltons invited visitors up to their country seat during the deer shooting season. Soon the estate would be playing host to a variety of guests, mainly from England, so it was imperative that all the fences, bridges, barns and outhouses were in good order. Later they would check the gunroom and the larder, and James would bring his Lordship over to see the Highland Garron ponies used for bringing down the dead stags and deer from the hill.

Lady Walton, with Dolly at her side, was having her own tour of the grand old Lodge. It was an imposing building of smooth, grey stone, built in a baronial style, with Ionic columns framing the large double doors. Three steps led down to the circular driveway, and Lady Barbara inspected the delightful display of dahlias planted in the centre. 'They are just like a carpet of brightly coloured pompoms!' she enthused. She paced the garden with a sense of purpose, noting the thick, glossy foliage of the rhododendrons and azaleas that lined the driveway to the main road. Around the perimeter of the house she frowned at the straggly branches of the buddleia and the forlorn forms of the laburnum and cherry trees. A harsh wind had stripped the leaves and the trees looked naked and bereft. In contrast, the herbaceous border was a riot of colour favouring the secondary hues of autumn. Montbretia, hebe and golden rod grew beside towering bushes of protective escalonia. Bunches of scarlet rowans adorned the mountain ash trees which flanked both the main gate and the side one leading down to the sea. It was a bird's paradise, for this year saw a heavy crop of blood-red berries scattered like jewels on the cotoneaster. The garden appeared to be lit up by beacons of autumn enchantment. Lady Barbara was particularly pleased to note the pots of exquisite red dahlias framed against bronzy-black foliage. 'Ah!' she cried triumphantly, 'my pride and joy, the Bishop of Llandaff!'

Dolly smiled, quite failing to appreciate such adulation for a few straggling plants. She longed to get back indoors and join Lottie. The two were employed each year to help with housekeeping duties when the Lodge was being used. Fresh linen had to be aired, beds prepared, and dust covers removed from the rose-patterned chintz furniture in the sitting room and conservatory.

As the tour of the inside of the house progressed, her Ladyship noticed the peeling paint and the dilapidated skirting boards and she vowed that she would employ a carpenter and painter to give the bedrooms a new lease of life before her guests arrived. Thus it was that Joker, just started on his career as a joiner, found himself in the Lodge, sawing strips of wood and learning how to fix sheets of plasterboard. In the weeks that followed, with her husband and ghillie out on the hill, her Ladyship found she enjoyed the view of the young man's muscles and his strong lean back. It was quite a tonic to her, a woman on the wrong side of forty, and so she spent as much time as possible interrupting him with her raucous voice: 'Jonathan! Come here and tell me what you think I should do here?' After he had satisfied her commands and had returned to his task, his boss Hamish could be heard tittering from the other room as the voice rang out again: 'Jonathan, come here and help me hang these curtains!' She made their morning coffee herself, for the cook she brought with her each year was too busy preparing the special banquets or making preserves and pickles for the larder. During their designated break, Hamish teased his young apprentice about the possibility of being a gigolo for her Ladyship. Joker scowled, knowing that he was going to be ribbed no end when he got back to the Pipers Inn. Life as a joiner certainly was not as he had imagined it.

He recalled that the first month of his time with Hamish had been spent learning how to make a coffin. 'For God's sake!' he had exploded, when his boss demonstrated to him how to rub down the wood and fit the pieces together, 'I didn't know I would be doing this. Gives me the creeps!'

Hamish had chuckled at the predictable outburst, and had reprimanded the boy. 'This is your bread and butter, lad; if you can provide this service to a community you'll never go hungry. I'll be initiating you into the other side of my business as well, but all in good time.'

'What!' Joker had cried, 'I don't have to wear a top hat, do I, and sit in front of the hearse, like you?'

Hamish had sniffed, 'Undertaking is a very important part of joinery; you'll soon find that out.'

In the next few months Joker proved himself to be a natural craftsman and soon perfected his techniques with the lathe, hammer and chisel. Having turned eighteen he was now permitted to drink in the pub legally at last, but Joker found that this was a mixed blessing. Donnie, Eck and big Donald Duff took great delight in referring to him as Lady Walton's poodle. He needed to find out just exactly what a gigolo was.

As October saw the nights draw in, and the tweed-clad men clambered out on the hills in pursuit of stags, Lady Walton conducted her own private stalking party. Poor Joker was her prey, and it was increasingly difficult for him to escape her clutches. She enticed him into her room with the pretext of fixing the hanging on the four poster bed, asking him to take off his shoes so that he could get up with her on to the mattress. She called for him when she padded out of the bath, hoping that he would come in and see her splendid body in all its white marble nakedness. Joker was at his wit's end and appealed to Hamish and his uncle for help. The older men just laughed at his plight.

'Just be careful, lad, for you don't want to offend her,' James advised. 'There's nothing scarier than a woman scorned, so they say.'

Hamish chortled beside him, 'Not to forget the wrath of the husband when he finds out you've been dancing on his bed with his wife!'

Joker sat with his head in his hands, wishing to God that he was back in the joiner's shop making a coffin.

The weeks sped by, guests came and went, and Joker and Hamish were summoned again to the Lodge. Lady Walton was making preparations for the Ghillies' Ball to celebrate the end of the deer stalking season. 'I insist that you join us for the dancing next Friday night,' she commanded.

'Right you are, Your Ladyship,' nodded Joker, almost tugging his forelock. He knew he was beaten, and there was no way she would take no for an answer. At least Uncle James and Victoria would be there, and quite a few of the locals had been invited as well. The kitchen was in a state of high alert as the cook had commandeered Kathleen and Lizzie from the Tea Room as well as Dolly, Lottie and Iona to help. There's safety in numbers, he thought. She's not likely to get me in a cupboard at the dance, not with all the fancy toffs about.

Lady Walton admired the platform they had finished building in the dining room. 'It's just perfect; I hope it's strong enough to cope with the band I've just booked,' she grinned happily.

'Where did you get them from, Mrs Walton, err... Ma'am?'

'Oh just call me Barbara, Jonathan; we don't have to stand on ceremony, you know!' and she brayed with laughter.

Jonathan coughed, his face as red as one of her precious dahlias.

'I just looked in the Yellow Pages and found quite a selection. I finally chose the *Angry Young Men*. Now what do you think of that! Quite a show stopper!' she trilled.

'They come from Muir of Ord, and the advert said that they play authentic Scottish tunes for every occasion. It seems they are a family business, so I'm sure they will be reliable.'

CHAPTER 37

The Ghillies' Ball was always a big night in the glen. James MacTavish, being the only true ghillie or gamekeeper to the Glen Gyle Estate, felt honoured that the ceremonial end of the stalking season was given such a high profile. Together with the other estate workers and prominent members of Drum Mhor's community, he and Victoria made their way up the rhododendron-lined drive to the Lodge.

The house was ablaze with lights, the doors wide open, and a beaming Lord Dickie greeted everyone with a warm handshake before ushering them into the vestibule. The guests were treated to the sight of a red tartan rug running all the way up the stairs from the hall. The painted eyes of aristocrats long since dead stared lasciviously at the plunging dresses of the village girls. A parade of stags' heads around the galleried landing reminded everyone why they were here and only Lottie Macdonald pursed her lips as she noticed a big cobweb floating from one grand beast's record array of antlers. She and her fellow workers, being paid as waitresses this evening, were dressed demurely in black dresses that hugged their ample hips and rode up with irritating regularity whenever they had to stretch up to reach an ashet or a tureen. The frilly white aprons only managed to accentuate their matronly figures.

Lady Walton had squeezed herself into a size fourteen dress, bought earlier in the year. She had treated herself to the luxurious red velvet back in March, when she had felt quite slim after an eight-week course of Pilates; she now regretted the many cream cakes and shortcake fingers she had devoured in the last month.

'Jonathan!' she hollered from the upstairs window, having caught sight of the young man standing awkwardly on the front step beneath her bedroom, 'Come here at once, I need you!'

Robert Ross and Wee Eck guffawed loudly. 'Better go, lad! If a lady has needs, you'd better see to them!'

Joker cursed under his breath and skulked his way up the back stairs towards his employer's bedroom. Politely he knocked but was mortified when he heard a groan behind him. Pivoting on his heel, he recognised her husband, Lord Dickie himself, puffing up the grand staircase.

'Oh, it's you, lad; young Joker is it not?' he said, staring at the boy in a knowing fashion.

'Yes, sir, My Lord. Lady Barbara summoned me.' Joker started to stammer.

'Very good, very good.' The older man stared at the closed door. Compressing his lips, he added, 'Well carry on, boy, just carry on.' Lord Dickie blundered on, a little unsteadily, towards his own room. He needed to recharge his toothbrush mug with just a little extra splash of Laphroaig. He didn't want Babsie seeing him tipple in public. She had notions that people around here might talk, though in his opinion there seemed damn little to talk about.

'Pssst, come in here, Jonathan, and do me up.' Lady Walton sidled towards him, enveloping him in an intoxicating cloud of Chanel No 5. Her zip was open and both halves of her dress hung open, teasingly revealing a white back naked to the crease of her buttocks. Joker nearly choked. She was standing in front of a full-length mirror and he could clearly see her reflection, standing like a warrior queen. She was awesome. Joker took in the tall and resplendent woman and, just for a moment, looked into the predatory eyes in the glass. Immediately she turned towards him and he felt her arms close like a vice around his chest.

'What did you want, Lady Walton?' the boy asked tremulously, turning his face towards the door, afraid that she might try and kiss him.

'Why, Jonathan, I just wanted you to do up my zipper; I can't seem to do it myself.' She gaily turned her back towards him again and presented her shapely rump. With one sliding move he pulled up the zip and concealed the view of her tantalising flesh.

'I must go, Lady Barbara; I think the band has arrived. They rang saying they were delayed, but would be here as soon as they could. I think I heard their car in the drive.'

'Wonderful, Jonathan; let's go down together, shall we? The least you can do is escort a lady to the ball.'

Joker found his arm clutched and he was marched to the top of the stairway. The assembled guests looked up and applauded as the lady of the house made her appearance in a lush, tight-fitting red dress, her hand hooked round the arm of her blushing apprentice. Hamish and James exchanged a glance, their lips twitching, as did the ladies in black.

'I doubt she'll be wanting any dinner; she looks as though she's saving herself for that tasty bit of crumpet,' snipped Dolly to Kathleen.

'That's if she's not had a wee nibble already,' Iona commented, her eyes gleaming.

Joker was correct when he said the band had arrived. The musicians unpacked their instruments in minutes, and soon slammed the doors of their blue Transit van, but were confused as to where they should go. Climbing the stone steps, they entered the hall and gazed about. Their faces showed signs of consternation.

The eldest man muttered to the youngest, 'Which one of these dolled-up birds is the lady of the house?'

Joker nudged Lady Barbara and she immediately took control. 'Good evening! Wonderful that you could make it. I expect you want to unpack your instruments and tune up, so to speak.' She looked beyond the first man's shoulder. 'How many of you are there?' she added.

'It's just us. I'm Willie John, and this is my uncle; he's called Big Willie. And this is my nephew…'

Lady Barbara cut him off as she dissolved into a gale of giggles, 'Oh please say his name is Wee Willie!'

'No, madam, he's Ewen.'

'Oh! Oh hello, Ewen,' and Lady Barbara burst into more peals of laughter.

'Where do you want us?' asked Big Willie, a touch gruffly.

'Well, on the platform, of course. I had it purpose built you know, though I must say I was expecting more of you. Are you sure there are just the three of you?'

'Aye, just the three, and we've never had any complaints before,' Willie John told her sternly.

'Quite, quite,' nodded Lady Barbara agreeably. She looked at the trio and looked pointedly down at the three boxes the men had put at their feet.

Willie John answered her enquiring glance. 'Two accordions and a fiddle; will that not do you?'

'My word, of course! Just the ticket, I should say; what do you say, James? We should be very well served with two accordions and a fiddle.'

James suppressed a smile and gestured to the aptly named Angry Young Men to follow him into the dining room, where already the trestle tables were groaning under the weight of a buffet. Haunches of venison, pink sides of salmon and glistening hams lay out ready to be joined by bowls of potato salad, purple beetroot and trays of broccoli, carrots and cauliflower. Even from across the hall he could hear the shrill voice of his hostess tell the assembled guests how appropriate she thought the band's name seemed to be.

'Well, Wee Willie looks an absolute sweetie,' she chortled into her glass of champagne, giggling as the effervescence tickled her nose, 'but the other two look as though they won't see sixty again. I suppose that would be enough to make any young man angry!'

Paula pulled up a chair in the conservatory and found she had a bird's eye view of the dining room. Smoothing her long cream dress, she reflected for a moment that this was her first opportunity to wear such a dress in Drum Mhor. She had brought it up from London but it had stayed in the back of the wardrobe for two years. Somehow the life she had chosen, working with Robert on the croft and keeping house for him, did not seem to demand much elegance. Since she had moved in with Rob, the cottage she had rented in the village had been let most of the summer to holidaymakers. Driving past last week she had noticed the outside had been given a coat of paint and the nettles had been removed. She had been vaguely intrigued, wondering if it had been let for the winter as well.

Paula smiled as she watched her friend Iona moving around the crowded dining room, helping people to sit at the small tables that had been borrowed from the hall and covered with white cloths. Dolly wheezed into the room carrying another tray of poached salmon, her face flushed with exertion. Paula could see the black skirt taut across the older woman's Rubenesque thighs. Lord Dickie had noticed too, and Paula gasped when she saw his Lordship place two hands firmly on her rear end. Dolly whirled around ready to give the offender a mouthful of abuse, but seeing whose face it was leering at her, she smiled querulously and bustled back to the kitchen, where no doubt she would give vent to her indignation. Paula's eyes narrowed at the sight of that strumpet of a woman who had so beguiled James and who was now flagrantly making a fool of him. Tawny eyes flashing, she followed Victoria's progress across the room. Dressed in a vermillion silk dress that plunged deeply at the front and barely covered her perfectly formed buttocks, Victoria tossed her fairytale hair back from her shoulder and flirted gaily with two English bachelors who were laughing raucously, trying to outdo each other to gain her attention. Paula muttered to herself, forgetting where she was.

'Well, my beautiful lioness,' Robert interrupted, 'is this what you do when I leave you alone?'

'What?' Paula asked crossly.

'Sit and mutter in the gloom, chewing a piece of celery like one of his Lordship's horses. What has made you so angry?'

'That wicked girl. Look at her! She's leading those two nice young men a pretty dance, and there's poor James over there, standing all alone.'

Robert glanced over and his eyes swept across the room, finally resting on Elvis and his wife, seated demurely at a table with Wee Eck.

Elvis was dressed in a pin-striped double breasted suit. His face was red and he looked hot and embarrassed. Without his van and uniform, he seemed reduced somehow, lacking his usual confidence and bravado. His head twitched and his hands clenched and re-clenched as he, too, watched Victoria laughing uproariously with those two posh bastards. His wife, Betsy, sat almost glued to his side. She was looking mean, her lips in a grim line turned down at the corners. He suspected that she had heard the rumours. No doubt her good friend Isla felt that it was her Christian duty to inform her poor friend about the things folk were saying. There could be no other reason, Elvis thought bitterly, because for the first time in history his wife had announced that she would be accepting the invitation to the Ghillies' Ball. Elvis would not be going alone after all. Sitting beside him now, with gritted teeth, Betsy looked like a prison warder in her staid coffee-coloured dress. Her hair was screwed up tightly. The faded once-red curls had been newly permed, but held no bounce; instead they cowered like frightened caterpillars on the pink scalp.

'Oh dear,' remarked Robert, 'I fear trouble ahead. Just look over there,' and he gestured with his fork.

Paula bit down on her lower lip, then started to laugh. 'This might be quite an entertaining evening, don't you think?'

Eck, too, was looking dapper, dressed in his suit, restrained and respectful while sitting with Elvis and his wife. He wondered how he could get away and fill his glass. It was going to be a long evening if he was expected to survive on that bowl of fruit salad that they called a drink. Smiling warily at the estranged couple beside him, he made a beeline for the punch bowl. Winking at Donnie who, from habit, was guarding the area with the refreshments in case he missed out on anything, Eck produced a half-bottle of black rum from his inside pocket and proceeded to tip the contents into the brew.

'That should put a bit more kick into it,' he smiled smugly, his shark-like teeth grinning with satisfaction.

'You great idiot,' Donnie exclaimed, 'his Lordship's already poured a bottle of whisky in it. God knows who else might have tampered with it. Dolly and Kathleen said they had put in a bottle and a half of wine during the preparation.'

'Well, let's just have a wee taste then, shall we?' Eck dipped the ladle into the ornately carved piece of family silver and poured a good measure into a glass. His face broke into a wide, satisfied grin when he swigged back a mouthful. 'Oh by God, that will put enough fuel in a rocket to send it to the moon!' Eck wandered back to mingle with some of the invited guests who had been stalking this last week.

Donnie laughed in spite of himself and took an abstemious drink of Highland Spring water before assisting his hostess to fill three glasses with the doctored brew. He then watched Lady Barbara cut through the room like a red comet, carrying a small tray towards the Angry Young Men. The three sat at a table on the far side of the room, enjoying the feast and gearing themselves up for the dancing. Willie John, busy wolfing down a plate piled high with roast venison, accepted the drinks with a wary nod.

'My husband, Lord Walton, plans to make a short speech,' Lady Barbara told them regally, 'after which he and I will lead off the dancing as we always do. I'm very partial to *The Pride of Erin* waltz so if you would be so kind as to oblige…' She smiled, noting the dimples in Ewan's cheeks and fluttering her eyelashes at him.

'With the formalities completed, then of course it will all be in your very capable hands.' She nodded graciously at the two older men.

'Very good, your Ladyship; just you give us a wink when you want us to start.' Willie John took a reluctant sip of the fruity concoction. His face broke into an unaccustomed grin. 'I think this party is just looking up, lads!' He proceeded to remove the strawberries, grapes and apples from the drink and piled them onto the congealing gravy on his plate. He then upturned his glass and swallowed the amber liquid. 'I think we might enjoy ourselves after all!'

Grace from the Post Office had her eye on James MacTavish. A line of concern added itself to the other lines that traced themselves around her kind eyes. Delicately sipping her second glass of punch, afraid to drink too quickly in case she got tipsy, she felt emboldened to approach her old friend.

'It's a great ball, James, don't you think?' she simpered. 'You must be so proud, being the real stalker here amongst all these posh folk.'

'Oh yes, Grace, it's quite gratifying to see one's labours being rewarded,' James replied, looking at her with interest. Unusual choice of clothes, he thought, as he took in the outfit she had chosen for the evening. Grace was dressed in a mud-green Paisley dress, with a waistcoat knitted from a selection of colourful squares that had been darned together. The colours were garish and too strong for the postmistress's high complexion. She had strained her feet into a pair of green sling-back shoes with kitten heels, a size too small, that she had bought in a sale during the summer. Already the hard plastic was cutting into her prominent bunion. 'That's quite a fetching waistcoat, Grace; did you knit it yourself?' he asked kindly.

Grace coloured. 'Yes, I knitted it last winter, at the knitting club.' She gasped, realizing she had made an unspoken reference to Suzannah. Immediately memories of last winter made them both fall silent. Grace coughed, and blushed a mottled shade of pink. 'Well, I must go and see how Mrs Munro is; she's on her own as well,' she said pointedly.

'No, no, Grace, come and have a dance with me. We're old friends, and I see my future wife is otherwise engaged. She thinks parties are a place to circulate, or so she told me,' and he looked over at Victoria being totally encircled by that big toff, Rory. James could see the visitor was quite besotted and couldn't take his eyes off her.

Grace stiffened, feeling herself being clasped in the arms of her dream man. James propelled her confidently around the floor, and Iona, watching from across the room, smiled at the strange picture the two dancers made. It's a pity we can't feel love on demand, she thought, and sighed wearily at the sight of all the plates that still needed clearing. She was looking forward to getting Murdo up for a rousing eightsome reel later on.

Victoria was in heaven. She was convinced she was the belle of the ball. Touching little of the alcoholic punch, she floated in bubbles of conceited self-love, high on life, dancing the night away with partner after partner. She particularly liked being in the arms of Rory, the curly haired gent from the south, who spoke such cultured English and who told her he drove a Porsche. When asked where he worked, he had just replied in his clipped manner, 'The city,' as though that was all the information anyone required. Victoria was extremely impressed.

Elvis was not. Growing befuddled and braver with each mouthful of the 'girly punch' as he had sneeringly labelled it earlier, he pulled his staid, teetotal wife up to dance in a sedate *Gay Gordons*. Dragging her manfully through the throng of dancers, he placed them both behind Victoria and her fancy man. From that close vantage point he could appreciate the view of his young lover's naked thighs and see the outline of the skimpy underwear that she never bothered to wear for assignations with him. Elvis danced like a robot, giving no thought to his scowling wife beside him. His eyes bore down on the golden curls, the breasts bouncing as she twirled in time to the music. Forgetting himself, he lurched forward and whispered roughly in her ear as she glided past, 'Don't you forget it's me you love.' He came back to earth with a violent kick in the shin. His long-suffering wife's court shoe struck hard and he let out a howl of pain.

'Oh, well done, sir; I forgot we have to cry "Hooch" during the dance!' Rory shouted over the music, 'Wonderful evening; Dickie certainly knows how to throw a good party!'

James, unaware of the dramas unfolding on the floor, was concerned at the sight of Margaret sitting by the punch bowl, morosely ladling the lethal liquid into a pint glass.

'Now then, lassie.' James bent over kindly, removing the ladle from her hand. 'Maybe that's enough?'

'No!' She grabbed it back from him. 'It tashtes wonnerful, and I'm sho sho thirshty.'

James rolled his eyes, looking around for help.

Only Wee Eck, standing on the other side of the table like a soldier on sentry duty, responded to James's plea. 'Not a problem, James. I'm the man for the job. I can do it. I can shee to her.'

James saw Eck's glazed eyes and his heart sank. Oh God, he thought, I'll have to get them both out of here before they either throw up or collapse. Fortunately, just at the moment he was urging Margaret from her seat and trying to wrestle the ladle from her grasp, Lottie MacDonald appeared and took control.

'Come away, Margaret, you just come with me. I know what's wrong with you, in fact I know all your problems and drink isn't going to solve any of them. I saw what you were reading in the doctor's surgery and I think it's about time you gave that old nutmeg a rest.'

'Actually it's a chestnut,' interrupted James helpfully.

Lottie glared at him and, coaxing the girl up, she continued lecturing. 'If you still want a man, though God knows why, looking about me tonight,' Her eyes slashed into Eck who stared back at her, unblinking. 'what you need to do is go for a completely different type. That's the solution, take it from me. You must look for a man as different from Robert Ross as an Afghan hound is to a poodle.'

'Who's talking about me?' slurred Joker, 'I am not a poodle.'

'Oh, get away with you, lad,' James said irritably. 'What is going on here? What's happening to everyone? We've only been given champagne and the punch which only has a wee bit wine in it.'

Donnie, hearing the last, said, 'No, James, it's not just a wee bit of wine but a bottle of whisky and half a bottle of rum, God knows how much vodka, and about three more bottles of wine on top of that. Everyone keeps adding to it. There's enough to put everyone here under their seats, that's for sure.'

'Oh my God!' James winced. 'Lottie, you take Margaret, and Donnie here will take Eck; get them out of here before they vomit all over Lady Barbara's fancy carpets.'

'Where will we take them?' Donnie asked James as he hooked arms with Eck, now as stiff as a poker.

'Anywhere, but get them away from the Lodge.'

Donnie led Lottie and Margaret out of the house and down the steps. He pushed the drunken girl into the passenger seat of his car and wound down the window, then shoved Eck into the back seat. 'It's all right, Lottie, I'll take them back to my place; they can sleep in the spare room. They'll be fine. I'll check on them later.'

As the night wore on, Lady Walton whirled around the dance floor in the strong young arms of the men she coerced into dancing with her. She was oblivious of the various undercurrents that were drifting around the room and instead congratulated herself on throwing such a successful party. There was such a feeling of bonhomie, such an intermingling. Laughing girlishly, she trilled over the music to a now somewhat relaxed Joker, 'I'm so hot, Jonathan, shall we help ourselves to some more refreshment?'

Joker nodded, and with somewhat unfocused eyes, stared intently down into his hostess's plunging cleavage. Docilely he followed her to the punch bowl. Watching him sip from the proffered glass, Lady Barbara smiled before taking it back and draining it to the last drop herself. She then fished a strawberry from the bowl, heavy with liquor, and held it poised between her plump full lips. Joker stood mesmerised, the room swaying and reality receding. He could feel himself being enveloped by her arms, and as she steadied him, he thought he might drown in her stupefying scent. He eyed the strawberry still cupped in the hollow of her luscious lips. He wanted to be that strawberry, to be consumed by the siren in the red dress. Droning into her ear like a drunken bee, he suggested they do some adjustments to her zipper. 'If I can pull it up, I can pull it down,' he slurred. 'I just want to see you and eat you. I just want to bite your tits.'

Lady Walton giggled nervously, looking around quickly to see if anyone could hear. Running her fingers through her short hair, she cocked her head to the side, all the better to study the swaying youth in front of her, and decided that he needed a sharp blast of fresh air to sober him up. Not being averse to the odd dalliance, she thought a quick uncomplicated tumble with the lad might be fun. His earthy use of language certainly was quite novel.

Donnie watched the duo from across the hall and winked at the sober form of Hamish who was leaning wearily against the window frame. 'Your apprentice seems to be getting an all-round education!' he laughed.

'Aye, he'll get it from that one, but I have my doubts whether he'll remember any of it!'

James eyed Victoria as she continued to dance. She fluttered her eyelashes at every young buck in the room and certainly did not want for partners. He noticed she made a point of avoiding himself. To compensate for his state of solitariness, he pulled up a chair and sat beside Murdo and Iona.

The old friends felt giddy with the effects of the punch. Iona eventually deposited her unfinished cup on a window ledge, and instead nursed a pint glass of tap water. I need to keep my head clear, she thought. Paula, by contrast, had thrown herself into the dancing and was now being hurled about like a rag doll as the music whirled them into a frenzy. She was laughing wildly, frantically searching for the face of the man that would catch her next in the *Strip the Willow*. Gone were any inhibitions and Robert frowned when he saw a drunken gent, a stalking friend of his Lordship, slip his hand down over Paula's smooth gown, feeling the outline of her taut buttock. The Angry Young Men continued to play, chastely sipping water between the various reels and Strathspeys. The sullen demeanour which had hung like a cloud over them at the beginning of the evening had evaporated. Now, their faces wreathed in wrinkled grins, they nodded at the couples lurching their way around the floor. Only during their break did they partake in a glass of the lethal nectar.

James was not the only one that kept his eyes on Victoria. From across the room Iona spied Elvis sitting looking, she thought, damned sour. No wonder, Iona muttered viciously, for his wife, that beady-eyed old bird who could only crow holy lectures, sat looking at James's intended with an unblinking stare. Iona followed the gaze and sighed. There she was, Victoria, in all her glory, a vision of her own self-delusion. She carried her shameless head high, confident that her ability to bewitch the man she was with was enough to protect her. Iona knew that everyone in the village had talked in whispers at first about the liaison with the postman, but after the lads from the forestry had confirmed the suspicions, the rumours had spread like a spring tide. Only James had stayed blissfully unaware. Now here she was flaunting herself with another, under both James's and Elvis's noses. It must be great, she thought, to be young and incapable of guilt, without a care for anyone but yourself. Iona watched as Victoria disappeared out of the room with that big handsome hunk called Rory Webster.

She wouldn't have minded a whirl with him herself, if she had been a wee bit younger. Tall, he was, with a grand head of curly brown hair. Eyes like chocolate almonds and features as chiselled as a silent movie icon. Iona sighed again and looked instead at her own man. Oh well, she thought, glancing down at Murdo's thick thatch of iron-grey hair and big nose, broken in two places from a brawl when he was twenty. Better the devil you know, so they say. She leant over and gave her husband a spontaneous hug. 'What about a waltz, old man? Are you fit for that, you old *bodach*?'

Lord Dickie was too busy groping Kathleen in the pantry to notice his wife slip up the back stairs with the young joiner. Disappointed that his oily charms had not worked with the more resplendent Dolly, he turned instead to Kathleen whom he caught unawares while she was quite alone in the kitchen. The old roué, delighted with his new quarry, his face flushing like a beacon over the navy cravat at his throat, manoeuvred the proprietor of the Tea Room backwards into the pantry. Panting excitedly, he dropped the latch on the door. Without further ado he encircled Kathleen's quivering midriff and nuzzled her second and third chins. She smelt fresh and warm, like yeasty bread straight from an oven. Lord Dickie inhaled her home-baked aroma and, unable to stop himself, he burrowed his round nose into the cushion of her velvety white cleavage. Kathleen, her mouth open in shock and outrage, attempted to push him away, but to her horror she felt herself begin to tremble and her eyes roll back into their sockets. Still protesting, her struggles becoming feebler by the second, she let out a low moan. She admitted defeat when his Lordship, with expert ease, slipped one of her raspberry nipples into his mouth.

The hours ticked by on the clock in the hall. Only empty pint glasses and sticky punch goblets were left standing. Most of the guests had drifted off, overcome by the witch's brew that had befuddled even the most hardened of drinkers. By prior arrangement the Angry

Young Men played a desultory rendition of *Auld Lang Syne* at the midnight hour, then left the dais unnoticed. They packed up their instruments and, giving thanks that they had been paid by cheque at the beginning of the evening, they were able to drive out of the glen, content they had fulfilled their part of the bargain. All in all, they thought, it had been a cracker of a night. Somewhere an owl hooted and a hazy moon struggled in vain to break through the thick cobwebs of cloud.

CHAPTER 38

James MacTavish returned to the Lodge the following morning. He left Victoria sleeping, flushed pink in his bed. They had not spoken since leaving the party the night before. It was a grey sky that met him, and he greeted the dismal day with an equally leaden heart. The leaves swirled around his feet and the sharp tang of seaweed exposed by the low tide filled the air. Before stepping out of his cottage, he turned from habit to address the portrait of his mother, but remembered a touch regretfully that she had been relegated to the room that she had once slept in. James compressed his mouth into an uncharacteristically disappointed line. Sheets of cloud hurried across the sea, as though in a race with the foaming horses breaking on each crest. Above him, encircling the village almost as though they were saying farewell, he watched the greylag geese preparing to take their leave.

'That'll be them gone again for a wee while,' a craggy voice broke into his silent thoughts.

Turning, James saw the figure of Hector approaching. He was walking slowly, bent into the wind, with Charlie tied to a rope in his hand. The old man's eyes were narrowed, like a wildcat's, giving him a shifty, evasive look.

'Good morning, Hector,' James smiled, his face relaxing at the sight of the old shepherd.

'Did you have a good party then, James?' Hector enquired, looking away to sea.

'It was quite a party,' he replied noncommittally. 'Aye, I suppose you could say it was quite good.' James made a thing of looking out to sea as well.

'And what about the woman you got from the magazine, did she have a good time too?' Hector spat with a noisy hawk on to a boulder near the gate.

'Aye, she did.' James nodded, unsmiling. 'She's still flat out, fast asleep.'

Hector looked past James's shoulder and caught sight of a golden head of hair passing the bedroom window.

'Well, I won't keep you, James. No doubt you will have a lot to keep you busy up at the Lodge today.' He narrowed his eyes as he glimpsed Victoria's face before she dodged back behind the thin curtain. The old man went on, 'When are all the toffs heading for off?'

'They'll be on their way as soon as they fill their bellies with whatever the cook gives them. Nothing like a good fry-up to soothe a sore head.'

'Aye,' nodded Hector, sagely. 'There's a lot to be said for a bit of black pudding to get your head back to rights. When they've gone, you just give me a shout, James, if you need any help with the horses. I'm always happy to lend a hand.'

'Very good, Hector; now I must get on my way.' James climbed into the estate pick-up, waving his hand as he drove up the track.

Almost immediately James was out of sight, Victoria flung open the door. Hector scowled at the apparition in front of him. The woman's hair was bedraggled. His shifty eyes fluttered downward, taking in the long thin hands clutching a mint-green dressing gown around the slim body.

'What do you want?' she spat at him.

'Just passing,' muttered Hector, turning away.

'Well, go! I don't want you hanging around here.' Her words lashed him as effectively as the sting of any thistle or nettle.

Hector muttered oaths under his breath as he and the dog retreated down to the beach. The salt wind blew tears into the old man's eyes. He stood for a long time looking out to sea, following the flock of gulls diving and swooping in a big white cloud, like snowflakes in a storm. Sometime later Hector heard the sound of a car. He had not moved far along the beach, for he had been lucky to find three wooden fish boxes washed in by the angry tide and was smashing them up to carry home for his fire. Picking his way cautiously over the rocks, he struggled up the beach to see who it was that had driven down to see that wicked woman. The vehicle hadn't sounded like Elvis the Post's.

Hector crept up behind the boulders and saw a tall young man in a brown Barbour jacket and jeans leap out of a fancy grey car. He watched the stranger disappear inside James's house. Hector's old eyes opened up wide when he saw the strumpet march out carrying a suitcase and all sorts of clutter. Slamming the door behind her, Hector could hear her screeching to the man to put all her stuff in the car. In minutes the car doors were closed and the Porsche was speeding up the track. Not even a word of farewell, thought Hector. The old man coughed, then spat out a glob of spittle. 'Good riddance,' he snarled, and called to his dog, 'For the love of God, Charlie, would you come back here. What's the matter with you, always nosing amongst dead bones?' He got hold of his dog and secured him to the leash. 'Aye,' he said, giving the collie a loving cuff around its ears, 'dogs and motor cars, always just like their owners.'

James MacTavish spent the day trying to keep his face free of expression. The Lodge was in disarray, and poor Dolly, Lottie and Iona were struggling with mops and vacuum cleaners, trying to return the public rooms into some semblance of order. The Waltons' guests ate the full breakfast that a rather distracted Kathleen had managed to serve them. She shuddered as she placed plates of black pudding and greasy mushrooms, sausage, eggs and bacon in front of their florid faces. Thank God, she thought, the cook was back and was able to take control of her already gleaming kitchen. After breakfast the guests took their leave, shouting loudly to one another as they packed their cases into cars and roared off down the driveway.

Iona, on her knees cleaning out the ashes from the living room fire, was suddenly aware that one of the handsome beasts that had so monopolised Victoria the previous night was standing in the doorway hovering as though he had something to say.

'Good morning, are you off then? It's a good day for travelling,' she quipped cheerfully, hoping he would be prompted to say what was on his mind.

'Yes, I'm off. It's been great fun. Look, I'm sorry about my friend, Rory; he left without saying goodbye… '

He was cut off by Dolly, rushing in. 'Oh there you are, Iona, you'll never guess who I saw running down the back stairs!'

Iona's eyes flickered. The young man smiled awkwardly and, picking up his case, he mouthed, 'goodbye' and skipped down the steps.

'Well, what is it? Who did you see?'

'Joker MacTavish!'

'No!' cried Iona, her eyes wide with merriment. 'No prizes, I suppose, for guessing whose bed he was sleeping in!'

Dolly laughed delightedly. 'And I think our friend Kathleen has a story to tell too. She's mighty twitchy this morning and colours up as pink as that grapefruit she's been serving for breakfast.'

'Do you think the randy old stoat got our frightened rabbit last night?' Iona giggled.

'I'd say it was a night of passion for some, that's for sure!' and Dolly breezed out flicking her duster at the sombre faces of the ancestors nailed to the wall.

It was late in the afternoon when James MacTavish, with a heavy heart, returned to his cottage. He frowned momentarily, noting the darkened windows and the smokeless chimney. The sun was setting in a glorious orange ball, colour rolling down off the black hills into the blood-red sea. Wavelets trickled on to the sand, the scarlet ripples turning from petrol blue to bronze. James was oblivious for once to the oyster catchers and gulls gossiping in a leisurely way on the shore. Framed on a rock perched a heron. Still as a statue it waited.

James let himself into the house, immediately feeling its emptiness. Turning on the light, he walked through to the kitchen and saw that it was just as he had left it in the morning. He removed his deerstalker hat and poured himself a glass of whisky before wearily making his way through to the sitting room. There it was, the forlorn fireplace, full of ash and half-burnt peat. Sighing deeply, he plonked himself down on his leather chair and took a sip of the raw spirit. He then looked around his room. Gone were the throws and the cushions and all the other paraphernalia. Only the velour cover on the fish boxes remained with the same block of pristine writing paper. On the top page, James observed that she had in fact finally written something:

Dear James,
Sorry it didn't work out, but I think we both know we're not right for each other. I could never be happy here. Hope you find your ideal woman.
   Love, Victoria

James sat back and closed his eyes. A smile played upon his lips as he thought about the novel she had planned to write. Ah well, at least she wrote the ending, he chuckled. He was surprised at how relieved he felt to be free of her, and for the first time that day he leapt about his chores with lightness in his heart. First, he thought, I'll get the fire going, then I'll heat myself up a tin of pea soup. Pleased with his agenda so far, he started to hum. After that, he thought, maybe, just maybe I'll have another wee dram!

CHAPTER 39

A pale dawn filtered through the net curtains of the spare room in Donnie's cottage behind the Pipers Inn. Margaret opened her eyes sleepily, then blinked in panic when she realised she was in a strange bed. Beside her, an even stranger body was breathing heavily. She bit her lip, letting her eyes get accustomed to the gloom. A hot flush engulfed her, causing her to screw her eyes tight in an effort to block out the scene unfolding around her. It was as though a projector was playing back the events of the night in her mind's eye. They ran like a sordid film show. Wee Eck lay naked beside her, sleeping gently, only his ragged breathing disturbing the silence. Margaret looked down under the sheet and noted her own naked breasts. Oh my God, she whimpered silently, what have I done? Easing herself carefully out of the warm cocoon of bedclothes, she grabbed her once-smart trousers and silver Lurex shirt and tiptoed towards the bathroom. Hastily putting herself to rights, she went back into the bedroom to search amongst Eck's discarded clothing for her pale blue Puffa jacket. He had turned over and pulled the duvet over his head, totally unaware of her departure from his side.

Silently Margaret let herself out of the bedroom and found herself in a small passage leading into an open-plan kitchen. The smells of bacon frying and coffee percolating assaulted her queasy stomach, and her face, already almost green from nausea, blanched and she rushed back to the bathroom to rid herself further of the horrors of the punch bowl.

Donnie met her when she returned, smiling ruefully at her sorry state. 'Here you are Margaret,' he said kindly, 'a glass of

Alka Seltzer and two painkillers. Should work fairly soon, though I expect a blow from the sea would help the healing process along too!'

'How did I get here?' she asked in a small voice, gratefully accepting Donnie's ministrations.

'You and just about everyone else at the ball were hoodwinked by the fruit punch. It was loaded with just about every bottle of alcohol you can think about. Talk about a lethal cocktail. That Sergei bloke didn't have to go to London to meet with assassins; he could have stayed right here.' Donnie smiled sympathetically and raised his eyebrows enquiringly. 'I don't suppose you want a bacon roll?'

'No,' Margaret grimaced, 'but maybe I could have some black coffee?'

'Coming up,' he said, pouring two mugs from the glass percolator.

'And Eck?' she asked shyly.

'Absolutely out of it, he was. I just let you both lie down in the spare room. At least I knew you were safe and out of harm's way. James didn't want you sick on her Ladyship's carpets!'

'Oh,' Margaret nodded, beginning to see the whole embarrassing picture. She hoped Donnie hadn't seen how intimate she and Eck had become during the course of the night. Inhaling the revitalising aroma, she closed her eyes to block out the recurring visions of Eck pulling at her clothes and she in turn struggling to undress him.

Donnie broke into her X-rated thoughts. 'Do you want a lift home, Margaret? I could drop you off before I open up the bar?'

Margaret shook her head, blinking herself back to the present. 'No, as you said, I think the sea air might help me to revive. Though look at me, doing the walk of shame in my party clothes! Everyone will soon know that I haven't been home. No doubt Doris at the shop will be peering out of her window, or Kathleen.'

'I don't think you need worry, Margaret, your business is small fry compared to some of the goings on last night. Just having too much to drink is nothing compared to what happened between Joker and Lady Babs! I don't think Kathleen will be judging anybody else either!'

The two laughed into each other's eyes, and immediately Margaret started to feel a little better. Taking her leave, she slipped out of the side door and made her way along the beach, away from the main street of the village, and up through the whin bushes to where the crofts ran down from the road to the sea. As she clambered round the big boulders, she saw the grey Porsche speed off down the road and turn left, away from the village. She couldn't be sure, but was that not James MacTavish's woman in the front seat beside that toff from London?

CHAPTER 40

November passed with little incident. Rain fell, and the winds blew. Paula read in the newspapers about shattering headlines from other parts of the world. She felt so far removed from events that had once held her in thrall. Instead she learned how to bake bread. At night, with the two collie dogs dozing by her feet and the fire reddening her face, she watched Robert through half-closed eyes. She loved to watch his long fingers whittling fragrant wood while he sat at the table, surrounded by his tools. Slowly, as the evenings passed, the raw shape of a fiddle slowly came to life in his hands.

Last week Paula had rung Suzannah, begging her to come up for a holiday, or to spend Christmas with them in the glen, but to no avail.

'Why won't she come up?' Robert asked.

'It's her father,' Paula replied, 'he takes care of Anton while she works part-time teaching English. I think the old man has grown very fond of the little chap so she doesn't want to take him away for his first Christmas.'

Robert nodded, reaching for more sandpaper to rub down the wood to a finer grain. 'Maybe she'll come up in the springtime?' he suggested.

Paula shrugged. 'I told her all about the fiasco at the Ghillies' Ball and Victoria running away, but she just laughed and wasn't sorry for James at all.'

'Quite right, silly old fool,' agreed Robert. 'Serves him right. Fancy sending away for a wife from a magazine like that, and then inviting her to live in his home without even having a drink with her first. What kind of courtship is that?'

'I just hope nobody tells him of the gossip about Victoria and Elvis. That would really dent his reputation as the village Romeo.'

'Well it has anyway,' Robert replied. 'Everyone knows about it except James. Maybe he does though, and just wants to preserve some dignity between himself and Elvis. After all they have to live here for ever and they've been friends since schooldays. Best to let it go.'

Paula sighed noisily, 'I just wish he would go and see Suzannah.'

'He was a right idiot for letting her go in the first place,' Robert said emphatically. 'If he had married her when he had the chance all this fiasco could have been avoided.'

Paula got up and dropped a kiss on his forehead in passing. She padded through to the kitchen in her thick woollen socks and opened the cupboard to get the hot chocolate out for their evening drink. Immediately the dogs' ears cocked expectantly, and with tails wagging furiously they scampered through to stand attentively at their empty food bowls.

Rosie was constantly in a state of high alert. The autumn months saw her and Billy running around the village, performing their mother's errands, but secretly conducting their own clandestine spying operations. Clutching the listening device and a small notebook and pencil they hoped to hear some vital piece of information that would lead them on to an adventure. In reality, this usually proved too boring to interest them for long and so instead they ran down through the fields to the river where the thickest brambles grew. Gorging on the juicy blackberries and sweet wild raspberries, they plotted and planned their various missions. In fact, as it turned out, the most thrilling information came out of their own front room. It was a weekend, towards the end of October, and their father had just arrived home with his bus from a tour that had taken him up to Wick in the north of Scotland. He and their mother were watching the ten o'clock news on television. Earlier, just after supper, Billy had placed the small microphone just inside the sitting room door, and ran the extension wire along the hallway and into the cupboard where he and Rosie cowered as quiet as mice in their pyjamas. They had stuffed their beds with soft toys to make it look as though they were asleep. A loud cry alerted them to some possible notebook-worthy entry.

'Oh thank God!' their mother cried. 'They've got him!'

'Who?' whispered Rosie.

'Sssssh, listen, we might hear,' urged her brother, spraying saliva in his haste to listen.

'We should tell her,' Jenny said, 'let's go and tell her that the horrible man has been caught. She still gets nightmares, you know.'

'She's probably asleep,' her husband replied.

'No, I thought I heard them a while ago. I shouted at them to get to bed. I doubt they'll be asleep yet.'

Billy and Rosie froze. They didn't know how to get out of the cupboard without their mother seeing them, or to stop her finding out the ruse they had pulled with their beds. If she found out about the listening device there would be big trouble and it would be returned as fast as lightning.

The sitting room door opened and Jenny stepped out and turned on the light in the darkened hallway. Both children held their breath. Just as she stepped on to the first step of the staircase, the phone rang, and she stopped to listen.

'Jenny! It's for you; the Home needs to talk to you about some shift they need you to do tomorrow.'

'All right, I'll take it, and then I'll go upstairs and see Rosie.'

Breathing a sigh, the two spies sneaked out of the cupboard. While Rosie tiptoed up the stairs, Billy collected the spying equipment then followed his sister lightly up to the bedrooms. He tossed all the toys from his bed and snuggled happily under his duvet. It had been a good spying night.

Shortly after, his mother came in and, seeing him still awake, she told him to come through to his sister's room. There, with her arms around Rosie, she told them that the wicked pervert, as she called him, had been captured. He had attacked another little girl near Edinburgh, but had been caught when she had screamed. He was in prison now and he would never hurt anyone else.

Rosie shuddered and cuddled her mother. 'I'm glad, Mum. When I grow up I am going to be a policeman, you know, and catch spies and bad men.'

Her mother hugged her close, then kissing her tenderly on her cheek, she whispered, 'Goodnight, Rosie, God bless.'

Putting her arm around Billy, she walked with him back to his room and eyed the mess of jumpers and toys scattered beside his bed. 'Goodness Billy, what on earth have you been up to?'

'Nothing, Mum. Goodnight!' He presented his puckered lips to be kissed. Jenny looked for a moment at the tousled black hair and the long sweep of lashes on her youngest son's cheek. He's got the face of an angel, she thought fondly.

With winter approaching, there were fewer opportunities to sneak up on people, so Billie decided to keep his eyes and ears open for anything untoward happening in the village. He took note of strangers' cars, of unknown faces, and especially of lights that came on in houses that he knew were supposed to be empty. One Saturday afternoon in mid-December, he and Rosie were over at his Uncle James's. His uncle was involved in the big palaver of making a Christmas pudding. He had laid out the ingredients on the kitchen table only to find that the recipe demanded suet. Billy was despatched on his bike to the shop. Having satisfied Doris's curiosity as to why he was buying suet for his Uncle James, Billy made a fast retreat from the shop, leaving Grace from the Post Office and several other women discussing at length the latest titbit about their favourite man.

Billie jumped on his bike and swooped along the dark and deserted street towards the church corner, where several cars were parked under the hanging tree. Billy knew the minister was holding a rehearsal for the Christmas nativity later in the afternoon so that would explain the vehicles. Turning back towards the village, the boy's sharp eyes registered a flicker of light escaping from behind a curtain in the cottage that Paula had once rented. He knew it had not been re-let, but he thought perhaps it was being made ready for a holiday let, and whoever it was that cleaned it might have left a light on by mistake. Scanning the pure snow, still crisp from the heavy fall that had occurred during the night, the master spy made out two sets of footsteps leading up to the door. As silent as a shadow in a graveyard, Billie left his bike by the road and slipped round the side of the house, taking care not to scratch himself on the coarse thorns of the gorse bushes that had been allowed to grow wild and savage. Peering through a chink in the curtain, he could see the light that had at first caught his eye. He deduced from the flickering nature of the light that a candle was being used. Pleased with his discovery so far, he strained up to the window ledge, his ten-year-old frame stretched to the limit to see who could be using the house as a secret hideout. He knew that sometimes wandering tramps took refuge from the weather in empty holiday houses. There was no sound, only the muffled swish of a car as it drove towards the church. Billy decided to move a flower pot from the front door and stand on that. He would be able to see in, if he could just get higher. It was as he struggled with the clay pot, heavy with compacted earth, that he heard the voice of Donnie the barman.

'Is that you, Billy MacTavish? What do you think you're doing?'

Billy dropped the pot, causing a loud thud to reverberate through the silence. He saw Donnie walking towards him, carrying a torch. Big feathery flakes of snow were falling on the barman's shoulders.

'Well,' he demanded again, 'What do you think you're up to?'

'I saw a light,' Billie said, suddenly afraid of Donnie standing fiercely in front of him.

'Where?' Donnie asked.

'In there; I thought someone had broken in, that's all.' Billy stammered, suddenly feeing foolish.

Donnie gave a cursory glance at the cottage, noted the darkened windows, and cuffed Billy on the shoulder. 'You're imagining things lad, there's nobody there. Get off with you. Aren't you supposed to be at the church this afternoon?'

Billy nodded, then spoke up. 'I had to get suet for Uncle James. He's making a Christmas pudding, then we have to go to rehearsal after. The minister is doing the singers first. I'm a Wise Man.'

At this, Donnie's faced creased into his normal wide laugh. 'Wise is it? Well, I have yet to see much evidence of that where you're concerned, Billy MacTavish. Now scram! I'll get Kathleen to check on the house later on. She's got the key.'

Billy needed no persuading and was soon pedalling as fast as he could along the slushy road back to his uncle's cottage. Donnie turned on his heel and continued walking down towards the bar. The snow continued to fall, the large flakes completely covering the tracks to the holiday house in a thick white blanket.

Inside the cottage, Margaret started to giggle. She and Eck had clasped each other tight, shaking with trepidation, while Billy was being interrogated by Donnie outside. Only their white-ringed irises and shallow breaths betrayed their fear of being found out. Now, regaining their equilibrium, they gave way to hysteria. The candle had been hurriedly snuffed out, and Eck felt for Margaret, laughing into her wild bushy hair. He clumsily pushed her back on to the rough rug.

'We have to go,' whispered Margaret urgently. 'You heard Donnie, he's probably phoning Kathleen right now. Do you want them all to burst in on us like this?' Her buxom body was driving Wee Eck wild with desire.

'I don't care if they do,' he grumbled, 'I'm tired of all this sneaking about. Winter is not the best friend of secret lovers and neither is a fresh fall of snow. You don't need to be a maths wizard to count how many pairs of footprints led up to the door.'

Margaret struggled to get up. 'Come on, we should go. Leave me alone Eck, stop that now,' and she started to writhe in delight as his tongue travelled down her plump belly.

The rehearsals for the Nativity went well and the following week, on Christmas Eve, the church was full to bursting. The Reverend Wilson was gratified that so many of his flock had turned out on the snowiest night of the year. The young choir of angels sang, their soprano voices soaring into the lofty roof arches. The front section beneath the pulpit was brightly lit up, giving the impression of a living tableau. The congregation sighed as one when the players came on and took their places. Kathleen was very relieved that precautions had been taken to protect the lapis blue church carpet. Four large bed sheets had been laid down and were duly scattered with straw. Grace from the Post Office craned her neck to get a glimpse of Iona MacPherson standing uneasily beside Rosie. Referring to the cast of characters on the back of the carol sheet, she noted that Iona and young Rosie were the official keepers of the Virgin's donkey, borrowed from the estate for the occasion. James had been a touch reluctant to lend it, she heard. Apparently it was known to be a bad tempered beast, and there was a fear that it might charge and ruin the whole tableau. Both keepers were clad in striped tunics, with Irish linen tea towels on their heads. Grace noted that Billy performed well as part of the wise trio, and Donnie had been persuaded to act the innkeeper. No doubt to keep the lad in order, she thought caustically. Given half a chance that lad would be up to no good.

Meanwhile, away from critical eyes, Old Hector sat to the side of the front pew. His role was to keep an eye on the two sheep. The Reverend felt that the live animals would lend a sense of reality to the holy tale. Hector's dog, Charlie, sat alert at his master's feet, his eyes darting about, ready to savage any creature that dared to step out of place. Beside him, Lottie MacDonald sat stiffly. She had been to the doctor earlier, and he had given her some strong pain killers for her sciatica. Hector studied her sidelong, with shifty eyes.

She had the kind of face, he remembered, that had once been plain and unworthy of a second glance, but was now a perfect spider's web of creases. Her smile, when she occasionally allowed herself to find a bit of pleasure in life, caused lines to shoot from her eyes, like the rays of the sun. He thought she looked a fine and wiry woman. Couldn't understand at all why she haunted the doctor's surgery so much. Hector was a man who liked to interpret the different life maps he read on his neighbour's faces.

Towards the centre of the church, Dolly, Grace and Kathleen were unable to stop laughing. Try as they might, they couldn't hold the mirth in. Their shoulders shook, causing the pew to vibrate.

Betsy, Elvis's sour wife, turned her beady eyes towards them. '*Haud yer wheesht*!' she hissed in a savage voice.

Elvis fidgeted, afraid that they might be laughing at him. He had suffered a great loss of confidence in the last couple of months since his summer lover had left him without even a backward glance.

Paula, James and Robert craned their necks to see the children enact the Christmas story. James smiled fondly as toddlers struggled to free themselves from their young mothers' arms. Livestock unexpectedly baaed, ruining a well-rehearsed line. Paula waved at a distracted Iona who spent the majority of the pageant scowling at the donkey. Billy for once looked like a saint.

Dolly whispered into Grace's ear, 'Margaret's pregnant!'

Grace gasped, 'No!' and immediately passed on the message to Kathleen, whose eyes widened in surprise.

'Who?' the two women mouthed in unison, their eyes wide with surprise.

'Wee Eck!'

'No!' they gasped again.

'Ssssssht!' spat Elvis's irate wife.

Grace started a silent laugh that nearly took her off the pew. Her shoulders shuddered as her two friends turned to her questioningly. 'What?' they mouthed.

'I was thinking about the 144 condoms she ordered from the chemist in Kyle. Surely to God she didn't use them all up with Robert Ross? You would think she could have saved two or three for Wee Eck!'

The three women let out a loud cackle and were duly reprimanded by the Reverend Wilson as he scowled in their direction.

'She was saying the babe is due in July, which means they must have been at it since the Ghillies' Ball. Maybe they didn't have one that night. Mind you, I doubt they would remember!' Dolly sniggered.

Kathleen coloured slightly and turned back towards the lit-up stage. For a few moments she had her own memory of the pantry when his Lordship had cornered her so insistently. She coughed discreetly, fumbling in her handbag for her reading glasses. Studiously she turned her attention to the carol sheet.

Dolly and Grace gave each other a meaningful glance, and smiled discreetly. They too turned their eyes to the angels and sang along with the children.

That night Hector Ogilvie looked out at the bright sky above his house. Stars were rivalling the moon in their brilliance, and the ground glistened like fairy dust in the moonbeams. A plop of snow shuddered off a heavily laden branch. He grunted to himself as he entered his cottage and pulled off his new thick coat. Dolly had brought it to him from the Salvation Army in Inverness. It was very fine; 'cashmere' it said on the label.

Later, sitting by the dying embers of his fire, he took down his diary and wrote:

Good covering of snow on the ground. Fed the hogs. Heavy showers in the afternoon. Took a load of seaweed to Lottie. There's a new baby coming to the glen.

CHAPTER 41

Suzannah's hands were immersed in a basin of sudsy water. Sunlight was streaming through the windows on to the pine floor of her father's flat in Edinburgh's Dean Terrace. Humming along to a CD, Suzannah squeezed the soap from her pale pink sweater. Behind her, on a blue and yellow rug, Anton sat cross legged in a pool of sunshine. His blond hair fell in soft curls at the nape of his neck, contrasting with the shadowy blue eyes and thick lashes that fluttered on his creamy cheek. In his hand was a cat's tail. The chubby fingers maintained their grip in spite of the low, rising growl of protest coming from the duly offended ageing and very tolerant black cat.

'Let go, Anton; he'll scratch you,' warned Suzannah as the cat's distress eventually cut across the music.

'Pussy, come,' ordered the toddler. 'Come, Pussy!' and he tugged at the tail as though it was a rope.

Suzannah looked on in horror, expecting the irate animal to retaliate with a vicious scratch. 'Let go, sweetheart; Pussy wants to sleep now.' She walked over to unclench the child's grip. Anton's head shot up, his eyes turned towards the door, listening like a little bird with his head cocked on one side, his mouth open revealing his twelve teeth in an angelic grin. 'Postie? I get letters, Mummy?'

Nodding in agreement, Suzannah watched her little son run off with his rolling gait to the hallway to collect the mail. Left alone she smoothed the fur of the flustered feline. 'Well done, Puss. You are a good natured thing aren't you?'

Suzannah reflected on how well her father's elderly pet had coped with the dramatic upheaval in its life. She remembered how, fourteen months ago, she and her newborn baby and all her belongings had travelled down to Edinburgh in the back of a black limousine. Courtesy of the Consulate General of Ukraine in Edinburgh, she had been relieved of responsibility for dealing with the repatriation of Sergei's body. Her father had given her shelter and supported her during the initial months when she had been heartbroken, confused and angry. There had been accusations and questions following her lover's death, and an inquiry into the possible link between his death and that of another scientist in London. Suzannah had sworn to the police that she knew nothing of Sergei's activities in London, or of any sinister network he might have been involved with in Ukraine. She was confused when the police had mentioned the name of Tatyana, telling her that it was logged as being a number Sergei called often on his mobile phone. They had not been able to locate the woman. There was no trace of her presence in the flat she once rented in Earl's Court. Suzannah felt scared and so angry at having been duped. When her father took her to register the birth of her child, she recorded his name as Anton Richardson, without the middle name of Yaroslav that Sergei had wanted.

Suzannah had found it relatively easy to find work and was soon employed part-time as a teacher of English. Her father looked after little Anton while she worked, and he and his housekeeper enjoyed many pleasurable days walking the baby around Stockbridge and along the Water of Leith. During the intervening months Suzannah kept in regular touch with her friends from Drum Mhor, and so was able to keep abreast of the latest news and gossip. Paula seemed so happy, ensconced with her handsome crofter. Iona's telephone bills must have rocketed as she relayed the lurid details of the Ghillies' Ball. Suzannah gasped in surprise, and then laughed delightedly on hearing the various escapades involving Wee Eck and Joker and Lady Barbara. She noticed, however, that her friend was often reticent when it came to talking about James MacTavish.

'How is he, Iona? Is he OK? Is he lonely, now that his bride-to-be has left him?'

'Och, I don't think he's upset at all, lass,' Iona demurred. 'He's glad to get back to his lighthouses if you ask me!' Then she added slyly, 'I see that Grace from the Post Office has taken to calling on him again.'

'No!' cried Suzannah. 'Surely he's not going to take up with her?'

'How's the wee one?' Iona neatly changed the subject and Suzannah was left with the picture of James and Grace strolling around the garden, admiring the carrots and so on.

For the first few months after her return to Edinburgh, Roderick Carruthers had acted like a knight in shining armour. He had taken her to restaurants and to the theatre. He had allowed her to weep through films in the dark privacy of the cinemas and had been a huge support through the initial torture of the police inquiry. Roderick realised, however, that any romantic feelings he had once felt for Suzannah were now over. It did not take him long to tire of his former fiancée's baby. To him the child was an irritation, and with lips tightly compressed the busy city gent found he could not disguise his impatience with the demanding little sod, as he liked to describe him. It did not take him long to transfer his attentions to a young civil servant working in the Scottish Parliament. Roderick was one who appreciated a smartly turned-out escort with high heels and tailored clothes. Suzannah, by contrast, had rapidly gone downhill since becoming a mother, and did nothing for his corporate image. Suzannah, aware that her charms had waned, smiled ruefully at the now silent telephone. She was resigned to spending most of her evenings alone with her father, but had no regrets. She held no feelings at all for Roderick, although she would always be grateful for his friendship and dry sense of humour that had seen her through the initial dark months.

'Letters!' Anton announced, speeding into the kitchen on his little bare feet. He stretched up his arms and held out two letters, one in each hand.

'I wonder who this is from?' said Suzannah, examining the thick, expensive-looking envelope while dropping the gas bill on the table with a look of distaste. She slit open the envelope and pulled out a stiff white card. Her eyes lit up when she saw that it was an invitation and she grinned widely on reading the embossed gold wording. She and Anton were invited to Drum Mhor for the occasion of the wedding of Wee Eck and Margaret. Suzannah was delighted, and placed the card on the mantelpiece in the sitting room. It was to be in a month's time, in early April, and she happily ringed the date on her calendar.

She bundled Anton up in his brown dungarees and padded jacket, then pulled on her own red duffle coat, tying her hair inelegantly back into a simple pony tail. Grumbling, she carried the pushchair and toddler down the two flights to the ground floor, and struggled with the heavy outer door leading to the street. She let herself out of the tenement building and smiled at the unexpected brightness that hit her eyes. Winter was over, and she cheered up enormously as she strapped Anton into his stroller. His head was recoiling backwards, his eyes and nose screwed up tight as the sharp rays of the morning sunlight temporarily blinded him.

Suzannah walked over the bridge and past the restaurants and tempting charity shops. She made her way along the river bank until at last she came to the Botanic Gardens. She noticed that there were several people like herself out walking with small children, some elderly couples were sitting on benches, and green-clad gardeners were making a show of clipping shrubs and weeding the spring beds. She loved walking through the rhododendrons at this time of the year, their fat glossy leaves, so dark and vibrant, protecting the burgeoning buds bursting with promise of the rainbow colours to come. From somewhere in the jungle of leaves she could make out some deep laughter and wondered who could be hiding from prying eyes. Strolling on a little way, she decided to wait and see who would emerge. Before long, three lanky gardeners scrambled out from the bushes. Looking around guiltily, they brushed the leaves from their heads, and slapped the legs of their jeans.

Seeing her eyes on them, one of them coughed a little self-consciously and grinned. 'We were just having a fly smoke!' he said.

Taking up his trowel and trug, the one who spoke to her moved over to the black beds where only small shoots were making an appearance. 'This will be full of trillium soon,' he told her helpfully. 'It's my favourite flower in the whole garden.'

'What a wonderful job you have,' Suzannah replied, 'surrounded by so much beauty and peace. I don't know what my favourite flower is, but I'll certainly come back and look at your trillium when it blooms.' She continued wandering along the paths, past the pond where they stopped to look at the ducks.

'Bye bye, birdie,' Anton shouted, causing a lady walking on her own to smile.

Stopping under a magnificent oak tree, still sombre and stark in winter hibernation, Suzannah finally let her straining toddler out of the pushchair. She put down a plastic table cloth and covered it with a tartan rug. Anton sat for just a moment, content to share an apple with his mother, before his flashing blue eyes registered an inquisitive squirrel and immediately he was off. Two magpies strutted nearby and Suzannah instinctively counted and breathed a sigh of relief. 'One for sorrow, two for joy,' she said, feeling just a little foolish. 'Joy!' She tasted the word on her tongue; a wonderful word, she thought, it conjures up the feeling of exuberance when leaping out of bed and racing to the curtains to see what the day brings. 'Joy!' She breathed in deeply, and then exhaled, closing her eyes tightly before looking up at the naked branches silhouetted against a glorious cerulean sky. Since receiving the wedding invitation she had felt a sense of yearning, a gnawing in her heart to go back to Drum Mhor. She knew she wanted to go back, but always she had the fear of how she would cope. In Edinburgh she was dependent on her father to help her with her son. How could she afford to rent somewhere? It was impossible. Yet she longed to hear the bleating of the sheep, to feel the presence of the dark hills, and to see the rolling waves where the light reflected the constant changing moods of the sea and sky.

'Come here, Anton! Come and give your mummy a cuddle, we're going back!'

CHAPTER 42

Hector remembered helping to build the old dry stone dyke with his father and other men from the village. He had been just a boy then when he had gathered the stones and learnt how to place them, carefully weighing and slotting each into its own space. They had built it to surround the kirk initially, but then continued the wall so that it ran round the corner and on up through the village. He looked through crinkled eyes at the wall, still standing fine and true after sixty years, though it was now grown thick with emerald-green mosses and patchy grey lichen. He ran his gnarled hand familiarly over a particularly large stone placed near the church corner. There was no mark to be seen, but he remembered how, one summer's afternoon, he had scratched his and Kate's names into the dark orange crottal that grew thick on the stone. Aye, lass, he thought, it won't be long now before I join you.

The road opposite was a blaze of dazzling yellow light. Bushes of broom seemed alive with the buzzing of bees. Beneath all this flamboyance sheltered the shy, nodding heads of the bluebells. It was a beautiful day and the sun glinted on the calmly rolling sea. Tiny puffs of cloud seemed to sit in the bluest of skies. Gulls wheeled and shrieked at the persistent clanging of the church bell.

Today Wee Eck waited at the altar for Margaret. Dressed smartly in his one and only suit, his shoes shined to a mirror's gleam by his devoted mother, he stood proudly at the front of the congregation. His hair was slicked back and his nails scrubbed clean. Only the persistent use of the ironed square of a handkerchief across his damp brow betrayed his nerves. That and the continual muttering to his best man.

'God, I hope she doesn't decide to marry you when she gets up here.'

Robert Ross had at first declined to be best man, given his long history with the prospective bride, but Eck had reassured Robert and Paula that he and Margaret were the real thing, and nothing would interfere with their destiny.

'We are made for each other. It just took us a bit longer than most to find out.' He had winked at Paula then. 'We'll just keep all the history in the cupboard, eh?'

So Robert stood tall beside Wee Eck and suffered his nerves and listened to the ticking of the clock. The organist looked in her wing mirror at the door for a signal that the bride was about to make her entrance. Around the church people fidgeted and whispered as outfits and hats were scanned critically.

Dolly commented to Lottie MacDonald, 'Look at Grace, would those be leg-of-mutton sleeves do you think?'

Lottie peered around the tall body of Elvis in order to get a closer view of the offending blouse. She snickered, 'Blushing pink! Mutton dressed as lamb, I would say. Look at her, making googly eyes at James MacTavish. Does she have no shame?'

Dolly sniffed in agreement and together they sat up a little straighter in their pew. They had spared no expense at all in their outfits. Both had chosen from the mail order catalogue and had waited with bated breaths for their new gowns to be delivered. It was always a gamble, seeing that the clothes modelled were always on skinny slips of girls with no hips. Dolly need not have worried, for the large yellow smock covered all her ample curves and showed off her fine legs. Her head was crowned with a wide black straw hat, for she felt it added just a dash of glamour to the church. Lottie had opted for a more conservative style. She wore a hyacinth-blue pleated skirt with a matching jacket. Her white felt hat was a touch summery, she thought. Further along the pew, Kathleen was sitting with Lizzie. Kathleen was a vision in green. Her emerald satin shirt shimmered and clung to her buxom shape, outlining the spongy pocket of flesh that had collected around her stomach and hips. She wore a navy and green floating skirt and felt positively girlish in her little Alice-band hat that bounced with flighty green feathers. Her silver hair was styled into a perfect globe. She smiled sweetly along the row to her two friends. They couldn't wait to see the bride.

James MacTavish kept his eyes forward. He sat down near the front with Iain and Jenny and their family. Rosie was next to him and her eyes were like saucers, taking in all the pomp and ceremony of a village wedding. He could see Paula, dressed in a sea-green pashmina over a mauve silk dress, sitting in the front with Wee Eck's mother, a funny old lady, dressed all in red. Across from them were Margaret's family. Looking around he tried to see Murdo and Iona, but had no luck. Seeing her catch his eye, he smiled a little hesitantly at Grace from the Post Office. A strange outfit, James thought; where does the woman get her clothes? Grace was wearing a hot pink dress with puffed sleeves and alarmingly big white buttons. It was sort of thing young Rosie might choose, James thought, looking away hurriedly in case she thought he was leading her on.

At the very back, slipping in late, came Iona in a beautiful silver suit, with Murdo spruced up beside her. On her other side was Suzannah and between them was Anton. Suzannah wore a simple dress that shimmered in sky blues and pinks. It fell into swirls around her thin figure, and her long silvery hair was loose, hanging like a curtain down her back. Her blue eyes scanned the church.

At last the organist spotted the Reverend Wilson sweeping into view in his long flowing robes, whereupon he signalled for her to begin playing the bridal march. She crashed her fingers down on the keys and the sedate music thundered out. The congregation rose and the procession began.

Wee Eck swallowed and whispered to Robert, 'Well, here goes. Have I got time to run?'

Margaret glided in on the arm of her father. She was dressed in a sweeping empire gown of snowy white. In her hands she held an extra large bouquet of deep red roses with cleverly arranged whispers of baby's breath. Her long gauzy veil softened her harsh features and wiry hair. Pregnancy hardly affected her already full figure; her general roundness concealed her condition. Nobody seeing her for the first time would ever suspect that the bride was already six months along the way. If truth be told, Margaret was not the first bride to walk up the aisle of Drum Mhor church in the family way.

When her father placed her hand into Eck's it seemed like the signal for every woman in the church to start sniffing. The Reverend Wilson looked around in concern at all the tissues dabbing wet eyes, and his words were punctuated with a cacophony of noses being blown.

After the ceremony James stepped out of the church into the sunshine.

'I thought it was supposed to be a happy occasion,' the Reverend observed, 'but I'm convinced they cry more at weddings than they do at funerals.'

James shook his head, 'Aye, well, women are a funny lot, spend all their time wanting to trap us, then when they catch us they start to cry.' Then he muttered, 'And some of them just run off.' Just then he saw Suzannah by the old wall, the sea behind her and the mountains looming in the distance. A soft breeze caught wisps of her hair and blew the fine silvery strands off her shoulders. Just as he was devouring her with his eyes, the church bells rang out, and the newly married couple urged everyone to gather round for a photograph. Sighing, he moved over to where Paula was standing alone with the little old lady in red.

It was not until after the meal, served on trestle tables in a marquee outside the Pipers Inn, that James was finally able to talk to

Suzannah. The men were clearing away and Donnie's friends from the Isle of Skye were tuning up their fiddle and accordion. Rosie was introducing little Anton to some of the other toddlers in the room.

'I didn't know you would be here?' James smiled at Suzannah uncertainly.

'They sent me an invitation. I expect Paula put them up to it, but I'm so glad I came.' She looked out of the flapping doorway, over to the sea. 'I missed it all so much.'

'Why didn't you come back for a visit before, then?' James persisted.

Suzannah flicked her hair. 'I have to work, so my father takes care of Anton. It's been quite difficult.' She didn't say that the thought of James with another woman might have been a major factor in her decision to stay away. 'How have you been?' she asked pleasantly.

'Oh you know, busy with the estate, and I've been getting my garden all set for planting. Nothing much really.'

He sighed, for once tongue-tied. He felt awkward, and yet how could that be? This was Suzannah, the woman who had been flitting in and out of his thoughts for nearly three years now. Here she was in front of him, and all he could talk about was his garden. Next thing he would be boring her to tears telling her about his new linoleum.

'Are you staying with Iona?' he asked.

'Of course, she insisted.' Suzannah smiled. 'Paula wanted me to rent her old house. Apparently it's been vacant for months, but as I drove past I see that someone's living there. Do you know who's taken it?'

James rubbed his chin and said thoughtfully, 'A lad from the south of England I believe. Quiet chap, he's a poet or a painter, or something like that.'

Suzannah smiled as she recalled that James had been the official painter for the drama production. She reminded him of that, her blue eyes sparkling.

With gentle laughter and carefully resurrected memories, the two tentatively attempted to build a bridge back to where they had once been.

Watching them from across the other side of the tent, Iona and Paula linked arms. 'What a grand day,' exclaimed Iona, 'God obviously smiles upon his own, and just look at Wee Eck; he's like a wee lamb with a frisky tail.'

'He is,' agreed Paula. 'It's funny how things work out, isn't it? I mean, who would have thought that he and Margaret would have been such a hot item. We gave them a punch bowl for a wedding present as a nice memento of how they met!'

'And you and Robert too, don't forget. What are your plans?'

'None at all, we are just happy the way we are. I have plans for another drama this autumn. I've ordered the Philip French book of plays, so we can look through that and decide what would be a good one. In the meantime it's just looking after the sheep. How are your lambs coming on?'

'So far so good, we've had two sets of twins so that's a good sign. Oh, listen! There's the music, I'm going to get that handsome young lad up to dance.'

'Which one?' asked Paula, frowning, quizzically casting her eyes over the crowd of forestry workers who had been invited for the dance after the wedding feast.

'You just watch!' and Iona walked around the room.

First to take the floor were the bride and groom, and Margaret and Eck danced close, staring into each other's eyes with everyone clapping as they circled around. Iona sidestepped her husband, whose frown was replaced with a wide grin when he saw her pick up young Anton, his chubby sweet face beaming as the strange lady whirled him around in time to the music.

Seeing her son in Iona's arms, Suzannah felt awkward standing alone.

'I would be very honoured if you would care to have this dance with me.' James MacTavish stood in front of her.

Suzannah blushed and rested her left hand on the scratchy shoulder of his jacket and placed her right in the warm calloused hand that he offered her. He pulled her close, and she was aware of his breath on her cheek. They moved around the tiny wooden dance floor as one, oblivious to the village gossips noting their every step.

'You'd think he'd have learnt his lesson,' quipped Kathleen.

'And look at her, away for a year and a day, then coming back up here to flaunt that spy child at everyone,' muttered Lottie.

'Grace's face has gone as red as a Russian flag,' noted Dolly. 'Do you think she might explode with rage? That pink dress she's wearing might burst with all that internal combustion!'

Later, walking back to the cars, Paula hugged Suzannah and whispered about the new artist that had taken up residence in the village. 'He is very private; he has all these canvases lined up in the room but all facing the wall, nobody knows what he paints. It's all very intriguing.'

Suzannah pushed her friend playfully. 'No doubt you'll find out soon enough. I'm sure that you'll have him roped into your next performance. Nobody gets to stay private here!'

'True,' agreed Paula. 'I remember I was so shocked at first how everyone gossiped here, I thought their lives must be so small if all they had to do was talk about me. Remember how indignant you were when you first arrived and had that rude introduction to old Hector? But somehow I don't mind so much anymore and I feel I've become part of the rhythm of the way of life. Maybe it's a better way of life, knowing that people know you and care about you. I somehow feel more valued here than I ever did in London. I mean only a handful of people cared whether I was alive there, let alone happy or sad. Here I can lie and listen to the bees up in the lime and sycamore trees and know that I will be missed in a few hours. I know that if something happens I can call a neighbour, but best of all I have Robert.'

Suzannah studied her friend's face, still so lovely, the toffee-coloured hair long and wavy, the face free of makeup and just a dash of freckles across the nose. Suzannah nodded in agreement, but added a touch ruefully, 'The danger of that is people will make up what they don't know, just to add a little spice into a sometimes dull existence.'

Spontaneously Paula stepped forward and hugged her friend close. It was in this way that Iona found them when she approached carrying Anton, fast asleep in her arms. The moon was shining through the still, leafless trees, and she looked at the two faces lit up by the pale light.

'Well, what were you two gossiping about?' she asked tersely.

'Paula was telling me about the new guy that has moved into that holiday house, the artist? She was saying that he keeps all his pictures covered up. We were wondering what he might be hiding.'

'Oh I can tell you that, you just had to ask me, lassie!' Iona crowed importantly.

Immediately Paula and Suzannah exchanged a knowing smile.

'Just yesterday, Doris was delivering some groceries that he had ordered,' Iona leant forward, conspiratorially, 'and when he was in the kitchen getting some money to pay her, she couldn't help herself, she just had to have a wee peek. She said she looked at one, and couldn't believe it, so she looked at another, then another, and then another. All the pictures in the room were of the same person, done in all sorts of different colours and different techniques.'

'And?' prompted Suzannah, her eyes out on stalks. 'Who were they of?'

Iona looked about her, as though to protect the trees from what she was about to say. 'They were all of Elizabeth Taylor! Honest to God, how weird is that?'

CHAPTER 43

Suzannah only had a week to spend in Drum Mhor before she was due to return to her teaching job in Edinburgh. She spent the precious days sitting around the table with Murdo and Iona, drinking coffee and learning at first hand all the news of the glen. In the perfect April weather Suzannah helped Iona plant out her little seedlings into the prepared earth. Eyeing a blackbird twittering on the fence, the older woman flung him a worm, which he pecked and pulled like piece of elastic with his beak and sharp toes.

Anton watched in horror as the wriggly morsel was eventually gulped down. 'Spaghetti, Mum, Anton wants spaghetti!'

Suzannah inhaled in great gulps the mingled smells of the dark, damp earth, the pungent hay and the ever present tang of the ocean. Breathing in mouthfuls of the cold, crisp air, she filled her lungs, relishing the sheer joy of being alive. With lambing time upon them, the two women patrolled the field checking on ewes straining in their labour, swinging Anton between them as they walked. During this time the child learnt a lot about sheep. He discovered that they were noisy and woolly and had very boisterous babies. He laughed at their antics while looking through the wires of the fence and Iona let him hold a bottle for the orphan she was feeding by the Rayburn in the kitchen. Suzannah cried out in alarm when she saw the child put the teat in his own mouth and drink up the milk while the baby lamb cried pitifully on its rug.

Every day Suzannah loved to walk along the road to the village, pushing her son in his pushchair and stopping to talk to the various people she met along the way. Everyone wanted to be introduced to such an adorable child. It was on one such day that she met old Hector, on his way home from the bar after his customary three pints of Guinness. He was walking with the aid of his rickety bicycle, leaning on the handlebars to keep his gait steady. Drunkenly he called to her and when she approached, he leant over, breathing his fumes over the blonde curls, and pressed a pound coin into Anton's small pudgy hand.

'There you are, wee laddie, put that in your piggie bank,' he said, smiling inanely. Then eyeing Suzannah he rolled his drunken eyes and leerily looked at her sideways. 'You know where to find me, lassie, if you should be looking for a man. I've had no complaints yet!' and he dragged on the string that was tied to his dog's collar and pulled hard. Charlie came reluctantly out of the ditch, his mouth full of some unspeakable object, and followed his master as he wove his precarious way up the road.

On her last day in Drum Mhor, the weather changed. A brisk wind had got up, driving the sea into a choppy fervour. The sky looked as though it had been wiped with a grey dishcloth and ominous black clouds loomed on the horizon. Suzannah and Anton took their final walk down to the beach. It was deserted except for the oyster catchers and gulls dancing around the shore.

Anton ran towards the birds, his arms outstretched in a valiant attempt to catch them, but missing his footing he skidded on some slimy seaweed and fell heavily on to the soft sand. His little face puckered in surprise, and for a few seconds he knelt looking at his hands, considering whether to cry or not. He looked towards his mother, for reassurance, but for once she seemed unaware of his plight and his small mouth turned down and his blue eyes grew damp. Suzannah stood apart from him, her eyes focused on the distant horizon. She was standing perfectly still, her profile sharp as carved stone; Anton was mesmerised by her long hair blowing like creamy coloured ropes in the wind.

'Well good day to you,' a kindly voice spoke to him. James

MacTavish knelt down beside the little boy. His twinkling eyes looked into the sad little face and he went on, 'I know everyone here in this village, you know, and I even know your beautiful mother there, trying to talk to sea captains as she likes to do, but I don't think I know you, little fellow. We've never met properly. I think we have a lot to learn from each other, and I think I would very much like to introduce you to my mother. Do you know,' he went on, 'she likes to sit above the organ up there in my wee house? What do you say, Anton, would you like to bring your mummy and have a cup of tea with me and I will show you my special lighthouses?'

Suzannah turned and watched James talking to her son, the lovely lilt of his Gaelic accent acting like a soothing balm.

James looked up at her, and their eyes met.

'You once promised to take me to see a lighthouse,' she said softly.

'And I will, lass, I will.'

Lightning Source UK Ltd.
Milton Keynes UK
UKOW051455130812

197469UK00001B/15/P